IN THE CENTER OF THE NATION

DAN O'BRIEN

AVON BOOKS ▲ NEW YORK

AVON BOOKS
A division of
The Hearst Corporation
1350 Avenue of the Americas
New York, New York 10019

Copyright © 1991 by Dan O'Brien
Cover illustration by Kim McCarty
Inside cover author photograph by Patty Grimsbo
Published by arrangement with The Atlantic Monthly Press
Library of Congress Catalog Card Number: 90-19742
ISBN: 0-380-71702-6

First Avon Books Trade Printing: September 1992

AVON TRADEMARK REG. U.S. PAT. OFF. AND IN OTHER COUNTRIES, MARCA REGISTRADA, HECHO EN U.S.A.

Printed in the U.S.A.

OPM 10 9 8 7 6 5 4 3 2 1

For Carl Navarre

IN THE
CENTER
OF THE
NATION

▲

PART ONE

ONE

Coming from either direction the land changes before you have a chance to get ready for it. Traveling eastward, you see the grasslands for the first time from several thousand feet up in the Rocky Mountains. You come around a turn intent on the ruggedness of the mountains, and suddenly the pine trees, rocks, and fast-running water are gone. Below you, though still fifty miles off, is the flattest, smoothest, most treeless stretch of land imaginable. And if you're traveling west, you've just gotten used to the fertile, black soils of Indiana, Illinois, and Iowa, just come to expect the neatly painted, prosperous farm buildings surrounded by cultivated groves of trees, when you come to the Missouri River, and it all goes to hell. Suddenly the order is gone, the prosperity scattered. When you get the feeling that the whole world can see you but no one is watching, you have come to the grasslands of North America.

They roll up out of the Missouri River breaks and flatten, with few deviations, for six hundred miles. Since the beginning the grasslands have reminded Europeans of an ocean, an ocean of grass. But, of course, they were as far from the big water as they would get. Maybe knowing that, but still having the feeling that they're floating, unable to reach anything familiar and solid, tends to drive people crazy. And maybe it's that craziness that makes some people move the way they do when they come to the grasslands: from one river drainage to the next, from town to town, right through the grasslands. Get away, fast.

Things have always moved out here, but usually in a circle. Like the geese, the ducks, the Indians, the buffalo. My God, the buffalo! Millions, weighing a ton a piece, turning grass into meat and moving on. Not moving through like the ocean people, but moving in huge, annual circles and coming back to the place where they have always been. Moving along the Missouri when they felt like it, turning to the west and grazing along the Cheyenne River, staying on the benches to the south, eating the wheatgrass, the bluestem, the switchgrass, and fescue.

For ten million years they moved like that, until Europeans came and said that all of it had to belong to someone. The buffalo were killed. For trespassing? Who knows? Only the birds, those that survive, still move in grand swirling migrations that take them thousands of miles south in winter and thousands of miles north in summer. They move back and forth with the seasons, perpendicular to the path of the people on the interstate highway.

There used to be hundreds of trails, each with its own idiosyncrasies. But now there are really only the three highways. One runs across the southern part, as straight as humans can build, from Omaha on the Missouri to where the Unita Mountains rise up and then fall into the Great Salt Lake Valley. The builders clearly wanted to spend as little time as possible out here. They were some of those ocean men and felt dizzy on the grasslands. They sighted down their transits at Omaha and didn't look up until the last bulldozer had topped the pass above Salt Lake. The other two highways are farther north and run a couple hundred miles apart and pretty much parallel until they come into sight of the Rocky Mountains; then they converge. It's as if the highways, or the men who built them, started out with purpose and courage but halfway through lost their nerve and built toward each other. Once the highways come together at Billings, they never separate until they are

4

through the grasslands, past the mountains, and into the fertile Northwest.

People travel those three highways by the hundreds of thousands but seldom stop in the grasslands for anything other than food for themselves and gas for their cars. It's mostly in the summer, carloads of families crossing the grasslands only as a consequence of wanting to get someplace else. Vacation pioneers, heading for the mountains or the opposite coast, telling themselves that the crossing won't be that bad. A few handle it well, but most feel the crush of too much space. Parents feel more protective for no apparent reason. They glance uneasily around their little car camps along the highway. There is only the grass, an occasional bare butte, scattered sage, and the wind. Maybe it's the wind that makes them herd their brood back into the car, look once more around them, then leap behind the steering wheel and drive on.

They drive too fast. Straight down Interstate 90 toward the distant Black Hills, where they have heard there are trees. They feel the loneliness and they don't like it. They stop at Harney, South Dakota, for gasoline, cowboy hats for the kids, or a miniature stuffed buffalo for a cousin back in Baltimore. As they get back into the car, they notice the Badlands looming off to the south. They stare for a while at the starkness. They may point out the bare, eroding soil to the kids. They may tell them, for their education, that nothing will grow there, that the land is worthless. But when they get back into the car, they don't take the kids to show them; they don't drive toward the Badlands. They stick to Interstate 90 because they are afraid of what they might find on the dirt roads that wind away from the highway.

But it would be better for the kids to take the first turn west of Harney. There, toward the south. The locals call it the bench road. Follow it past the wind-blown buttes, through the twisted landscape. Show the kids a cutaway of the earth. Show

5

them what's inside. Show them mule deer, antelope, and beef cattle standing, staring at what seems like nothing. Show them a morning in March, a morning during the first false spring, when the snow promises to melt in the late afternoon. Show them the way yesterday's puddles froze hard in the night and how still it can be just after sunrise. You're early enough so the kids will learn that the wind can be gentle. They'll learn the sun is almost always huge and yellow-red as it peeks over the moonscape of the Badlands. Look yourself. See the new sun sending countless shadows of different lengths across the land?

Go on down the bench road. See how the land falls off toward the west, draining to the Cheyenne River beyond? There are four major draws that drain this bench between the Badlands and Cheyenne. There is a small creek in each draw, and that's where the few trees live, where the water is. The draws are the female part of this country, the fertile part, the constant. Everything that is alive here owes its existence to those draws. But drive on. There on your right, the silly sign built from old car parts. And farther on, see the chain link fence not fifty feet off the road on your left. Look close. Those are antennae sticking up. Not much sign on the surface, but there's a missile down there. Did you expect to find your government keeping vigil? But drive on. Take the dirt road that leaves the gravel there where the wind has gnawed the earth away. It leads to a set of ranch buildings. Here the sage smells sweet on cold spring mornings like this. It has smelled sweet since long before the house or the barn or the corrals were built. It's the Kiser place. A poor place, wanting paint and repair, but a proud place, stark and defiant as the country that surrounds it. Park the car there beside the workshop. Notice the woodsmoke trailing from the chimney and a stock dog sleeping flat on her side near the porch. The dog's name is Babe. The colt in the corral is Dancer, and he slides his feet as he walks, slides the rear hooves so far ahead that it looks as if they might hit his front hooves. But they never do. The muscles of his shoulders ripple under a black winter coat that is showing signs of shedding. He carries his head low, and it bobs as he moves. The head is small and the neck developed so that every muscle can be seen. Dancer's ears come up and Babe jumps to her feet. Watch John Kiser come out of the house.

He's an old man, nearly seventy-five, but still strong and leathery. He is thin and has not shaved for a day or two. But he's smiling and looks out at the morning you just drove through. It's that view that keeps him getting up every morning. It's the payoff, he thinks. He turns from the rose-colored sky, and Babe leaps to meet him. He catches her by the scruff of the neck, gives her a playful shake, then swings her a couple times and lets go. The dog lands on her feet and barks once before she follows toward the corral, where Dancer waits, standing off in a corner watching over his strong rump.

Kiser leans on the corral rail and looks at the horse. He's as nice a colt as the man has ever owned, and he's learning fast. Casually Kiser takes the lid off the oats barrel beside the corral and sees the colt look with interest. He's trying to play hard to get, the man thinks. A damned good horse, he thinks, but still a horse. Too big and strong for his age but still just a horse. He dips the coffee can until it is half-full of oats and shakes it. Dancer turns slowly and begins that wonderful sliding walk across the corral. The man watches and smiles. If horses weren't suckers for oats, he thinks, we'd still be afoot.

Kiser slips the halter over Dancer's head while he's eating. He rubs the blaze on the horse's head. Now he eases the gate open and leads Dancer to the hitching rail outside the tack room. He puts the bit into Dancer's mouth, slides the bridle over the ears, and curries the coat, combing away the loose hair, before he eases the blankets and saddle into place. You'd never know that colt was started just last fall and has been ridden only a dozen times this spring. Just since calving season

7

started in early March, and he's already a decent cow horse. The man tightens the cinch and picks up Dancer's feet one by one. He strokes the horse's neck.

Elizabeth, the part-Sioux girl that Kiser took in, along with her young son, ten years before, comes out of the house. She's going to the barn to milk the cow. And behind her is the son, Kyle. His job is to feed the heifers before he walks out to the road to catch the bus for school in Harney, forty-two miles north. They go into the barn while Kiser makes final adjustments on the saddle. He fastens the rear cinch and sees that his rope is in place. He hears the old man, his hired hand and friend, Pete Rienrick, moving around in the bunkhouse. Then he leads Dancer away from the hitching rail. See how he strokes Dancer's neck again before he takes hold of the stirrup with his left hand? He talks to the horse as he swings up into the saddle.

The horse is tranquil as the man settles his weight in the middle of his back. The man is square in the saddle, with both feet in the stirrups. He nudges the horse with his spurs and lightly turns his head with the reins. The colt moves mechanically. They have done this before, and the man is proud of the way the colt moves fluidly toward the calving pasture. But today, after yesterday's thaw and the freezing night temperatures, there is ice, and the colt's left rear hoof slips as he shifts his weight to his right front. This in itself is nothing. He still has three feet on the ground. But it frightens the colt, and he tries to hop away from the slippery spot. Now the right front hoof finds a second patch of ice and slips out, too.

Kiser is old and wise. He has been in this position a thousand times and knows that it is best to sit it out. He keeps his weight centered to help the colt regain his balance. But now the colt is scared and naturally wants to get rid of his load. He tries to buck but has no footing. The man feels the colt start down. Falling is the one thing about horses that scares Kiser.

He feels the colt fighting the fall: down on the left, regaining balance, then toward the barbed-wire fence, and finally, the worst thing possible—they start to go over backward. The man knows that the colt will come over on top of him, and this is very bad. What he does not know is that the saddle horn will be forced into his guts, and the weight of the horse will crush his pelvis and break his back.

The colt pauses high in the air before he topples backward and the man realizes that he will be hurt. But even then, in the instant before the fall, there is no way to know that this terrified colt will fall with enough force to paralyze Kiser forever.

Listen. You can hear the colt squeal; you can hear the grunts as he fights to get his feet under him. Can you hear the hooves chipping the ice as they claw for footing?

Elizabeth hears it and knows that something awful has happened. She and Kyle run from the barn in time to watch the colt stumble to his feet, leaving old John Kiser twisted and still in the ice and mud. The colt jogs a few yards off and stands quaking at the fence. Now Pete Rienrick is coming from the bunkhouse, no shoes on and suspenders over his underwear top. They all slow to a halting walk as they approach the body. It is motionless and they kneel, but it is clear that there is nothing they can do. The boy goes to catch Dancer; Babe sits down in the driveway confused, whining softly. Elizabeth and Pete stare at the body until Elizabeth pushes Pete toward the house. "The telephone," she says. "Call the ambulance."

Don't move. Don't start the car. Don't try to sneak away. Sit back in your seat and watch. Let the kids see what will happen here. It's more important than you think.

Kyle stands near the corral holding Dancer's reins. See how their young shoulders touch? They do not want to be near the crippled body. Pete Rienrick looks down on his friend of forty years and shakes his head until Elizabeth pushes him again toward the house. She touches John's gray hair as if to comfort him, but his eyes only stare upward, as immobile as the boy and the colt. Elizabeth smiles but cannot keep her eyes on John's face. She looks out toward the east. The sun is above the butte now, and she knows that the day is going to be warm. She also knows that now her world will be different, and she is frightened. The wind is coming up, and she can feel it moving through her hair. She begins to wonder what they must look like from above, surrounded by nothing but grass. Miles and miles of grass. And the wind. How very lonely it must appear.

▲

PART TWO

PART TWO

▲
TWO

Larry Sorenson stood at the door of his office and watched the evening sky. It was starting to cloud up, and the wind was still coming from the southeast. Only a few stars were visible, and it was not as cold as it had been the evening before. Sorenson glanced up at his bank's sign and saw that it read thirty-three degrees. It had been two degrees off ever since he'd had it erected. The sign had been a real addition to the community. It had lessened the people's feeling of isolation. The bank sign was just like the ones in Rapid City and the ones they see on television. It gave the people more pride in their community. It didn't really matter that the temperature was a little off. The strange thing was it read two degrees high in the winter and two degrees low in the summer. But the citizens of Harney had adjusted. Sorenson saw thirty-three degrees but read thirty-one. It was six fifteen.

Mrs. Murray drove past him and parked in front of the bank. She would be bringing her weekly deposit from the gas station to the night teller. She was dressed the way she dressed when it was below zero and held her deposit with both hands, out in front of her, as if it were alive and capable of wiggling out of her grasp. This time of year the deposit would be about three hundred dollars. Sorenson knew because he was Mrs. Murray's banker and knew how much the gas station made, how much the Murrays owed on it, and how much they had in the bank. He knew those things about most of the people in the Harney area.

Sorenson's family had owned the only bank in Harney for over fifty years. He had worked in the bank almost forty years himself. Since the interstate highway came through, some people did their banking in Rapid City, but he still got most of the local business. Sometimes he thought that he had too much business. He was getting older and thought about retiring, but he didn't know what he'd do with himself if he retired. He'd never acquired a hobby. His only daughter, Loni, was married but had no children. She never came back to Harney anyway. There was no golf course in Harney, so he'd never learned to play. If he retired, he'd probably end up hanging around the house and driving his wife, Karen, crazy. Besides, even though he'd done well in this community, only now was he gaining the contacts to really help. It would be nice, he thought, to put a really far-reaching plan together, a big deal, something that would put Harney on the map, make it a good place to live for generations to come.

Mrs. Murray waved to him as she stood in front of the night teller. She would want to talk after she dropped the deposit into the slot. He turned back into his office and shut the door before she had the chance to come his way. He sat on the corner of his desk and rubbed his face. He felt off balance, as if he were catching a cold or had drunk too much coffee. It felt better if his eyes could focus on something farther away, so he looked out the window. Mrs. Murray was pulling away from the curb. There were two other cars parked across the street but no other sign of life. It looked more like winter out there than early spring, and for an instant Sorenson thought he had lost nine months, that spring and summer had not happened this year and winter was starting over.

There was still a lot of work on his desk, but he knew he was done working for the day. He took his coat from the rack in the corner, put his hat on the back of his head, stepped out the side door—in case Mrs. Murray had circled the block—and walked around the building to his car. He had always parked in the alley. In the beginning there had not been enough cars in Harney for anyone to notice. By the time parking had become an issue, everyone was used to his car being there, and no one ever complained.

He drove a cream-colored Impala. It was four years old and had just over eighty thousand miles on it, but the body was in good shape, and the engine seemed to run well even though Karen complained about some noise. Most of the miles had come from driving back and forth to Rapid City. Rapid was seventy miles away, and ever since Loni had gone off to college, Karen seemed to make the trip a couple times a week. She had her own Toyota, but she said she liked the bigger car for the open road.

Sorenson slid behind the wheel but did not close the door right away. He sat in the car with his feet still out in the alley. The wind was blowing from the south and had not changed direction for two days. Sorenson turned his face into it. He took a deep breath and let it out slowly. The air was still fairly warm, and it seemed full of moisture. The wind was bound to swing and start coming out of the west soon. That could mean snow, Sorenson thought, spring or no spring.

He had left the keys in the car. He always said that it was easier to find the car than it was to find the keys. You can call the police if you lose your car, he joked to Karen, but she had chided him about this habit for years. She pointed to the television ads that warned against it. She told him that he would be sorry someday. Until he'd finally gotten the satellite dish and started getting all those channels and all those advertisements and public announcements, it seemed to Sorenson that car theft was not a problem. It was as if the television had created it. But, of course, things were changing. No one knew that better than Larry Sorenson, and he suspected that his defiance about leaving his keys in the car was really only a way of

15

irritating Karen. It was something he had caught himself doing. Maybe it was because in the last few years she had begun to seem even younger than she was. She didn't look or act like the wife of the town's leading citizen. She had stayed active and vibrant, and even though Sorenson took pride in her as his wife, she sometimes made him feel uncomfortable. Maybe deep down he felt she found some pleasure in pointing out that he was twelve years older than she was, and maybe that's why he sometimes did things to irritate her. The truth was, he didn't know why he did it.

Sorenson pushed those thoughts out of his mind as he drove around the corner to the front of the bank. It was still thirty-one degrees. There was a light out in the north side of the sign. He'd have that fixed first thing in the morning. Sorenson passed the Badlands Café, Ottmyer's clothing store, the Coast to Coast store, and Montgomery Ward. He considered turning onto the service road and going out to the sale barn to see how the bred-cow and heifer sale was progressing, but when he got to the interstate, he turned around and stopped with his car facing the city-limits sign:

HARNEY, SD
POPULATION 1456
ELEVATION 2943 FT
HOME OF LONI SORENSON, MISS SD 1979

Sorenson questioned the population figure. They had certainly gained some since the sign was put up. It had been only five years, but already the paint was beginning to peel. Perhaps he could have the population raised a little when they repainted the sign. He looked beyond the sign and saw that a few lights were starting to come on in town. The cattle sale would be nearly over. He drove back down Main Street. There were two vacant stores between Murray's gas station and

Thompson's Café. Farther north he passed the Shoe Shop, Jorgenson's Bakery, and the Blue Note Lounge. There were a couple more vacant buildings before he got to the new ice cream parlor and then to the Enchanted Forest, which was perhaps his greatest contribution to the community.

The Enchanted Forest had been just a field before he and Cleve Miller organized some investors to put up the money to start a tourist attraction. Thousands of people streamed past Harney every day on the interstate highway on their way to spend money in the Black Hills and Wyoming. It hadn't taken much foresight to see that Harney would be a better place if those tourists would leave a little of that money there. He and Cleve had hired a string of managers, and finally the land had been sold to a hard-working young man eight years ago. Their financial interest ended then, but they stayed active as advisers to the business. The Enchanted Forest had been a good experience and good for the town.

It had started simply. They constructed a building, brought in a few hundred tons of petrified wood from the Badlands. They had fashioned a sort of garden of the stuff, complete with rock castles and fountains, then filled the building with souvenirs and erected hundreds of humorous road signs to draw the people off the highway. A lot of people had laughed when they started, and it had been slow at first. They had to mount a sizable lobbying campaign to keep the state from following the federal highways beautification plan, but in the end they had made money and brought even more money and jobs to their community.

Before the Enchanted Forest started pulling people off the interstate, the town was dying; the kids were all moving to Minneapolis and Denver. Now Harney was doing better than almost any other community in the area. But still things could improve. Sorenson turned his car around and drove back up Main Street. The vacant buildings saddened him. He knew the families that had run those businesses and felt a sense of his own shortcomings as a financial leader when they had failed.

When he reached the other end of Main Street, he turned his car around and stopped so that he could see almost all of his town. In a lot of ways his job was thankless, but there were rewards, too. He looked down the street. It was a nice, warm little town.

▲
THREE

As a boy Ross Brady dreamed of horses. They came to him in billowing clouds above a prairie that he had never seen, and they moved like birds toward him as he stood wide-eyed and all alone. Their necks would sometimes arch defiantly and show him a strength that he had only imagined. At other times they would come gently to him, and he would touch their faces and find them softer than anything he had experienced in his young life. And he would awaken with a glaze of sweat on his forehead and a longing he could not explain.

The longing never left him. Twenty-five years later, even as he looked from his kitchen window at the prairie that he had once only imagined, he could still feel the longing as a thumb-sized spot of pressure just above his heart. Because the life he had built in this land so far from his childhood did not ease that pressure, he wondered whether he had made a mistake. It was a long way from the populated Pennsylvania countryside where he was raised to the Badlands of South Dakota, and he was no longer the thin boy who dreamed of horses.

Now he was a mustached man in his mid-thirties sitting by the wood stove in the kitchen of his own house on Sweet Grass Creek. Outside the early spring wind was pushing the brown grass down in front of it. The sky was perfectly blue, but Ross Brady knew that it was cold. He had already been outside that morning to feed the horses that he would need when he checked his cows later that day. The cows had begun to have their calves two weeks before. Eight calves had been born so far, and none had needed help. They would begin to come faster soon, and Ross knew that in the next month he would get up to eight calves in a single day. If he was to get ninety-five live calves from his hundred cows, he would have to watch them closely. If he lost more than five, he would have to count on the price of cattle rising if he was to make his land payment in the fall.

The land payment. That was something that had never been in his childhood dreams of the prairie. He had somehow imagined ranching as a cross between his father's stable truck farm on the outskirts of Philadelphia and a Western movie. His expectations had not been extravagant—he had never thought of this little ranch as the Ponderosa—but from time to time the realities of his life oppressed him. He lived alone now that Linda was gone. It was not the way he wanted it, not the way he had imagined it. It was not healthy, and he wondered whether it would eventually make him crazy. Everything had been different before Linda moved back to Los Angeles, and he knew that it was the memory of her presence that was making it hard for him to get started that morning.

But this crush of inertia was not unusual. It happened to him often. Sometimes it was a general malaise, a weight of dreaminess with no focus. But this morning it was centered on a word. *Desertion.* It had been in his mind since he woke up. It had been in his dreams.

He had begun to wonder whether certain lives were drawn to words and the concepts behind them. *Challenge, fellowship, loneliness.* He had known lives that attracted those words, that were lived in such a way that those concepts turned up time and again. Could it be that for him the word was *desertion?*

He thought it was a nasty word. *Desertion.* It was not exactly what Linda had done. They agreed it was best, and besides they were still married, still very close. Ross rubbed his face. This was silly; he had work to do. He had to break away, get outside. But he couldn't move. *Deserter.* Yes, he was a deserter. A military deserter. But that was in the past. He had been given amnesty. It was over, and besides it had never seemed as ugly as the word. *Desertion* again. If he were to leave this place, would it be desertion?

He stood up from the chair he'd been sitting in too long and moved close to the window. He wanted to go out there, feel the cold wind against his skin, but Linda was still in his mind, and he would be able to do nothing until she was finished with him.

Over ten years ago they met at the University of British Columbia. It was 1972, only a month after his father had become suddenly sick. Ross had just returned from a clandestine trip to see him. It was difficult to get in and out of the country then. It had been a bad trip and, though Ross didn't know it, the last time he would see his father alive. He returned to the graduate course in biology that he would never finish, and the first day back he met Linda. She was just beginning in music, a tall, graceful girl from LA studying the arts in Canada. When Ross first saw her, she was dancing. And that is the way he has pictured her since: the exercise room near the racquetball courts, black leotards and sleeveless sweatshirt, the hair pulled back starkly, the face as beautiful and classic as her movement across the floor. He stood in the doorway and stared, sweaty from his racquetball game and the racket limp in his hand. He watched her swirl, and ever since, he has been able to conjure up the exact movements she made that first day. To become a professional dancer was her dream, and now it looked as if it might come true. She had called the day before from LA full of excitement about an audition with a small California dance company run by a woman named Barowitz.

The audition had gone well. Anita Barowitz herself had taken Linda aside and told her how well she'd done. They were looking for someone just like Linda for a tour that would start very soon. Ross was glad to hear that she was doing well. Her voice on the telephone was a cure for the late-winter blues Ross had been feeling. If they hired her, she would perform with the troupe one night in Denver. "You could come down," Linda said. Her voice was tentative, hopeful, but with a hint of sadness.

"It would be good to see you," Ross said.

"Yes, it would be very good."

She asked about the cattle, and Ross remembered how concerned and helpful she had always been at calving time. Then she talked about her family, how nice it was in some ways to be home. Her father and mother were fine, and they sent their love. Her brother, Stewart, had sold out of the latest company he had started and was taking some time off. "He needs to get out of LA," she said.

"Send him out here. I could use some help."

"Stewart is not exactly a cowboy."

"Neither was I," Ross said.

Ross didn't think there was any chance of Stewart Bergman coming out to help on the ranch. It had been four years since Ross had seen him, and unless there had been a remarkable change, Stewart was not the type to pitch hay or shovel manure. He smiled at the thought of the Bergman family. They had been so kind to him, understanding what he had done in the face of military service, filling in for his mother and father after they had died within a year of each other. That was a short time after he had married Linda and a year before he had taken her to what Mr. Bergman described as "the end of the earth." He wondered what they thought of him now, with Linda home the way they had probably always hoped. He knew they would call it a separation—never desertion—with a divorce implied for the future. It embarrassed him to think about it, and he forced himself to push away from the kitchen window. He was wasting time and should go out among the cattle, see whether there was anything going on. He opened the stove door and stirred the coals before throwing two more sticks of wood on top.

Coming from the house, he zipped up his coveralls. The wind was still strong, and Ross sniffed it for moisture. But all he could smell was the smoke that the wind sucked from the chimney. The house nestled in the draw that Sweet Grass Creek had dug for itself a hundred centuries before, and so it was protected from the worst of the wind. Ross pulled his cap down and wrestled his overshoes over his boots. He sniffed again at the air. If there was moisture in the clouds building slowly in the west, it could come in the form of snow. The temperature was probably above freezing, but it would drop into the teens before the night was through. Ross slid into the pickup, and the wind whined in the gap between the window and door. He started the engine and sat, letting it warm up. He'd check the cattle from the pickup first.

Ross Brady's land was one of four ranchers on the bench that lined up to the east of the Cheyenne River, each one arranged around a separate tributary that drained the Badlands. The ranches were all small, just over two thousand acres each, and Ross had learned that a ranch that size was barely big enough for making a living. In fact, like his neighbors on the bench, there were years when Ross lost money, and even when it was averaged out over the eight years he had been there, his income was just below the amount he had read was considered the poverty line. That had surprised him. He imagined that he did not have as much money to spend as some of the people he went to college with, but he never thought of himself as poor.

He had known from the start that money was not the

reason he had come to the edge of the Badlands. It was the bigness, the stark beauty that attracted him. He had come for the freedom he felt here, a freedom he now thought might have been imagined. Romance was part of it, but being able to drive his pickup out over his own land and look at his cattle was part of it also. And that was real, if only partly true. The truth was, it was not exactly his land. He still owed the First Bank of Harney almost as much as the land was worth. The payments seemed designed to cover only the interest. The principal never seemed to decline. Still it was his place, even though most people in the area persisted in calling it the Swenson place.

Exactly why they called it the Swenson place was a bit of a mystery to Ross. He had not bought it from a Swenson. He had assumed the loans of a man named Miner, whom he'd never met. Miner had bought it from a Howard. It was Howard who had bought it from Oliver Swenson. But in studying the abstract of title, Ross found that even Oliver Swenson was not the first to own it. In fact, the ranch was comprised of ten homesteads, eight of which were patented by people named Swenson, two by Jorgensons. Some of the homesteaders were women, which probably meant that everyone in the Swenson family old enough to file on land received title to a hundred and sixty acres. The rule was that every homesteader had to improve the land. There were some areas of the ranch that were never homesteaded, but Ross had found the ruins of eight of the original ten homes.

From the top of the first ridge Ross counted sixty-eight head of cows on the flat where he would feed them later that day. Most were lying down, and none looked as if she needed anything. The remaining bunch was probably farther down the ridge, in the buckbrush at the bottom of the draw. If he continued down the ridge, he would be able to see them from one of the indentations left from the dugout home of a homesteader. He was in the habit of stopping every time he came near one of the ruins, sliding off his horse or getting out of the pickup, and moving to what must have been the front of the home. They were all, except for the house he lived in, merely holes in the ground. The rafters that had held up the ground-level roof had no doubt been cut from the cottonwoods along Sweet Grass Creek and had long since rotted away.

There were twenty-one head lying in the buckbrush, where he suspected they would be. Counting the eleven first-calf heifers back at the barn, all the cows were accounted for and looked contented. The wind was still cold as Ross got out of the pickup and pulled his cap down. He moved to the front of the old homestead, where you could see over half of Ross's land: most of the calving pasture, part of the summer pasture, and a mile of Sweet Grass Creek winding down to the bottoms, and finally the Cheyenne River. It was a view that he had enjoyed many times. But every time he stood there, in front of the shallow, twenty-by-twenty-foot impression in the ground, he could not help looking at the immediate area, the paltry hundred and sixty acres that surrounded the dugout. He did his best to see it the way the homesteaders had seen it, but all any straight-thinking man could see from the doorway of any of the homestead ruins was a great deception and the bitterness of broken dreams. Ross knew from experience that it was almost impossible to make it on twenty-two-hundred acres. To try to raise a family on one hundred and sixty was insane.

During the thirties Oliver Swenson slowly bought out his brothers and cousins for fifty cents an acre. The brothers and cousins packed up for California, but Oliver, an old bachelor whose requirements were small, stayed and put together a real ranch. He ate venison and grew his own vegetables for ten years after his family moved on. Then the war came, and the price of beef went up. He made good money in the early forties, but Oliver Swenson was smart enough to know that financial prosperity on this land was an artificial thing. He fixed the house up and waited for a soldier with more money than brains to come home from the war. That's where Howard came into the picture painted in the abstract of title. He showed up in Rapid City in the spring of '46 with a strong back, an unshakable belief in the American dream, and enough combat pay from months of fighting in the mud of the Pacific Islands for a down payment on a ranch.

Howard was the first to take out a loan from Larry Sorenson, the young loan officer at the First Bank of Harney. Howard ended up with a monstrous mortgage that he was never able to pay the interest on; Oliver Swenson bought an artichoke farm in Castroville, California; and the new loan officer at the First Bank of Harney got a bad loan that he was able to pass along for nearly forty years. Ross could see parallels between himself and Howard, as both their down payments were absorbed by the bank. He wondered whether he would one day be just another name on the abstract of title for this tiny sliver of grasslands.

The sun was high enough now and the sky so perfectly clear that Ross could feel some warmth on his face where the wind did not hit. There were a few clouds north. He should go back and start hauling hay out to feed the cattle because he wanted to get them fed by noon and go through them on horseback for a good look before the sun began to turn pink. He studied the clouds in the west. Would they get some moisture? Ross didn't think so. He took one more look at the cows below him in the buckbrush and noticed a mule deer standing motionless beyond. In a month there would be lots of calves in this pasture. The fawns would come later. The birds would be back by then. The place would come alive with color and life. But now it was still winter-dull. He turned and peered into the dark hole that had once been a home for a family. He could not help wondering whether there had been children, whether they had laughed and played the way he had back in Pennsylvania, whether their Christmases had been warm and bright. What had become of them?

The summer of their second year on the place Ross had ridden to the top of this hill and been startled by a blast of bright yellow. It was an ancient primrose bush that had gone wild but was perhaps more vigorous now than ever. He had never seen roses like that before and assumed they were brought from the old country. That summer day he had gathered a handful of the small flowers with the needlelike thorns and carried them back to the house for Linda. The horse had stiffened when Ross approached with the shield of yellow, but finally he stretched out his nose to smell them, deciding they were safe to carry home.

Now Ross moved to the tangle of brown sticks that he knew was the rosebush. The winter left it bare, and there was no way to guess what it really was except for the circle of stones that formed a border between the bush and the native grass. He touched one of the stones and tried to imagine the woman who had gathered them ninety years before. It was not a place for most women. Not then or now. She must have seen the roses as a tiny speck of what she had left behind. Ross inspected the rose branches for signs of green though he knew it was too early in the year. She stood right here, he thought, hundreds of times, looking for a sign of spring. Every day she would try to spend a few moments by herself, drawing energy from this tiny garden. Ross wondered whether she ever learned to draw on the land that surrounded the homestead. He wondered where she went from here, whether she'd found joy somewhere else. He wondered whether, thinking back on this place, she remembered the beauty of the view or thought of it only as a cruel little home on a windy ridge.

▲
FOUR

There was a single light burning in Larry Sorenson's house. He stopped the Impala under the carport he had built onto the garage. They kept the Toyota inside the garage because it was newer, but Sorenson was sure it was gone. Karen was seldom home when he arrived. He sat looking across his backyard, into his kitchen through the large window above the patio. The light came from over the stove. It was yellowish and gave the appearance that it was left only to create the illusion of the house being occupied.

As Sorenson pushed open the back door, he felt the same nausea he had felt earlier in his office. He did not turn on the overhead light. Instead he walked to the center of the kitchen and looked around at what the yellow light from over the stove did to the furniture, appliances, and Congoleum. The whole kitchen was new in the last two years, but now it looked old, faded like newspapers from the Depression. He pulled his coat off and laid it over a chair. Then his eyes caught the message on the refrigerator.

Now he turned on the overhead light and stepped close enough to read the note pinned to the refrigerator door by a very red magnetic tomato. Karen had gone to get some things from the grocery store. There was no surprise in that, but at the bottom of the note, scribbled in the corner as if to say, "Oh, by the way," she had added a telephone number and a name. John Higgins was the president of Brome Mining Company.

Sorenson snatched the note from the refrigerator. The

magnetic tomato flipped off and skittered across the Congoleum. John Higgins had called him at home. He looked hard at the note. "Call him," it said. Sorenson lowered the note and exhaled. He smiled, feeling much better. John Higgins was a very important man, an Australian who ran one of the biggest businesses in South Dakota, one of the biggest gold-mining operations in the world. And he'd called Sorenson at home. He'd met Higgins a few times. They had both been on the governor's committee to promote a waste-disposal site in the caverns of the Badlands. They had not been successful, but Sorenson had been impressed with Higgins. Now Sorenson folded the note as he thought. He tapped the folded paper against his chest absently, then smiled again. Maybe Higgins had been impressed with him, too. He would call Higgins right away. He turned toward his den and saw the tomato magnet on the floor. It had slid under the kitchen table. Sorenson had to get on his knees to reach it. Before he left the kitchen, he reattached it to the refrigerator, exactly in the center of the upper door.

He had already dialed the number when it occurred to him that this might not be a good time to call a man like Higgins. Sorenson was suddenly panicked and glanced at his watch. It was ten after seven. Before he could decide whether that was a good time or not, Higgins answered the phone. Sorenson knew it was Higgins by the accent, which had always been disarming to him. It made what Higgins said seem upbeat and indisputably true. It was not a British accent as Sorenson had at first assumed. It was Australian, very positive and filled with a pioneer spirit that fit well in the American West.

"Hello," Higgins said again.

"Hello, John? This is Larry Sorenson out at the First Bank of Harney."

"Larry, that was fast work. I only called an hour ago. I see your wife got the message to you."

Did that mean there had been some doubt in Higgins's mind that Karen would give him the message? Had she been rude? "Yes, just got in from work. You didn't try me there did you?"

"No, Larry. To tell the truth, this is about something I'd like to keep private for at least a while."

Sorenson's breath caught in his chest. "Yes?"

"Do you think you could come into Rapid City some day soon? I'd like to talk."

"Of course. Could you give me some idea what it's about?" Sorenson tried to keep his voice even. He heard the back door open. Karen was home.

"No details over the phone, but let me just say that our Development Department presented the results of a rather involved study to me this afternoon. It's been ongoing for several years, and I was very pleased with some of the projections. And I think you'll be pleased with what they're saying, too."

Sorenson took a second to calm himself before he spoke. "It sounds very interesting. Am I to understand that Harney could be involved?"

"Yes," Higgins said. "We're talking jobs here. The kind of thing that could change the whole area. Keep the kids at home, change everything for the better. But I don't want to say any more on the phone, Larry. You understand."

"Certainly," Sorenson said quickly. "I could come in any day."

"Would Thursday for lunch be all right?"

"Fine," Sorenson said. It was Monday. He had hoped Higgins would pick Tuesday or Wednesday.

"Good. Let's say the Hilton at twelve thirty."

"Twelve thirty. Fine. Yes."

Sorenson replaced the receiver gently. He heard Karen moving around in the kitchen, but he remained sitting quietly,

31

forcing himself to relax. This thing with Higgins could be very big, and it had just fallen into his lap. He marveled at that for an instant, then told himself that he might be getting his expectations too high. If he'd learned anything in the banking business, it was that things have a way of falling apart for tiny reasons. Then he began to wonder again whether Karen had been rude to Higgins. He'd had deals fall apart for smaller offenses than a rude wife. In recent years it had become a juggling game with Karen. He wondered whether she had treated Higgins the way she had treated Cleve Miller. The chances were great that he would bring Cleve Miller into whatever Higgins had in mind, and Karen had never liked him.

Sorenson shook his head. Not liking Cleve Miller was hard for him to understand. Sure, Cleve could be provincial, and he had some strange ideas, but he kept them to himself. Besides, for better or worse Cleve was one of Larry's oldest friends. They had grown up together, gone off to college together. They'd seen each other through good and bad times. It had occurred to Sorenson that his friendship with Cleve was the reason Karen disliked him, and he had brought that up a few times when Karen attacked Cleve unfairly. But Karen always went back to the Sarah Looks Back affair. Sorenson had explained many times that she was misinformed, that it was fifteen years ago now, that Cleve was going through a rough time in his life then. It was before he'd stopped drinking, when farm prices were low, and before he'd gotten his real estate license. The Sarah Looks Back incident had taken place before he'd found his way back to the church. Contrary to what Karen believed, Cleve had taken no active part in what happened at the Blue Note Lounge. If he made a mistake, it was that he didn't stop what was going on. But Karen would not listen to reason. She refused to allow Cleve in the house on the grounds of an unfounded rumor.

What had happened was this: Cleve and a couple of his rancher friends were drinking beer at the Blue Note in Harney and were approached by an old Indian woman, Sarah Looks Back. She was a known alcoholic, and she wanted them to buy her a drink. They weren't going to buy her a drink, but Sarah kept bothering them until someone said, "OK, but we have to work for our drinks; what can you do for yours?"

Sarah thought they were talking about sex, but of course they just laughed at that. "No," they said. "Entertain us."

She tried to sing, but she was very drunk and the only songs she could remember were Lakota chants, so they told her to go away. But she wouldn't, and finally a man finished his beer and handed Sarah the bottle. "Here," he said, "piss in this bottle and we'll buy you a beer."

Sorenson swiveled in his chair thinking about the scene. Cleve should never have allowed it to happen, he thought. That was when he should have stood up. Cleve was a big, strong man and could have stopped it. But he did not. It became the funny thing to do at the Blue Note. Sarah would squat in the middle of the floor between the tables and the dance floor and fill a bottle for a drink. When the white women heard about it, they complained and Sarah was barred from the Blue Note.

Loni had been only a girl then, but strongheaded like her mother. Sorenson remembered how pretty she was, how pretty they both were. Their response had been out of proportion to the situation. Karen had made a point of finding out who had been in on Sarah Looks Back's humiliation. When she found that Cleve had been there, Karen forbade his coming into her house.

What happened to Sarah Looks Back had been a horrible thing, Sorenson agreed. But to attack Cleve Miller, to blame him for it, was grossly unfair. The way his wife had acted had been embarrassing for Sorenson, and now as he sat in his den, he wondered whether that had been the beginning of more misunderstandings, whether everything that came after couldn't be traced to that one great injustice.

Suddenly Sorenson was overwhelmed by a desire to make it all right. He wanted Karen on his side in this thing with Higgins. He wanted her on his side the way she had once been. With that on his mind he moved quickly from his den toward the kitchen. He had heard the clatter of pans a moment before. Now, as he came down the hall, he could hear Karen chopping something for their salad. The overhead light had been turned off, and Karen stood over the stove bathed in the yellow glow. The chopping board was on the stove. A small pile of diced radishes lay in one corner, and Karen had started on a carrot. Sorenson stood in the doorway and watched her. The light made her look older, but she was still beautiful, still the girl he had married, still Loni's mother. He wanted to tell her about Higgins, and just thinking about it made him smile. As he stepped into the room, he turned on the overhead light. But she only squinted at him as if he had interrupted her, as if, just now, cutting that carrot was very important.

▲
FIVE

Most of the people who lived on the bench agreed that Tuffy Martinez was a coyote. He drank too much, and bad luck followed him like an orphaned lamb. But he was good-natured, loyal to his friends, and capable of putting in a day's work, especially if he could do it from the back of a horse. He was also handsome. His Sioux and Mexican heritage had combined to give him huge, dark eyes and shiny black hair that he wore cut short for an Indian but long for a white man. Perfect white teeth made his smile hard to resist. Before he had to sell his cattle, he, like everyone else, was busy in the spring. Now spring didn't mean much to him, but a bright, crisp morning with no wind like this one still reminded him of that busy time of year. Even though he had drunk too much the night before, he was awake and outside leaning against his pickup not long after the sun was up.

A month earlier he had sold the best horse he ever had to Ross Brady. The horse's name was Bozo, and he had sold him too cheap. But Tuffy had no use for him, and he didn't want Bozo to stand around in a pasture going downhill. Ross didn't have the money Bozo was worth, but Tuffy wanted Ross to have him. They were both special to Tuffy, who figured he'd made a pretty good deal. He wanted Bozo to have a good home, and he wanted Ross to have a good horse. But with Bozo gone, Tuffy's only remaining responsibility around the place was to give Clyde, his cat, a bowl of milk, a can of cat food.

It doesn't take long to do the chores anymore, he thought

as he watched the sun peek for the first time that day through the cottonwood branches east of his yard. He had no plans for the day but thought he might go over to Cleve and Edith Miller's house and see whether he could help with something. Maybe Cleve needed help feeding his cows, though Cleve was probably working on his haying equipment. Cleve was the only man Tuffy knew who fixed his equipment before he needed it. This habit was annoying to Tuffy, probably because he knew it was one of the reasons Cleve Miller was doing a little better than most and that his own lack of such habits was the main reason his cattle had been sold. If Tuffy hadn't inherited his ranch from his parents, who acquired most of it when the reservation was divided up between individuals in the tribe, he wouldn't have a place to live now. But unlike everyone else on the bench, Tuffy owned the land outright and had no payments to make.

He'd lost money on cows and had learned that it was safest to lease his pastures to others and live on the lease money. It was a poor way to live, but it was better than borrowing money and risking the place. Tuffy turned up the collar of his jean jacket against the cold. He opened the pickup door and pulled himself onto the seat. When he turned the key, nothing happened. He tried again, but still nothing. The pickup wasn't that old. The battery, he thought, was a summertime battery. No guts. The old International tractor was down by the shed. He could jump the pickup with the tractor. But there was no guarantee that the tractor would start. He slid out from behind the wheel and stood for a moment with his hands in his jacket pockets. It was cold, bad weather for gutless batteries. But the old Harley-Davidson didn't need a battery to start. It depended on leg power.

The barn door was frozen shut, but one kick freed it. Tuffy had trouble sliding the door open and thought, for the thousandth time, that he should fix the rail on which it moved. The door sagged when it got to the end of the rail. The boards on the barn were rotten, and the carriage bolts that held the rail had pulled loose.

The motorcycle was a thirty-five-year-old Harley 74, a little older than Tuffy. Its handlebars reminded him of a long-horned steer; it had a foot clutch, hand-shift transmission, and running boards to rest your feet on. The wide saddle seat was covered with sparrow droppings. Tuffy knew that the birds spent the winter roosting in the rafters of the barn. Clyde should be taking care of them, Tuffy thought. No, he should have shot them, should have sneaked into the barn on a cold night and gotten them while their heads were under their wings. He had thought about it a couple nights that winter but didn't have the heart to do it. Now he simply brushed the droppings away with his hand.

"Go for it," he said as he threw his weight down on the kick starter. The Harley never started on the first kick. "Go for it, you son of a bitch." He kicked it three more times and finally there was a deep Harley pop in one of the two cylinders. Tuffy smiled. "Come on, mother." The next kick yielded two pops, and on the sixth try the engine broke into a string of explosions as Tuffy nimbly twisted the throttle and eased the choke back.

Tuffy's place was the last of the four on the bench. Its southern boundary was the reservation. Upstream from him the land broke into the Badlands, and downstream lay the flat bench that grew the most beautiful grass in the county. The first stream that wound off the bench was Red Willow, and it ran through the middle of his place. Next came Cherry Creek, where crippled old John Kiser lived. Elizabeth Janis had title to the place now. Then the Miller place with Old Woman Creek, and finally Ross Brady along the side of Sweet Grass Creek. After Ross's place the land dropped into a homogenous plain where the grass was poorer and winter cover for cattle scarce. The bench was really only a six-mile slope wedged between the reservation and Badlands on the south and east and the open plains on the north. It was good cattle country because of the water courses. A county road ran along the east side of the bench, and the driveways to the four ranches peeled off it, winding their ways downhill and to the west.

Tuffy's teeth were chattering when he came to the intersection of his driveway and the bench road. He took the turn slowly. There was no gravel on his driveway, but there was a little on the road. Tuffy never liked driving motorcycles on gravel. He hated the thought of the front wheel going out from under him. The Harley was a big bike and almost impossible to hold up, so he took it easy. He'd heard of lots of guys breaking legs because of gravel. Lots of guys had been killed, too. Not only that, but it was really too cold to ride a bike. He was freezing, so he let her idle along the road and watched the land between the road and the Cheyenne River.

He had traveled almost two miles when he came to Kiser's driveway. He still thought of it as Kiser's even though John was a vegetable and Elizabeth ran the place. Kiser had been a smart old geezer and probably knew what he was doing, but it was a mystery to Tuffy how Elizabeth could manage the ranch. They were close to the same age, and he had known her and her twin sister, Tracy, since boarding school on the reservation. He considered her a real friend, but she was private and kept to herself. He had always thought of her as too shy to do what it took to run a ranch. But maybe it was just that he couldn't run a ranch himself and so he had a hard time understanding how anyone could. Tuffy thought about pulling in to see Elizabeth. Kyle would be at high school now in Harney, old Pete would be out feeding the cows, and Elizabeth would be busy, too. Maybe he'd stop back that evening around suppertime.

The Harley popped past the driveway, and on the open

stretch between Elizabeth's and the Millers' Tuffy cracked the throttle a little. The engine responded with a hollow rapping sound that echoed off the eroding buttes to the east of the road. Tuffy was going forty miles an hour before he lost his nerve and eased off. The wind was like ice. He coasted by the chain link fence surrounding the missile silo, just past the Millers' driveway. He could never remember whether it was a Minuteman or a Titan that was stored down there.

As he approached the Millers' driveway, he cut the power all together and coasted to a halt at the base of the huge iron sign that had been there for fifteen years. Tuffy had helped Cleve Miller with the welding. It was the only sign of any kind on that road for forty miles in either direction. They had built it in Cleve's shop, and they built it to last. It was eight feet long and supported by six-inch iron pipes scavenged from the oil fields in Wyoming. The sign itself was cut with a torch from boilerplate and trimmed with chrome car bumpers. Other pieces of bumper were welded onto the boilerplate and spelled out CENTER OF THE NATION in letters two feet high. Under the letters and welded to a horizonal piece of drill pipe was an old toolbox. Cleve had cut a slit in the top of the box with a chisel. The paint was worn away now, but the side of the box had once read DONATIONS. For his help Tuffy had been promised twenty-five percent of the take.

Cleve had originally padlocked the toolbox to hold it shut. It was probably some crazy Indian on his way back to the reservation who shot the padlock dead center with what must have been something like a .30-06, and now it hung useless in the hasp. Tuffy supported the motorcycle with his feet, leaned over, and looked into the toolbox. There was no money. There had never been any money, but still he had to agree with Cleve's statement of fifteen years before: "Cattle isn't really a business. It's a joke. The real business in this part of the country is tourism. Look at Mount Rushmore. Look at the Enchanted Forest. Made more money for Harney than all the cattle in the world."

Still, Tuffy had questioned Cleve. "But the Park Service has a sign up in Harding County that says that's the center of the nation. That's a hundred miles from here."

"Huh," Cleve said. "Do you think the government knows where the center of this country really is? Dirt's washing off into the ocean every day. Land's going down the Missouri River. This is just as likely to be the center as any place else." And so Tuffy had worked for six days helping Cleve build the sign. But nobody had put the first penny in the toolbox.

The Harley's engine popped every couple seconds while Tuffy checked the toolbox. When he twisted the throttle, the popping gained momentum, and Tuffy let his feet drag some gravel as he left the county road and headed down Old Woman Creek toward the Millers' house.

Tuffy saw Edith come to the window, but when she saw who it was, she went back to whatever she had been doing. She had never said much to Tuffy, but he got the feeling that she didn't like him coming around. He knew people thought he was a little wild, but Edith didn't need to worry about him leading Cleve astray. Cleve had been around a long time. He was a churchgoer, big, gnarled, and strong. He was absolutely sure of himself since he quit drinking.

The Millers lived in a square, modular home they had built ten years before. That was about the time Cleve had taken up real estate. He'd made a little office in the new house, but Tuffy didn't think he ever sold much. The original homestead, now going to ruin, was on the other side of Old Woman Creek, half a mile from the new house. Tuffy had always liked the old two-story place and never understood why Cleve had abandoned it for the box they lived in now. It was more modern and closer to the road, but still it seemed a shame to let the old house fall to pieces.

Cleve had heard him coming and was walking out from behind a combine with a greasy hand held high. He was an older man, tall, with a long Adam's apple that he seldom got shaved properly. Tuffy let the Harley idle down and rolled to a stop. "Just the guy I'm looking for," Cleve said. "You used to have an old Gleaner combine like this behind your shed."

Tuffy nodded. There had always been a combine sitting behind his barn, but nobody on the bench raised grain except Cleve. Tuffy had never known why the combine was behind his barn. He had never really thought about it. "Yeah, there's a combine out back."

"Does it still have bearings on the main axles?"

"Might have," Tuffy said. "I'd have to look." Cleve frowned, obviously disappointed in Tuffy for not knowing everything about the combine. "You're getting ahead of yourself, aren't you? Grain won't be ready for five months."

"Probably won't even get any grain. Probably won't rain," Cleve said.

"Hell," Tuffy said, "it's dry now, but wait. About June those black clouds will come rolling in and dump a hat soakin', frog drownin' turd floater on us."

Cleve snorted. "Even if it does rain, it'll likely come with hail and smash all the grain flatter than a cow pie. And if things work out right and I get some grain, the Jews in Chicago will buy it for nothing. What's left the government will take." He looked back at the combine. "Shit," he said.

"Why bother?" Tuffy asked.

"Have to do something," Cleve shouted, "Real estate's gone to hell. Can't expect to get ahead if you don't do anything."

Tuffy could see that Cleve was in one of his moods. Cleve

was a good man, but when things went badly, he would often rave about everything he could think of and wasn't pleasant to be around.

Tuffy always figured Cleve was like this because he was raised in the thirties. It seemed as if the men who lived through the Depression were always scared that things were going to go to hell as they had then or because every so often they looked around and saw that things had never really gotten better. Tuffy had come to the Millers' thinking he might be able to help Cleve and maybe make a few bucks, but now it occurred to him that working with Cleve that day would not be much fun. Besides, he was hungry. "You got your cattle fed?" he asked.

"Yeah, fed them early," Cleve said.

"You want to go over to Milo to the Dust Buster with me?"

The Dust Buster was a beer joint strategically built on the edge of the reservation. Alcohol was illegal on the reservation, and business at the Dust Buster was brisk.

"It's a little early to start drinking, isn't it?" Cleve frowned. He was definitely in a self-righteous mood.

"They got food there," Tuffy said. "Hop on." He motioned toward the back of the motorcycle, though he was sure Cleve wouldn't get on.

"In a pig's eye. It's got to be cold as a witch's tit on that thing. You're crazy if you think I'm going to ride eighteen miles on the back of a chopper with a damned Indian to get a frozen pizza."

"You should try it, Cleve. It would set you free."

"You really hungry? Let's go into Harney and get a real breakfast."

Tuffy smiled. "Sounds good. Hop on."

"Screw that goddamned thing. We'll take my pickup." Cleve waved for Tuffy to hurry.

Tuffy knew Cleve had a five-year-old Ford Crown Victoria

in one of his sheds, left over from the beginning of his romance with real estate. "Let's take the big car," he said.

Cleve waved the idea away. "Come on; hop in." He pointed to his dented pickup.

Tuffy glanced toward the house as he got into the pickup. He expected Edith to be watching, but she wasn't. Harney was forty miles away, and they'd be lucky to be back by noon. Tuffy didn't know for sure because Edith didn't talk to him much, but he figured she'd disapprove.

▲
SIX

There were two wells and three stock dams on John Kiser's place. But the dams were in the summer pasture, and both wells were near the house, so in March, when all the cows were in the calving pasture, they were watered from Cherry Creek. Sometimes at that time of year there were a couple of places where the ice was thawed and the cattle could drink. But this year the nights had been a little colder than usual, so Pete Rienrick had to chop ice every morning.

Pete parked the pickup on the hill above the first bend below the house and walked down to a wide spot in the creek to chop a hole. He had chopped ice every winter since he was ten; that was over sixty years ago. He'd done it for twenty years for John Kiser before the accident. He'd helped Elizabeth since then, chopping the wide hole in almost the same spot every time. It was always the same: he parked the pickup in the same place if there wasn't too much snow, and he walked the same path to the creek. He always wore coveralls over his thin white body, but in recent years he'd taken to wearing an extra pair of pants and a shirt over his usual clothes and under the coveralls.

His left hand, the withered, useless one, was tucked away in a mitten and swung unnaturally at his side. (There were a few traces of snow from the night before.) The sun had been up only a few hours, and there was little wind, but the cold of the night still hung in the draw. The cows saw Pete walking toward the creek; their breath steamed as they lurched to their feet and began to amble toward him. Their mooing and movement was contagious, and before Pete was halfway to the creek, cows were coming from every direction.

Pete stopped near the creek and watched the ridges to be sure that the cows that were on the other sides were coming, too. He wanted to be sure that they all got water before the hole froze over again. Two strings of cows snaked their way toward him, one from the south and the other along the north ridge. Two old cows stood guard on the hillside, giving no signs of moving toward the water, and Pete knew that they had their calves hidden in the chokecherry bushes at the bottom of the draw. They would not come for water until the calves were a few days older.

Now he stepped to the edge of the creek and tipped the ax off his shoulder, letting it hit the ice first. A long shard of ice snapped out beneath the blade and skittered across the frozen creek.

It had been very cold the night before. The trench Pete had chopped the day before was refrozen as solid as the rest of the creek. He picked up the ax and let it fall again. This time it hit exactly along the line of the new ice. The ax came up again and pecked at the ice six inches farther along the line between the old and the new ice. The trick was to cut almost through along the entire perimeter of the trench before you broke into the water for the first time. If you did it just right, the ice came out in large pieces, and you didn't splash freezing water on yourself.

The cows were still coming. The bold ones stood only a few feet from Pete as he worked. Some of the shy ones, who had just calved or were about to, stood off and watched. They held their heads high and craned their necks. These cows made no noise. Their eyes were big and alert. Having newborn calves had made them forget that their ancestors had been domestic for thousands of years. They were not docile like the cows that were still weeks away from calving. These cows that stood their ground were ready to run or fight.

Pete worked steadily, raising the ax with one arm and bringing it down accurately. He finished scribing the hole, then straightened up and let the ax blade rest on solid ice. He was feeling his age. He couldn't remember when he had not awakened stiff and sore. Under the collar of his two wool shirts he wore a black silk scarf tied around his neck. With his right hand he pulled the scarf out and over his nose so he could breathe through it. He was breathing too deeply, and without the scarf the cold air stung his lungs.

After he had caught his breath, he lowered the scarf and watched the air he expelled form a thick cloud that drifted away on the light breeze. He coughed twice, deep and jagged, then began to call the cows. "Here, Boss! Here, Boss!" He raised the ax and let it fall with the flat of the blade hitting the center of the block of ice he had chopped around. The force was just right, and the block cracked loose and bobbed free in the water of Cherry Creek. He divided the slab into three pieces with the ax and pulled them out one by one.

The cows pushed in around him. Pete looked into the water and wondered whether it was true that there was gold in the small streams that fed the Cheyenne River. A crew had come through the year after John was crippled and drilled test holes all over the bench. Pete figured that they had waited until John Kiser was stuck in a wheelchair, slobbering on himself, before they made their move. They knew that if John was sound, he'd never let them on the place. But Elizabeth, even though she might not have wanted them around, couldn't be as tough as John. They'd talked her into it in minutes.

Pete tried to see to the bottom of the pool, but cows had begun to drink and the water was too agitated for him to be able to see clearly. The cows jostled him as he pushed out between them. He knew the mean ones and stayed clear of their hindquarters and lightning back kicks. "Get over, girl," he said; "ah, move it!" And he prodded them with the flat of the ax head.

Pete looked closely at the cows, reading their ear tags and looking at their udders to see how close they were to calving. There were nearly a hundred and fifty cows in the pasture, and most were ready to have calves. But Pete had no trouble telling them apart. "Twenty-eight," he said out loud. "You snaky old bitch. You're getting close." He faced number twenty-eight and asked earnestly, "You planning on takin' your calf up into the northwest draw again this year?" They looked at each other for an instant, and the cow swayed from side to side.

The first group of cows was watering, and number twenty-eight was waiting her turn. When Pete moved toward the pickup, she hopped sideways and bucked playfully. "Feeling your oats," Pete said. He nodded and looked at the sky. "Must be weather on the way. Tomorrow it'll snow like hell." When he got into his pickup, a healthy, younger John Kiser was sitting in the seat beside him. "Looks about like the day you got busted up. Hell," Pete said, "couldn't do it on a nice summer day." He laughed. "Hell no, you wouldn't call it quits if the sun was shining and warm, would you?"

John laughed, too, and looked out the side window. Pete followed his gaze. The sun was pale in the eastern sky. About average for March, Pete thought, as he started the pickup. He was seventy-six and had lived in this country his whole life. He had seen March days that got up to eighty degrees, seen it where the grass was starting to green up and grow by this time. But he'd seen three feet of snow, too. He'd seen it twenty degrees below zero on Good Friday, and Good Friday was still three weeks off.

A few cows stood in front of the pickup. He had already fed them, but there were always a few who could eat all day. He didn't blow the horn because that was their dinner bell and would just make things worse. Instead he eased the pickup forward and bumped them with the grill. These cows were the biggest of the herd. They were barrel-shaped, three and a half feet wide, and they weighed up to sixteen hundred pounds. When he bumped them, they didn't move. They looked over their round hindquarters at him and bellowed. If they could, Pete thought, they'd hold me up and stick a gun to my head for a bale of hay. He pressed the accelerator and bumped a couple that were directly in front of him. They all moved except one fat Hereford. Pete let the pickup roll tight against her flank, shifted to four-wheel drive, and began to push. She straightened her legs and set her hooves, but the pickup was too strong, and finally she waddled out of the way. But she turned as Pete passed so that her face was only inches from the window on the driver's side. She gave one last bellow of protest and sprayed the window with slobber. Pete took note of her ear-tag number. "Ninety-seven," he said to himself. "Crazy old bitch."

▲
SEVEN

Elizabeth saw the pickup bouncing across the pasture as she stood in the lot behind the barn. Kyle had checked the heifers when he fed them before taking the other pickup to high school in Harney, and it was Elizabeth's turn to check them now. She traded off with Kyle, every four hours, with the two A.M. check falling to her. She was up again at five-thirty to wake Kyle, milk the cow, and get a breakfast ready before Pete was ready to go out to feed the cattle. Before she fed John, she would usually have to spend some time talking Kyle into going to school.

Kyle hated school. He was a good kid, but he had trouble learning some things. The truth was he could hardly read, and even though Elizabeth had tried to help him, he had never improved. He was very embarrassed about it, and sometimes Elizabeth wondered whether she was right in making him go to school. It was always hard for her.

But lots of things in life were hard. Taking care of John was hard. Not so much the bathing him or feeding him or lifting him in and out of his wheelchair as just watching him sit motionless, staring without blinking an eye. She wondered what he saw, what he thought about, and it made her tired. Every spring Elizabeth would often experience a sinking feeling about this time of day. She stepped from the lot and moved away from the buildings toward the cottonwoods along Cherry Creek. If she followed the trees for three miles, she would come to the Cheyenne River. If she walked up the draw, she would come out in the bull pasture, where the land flattened into a productive hay pasture.

She stood just at the edge of the trees until she heard the pickup approaching, then she moved toward higher ground.

The ground had begun to thaw, and the gray gumbo soil squeezed out around her overshoes. She angled to the left and slipped on the thawing bank as she climbed over the exposed roots of an ash tree. Suddenly she felt like a little girl again and remembered when she was a seventeen-year-old from the reservation with a year-old son, no husband, and nightmares that wouldn't let her sleep. When she had first come here to live off the kindness of John Kiser, she had gone to the bull pasture to hide. She had used this pasture as a hiding place after John Kiser's accident, too.

Where the draw spread out into the bull pasture was a huge limestone rock shaped like an egg. This was her special place. She had spent many hours here while Kyle was growing up. She imagined that if Kyle were ever to seek a vision, this would be the place. From her perch on top of the rock she could see the Cheyenne River. Sometimes before the bulls were turned out with the cows in June, they would come around when she sat there. They acted like they didn't know she was there, but of course they did. Their haughty ways didn't fool her. She was sure they came so she would not feel alone. And sometimes a badger would come and sit on his ridge and watch her. When he came, he was on his best behavior. He never came close like the bulls because he was wild and had a reputation to uphold, but she knew he came for the same reason.

She thought of Pete and Kyle. She enjoyed getting up at two o'clock to check the heifers. It made her feel good to let the others sleep, and besides, it gave her a chance to watch the night sky. She had once tried to count the stars, but the more she counted, the more she concentrated on the pinholes of light, the more stars became visible. Now she knew it was an impossible task. You could count forever and still there would be more. But even realizing that, she sometimes counted a few when she went out at night. It made her feel good to count stars, take care of the heifers, and let the men sleep. They had both been tired since the spring routine started. They were men, she thought; they needed sleep. And it popped into her head before she could stop it that because they were men, they would die suddenly; Kyle perhaps before his time. Honorable old age, it seemed, was not meant for men. Women, like her mother, at least have a chance to grow old and wise and come to be respected. But it never seemed to happen to the men. If they didn't get hurt or go crazy, like John and Pete, they got bitter, mean, impossible to live with. Or something small and stupid would kill them. Her father had died in a pickup accident on a road he had traveled every day for years. It had happened a month before his forty-eighth birthday. John Kiser had been crushed by a colt on a lovely spring morning. Kyle was seventeen—would he live a long life? Then she remembered the first time she saw John Kiser.

Charley Janis, her father, had been a friend of John's. They were roping partners for years, and because they worked well together, they were asked to help at a big roundup and branding near Wounded Knee. It was the largest branding Elizabeth had ever been to: eleven hundred cows and their calves. It took three days to gather, brand, and vaccinate them all. There were thirty men to help, and many of them brought their families.

Elizabeth and her twin sister, Tracy, slept in the pickup box, and Charley and their mother made a bed on the ground. The sons of the men who were working helped where they could; most of the daughters busied themselves with cooking but spent as much time as they could at the corrals watching the young cowboys who would show off for them. Some of the more courageous girls arranged to meet their favorites in the evening after the work was done. Elizabeth had been much too shy for that sort of thing, but Tracy was anything but shy. She was also, unlike her twin, beautiful. That combination of personality and beauty brought the boys around in swarms. And when they came, Elizabeth would hide.

That is how she got to know John Kiser. He was often quiet, too, and would sit in the light of the campfire and listen to Charley tell his famous stories. John's smile would explode out of him at the punch lines, and he would push his hat to the back of his head and laugh. Elizabeth sat between the two men feeling safe as she listened to the stories, and she would smile down toward the ground at the jokes. And they would drink whiskey until Charley was drunk, which never took too long. "Work like a Frenchman; drink like a Sioux," John Kiser would say of his friend. That would bring a laugh from the Indians around the fire. John was a white man and a tough white man, but there was something about him that made Indians feel they could be themselves. There were no wooden Indians at his fire. He had the sense of humor of a Sioux, and everyone knew he was different, that he belonged in this place. No one could deny feeling that when John Kiser was around, there seemed to be a chance that things would turn out all right.

People would ease around their fire to listen to the two men kid each other and laugh, and Elizabeth remembered looking up to see Louis White Horse with his arm around Tracy. It had frightened her because she thought her father might get angry. But he did not. Could that have been the night Tracy met Louis? She shivered to think of it, then shook her head and smiled fondly as the memory of her father came back into focus.

Charley Janis had never amounted to much in the eyes of the world, but he had been a wonderful father. He always said that his only real claims to fame were his women. He had married a girl from Whiteclay, Nebraska, with very light skin and said that she was the reason his daughters looked like movie stars. The way he said it made even plain and gangling Elizabeth believe it.

Once Elizabeth had told John Kiser what her father had said, and John had nodded. "Nice women," he'd said. "But he had a lot more going for him than that." It was a year or so after Charley's pickup had overturned and killed him, and John still had a tendency to be wistful when he spoke of him. "The man could rope," John said. "The man could rope like nobody's business."

Of course, there was the negative side, Elizabeth thought. His habit of drinking until he couldn't function was well-known. And his attraction to women was not always limited to his wife. Though he always provided for his family, he found it hard to work a steady job. It wasn't that he was lazy or that his drinking got in the way of his working. He never got mad and quit. The boss never got mad and fired him. Usually when it came time to quit a job, Charley just didn't show up. It was not unheard of for him to wander off in the middle of the day and never come back. This quirk drove employers mad. They were mostly white, and they would blame it on Charley's Indian blood. The ranchers that Charley worked for never understood this little quirk, and though they finally saw humor in it and seldom hesitated to hire him back, they always treated Charley as if there was something wrong with him. That is the way Elizabeth remembered white people treating her father, and maybe that is what made John Kiser stand out at the branding near Wounded Knee.

The branding had been in May, and most of the calves were small. The ropers walked their horses into the bunch and, with good-sized loops, caught the calves around both back legs. They dallied the rope around the saddle horn and turned the horse toward the opening in the pen. As they dragged the calves out, teams of men grabbed them, took the ropes off, and held them down while other men and women descended on them with syringes filled with vaccine, castrating knives, ear tags, and red-hot branding irons. It took only a minute until the mother cows, who had already been vaccinated and stood waiting outside the corral, were rewarded. The calves jumped up bawling and scurried out to their lowing mothers.

Those were the spring calves, a couple months old, weighing maybe a hundred pounds. They were calves like the hundred and fifty Elizabeth would have to find a way to get branded in six weeks. It was a big job, and she always worried that they would never get it done. But with the help of the neighbors, especially Tuffy Martinez and Ross Brady, they always seemed to manage. At least they would not have to worry about calves born in the fall. At the Wounded Knee branding there had been fifteen or twenty of those, weighing over five hundred pounds. They were not about to be dragged away from the rest of the herd by the back legs and held down by two cowboys while people cut, burned, and stabbed them. They were half-wild, not babies anymore, and carried with them the wisdom and strength of a winter on the grasslands. Those were the cattle that the boss sent Charley Janis and John Kiser into the pen to rope.

They did it the old way. Charley shot small loops into the crowd of calves, neatly roping the big calves around the horns, which had already grown to a length of eight inches. Then he turned his horse, who lowered his rear end and strained to pull the calf, bucking and bawling, into the center of the corral. As Charley turned the cattle, John, older and more patient, rotated the large heeling loop and waited for the exact moment when he could snake it out and catch both hind legs. When the rope found its mark, both horses moved away until the ropes went tight and the calf toppled onto its side. The horses and men stood motionless as the ground crew worked. Elizabeth remembered how the two men faced away from each other on their horses, how the muscles bulged and glistened with sweat, how the ropes, connecting the men through the living calf, seemed taut to the point of breaking. There has always been that image in her mind: two men erect in the saddle, motionless but still in control of the horses and the situation.

When the ground crew pulled the ropes loose and let the cattle free, the riders did not yell back and forth to each other with the bravado of younger cowboys. They did not even look at each other. They simply began to coil their ropes as they turned their horses slowly back toward the herd.

Her father had been riding Sugar that day; John had been on Bud. Elizabeth winced. Bud had lived until just two years ago. John had been looking for a replacement for years. He had been through a lot of horses, but the only one he thought might someday be as good as Bud was the powerful black colt that crippled him. She shook out of her mind the sound of Dancer squealing and tried to concentrate on that day, years before, when she had found herself staring at the men as they worked. It was as if they were one man—no words, no pretenses—and to her that day it had seemed strange. She had seen men work before, of course, but there had always been bantering back and forth, betting on the next throw of the rope, maybe drinking as they rode. It was her first experience with men at their best, working, doing things that needed strength and skill, but quietly, as if the work were more important than whether others noticed. Had she not known better, she would have thought that the two men did not like each other. But as she watched, she saw that they did. It was the beginning of her understanding of men. They glanced at each other, a nod here, a soft word there. For the men on the horses the women had faded away. They were at ease, with deadly accurate ropes and precision horsemanship. And Elizabeth had loved them both and wanted it always to be that way.

Now she watched the blue sky over Badger's Ridge and tried to force all the tension out of her muscles. The rigors of spring had made her tired, too. She drew her ankles up tight against her buttocks and rested her chin on her knees. She closed her eyes and thought about pleasant things: spring rain, newborn calves, running horses, and fields of tall grass. As she concentrated on those things, she heard the bulls moving slowly toward her. She kept her eyes closed and let more of the tightness in her arms and back drain away. The bulls' hooves clicked as they milled around the rock, and she heard a few of them groan as they lay down. In a moment she heard the slow sound of the bulls chewing their cud. Their male smell soaked the air.

When she opened her eyes, the badger was on his ridge. He sat like a dog, watching her from a safe distance. His eyes glistened from the center of his thick winter mane, and Elizabeth knew that he had no tricks in mind. She smiled as she considered what the other animals would think if they knew that he had met her like this for so many years. She hoped that the badger knew how much she appreciated the risk he was taking.

▲
EIGHT

Linda's father was concerned about his only son. "He should never have quit that telephone company," he told Linda. "He's a good boy, your brother. There's not a thing wrong with him." He shook his finger in Linda's face as if she might disagree with him. It was the way he had always acted when he was frightened. They were sitting in the living room of Linda's apartment. Linda had not been awake long.

She had just finished stretching when her father walked in with only a knock and closed the door behind him. He had helped her find the apartment and had kept a key. To him it made perfect sense that a father should have a key to his daughter's apartment. They sat on the couch, Linda in sweat clothes and her hair pulled back, and her father trim and scented in his suit, an open collar, and white shoes. He leaned forward with so much sincerity that Linda felt herself wanting to hug him. He was tanned, and his thinning silver hair was combed back perfectly. He looked like the successful business-man that he was, but his face drooped in a pout that Linda knew meant he wanted her to do something about Stewart.

"He won't listen to me," her father said.

"It's still his company."

"Forty percent only."

"OK. But he's the one who got it going. Just like the other companies he helped start. He's done very well."

"Yeah, yeah. But money isn't everything. This jumping from company to company, I don't like it."

"It's the way things work now, Dad. He'll get going again. He's done this after every job change."

"Never like this. He spends all day in bed." Her father leaned even farther forward. "God knows what he does at night. Drugs, alcohol; who knows?" He looked into Linda's face. "Go talk to him. I know you're busy with the dancing, but go talk to him. You were always close. It was so nice. Please. Talk to him."

When she got to Stewart's house, he was lying on the floor watching Donahue. Linda pulled the blinds open to let in the morning light as Stewart rolled to a sitting position. The ocean was only a few hundred yards away. She watched a surfer catch a small wave. When she turned back to Stewart, the sunshine was in his eyes. He rubbed his face, and she could almost hear the sound as he passed his fingers over his whiskers. "Sis. What's happening?" He wore a bathrobe and huge woolly slippers on his feet.

"That's what everyone is wondering. I was sent to find out what your problem is."

Stewart shrugged. His hair was a mess but he was smiling. "Problem?"

Linda gestured toward him. "Look at you. What are you doing?"

Stewart mimicked her gesture toward the television. "Learning about codependent dyslexics."

"Ha ha."

Phil had just stuck a microphone in the face of a sobbing woman. Linda covered the distance to the television in two steps. She looked for the power switch.

Stewart pulled the remote-control box from his bathrobe pocket. He held it up to tantalize his sister. Linda smiled. "Turn it off," she said. They looked at each other for what seemed a long time. There was a touch of defiance in Stewart's eyes. Donahue's audience was applauding something the woman had said. The defiance slipped away. He switched off the television.

Linda nodded. "We better have a little talk," she said. "You got anything out in that kitchen for breakfast?"

Stewart's smile was weak. "You like stale bread and moldy fruit?"

"Take a shower. I'll make coffee."

She found all the makings for coffee except the filters. The kitchen was a mess. A week's worth of dishes were piled in the sink. There were a few empty beer bottles and a bottle with a half-inch of cabernet left in the bottom. The cork was gone, and the wine smelled thick and sour. Linda used a paper towel for a coffee filter and began to straighten up the place. The water pressure was low, and she suspected that Stewart had just gotten a shot of cold from his shower. Justice, she thought.

There were some clothes hanging on the kitchen chairs that she gathered and began to fold. Stewart had apparently undressed in the kitchen. The sweater was still clean, a cardigan, very nice, but the pants were wrinkled, and she pulled the belt out and emptied the pockets on the counter. She laid the billfold and comb beside the loose change and the tiny ivory-handled pocketknife. There was a button, a matchbook from a nightclub, and a small plastic device that looked like a pencil sharpener. But it was no pencil sharpener. Linda picked it up and looked it over. There were two clear plastic chambers, one much larger than the other, and a small lever that emptied one chamber into the other. It was a cocaine bullet, shaped to fit into a nostril. All the cocaine had been sucked out.

When Stewart came into the kitchen, the table was clean except for the bullet, which was sitting upright in front of the chair Stewart used. When Stewart saw the bullet, he looked up at his sister and smiled like a little boy.

Then they talked.

And as he mumbled about being bored and feeling useless, she thought of Ross. She had already decided to let Stewart get everything out, and then she would suggest he take a couple weeks and go see Ross. Time with Ross might get Stewart back on track. It would be a couple weeks like none other in Stewart's life. It would be good for him to see that there was something more than late-night clubs, fancy clothes, and Sunset Boulevard. Stewart and Ross were very special to her, and she wanted them to get to know each other, something they had never had a chance to do. But all of that was only part of the reason she wanted Stewart to spend time with Ross. The other part was her own desire to keep her link to Ross alive. She nodded as Stewart talked, but her mind was miles and years away.

South Dakota was a beautiful place, with values that were straightforward and honest. Again she thought it would be good for Stewart. But a memory nagged her as she pretended to listen to her brother describing his jumbled life. There was a small incident, an impression really, that probably only she was sensitive to, but she could not forget it. When she thought of the place where she had tried to live with her husband, the feeling she had in Cleve Miller's little real estate office that first day came to her.

It was the simplest of things, and many times she thought she imagined it. Ross had decided, because of his need to live away from people, that he wanted to start his new life in the United States on the edge of the Badlands. In those days there had been a small market for ranches, and Cleve Miller had a few listed, but they were leaning toward putting all of Ross's inheritance down on a ranch that was being foreclosed on by the Farmers Home Administration. Cleve was a big, middle-aged man but gentle and soft-spoken. Even so, there was something about him that had bothered Linda, something that she came to find everywhere in that country. There was a darkness hidden in the pleasant smile, a darkness Ross never noticed and that she had never been able to explain. Cleve had tried to talk Ross out of buying near the Badlands. "I know this country." He waved his hand to indicate the direction of the ranch Ross wanted. "Hell, I lived here all my life. It's simply not a good place to be." Cleve's smile made her think of her grandfather, except for the glint of gold in the black recesses of the mouth. "The reservation is only ten miles away and that's a mess. It's best to stay with the pure breeds in this country," he said earnestly. He smiled again and Ross nodded.

Sitting in the chair in the real estate office, she had felt naked, as if everyone were staring at her body. And it was this feeling that never left her, that drove her away from South Dakota as much as did the lack of an opportunity to dance.

That was the bad part of her years out there. It was something Ross had been numb to, probably because he wanted so desperately to come back to America. Also, he was drawn to the land, to the solitude. She always thought that the chance to fade into the landscape had seduced Ross. She felt it offered him a way to ease back into society, and she had gone along with it. She never thought it would last. Neither of them understood that place. To Linda it was obvious that until a person understands a place, he or she does not belong there.

But Stewart would likely never feel what she had felt. He would love the big blue sky, the horses and cows, and the simple life. She imagined him pitching hay from the back of a truck, and she smiled. Stewart smiled back. He was winding down, starting to joke and poke fun at his situation. She told herself that Ross would be good for Stewart. Ross saw only the beauty and the romance. That's what he would show Stewart, and that is what Stewart needed. When Stewart mentioned something about how his life had no adventure, no real pizzazz, Linda saw her chance. "What you need," she said, "is a vacation, a little change of scenery."

▲
NINE

The prevailing winds over the grasslands are westerly. Ninety percent of the weather comes from the west or the northwest. It is the rotation of the earth that sets these great blankets of air moving down from the frozen tundra, over the northern Rocky Mountains, and onto the grasslands. The wind is something that the inhabitants of the grasslands must endure. The natural residents do not seem to mind; they have evolved to withstand and even use the wind. The jackrabbits build their shallow forms on the southeastern side of yucca plants and back into them so that their tails touch the yucca. There they sit on the windy days, in comfort, facing the direction into which their scent fans out. Before they are in danger, they will see any ground predator that can smell them. By remaining still beneath the yucca, they do not attract the streamlined ferruginous hawks and golden eagles, which have learned to ride the air high above the earth and to stoop, with the wind at their backs, at speeds that the jackrabbit cannot comprehend. The wind plays a part in almost every drama on the grasslands, and everyone who knows the land is constantly aware of its direction and velocity.

But the wind does not always come from the west or northwest. Sometimes it comes from the southeast. Usually this means low pressure is lingering over the mountains of Colorado. It can bring lovely spring snow to the Rockies, and the skiers are delighted. The winds around that low pressure move counterclockwise. There is a huge cyclone effect in the center of the mountains that spirals out beyond the mountains to the canyon lands of Utah, the grasslands to the northeast, and as far south as the Gulf of Mexico. At the same time high-pressure ridges often cover most of Minnesota and radiate their clockwise winds equally far in all directions. Minneapolis will enjoy unseasonably nice weather. The result is a corridor seven hundred miles wide and stretching from the warm, moist Mississippi Delta to the foothills of the Rockies in central Montana. When this happens, the counterclockwise winds of the Colorado low and the clockwise winds of the Minnesota high are going in the same direction along the corridor that blankets the entire grasslands. The winds begin to mingle over Louisiana and suck the Caribbean's warmth and moisture into the corridor and toward the northwest. In a sense, they reverse the flow of the Missouri River.

The ranchers around Harney, South Dakota, had been testing the air for days, finding familiar signs in the combination of wind and pressure. The wind would soon be warmer, coming from the south, but the rabbits would not move to the other side of the yucca. The rabbits were waiting it out because somewhere in their primordial memory they knew that the wind would soon change again and would begin to blow hard from the north. The temperature would drop as the Colorado low moved over the grasslands, and as the center passed over them on its way eastward, the counterclockwise movement of air would mean a northwesterly wind. Depending on what kind of weather was farther north, the temperature could crash, and all the moisture from the gulf that had been sucked northward could condense and fall on the grasslands in the form of snow.

The rabbits would stay were they were. They would not worry even if they could. But the men of Harney were uneasy. They asked whether the wife had plenty of groceries. In their minds they figured how much hay was left in their stacks. They thought how glad they were that they hadn't moved the cattle away from the buildings for the spring, or cursed the fact that they had. Those who had satellite dishes tuned to the weather station and watched the representation of the huge Arctic cold front move across the Rocky Mountains of British Columbia and knew that conditions were perfect for a spring blizzard.

Ross Brady had been on the grasslands long enough to feel it, too. He stood on his front porch and tasted the change in the air. This was one of the things that he liked about living in this country, weather that not only changed gradually with the season but had the potential for creating a spectacle. He told Linda once that it was like living beneath a drive-in theater that showed unscheduled movies by Cecil B. DeMille. But, of course, it was different from that, better in fact, because the weather on the grasslands was real. The thunderheads that formed to the west in the summer could take your breath away. The stillness that preceded them and the grandeur of the swelling dark clouds towering over the whole world affected Ross deeply, made him feel that he was actually part of his surroundings and calmed him in a way that made it possible for him to accept the violence of the winds and hail that swept in with a force that was unimaginable.

It was part of what had brought him to the grasslands. It was what set him apart from what should have been his heritage. But the panoramas—sunsets and sunrises, the wind, the weather—and daily contact with things that he had dreamed of as a child still did not seem to satisfy him. He thought about the rolling, tree-covered hills of Pennsylvania, of a city life in which you could buy anything you needed, of family, and of houses where the water always came out of the tap the way it was supposed to, and though it left him unmoved, he would search those memories for a hint of what was missing in his present life. The obvious answer was Linda, but Ross had never trusted the obvious. If he had, he would have settled into running his father's truck farm after his parents died. He wouldn't have sold out and put the money down on a ranch at the edge of the Badlands.

▲

TEN

Tuffy had gotten very drunk, but he figured he deserved it. He'd spent the night in Milo at the Dust Buster and driven back to the ranch after closing. It was two thirty when he pulled up beside the house. He sat in the pickup and tried to gather his thoughts. This was a critical time. He had made the same mistake too many times and ended up with a dead battery. He told himself, out loud, to turn off the ignition and the lights.

He finished the beer he was holding and tossed it into the back of the pickup, along with a hundred others. Where was Clyde? he thought as he climbed the three steps to the kitchen door. Goddamned cat was never home. After he had flipped on the kitchen light, he stuck his head back out the door and called into the night. "Clyde, you dirty son of a bitch, where are you?" The cat answered from the darkness with a sharp meow. "Get in here, you old bastard." Tuffy held the door open, and the yellow tomcat shot through.

Tuffy stood for a moment in the kitchen doorway and rubbed his face. He had had another rough time at the Dust Buster, and he was trying to remember exactly what had happened. Clyde jumped onto the counter and meowed for his dinner.

Tuffy didn't want to think about those guys in the bar. The only decent human being there that night, he thought, was Ruth Albertson. She was the tough, heavyset older woman who owned the place. She liked Tuffy. The rest were just punks.

Won a buckle or two at some pop-stand rodeo and all of a sudden they're big deals. Then he remembered what had happened. They had stolen his hat when he'd laid his head down on the bar. They'd put it upside down in the toilet so the seat held the brim and let just the crown touch the water in the bowl. Everyone had gotten a big kick out of it when he'd come out of the men's room wearing the hat with just the very top wet. Tuffy had been mad but now he smiled. It was a pretty good trick, he thought. And it could have been worse. Clyde meowed loudly.

"Yes, sir, Mr. Clyde," he said. "Coming right up."

He took a can of cat food from the cupboard and opened it with the can opener that hung on a nail by the sink. "Don't know how you can eat this shit," he said. "I mean, give me a baby bird or a dead rat any day." Clyde had jumped to the floor and was rubbing against his leg. Tuffy looked down at him. "You crazy bastard, you love this stuff, don't you? This is the stuff they sweep up at the tuna cannery. Fish lips." He looked at the top. "Eighty-nine cents," he said. "Christ, a house full of mice and you got to have a gourmet dinner." He dumped the can in Clyde's bowl. "I'm going to bed," he said. "Don't stay up too late."

Tuffy wanted to brush his teeth. It was one thing that he always did before going to bed, and just as he had with the ignition and the headlights, he had trained himself to remember. There was a large spiderweb in the corner of the bathroom, and Tuffy checked it for flies. There were no new flies, and Tuffy concluded that the guys in the bar had been right. There was no early spring in store for this year. He spread a little toothpaste on his toothbrush and began to brush. His reflection in the mirror was not clear: the glass was dirty, and one of the overhead bulbs was burned out, but Tuffy could see that he looked rough. It had been a bad night at the Dust Buster.

First, Cleve Miller had come in from one of his night rides along the bench road in his old Crown Victoria and talked to him about fighting the bank and getting his cattle back. When Cleve talked like that, it made sense. The Jews ran the banks and the grain elevators. They controlled all foreign grain sales. The cattle markets moved just the opposite of the grain markets, so they had control there, too. The only thing they didn't have yet was the land. Their plan was to take over by foreclosing on bad loans. Of course, since they controlled all the markets, they could make anybody's loan bad. Cleve said the country was at a crossroads, that it was up to the decent, simple people to make a stand. He had Bible verses to prove all this.

Since the money that the bank had lent him was not backed with gold, it was illegal tender anyway. The bank had really lent him nothing of value, and they had taken something of value to satisfy the debt. It was a pretty slick deal, Cleve said. They take our property as collateral for worthless notes, inflate the price of everything so you can't pay them back, then foreclose.

Tuffy spit into the sink. It seemed more complicated when he thought about it alone. He guessed he wasn't cut out to understand world economics. He cupped his hands, sucked in some water, and rinsed his mouth. He spit again and reached for the soap. But the soap was not in the tray. "Goddamn," Tuffy said. He shut the water off and turned to the shower. The soap wasn't there either. "Goddamn!" he yelled and stormed out of the bathroom.

He stopped in the kitchen long enough to take a flashlight from the top of the refrigerator and to glare at Clyde, who was finishing his dinner. "You lazy fucker," he said to the cat, then pushed out the back door.

As he crossed the yard to the machine shop, Tuffy noticed that the wind was warm, southerly, but the weather didn't concern him. What did concern him was his soap. He stopped in front of the gas pump. The co-op had cut off his credit two years before, and when the thousand-gallon underground fuel tank had gone empty, he had stopped using the pump all together. Now he knelt over the filler hole and unscrewed the cap. The tank had rusted out at a seam eight feet below ground level. As Tuffy peered into the filler hole and adjusted the light on the bottom of the tank, he could see that the pack rat had pulled more cactus through the rusted place. The pile of trash at the bottom of the tank had expanded to a ball four feet in diameter. On his knees and one hand he directed the light past his right ear so he could study the cactus, bailing twine, and horse turds. He inspected every corner of the nest. Finally he found his soap. It was tucked away neatly between a ballpoint pen and his original set of pickup keys.

By the time Tuffy got back to the house, he was beginning to feel very tired. He felt a headache coming on and took the bottle of aspirin from one of the kitchen cupboards. Clyde had finished eating and was gone. He had a secret place in the house where he went when he didn't want to be found. Tuffy peeled his shirt off as he walked down the hall to his bedroom.

It was cold in the back of the house, and he turned on the propane heater beside the bed. The bottom fitted sheet had come off the mattress again and was tangled with the wool blanket. Tuffy sat on the bed and pushed each boot off with the opposite foot. He slid out of his pants and reached for the lamp on the bedside table. But before he turned the light off, he opened the thin drawer below it and took out a 1975 high school yearbook. He turned to page twenty-four and looked at the only picture he had ever had of Loni Sorenson.

She'd gone on to college just after the picture was taken. Then she was a beauty queen. Tuffy had heard that she was married now to a lawyer in Minneapolis. He held the picture very close to his face. It was not a good picture. Her smile seemed stiff, but her hair was curly and thick, just the way he remembered it. Now he closed the book, laid it back in the drawer, and turned off the light. Before he felt asleep, he felt Clyde jump on the bed and curl up in the hollow at the back of his knees.

▲
ELEVEN

Though Elizabeth had not had the dream for a long time, she knew that it would come that night. She had never told anyone about the dream except Tuffy, and that was years ago, when the dream visited her much more often. Dreaming that dream had to do with life being too good. It came when things were going well, like now, with the easy spring and no problems with the cattle. There was something about everything moving along without a hitch that triggered it. It was as if she had to pay for her prosperity. A day or so before she had begun to feel anxious, as if there were something unpleasant that had to be done.

That night she stayed awake as long as she could, until she was exhausted. It was just before three o'clock when she dozed off, still dressed, with the light on. And the dream came the way she was afraid it would, within minutes of closing her eyes.

It began the way it always had, with a sickening feeling in her stomach. Then there was the strong hand at the back of her neck and the fingers paralyzing her. In the dream she felt the hard slap and heard the dress tear. She felt the cut below her right breast where her bra was ripped away. This time it lasted long enough for her to feel the hands, like two vises, around her wrists and the prickly straw of the barn floor against her back. Mercifully she awoke with a whimper before she felt the weight on top of her or smelled the sweat and whiskey close against her face.

▲

PART THREE

PART THREE

▲

TWELVE

The barn on the old Miller homestead was now just a pile of siding, shingles, plaster, and two-by-fours. You could still see where the corrals had been and the shed that burned because of an electrical short while Cleve was at college. There wasn't much left of the old place but the house, and thinking of it always made Cleve feel lonely. He seldom went over to the old place.

The land Cleve Miller had inherited from his parents was good cattle country. All the land on the bench was. But cattle country had no value. If they could raise crops, it might be different, but though Cleve tried, it rarely panned out. The truth was that it was tough making a living on the bench. Cleve kept some mother cows, and if the cattle market looked good, he bought yearling grass cattle and ran them for the couple hundred pounds they would gain. He had friends who operated feedlots in the eastern part of the state, and he sold the yearlings to them to fatten on corn.

But the old ranch had never really amounted to much. There was certainly no real money in it, and Cleve never really enjoyed ranching anyway. He'd never found satisfaction in it the way some seemed to, and he had realized, even as a child, that the economics of agriculture would eventually push most people off the land. His parents realized that, too, and encouraged him in his schooling, where he had always been a standout. They believed it was the way out, and maybe they had been right. Maybe if he had stuck it out, he'd be the doctor that his father had always wanted him to be.

Cleve Miller sat at his desk in the part of his house he called his office and looked at the picture of his mother and father hanging on the opposite wall. The couple stood in front of the old house with looks of calm determination on their faces. Cleve remembered how shocked he'd been when he'd seen Grant Wood's *American Gothic* in an art appreciation class at the university. The man in the picture looked so much like his father that it had startled him. He almost said something to the professor, but he had been too shy then. The professor spoke fast and didn't give anyone much time anyway. But Cleve could always remember the look on that man's face by looking at the picture of his father.

Alvin Miller had been the last of the truly free men, Cleve thought. He was lucky to have lived when he did, when self-reliance mattered. He was lucky to have died before the federal bureaucracy got so out of hand, before the country started down the evil path it was on now.

Evil. There was no other word for what Cleve Miller saw in his everyday life. The world had been slowly slipping toward hell since he could remember. Though he hadn't recognized it then, he'd seen it first in that last year of college: the greed of the doctors at the hospital where he'd worked for a semester to see whether medicine was what he really wanted. He'd decided against it because of those doctors, half of them unable even to speak good English but pulling down disgraceful salaries. If he had stuck with it, he would be making money like that now himself. But he had refused to kowtow to those doctors, Milofsky and Berger. He would never forget their names. They were surgeons and controlled the small hospital where he had spent those three months. They were arrogant and abrupt, looking down on him because of his country background. It was later, when he'd started reading, that he'd realized that Milofsky and Berger were just part of something much bigger.

Cleve looked at the registered letter on his desk. It was from the attorney of the man he had sent his yearling cattle to last fall. The cattle had been worth nearly $200,000 when they left Cleve's pastures, but he had never received any money for them. The registered letter was to tell Cleve that the man had taken bankruptcy. Somewhere in his files Cleve had several letters from the bank in Rapid City where the cattle were financed. They wanted their money, $163,000 that Cleve did not have.

He pushed back in his chair and rubbed his face. None of this really surprised him. It was just the world slipping one more notch toward hell. If he had financed the cattle with his friend Larry Sorenson, there might be something he could do. But he liked to keep part of his business confidential. He should have known better than to deal with the bankers in Rapid City. They were connected to bankers as far away as Europe. They couldn't care less. He was in the worst trouble he had ever known, and there was nothing he could do about it except have faith in the Lord that he'd get through somehow.

But the injustice of it swelled in Cleve's chest and occasionally pushed into his throat. It made him feel as if he might cry. But he knew it was the way of things. Good people were always being tested. It was the evil ones who had it easy in this life. Dr. Milofsky and Dr. Berger could probably write a check for the $163,000, but Cleve Miller wouldn't trade places with them. There was another life to consider. There was a Judgment Day to think about.

▲
THIRTEEN

Tuffy got a call from Ross Brady early the next morning. The telephone rang several times before Tuffy realized what it was. He was bouncing off the hallway walls on his way to the kitchen when he saw through the window near the front door that the sun was just coming up. Tuffy was not fully awake but still he knew that he had a pretty good hangover. As soon as he said hello, he looked at the clock on the kitchen wall. It was five thirty.

"I tried to call last night about ten, but you weren't home yet," Ross said.

"I was at Milo. Training session at the Dust Buster." Tuffy's voice was hoarse.

"How bad you hurting?"

"If I don't bleed to death through the eyes, I'll make it," Tuffy said. "What you need?"

"I have to go to Rapid to pick a guy up about one thirty. I could use some help with the chores."

"Jesus. I sit around with nothing to do for weeks, and as soon as I get a touch of the Dust Buster flu, you call up and need some help." Tuffy enjoyed complaining a little. He smiled into the phone.

"It's just that this weather might turn rotten, and I wanted to be sure everybody's got plenty to eat in case it gets cold. Thought I'd double up on the hay. It would go a lot faster with two guys." Ross knew that Tuffy would come and just wanted to be coaxed. "I'm putting the coffee on right now."

"Coffee?"

"Yeah, and pancakes if you hurry."

"If I can get the pickup started, I'll be there in twenty minutes." Tuffy put the receiver down without waiting for a reply.

In minutes he was sitting in his pickup with his hand on the key, asking Wakantanka for a little help getting the engine to turn over. He looked in the four directions, down at Mother Earth, and up to the sky. "Come on mother," he said and turned the key. When the pickup exploded into life, he looked up at Father Sky and said, *"Hau."* As the pickup warmed, he dug through the glove box searching for a bottle of aspirin.

They drank the coffee and wolfed down the pancakes. Tuffy would have liked to take a little longer in the house, but Ross was in a hurry. Tuffy made a few moaning noises, but Ross paid no attention.

It was nearly freezing when they came out of the house. The air, along with the coffee and the food, made Tuffy forget about his head. Ross started the grapple-fork-equipped John Deere while Tuffy drove the flatbed pickup to one of the fifteen haystacks lined up inside the fence that separated the farmstead from the first of Ross's pastures. There were two pitchforks sticking upright behind the pickup cab, and as Tuffy took them down, he saw that the cattle were already beginning to trail toward the level place a quarter mile away where they were used to being fed.

Once Ross got the tractor rolling, he pointed it toward the first haystack and lowered the grapple gradually, so that it touched the ground just as the tractor drove it deep into the hay. When the grapple rose, it looked like a giant animal with several hundred pounds of hay in its mouth. Ross backed away from the stack, then moved forward until the grapple held the hay over the bed of the pickup. When it was just right, he released the load, and Tuffy, who was in the cab trying to tune the radio, felt the pickup shift as the hay settled onto the flatbed. The tractor took three more huge bites of hay. Ross arranged them on top of the first one so that when he was finished, the pickup looked like another haystack.

Ross let the tractor idle, jumped down, picked up the pitch forks that Tuffy had placed out of harm's way, and drove them deep into the hay. When he got in on the passenger's side, Tuffy was frantically trying to tune the radio. Though he twisted the knob violently, a symphony played on without a quiver.

"Son of a bitch won't work," Tuffy said and banged the dash.

"It's locked on one channel," Ross said. "NPR."

Tuffy looked up from the radio dial in disbelief. "NP-fuckin'-R?" he asked.

"Yeah, they'll have news on in a few minutes."

"Great," Tuffy said as he sat upright in the seat and shifted the pickup into low.

They crawled through the first gate and down into the ruts leading to the second gate, which was shut. There were a few inches of slippery mud, and the tires spun for a moment. Ross hit the transfer case shifter with the heel of his hand as Tuffy depressed the clutch, and the pickup bucked into four-wheel drive. The spinning stopped, and the pickup's engine growled under the load. The brakes moaned as Tuffy eased the pickup to a halt so Ross could open the gate.

Ross had opened that gate a thousand times, and every time he told himself that he should bring the fence stretcher next time and loosen the wires so it would not be so tight. It was a wire gate like almost all the gates in that country: four fifteen-foot strands of barbed wire strung between two sticks and held there with a loop of wire nailed to a gatepost sunk deep into the ground. He always had to get his shoulder against the gate stick and push with his legs while he used his right hand to flip the loop of wire that held it closed. When he finally got the gate open, he tossed the gate stick in a neat arc that kept the wires stretched out so they didn't tangle. He swung back into the pickup as Tuffy drove it through.

The cows began to crowd toward them as the two men gained the high ground of the feeding flat. The news program started, and the commentator was discussing the demographic shift in the AIDS epidemic from white homosexuals to blacks and Hispanics. "It'll be us Indians next," Tuffy said as he downshifted into low range and opened his door.

Ross already had his door open but paused before stepping out. "Probably not," he said. "They say IV drug use is the big factor."

"There are needles on the res," Tuffy said. "Besides, we don't need needles. We can catch shit like that from infected blankets."

They left the pickup idling in gear and clambered onto the slowly moving load of hay, each taking a pitchfork as he went. When they got to the top of the hay, they looked out over the pasture to be sure that most of the cows were coming. It was a lovely morning. The sun was ten degrees above the eastern horizon, and the twisted shapes of the Badlands were magnified in the distance. The wind still came from the south. "Look like we'll get some weather to you?" Ross asked as he sunk his fork into the hay.

Tuffy was just sending the first forkful off to the milling cows. He glanced at the western horizon. "Hard to say. But it don't look real good."

The pickup inched across the flat, and the pile of hay was scattered behind it. By the time the hay was gone, all the cows had arrived, and Ross and Tuffy returned for a second load. They spread this load in a line paralleling the first, to disperse the cows and keep the more dominant ones from getting more than their share. By the time they finished, Tuffy had broken a sweat and taken off his jacket. "This is too reminiscent of work, Rossy boy."

They leaned against the hood, catching their breath. "I really appreciate it," Ross said. He looked at his watch. "Just right. Need to ride out through these cows quick, feed the heifers, then change my clothes and head for Rapid." He watched Tuffy's reaction, already knowing what it would be.

"Ride the cows?" Tuffy said.

"Yeah, take a good look. See if anybody's got trouble."

"You got Bozo in the barn?"

"Sure."

"Maybe I could check the cows while you feed the heifers."

"I was hoping you'd say that. Otherwise I'd be late for Stewart's plane."

"Stewart who?"

"Stewart Bergman, Linda's brother."

"Your Linda?"

Ross laughed, shook his head, and shrugged. "Not exactly my Linda, but the Linda who used to live here."

Pulling on a clean shirt, Ross stepped from his bedroom and saw that Tuffy had returned from checking the cattle. He sat at the wood stove in the kitchen. The stove door was open, and Tuffy was poking at the coals with a piece of wood.

"Any problems?" Ross asked.

"Nope. Everybody's fine. And old Bozo is as good as ever. Should have never sold him."

"You know you can buy him back anytime you want."

Tuffy looked at Ross. Ross said nothing and at first thought

Tuffy missed his horse. But then it dawned on him that Tuffy wanted to ride along into Rapid City. Ross walked to the window and looked at the sky. "Doesn't look like we're going to catch hell quite yet."

"No," Tuffy said. "Maybe tonight or tomorrow. Maybe we won't get nothing."

"You got something on for this afternoon?" Ross asked.

Tuffy laughed. "Soap opera at one o'clock."

"Why don't you go with me to pick up Stewart? I could use the company."

Tuffy looked up from the stove. "Hell, you're all duded up." He faced Ross, held his arms up to show the holes in the elbows of his shirt, and frowned. "I look like I been roped and drug."

Ross shook his head. "You want to borrow a clean shirt?"

Tuffy smiled. "That blue one with the pearl snaps."

When they got to the county road, Ross started to turn left, but Tuffy reached out and stopped the steering wheel. "Are we running behind?" he asked. The shirt was a little small, but with his hair wetted down and the hay brushed off his jeans and hat, Tuffy looked pretty good.

"No, we got time."

"Then let's go through Milo and up Highway 44. It's a little longer, but the scenery is nicer."

"You mean there's more beer joints."

"That's what I said. The scenery is nicer."

Ross shrugged and made the turn to the right. They passed the Miller place, Cleve's sign, and the missile silo, then curved up the bench road past Elizabeth's driveway. Ross slowed as they came to Tuffy's mailbox. "You need anything?" Tuffy didn't say anything, but with three salutes that began at his forehead and ended up pointing down the road, he motioned Ross to go on.

They moved between the eroded buttes and down the grassless draws. There was no sign of humanity, and the road swung onto the reservation for a few miles, then back onto state land, and finally a few trees on the horizon alerted them that Milo was just ahead. "It's bad country," Tuffy said.

Ross had played this game with Tuffy before. "Dry," he said.

"Man could die of thirst."

"Wait," Ross said. "Is that a town up ahead?"

"Sweet Jesus, sweet Jesus," Tuffy said. "We've been saved." And Ross pulled the pickup off the gravel and onto the dirt parking lot of the Dust Buster, which was really just one end of the Milo grocery store.

Ruth stood at the window, and when she saw Tuffy jump out, leaving Ross in the pickup with the engine running, she disappeared only to meet Tuffy at the door with a twelve-pack of Coors Light. They were on the road again in moments. "Just like the fuckin' pony express," Tuffy said as he popped a top and handed a beer to Ross.

From there the road bellied down a long, barren grade toward the west. It went through a corner of the Badlands National Monument before it hit Highway 44 just north of the town of Scenic. They turned onto 44 heading toward Rapid, and Tuffy popped the top off two more beers. He handed one to Ross and with closed eyes smelled his own. "My headache is starting to go away," he said. Then, "What's Linda's brother coming out here for?"

"Linda said he had to get out of Los Angeles," Ross said. "You know how those people are: they think this is a sort of summer camp. I suppose he needs a shot of nature."

"You don't sound too enthused."

Ross shrugged. "I don't know."

"Seems like Linda's got a lot of nerve, asking you to baby-sit her little brother."

"He's no kid. I could have said no."

"You guys still talk, huh?"

"All the time. Why not?"

Tuffy sipped his beer. They were just crossing the Cheyenne River, fifteen miles upstream from the bench. The cottonwoods were leafless gray tangles of branches. The river itself was a small trickle winding over sandbars. There hadn't been much snow, so the river hadn't swelled from run off. It was hard to believe that in some years this tiny ribbon of water could turn into a half-mile-wide flood.

They came out of the river breaks and saw the Black Hills squatting dark on the western horizon. The ranches were closer together and more prosperous-looking. Cattle were bunched up close to the buildings, and some already had shaky white-faced calves on the ground. There was some winter wheat on the north side of the road that was beginning to grow. It was the greenest thing they had seen since the middle of last summer. Tuffy and Ross watched the wheat as they passed. They knew that farming ruined this land in the long run, but the wheat was pretty, and they had to admire it. Someone had done a good job of getting it in at the right time. The rows were straight, and the wheat was coming up thick. "Come harvest time," Tuffy said, "that guy's going to be smiling like a skunk eating yellow jackets."

The Black Hills grew larger as they drove west, and by the time they came to the airport turnoff, the hills dominated the entire horizon. The airport was ten miles east of Rapid City, but already they felt as if they had driven through a time warp. The airport approach was a new, clean, four-lane highway with huge signs pointing to a half dozen different parking lots and airlines. Ross negotiated the turns without much hesitation while Tuffy shook his head. They sat in the pickup and finished their beers. When a United Express jet appeared from the south, they stepped out into the breezy parking lot. "That must be Stewart," Ross said.

"He's right on time," said Tuffy. They moved across the street and through the automatic revolving door of the terminal.

Neither Ross nor Tuffy knew exactly what to look for. Ross had seen Stewart only a couple times, and that had been years before. Tuffy could only think that he would look like a male version of Linda. If that were the case, he thought, he would be easy to pick out. Just look for a tall, graceful brunet. But no one of that description came through the gate. Ross and Tuffy leaned against the wall across from the gate until all the passengers had come through. There were not more than twenty people: several couples, three air force men coming back from leave, a dopey-looking kid in cowboy boots and ten-gallon hat, and a couple of single women. Ross and Tuffy looked at each other and shrugged. As Tuffy was suggesting that since they were this close to Rapid they might as well go into town and have a few beers, the dopey-looking kid walked up to them.

"Ross?"

Ross nodded.

"Qué pasa?" Stewart said as he stretched out his hand. "Long time no see."

Ross and Tuffy looked at Stewart without speaking. He was short. His dark, curly hair stuck out from under the obviously brand-new, wide-brimmed cowboy hat. He wore a western-cut shirt with pointed pockets and snaps, and his new denim jacket matched the jeans, which were tucked into the tops of his new boots. His glasses were thick, black horn-rims. He pushed them back up his nose with his middle finger several times before Ross or Tuffy could think of anything to say. Finally Ross took Stewart's hand. "This is a neighbor," Ross said. "Tuffy Martinez."

Stewart took Tuffy's hand. "Nice to meet you, Tuffy."

Tuffy let him pump his hand. "You don't look much like your sister," he said. There was a pause and Tuffy went on. "Why don't we go into Rapid for a beer?"

"Great idea," Stewart said. "Just let me get my bags, and we can head out." He smiled and shook his head. "Goddamn," he said. "It's good to be here."

They started about two o'clock at the Crystal Lounge. Two old ranchers in Stetsons sat talking at a table near the dance floor. The bartender read a newspaper not far from a middle-aged woman with three cocktail glasses lined up in front of her. It had been bright outside, so the darkness of the bar blinded them. They stood near the front door blinking and peering into the corners of the lounge for more people, but it was a weekday afternoon. There was no one else.

Tuffy led the way to the bar. The older men stopped their conversation and watched them move across the corner of the dance floor. Tuffy and Ross knew they were looking at Stewart, who walked between them with a completely inappropriate smile on his face.

"I'll have a Coors Light," Tuffy told the bartender, who looked up but still leaned against the bar over his newspaper.

"Me, too," said Stewart.

"Make it three," Ross said as he laid a five-dollar bill on the bar.

Tuffy called after the bartender, "Is it always this crazy in here?"

"You want action at two o'clock in the afternoon, go over to the Boot Hill and ride the mechanical bull," the bartender said over his shoulder. "The band doesn't start in here for seven hours." He was an older man, nearly bald, dressed in a white shirt and dark pants. He did not seem happy with his job.

"Well, you got a jukebox, don't you?" Tuffy said.

The bartender was coming back, popping tops as he walked. "Sure," he said as he put the beers down and reached under the bar for the dice cup. He put the cup down hard in front of Tuffy and started to pick up Ross's money, but Stewart handed him a twenty.

"Horses?" Tuffy asked. He picked up the cup, put one hand over the top, and began to shake it over his head.

"Horses," the bartender said as he turned to the cash register.

Tuffy closed his eyes and shook the dice cup violently above his head. "Hey, hey, hey," he said.

Stewart, who had been watching this closely, looked at Ross. Ross shrugged and sipped his beer. He noticed that Tuffy had gotten the attention of the woman at the end of the bar. She looked on with some interest. Ross guessed that she was in her mid-thirties. She was probably a little drunk but sort of pretty.

The dice came out two sixes, a four, a two, and a one. Tuffy looked up. "Nothing wild," the bartender said.

Tuffy left the sixes on the bar and rolled the other three dice. He picked up another six, left it, and began shaking the remaining two dice with even more vigor. Over his head, beside the left ear, the right ear. He banged the bottom of the cup on the bar. "Hey, hey, hey." One more shake and out came the dice. No sixes. "Shit."

"Four in a week," the bartender said as he scooped up the dice and looked around the bar. He pointed at the woman's drinks. "How you doing?"

She had a drink and a half still in front of her. "Fine," she said.

The bartender rattled the dice and let them out. Four sixes and a two. "Horse on you," he said and scooped the dice for another throw. He won that round just as easily, and Tuffy spun on his chair and headed for the jukebox.

"Play A7, then B11," the woman said. She smiled, and for an instant Ross thought she was looking at him. It was hard to tell just where she was focusing, but in an instant he realized that she was looking past him. When he turned, Stewart had his hat pushed back and was smiling back at her.

Bob Seger's "Like a Rock" began just as Tuffy came back to his stool. Stewart tried to say something, but Tuffy held up a hand to keep him quiet. "Listen," he said. "This son of a bitch sings to me." He bowed his head and listened to the first verse. Then he turned his eyes up to the woman who had asked him to play the song. "You got taste," he said.

Two beers later she was sitting between Stewart and Tuffy. Her name was Twila. She'd worked as a topless waitress in a bar out by the air base. But the bar had gone broke, and now she worked at Wendy's. She kept saying, "Hot and juicy, cousin Lucy." Stewart and Tuffy cracked up every time.

An hour and a half later they had bought a couple more drinks, the ranchers at the table had bought them one, and even the bartender, who seldom looked up from his newspaper, had bought a round. The jukebox had been playing steadily, mostly B11, which was a country song about a Christian woman who had just seen her husband disappear into a motel with her best friend. Twila seemed to identify. She had told Stewart and Tuffy the whole story. Ross had not been able to hear exactly what had happened to her, but Stewart and Tuffy seemed genuine in their consolation. Tuffy patted her on the back a lot, and Stewart looked into her eyes and nodded his head. He looked ridiculous in the cowboy hat, but Twila did not seem to notice.

"You're an Indian, aren't you," she said to Tuffy.

"Part."

"Which part?" she giggled. Tuffy smiled. "No, really," she went on. "I'm part Indian, too."

"Which part?" Stewart said and they all laughed.

"No, really. My grandfather was a Chippewa or something." She did not look one bit Indian. "Maybe a Cheyenne."

"I'm Sioux," Tuffy said.

"How come you got a Mexican name?" she asked as if she had just caught him in a lie.

"Lots of Sioux have Mexican names," Stewart said. Everyone, including the bartender looked at him. He shrugged. "The Mexicans that brought the mule trains up from Santa Fe a hundred years ago stayed and fathered children."

Everyone looked at Tuffy to confirm this. He looked at Stewart, then at Ross. "Sounds right," he said.

"I read it in a book on the airplane," Stewart said.

"Let's go to an Indian bar," Twila said. Ross and Tuffy straightened up. Stewart pushed his glasses up his nose and smiled.

Ross shook his head. "I don't know."

"I know I'd enjoy it," Stewart said.

Tuffy held up his hands. "We could go down the street to the Oasis," he said. Then he turned to Stewart. "But you can't go looking like that. We'd be asking for it."

"He looks cute," Twila said.

"He'll get us beat up," Tuffy said.

"Yeah," Ross said. "The pants got to come out of the boots."

"He can leave the new coat in the pickup and roll the sleeves up on the shirt." Tuffy reached over and took the oversize, fashionably shaped hat off Stewart's head. "But the hat," he shook his head, "will have to be gurred."

"Gurred?" Stewart asked.

Tuffy and Ross nodded. The ranchers turned in their chairs. "It would be the best thing," Ross said. And Tuffy began to wad the hat up like an old hamburger wrapper. Ross joined in, and together they forced the hat down to the size of a soft ball. Twila gasped when they dropped it onto the floor and began to stomp on it. The ranchers began to laugh, the bartender smiled, and Stewart looked on in disbelief.

After the gurring, Ross straightened the hat out and slapped it across his thigh. Tuffy brushed it off and stuffed it back on Stewart's head. They stepped back and began to nod. "Better," they said.

▲
FOURTEEN

Kyle and Pete had ridden out at five thirty in the afternoon to check for new calves and to drive the cattle down into the draws. Most of the cattle were already in the draws, and it didn't look as if any were going to have a calf soon. Pete looked at the sky and cursed to himself. The date you put the bulls in with the cows was critical. The cows would start to calve 280 days later. They didn't wait for nice weather, so it was always a gamble. The earlier you started, the bigger the calves would be in the fall, and the more money they would bring. But if you started early, sometimes you got caught by a calf-killing storm. Sometimes you didn't. Maybe it really didn't matter what you did, Pete thought. It was up to Elizabeth anyway; she called the shots, and she knew as much as anyone. Pete didn't make decisions, and that suited him fine.

They were on their way back to the house for supper when Pete's horse, Barney, nearly stepped on a jackrabbit. Kyle, on Jake, was angling to join Pete and Barney when the rabbit jumped. It didn't run wildly from the horse's hooves, and the horse paid no attention to it. The rabbit simply bounced a few yards to one side and stood on its hind legs. Pete took a quick look down at the form on the southeastern side of the yucca bush where the rabbit had been. The form was a dish in the earth that looked as if a foot-long piece of pipe had laid there long enough to kill the grass and make a dent. Just rabbit-sized, Pete thought. Doesn't look that uncomfortable.

But he couldn't understand how a nervous little varmint like a rabbit could sit there for sixteen hours a day.

The rabbit stood on its back legs and checked the air as Pete rode past. Its fur was still mostly white, and as Pete glanced at it, he thought, Snow is coming. He lightly touched Barney with his spurs, and the horse broke into an easy lope to catch up with Kyle and Jake. Barney's lope was smooth as a boat ride. A lope like that was one of the things that Pete truly enjoyed about horses. It was what he would miss when he was too old to ride.

He watched Kyle riding on the side hill ahead of him. Pete had never been able to ride like that, so relaxed that it appeared lackadaisical. But Kyle was not lackadaisical. He was just so in tune with the horse that they seemed to be one animal instead of two. Kyle was just a kid, but it was clear he was going to be built like his mother, tall with a little stoop to his walk and wide, flat hands. And he'd be shy, too. That was the Indian in him. Learned it from his mom, aunt and uncle, and the grandmother down on the reservation. Pete never minded that Indian shyness the way some white men did. He guessed he'd learned to appreciate it by hanging around old John Kiser. In fact, though as a German he'd been raised to look a man in the face when he talked to him, he kind of liked the way Kyle never would look grown-ups in the eye. It was their way of showing respect.

Pete caught up to Kyle just as they came to the gate. Kyle had already swung off Jake and waited as Pete and Barney rode through. He led Jake through, stretched the gate closed, flipped the wire over the post, and swung back aboard with no effort. "Boy," he said as he came abreast of Pete, "I'm hungry."

"What's new?" Pete said.

"Mom said we were having chicken tonight. Sounds good, huh?"

"Huh," Pete said.

"If it snows," Kyle said, "maybe I won't have to go to school tomorrow."

"You'd do anything to get out of school."

"I hate it," Kyle said. "I bet you would have, too, if they'd had schools when you were my age."

"We had schools, smartass." They rode on toward the house. "But you're right," Pete said. "I quit long before I was your age."

Kyle's Aunt Tracy and Uncle Louis White Horse were just coming out of the house as they reined their horses up in front of the tack room. They had left their year-old baby with Elizabeth while they went into Harney on business, and they had come to pick her up. They had two boys in school down at Rocky Ford. The boys rode the bus and didn't get home until late, but they had probably been home for an hour by then, and Tracy was trying to hurry Louis along. Louis liked whiskey, and it was easy to tell he'd been drinking. They still had an hour and a half drive ahead of them. Pete and Kyle waved as they pulled around the driveway and passed the hitching rail. "You boys try to stay warm tonight," Louis said through the window.

Kyle, who was closest to the pickup, said, "Oh, we will. You keep your own self warm."

Pete stood between the horses and pulled on Barney's cinch. He had never liked Louis. "Hope you freeze your ass off," he mumbled. No one heard him except Kyle, who laughed.

Elizabeth had not done as much that day as she had hoped. The baby had kept her busy, and John appeared to be uncomfortable. She had moved him several times. He seemed happiest looking out the window toward the west. Now she rushed to get supper on the table. From the window over the sink she could see Pete and Kyle slide the saddles off the horses. Kyle draped the halters over his arm and took a saddle in each hand. It was a pretty good load for him, but she knew he was doing it because Pete, with his withered arm, would have had to make two trips.

She filled water glasses for Pete and herself and took them to the table, then put an empty glass and a quart of milk at Kyle's place. When she got back to the window, Kyle was nearly to the house, but Pete was still at the hitching rail with the horses. Dancer stood in the corral next to the tack room, as close to the other horses as he could get, and watched Pete brushing the sweat away from where the saddle blankets had been. It was not unusual for Pete to stay with the horses like that. Some times he would stand out there for an hour brushing and talking. He had missed many suppers that way, but there was no hurrying him. They had learned to go on without him. He would come in his own time. Elizabeth had to smile at him. He talked to himself and raised his good hand for emphasis. But then Kyle was in the mud room pulling off his boots and coveralls, and she moved to the oven to get the chicken.

"You're just an ornery old son of a bitch," Pete said to his father, who leaned against the barn.

"You would have never said that when I was alive," his father replied.

"Well, hell no. You'd a thumped me a good one. But I can say it now. You're an ornery old son of a bitch. Now go on, and let me finish rubbin' these horses down."

He took a few swipes at a piece of mud on Jake's shoulder and heard a horse nicker. It was Dancer, with his head over the corral rail near the feed barrel, asking for a scoop of oats. Pete stopped brushing and looked at the young horse. He was still young, coming seven. Pete thought, Maybe I should have shot

95

him. But it hadn't been the horse's fault. Pete let the curry brush drop to the ground and moved closer to Dancer. He put his right hand into his left armpit, squeezed down on the glove, and pulled his hand out. Slowly he reached out and touched the colt between the eyes. Dancer jumped back, though not far. In an instant the nose was back over the oats barrel, and Pete rubbed the forehead gently.

"Still like your goddamned oats, don't you?" Pete took the lid off the barrel and offered the colt a scoop of golden kernels. Dancer pushed his face into the can and chewed steadily, moistening the grain and releasing its rich odor. Pete held the scoop with his right hand and, since the left was no good, leaned over and touched the colt's face with his stubbly cheek.

▲
FIFTEEN

Before they had finished their shrimp cocktails, John Higgins's assistant produced a preliminary study based on borehole testing, transportation estimates, and projected future markets for precious metals. He handed a copy to Sorenson and one to Higgins, who laid it beside his plate. "Look that over at your leisure, Larry," he said. "Just let me bring you up to speed with what Brome has been up to." He pushed his shrimp cocktail away and winked. "Of course, this is all confidential. You'll be the first nonmanagement person to hear about this."

"Of course," Sorenson said.

They were in a private dining room at the Hilton Hotel. The room seemed to be reserved for Brome meetings. The waiters came and went discreetly. No one spoke while they were serving.

"Brome Mining Company has been researching the possibilities of expanding its operations. As you know, most of our activity is here in the Black Hills themselves. There's fairly new technology that allows us to strip out riparian areas and leach the metals, particularly gold, with acid." Higgins took a small bite of his scrod. "We push the ore up into piles and sprinkle cyanide over it."

"Cyanide?"

"Yes," Higgins said. "It washes out the gold. We collect the ore in ponds and extract the minerals. It's very economical compared to hard-rock mining. How's the fish?"

Sorenson had forgotten about the meal. "Fine," he said and took his first bite of the entrée.

"There's ore in a lot of the creek bottoms around the Black Hills," Higgins said. He motioned to his assistant, who laid out a small map for Sorenson. "But economically the most feasible deposits seem to be out your way."

Sorenson had no difficulty recognizing the map. It was Harney County. The shaded area of the map was south of Harney. The darkest shading encompassed the area known as the bench.

"As you can see, we feel the country south of the interstate has great potential for mining. They won't let us on the national park right now, but if we can show profit on the land just north of it, they might. There is also a possibility of finding some marginal sites closer to town. But the heart of the project is south, those four little creeks that drain into the Cheyenne River." Higgins tapped his pencil on each creek: Red Willow, Cherry, Old Woman, and Sweet Grass. "That area's key to this development. To ensure that this thing goes ahead, we should have mining rights on at least half of that ground."

Higgins let what he had said soak in as he finished his scrod. Sorenson looked at the map for a long time, trying to remember who owned the four ranches in the shaded areas. He was only sure of one: it belonged to Cleve Miller. That was a tremendous stroke of luck. Sorenson's scrod was cold, but he took a bite anyway and sipped at his water.

"In searching the public records," Higgins went on, "we noticed two of the most important ranches are at least partly financed at the First Bank of Harney." Sorenson nodded solemnly although he was furiously trying to remember who lived on the ranches and the status of their loans.

"And that's why I wanted to get in touch with you. I know how civic-minded you are, and I knew you'd realize what this could mean in terms of jobs. Of course, we'd like to get this thing put together before we take it public. You know how things can get fouled up if John Q. Public gets wind of an economic development project." Higgins laughed. "We've been through that, haven't we, Larry?"

Sorenson laughed, too. But then Higgins became very serious. He leaned toward Sorenson. "There's tremendous opportunity here, Larry. It could mean an end to the depression your town's been in for thirty years. People will move in. Families will be able to stay together. Nobody will have to leave to find work. The whole structure of Harney will change." He straightened up and his voice became softer. "Someday there will be gold mining in Harney County. Someday technology will make it feasible to mine all that country. But if we're going to see it in our lifetime, we need a nucleus. We need two of those four ranches in our pocket before word leaks out."

▲
SIXTEEN

The wind was still southerly, and the sky was clear. That meant the nice weather would hold. Maybe they would get through calving without a storm, Ross thought, but then they would be short of water for the summer, and that would be worse. Ross was the only one of the four who looked up as they walked to the front door of the Oasis bar. He had never been inside the Oasis and knew that he was going now because he had had just the right amount to drink. He held the door for Twila and Tuffy, who hung onto each other as Tuffy tried to teach Twila a few words of Lakota. Stewart swayed along behind them in his not-so-new hat, looking only a little out of place. Smoke and the sounds of the jukebox poured out onto the street. Before Ross followed Stewart in, he took one last look at the sky and noticed a small cloud drifting across a corner of the moon.

The Oasis was packed. Several couples danced shakily to the jukebox, both pool tables were in use, and people jammed the bar and the booths. Most in the crowd were Indians, but there were several blacks, almost certainly from the air base, and a half dozen whites.

Tuffy got beer, and they found a stool at the bar for Twila. They had been standing there only a minute when a big, drunk Indian, carrying a pool cue and wearing a fatigue jacket, came over to Tuffy. "Martinez, you fucking wimp," he said.

Tuffy looked for an instant before he recognized him. "Santee?"

"Hey," the Indian said and they shook hands like brothers. "Goddamn."

They began to talk and laugh. Everyone in the bar seemed very drunk to Ross. The pool players danced between shots, and several people were slumped in the booths with their heads on the table. Tuffy introduced Santee around, and he shook hands and smiled. He wore a red bandanna around his head, but still there was sweat around his eyes and on his cheeks. He was not as drunk as some of the others but was very hard to understand. He said something to Ross when they shook hands, but Ross could not make any sense of it. When he took Twila's hand he said with great care, "I'm looking for a partner." Twila smiled weakly and drew back. He said the same thing when he shook Stewart's hand. Ross and Twila looked at each other, and Twila made a face.

"Sure," Stewart said. "You got your money up?"

"Hey," Santee said. He slapped Stewart on the back and handed him the cue. "Best stick in the house." Stewart pulled his hat down and followed Santee toward the pool table.

A short white man with a thin mustache and black hair that stuck out at all angles walked up to Ross and Twila. "You look like a nice couple," he said. "I'm going to be completely honest with you." Ross and Twila waited. "Have kids before you get too old. Could you spare a dollar?"

"Fuck off," Tuffy said.

"No," Twila said to Tuffy, then turned to the man. "I've got a dollar. I'll bet you have a family."

"No," the man said, "but I've got a terrible thirst." He squeezed up to the bar beside Twila. "My name's Anthony," he said. "You have lovely hair." Tuffy rolled his eyes at Ross. They turned away from the bar and watched Stewart and Santee play pool.

They were playing two sullen young Indians who leaned against the wall as Stewart shot. Santee held the beer and mumbled cheers that only he understood. Stewart pushed his glasses up with his middle finger and smiled. He, too, had had too much to drink. But he made his first shot, chalked up, and sunk another. "Hey," Santee said.

They could hear Anthony and Twila talking. "One time I was dying," Anthony said.

"One time you were dying?"

"OK, OK," Anthony said as if she had caught him in a lie. "A lot of times I was dying."

Santee sunk the eight ball, and the young Indians grumbled, then left through the back door. Santee and Stewart returned to the bar to toast their victory. Santee held his can high. Anthony looked at them. "Let me tell you about pool, Jackie Gleason, and nuclear fission," he said.

"Hey," Santee said.

Stewart bought another round. The bartender put the beers and Stewart's change on the bar. Someone yelled at Santee to bring his pale-faced partner and get ready to get their asses kicked. Ross took his beer from the bar and held it high. "Your buddy Santee is a pretty good pool player," he said to Tuffy.

"Bullshit," Anthony said. "He knows as much about pool as I know about God." He looked at Stewart's change. "By God, there's a dollar." He picked one from the pile and put it in his pocket.

Ross poked him in the shoulder. "What are you doing?"

Anthony put his hands up. "Easy," he said. "I ain't got no skiis, ain't got no gun."

"Cool it, Ross," Twila said.

"Jesus Christ," Ross said. He picked up the rest of Stewart's change, finished his beer, and ordered another.

Stewart ran the table. "Hey, hey," Santee yelled. The sullen Indians had come back in the middle of Stewart's run and glared at Santee as they put their money up to challenge the table. They did not look drunk to Ross. Their eyes were wide and angry.

Tuffy brought Stewart and Santee beers. Santee slapped Tuffy on the back. "We be humans tonight, ain't we?" Santee said.

"Shut up and break," said one of the Indians.

Stewart's shooting had attracted some attention, and a few people got up to watch Santee break. Although he hit the cue with all his might, the balls did not move much, and nothing dropped. Tuffy and Ross stood side by side. "Loose rack," Ross mumbled. Tuffy nodded.

The first Indian shot three big ones but left himself badly. Instead of trying the best shot, he played Chicago and left Stewart hooked behind the fifteen ball. Ross watched Stewart and noticed the look he gave the Indian. There was something in it that he had not seen in Stewart before. It was the look his sister used to have when she was minutes away from a dance performance. Stewart tried a difficult shot and missed. The other Indian put one down and missed. Santee sunk two and left a poor shot. When the Indian hooked Stewart for the second time, Ross turned back to the bar. "I think I'll get a twelve-pack to go," he said. Tuffy nodded and moved closer to the table just as Stewart shot a massé that ticked the two ball into the corner pocket and set him up to run the table.

Ross ordered the beer and leaned over to Twila. "I think we're about ready to go."

Anthony was talking. "It's really a case of the monetary hives. I need someone to help me scratch."

Twila turned to Ross. "Anthony said he'd take me home." She smiled.

Tuffy heard this and leaned back. "It's been lovely," he said and touched her face gently.

Ross gathered up the beer in time to see Stewart click the last few shots off with the pomp of a military man. The Indian who had hooked him grew tighter with every shot, and when Stewart slapped in the eight ball with just enough draw to leave the cue exactly where the eight had been, he snapped.

Ross froze, but Tuffy lunged before the Indian could swing his cue stick. As Tuffy took the Indian up against the wall, Ross saw that Stewart had jumped clear. Ross heard Santee yell, *"Hey, hey, hey."* Then everyone was into it. Stewart got away from the first Indian and tried to move out of the middle of things. Tuffy had the other Indian by the hair. As Ross was backing toward the door, he watched the second Indian twist around and tee off on Tuffy from the side. Tuffy took the haymaker and spun, dazed, out of the fray. With Ross on one arm and Stewart on the other, Tuffy was whisked out the front door. When they broke into the cool night air, it was snowing.

They were almost out of town when Tuffy held his hands up and commanded Ross to stop.

"Look at that," he said, pointing past the barricades near a construction site.

"What?" Stewart asked. He was silly from the excitement.

"On top of that pile of busted two-by-fours. It's an iron fence." The pile of waste lumber was in the gutter in front of a Catholic church. On top of it were six or eight sections of black wrought-iron fence, the kind used to surround cemeteries. "I been looking for a fence like that," Tuffy whispered.

"You going to start your own church?" Stewart thought that was funny but no one laughed.

"For the family graveyard," Tuffy said. "Let's load her up." He started to get out of the pickup.

"We can't steal it," Ross said.

"Sure we can," Stewart said.

"They're throwing it away," said Tuffy. His door was open. Snow was blowing in.

Stewart smiled. "It's just trash, Ross."

Ross hesitated but gave in. "All right," he said, "but hurry up."

Tuffy and Stewart loaded the fence two sections at a time. They were heavy, but the whole process took only a few minutes. Then they were back in the pickup popping beers, and Ross was steering through the light snow on the way out of town.

It snowed steadily but not hard all the way to Scenic. Stewart and Tuffy sang most of the way.

> *I can see you've heard the stories.*
> *It's written on your face.*
> *But it happened in another time,*
> *And in another place.*

Ross held the steering wheel with both hands and squinted at the road ahead. The snow reflected the headlights and cut the visibility in half, so he drove slowly. He held the can of Coors Light between his legs and sipped when he could. As the cans were finished, Tuffy rolled down the window and threw them into the pickup bed. He showed Stewart just how it was done. At forty-five miles per hour he would throw the can up and ahead of the pickup so that just as it disappeared in the dark above the headlight beams, it would begin to lose velocity and fall. It would go out of sight above the windshield as they drove under it, and an instant later they would hear it rattle into the bed behind them. Stewart was very impressed.

"Years of practice," Tuffy said.

"Let me try."

"We don't have any empty cans," Tuffy said.

Stewart chugged his beer. "Here."

They changed places so that Stewart was beside the window, and Tuffy gave a long explanation involving trajectory, velocity, English, and concentration. "It's the forty-five-forty-five rule. Forty-five degree angle and forty-five miles per hour. Put it right on forty-five, Ross." The window was open, and snow blew around inside the cab.

"You better make this," Ross said.

"Lean out as far as you can," Tuffy said. "Toss her up like you mean it."

Ross was cold. "You better make this."

"Now follow through, Stewart, baby."

Stewart let the can go. It sailed up in front of them, hung for a moment, then fell out of sight. Ross held the pickup at a steady forty-five miles per hour, Stewart rolled up the window, and they all waited to hear it hit the pickup bed. But it never did. After several seconds Ross stopped and began to back up.

"What are you doing?" Stewart asked.

"I forgot to tell you," Tuffy said. "Your brother-in-law is a little funny about this sort of thing."

"You missed," Ross said. "Now we have to find it."

"It's dark," Stewart said. "And snowing."

"We'll help," Ross said as he slowed the pickup.

They found an old and faded Budweiser can, and Tuffy and Stewart tried to convince Ross that it was the one Stewart had thrown. Ross didn't buy it. After five minutes they found the right can, jumped back into the pickup, and turned the heat up full blast. They finished the last three beers before they got to Milo, but no one tried to toss the empties into the back. There were a few cars in front of the Dust Buster, and a light still burned in the bar. Tuffy and Stewart wanted to go in for beer, but by then the snow was coming harder, and Ross had begun to worry about the cattle. Tuffy knew that he was right, that the snow could get worse, and so they compromised. Tuffy ran in for a final six-pack.

Tuffy was gone only a minute, and Ross and Stewart could see Ruth peeking out the door as he scurried back to the pickup. As they drove onto the bench, the snow became even thicker, and the wind shifted to the northwest and picked up speed. By the time they turned onto the half-mile driveway, little finger drifts were beginning to dance across the road. They didn't say much between Milo and Ross's driveway. Everyone was beginning to feel the beer. It made Ross and Tuffy think of other spring storms they had seen. Stewart was simply drunk.

The beginnings of drifts trailed off behind Tuffy's pickup. "You want to stay?" Ross asked.

"Might as well. Clyde has plenty of food."

The headlights swung around the yard and illuminated the buildings. "So this is the place," Stewart said.

"This is the place," Ross answered with some pride. He looked at Stewart's face and saw he had tried to picture the ranch from Linda's description. "I'm going to check the heifers," Ross said. "It would be just like them to start calving tonight. Tuffy, why don't you take Stewart in and get a fire started?"

"I need to see the heifers," Stewart said.

"You'll see plenty of heifers," Ross said. "What you need is to go to bed."

Tuffy took Stewart's arm and helped him out of the pickup. With both doors open, the wind drove the snow through the cab, and Ross had to pull his hat down to keep it on his head. "We'll go start a fire," Tuffy said to Stewart as he led him away.

The snow was in Ross's face as he walked to the shed. The flakes were still fairly big and wet. It was much colder than it had been, and though it was still not severe, Ross knew there was a chance things would get worse during the night. He was glad that they had fed the cows extra hay that morning. He hoped all the cows with calves were in draws and out of the wind.

The shed was open only to the south, so once inside Ross hardly noticed the cold. He turned on the light and immediately saw that a lot of the heifers had come in for the night. Cattle could feel things in the air. Ross counted them and found that they were all there. That could mean that the storm would be bad. But in the shed, with the gentle heifers staring wide-eyed at him and the heat from their bodies warming the place, it was hard to believe a blizzard was about to descend. He could separate the smell of the wheatgrass hay and alfalfa in the mangers from the smells of the sweet decaying manure and the breath of the cattle themselves. He reached out and touched a particularly friendly heifer on her broad, moist nose.

When the shed door opened, he turned with a start. For an instant the cold wind broke the spell, but as soon as the door went shut, the warmth wrapped around him again. It was Stewart and Tuffy. Stewart weaved slowly toward him, and Tuffy stood with his back against the door and shrugged as if to tell Ross that he had not been able to stop Stewart. "I forgot," Stewart was saying. "I forgot."

He was drunker yet and had pulled his cowboy hat down against the wind so that now he looked very different from the way he had looked when he got off the plane. "It's a big deal," he said. "I should have told you right away." He staggered toward Ross, and the heifers moved out of his way.

Ross took him by the shoulders and looked into his face. The face was vaguely familiar. "She got the job," Stewart said. "She'll be featured on the Barowitz tour."

Ross looked at Tuffy as if to ask if it were true. Tuffy showed no emotion. "She wanted me to tell you," Stewart was saying. "She's really looking forward to seeing you in Denver." The heifers were curious and had closed in around them. The friendly one was very close. Ross reached out and touched its nose again. Stewart smiled and reached out, too. The heifer did not pull back. She let them both touch her at the same time.

▲
SEVENTEEN

The wind continued to build throughout the night. By morning it blew a steady forty miles per hour, and the gusts were close to sixty. The temperature had fallen during the night, too. Sheltered from the wind, it was eleven degrees, but there was no real shelter, and the wind-chill factor made the temperature as low as fifty degrees below zero. The snow was hard to measure since the high places were blown clear while the draws and areas of relative calm were piled to a depth of several feet and packed hard as ice. The snow moved in swirls, making it impossible to tell the new snow from what was shifting from one drift to another.

The world outside Ross Brady's kitchen window was completely white. It was still very early, barely light, but Ross was up loading the stove. The view from the window did not surprise him because he had been awake for hours, lying in his bed, hearing the wind whistle and the house creak. Now he stood staring at the wall of white. He was wearing only a pair of blue jeans, and the hardwood floor was cold against his bare feet, but he could feel some warmth from the stove as the new wood caught fire. He wondered how long it would blow and hoped that none of his cows would decide to have calves in this. He turned to the sink and filled the coffeepot. He had not had enough sleep, but he couldn't go back to bed.

The coffee had just finished perking when Tuffy came into the kitchen from the living room, where he had slept on the couch. Ross sat at the kitchen table looking out the window but turned toward Tuffy as he entered. They smiled but neither of them spoke. Tuffy poured himself a cup of coffee and placed it on the stove while he opened the stove door and poked at the wood the same way Ross had only moments before. Then Tuffy sat at the table. "Fuck me," he said. It would be a long, tense, coffee-filled day of waiting.

All along the bench people sat in their kitchens listening to the wind. Cleve and Edith Miller pushed cooling bacon around their plates and tried to talk. But the conversations cooled as fast as the bacon. Cleve had been outside briefly just at first light to be sure the animals in the barn had plenty of feed. Edith had worried the entire time he was out. The stories of people losing their way in blizzards and freezing to death between the house and the barn were not myths to Edith Miller. It had happened to an uncle of hers in 1962.

She had asked Cleve not to go out, but of course he hadn't listened. It was silly to risk going outside in a blizzard, especially since a trip to the barn was really just a gesture, and they both knew it. The animals who needed the feed were the cows in the pasture, and even if there was a way to get to them, they would never come out of the draws to eat. As long as the chill factor was below zero, they would stand in the draws and lose a pound of weight an hour trying to keep warm. If they had a calf in this weather, it would die quickly. But Cleve had gone out anyway, and Edith had done everything she could to keep from standing at the window wringing her hands.

She busied herself with the breakfast but couldn't keep her mind off the chance that Cleve was taking. She began to think of risk and how catastrophe was just around life's next corner. It could strike at any time. Hadn't their only son been run off the road on his way into Harney on a beautiful spring day and broken his neck in the crash? After the injury he said it was impossible for him to stay on the ranch. Hadn't he gone to Oregon and never returned, although Cleve always hoped that he might? Hadn't their lives been changed in a minute? Hadn't everything they'd worked for, everything they were working for now, become hollow? And wasn't that the way it always was? The possibilities for the future vanished when you got close. Like hail. When the oats looked better than they had ever looked, when it looked as if they would make some money and be paid for all their effort, the hail always came. Pow, out of a clear, blue, summer sky, the hail moved through in minutes, leaving nothing high enough to reach the combine blades. It was always like that, and the Millers knew it better than anyone. They tried to do everything right, to work hard to ensure their reward, but still catastrophe swept in on them. And in the face of what was a fact, Cleve had bundled up in his coveralls, Scot's cap, and felt-pack boots and pushed out the back door like there was nothing dangerous waiting out there for him. Edith had stood over the stove thinking about what she would do if something happened to him. She had worked herself into quite a state by the time he came stomping back into the house.

Now she sat across from him, glancing up from her plate only occasionally to watch him. He looked old and weathered, she thought. But he was such a good man. He was honest, intelligent, and worked hard every day. Still he had never gotten ahead. If it wasn't one thing, it was two, she thought. And now this storm. If it passed soon, it might not hurt them. On the other hand, it could take all the profit out of the ranch for another year. She watched him cut off a very small piece of bacon and raise it slowly to his mouth. He chewed thoughtfully. The air in the kitchen felt heavy and stale to Edith, and she thought of summer, when the meadowlarks would return and they could open the doors and windows.

▲

EIGHTEEN

Still groggy from sleep, Stewart stood at the window and watched the snow drive by him horizontally. Somewhere there was a whistling. "Not exactly the sweep of easy wind and downy flake, is it?"

Tuffy grunted. He was reading an old newspaper.

"No," Ross said. "This is pretty western."

"Is this usual?"

"We get them once in a while." Ross said. "But they aren't usual."

Ross had been outside to check the heifers and to bring in more firewood. The heifers were cold but safe inside the shed. Between the shed and the house the visibility was down to a couple of feet, and the snow was more like ice. It stung when it hit Ross's already frozen face. By the time he was back to the house, his mustache was stiff with ice. He had sucked the ice away as he carried the firewood to the box beside the stove and was reminded that snow has no taste.

That was the first of several trips to the woodpile that day. Conditions did not improve. At noon Tuffy took a beer inventory to see when it would be safe to start drinking. "It would be easier not to drink at all than to get started and run out," he said. There were only seven beers, so they decided to wait. They played some pinochle when they were not tending the fire, and Ross did his best to act interested. But his mind wandered, and he had to be reminded to bid.

Snow still streaked across the window as the light slipped

from the sky. Several times Ross had noticed Stewart watching him and realized that he was trying to figure out what was expected of him and what was going to happen. Once, about four o'clock, Stewart had asked, in a lowered tone, if the drifts could cover the house. They had not been talking about the storm—neither Ross nor Tuffy had verbalized their fear that the cows might be pushed together in a draw and buried alive. But Stewart had seen the possibility.

Now Stewart and Tuffy were watching "The Cosby Show" on television. Ross washed the dishes from supper out of sight of the television, but he could hear some of the dialogue. Cliff was talking about the price of TV dinners. Tuffy had made spaghetti, and Ross thought how good it had tasted, how nice it was to be warm. He heard Tuffy and Stewart talking during a commercial.

"Bet you wish you were back in California," Tuffy said.

"It has crossed my mind."

"Give it a couple days. We'll have spring again." Ross could tell that Tuffy was trying to make conversation. His heart was not in it. "What did you do for a living," Tuffy asked, "out in sunny California?"

"Officially I'm in telecommunications," Stewart said. "In reality I do all sorts of things. I'm a *schlockmeister.*"

"A what?"

"A *schlockmeister.* I deal in things nobody needs."

"What kind of word is *schlockmeister?*"

"It's Yiddish. Jewish. I'm sort of a jack-of-all-trades."

"A master of none," Tuffy said. "I know how that is. Jew, Sioux, what's the difference?"

"It's really long-distance telephone service. Big deal since deregulation."

"Like Mountain Bell?"

"Sort of."

Ross knew that Tuffy was trying in his own way to make

Stewart feel at home. It was a hard thing to do with the storm pounding away constantly. Tuffy knew how serious it really was outside.

Ross was drying the dishes when Tuffy came into the kitchen. Cliff was still talking about the TV dinners. "What do you say we call around the bench, make sure everything is all right before the lines go down?" Tuffy said.

"I was thinking the same thing."

Ross dried his hands and picked up the telephone. There was a hum on the line, but they had a dial tone. "We're still in business."

"You call the Millers and I'll call Elizabeth," Tuffy said. "Edith will think I'm calling to ask Cleve to come out for a beer, and Elizabeth is too shy to talk to you."

"Is that it? Shy?"

"It's like that. Even with me sometimes and we grew up together." Tuffy poked at the coals in the stove. "She's better when there aren't many people around. She shuts down around strangers."

"I've known her for eight years."

"You're a stranger. You're from somewhere else. But hell, Ross, she likes you. She thinks you're all right."

"She talks to me about three times a year."

"Don't mean she doesn't like you. Hand me the phone."

Ross watched as Tuffy dialed from memory. Tuffy had been right, the most Ross would have gotten out of Elizabeth would have been a yes or a no. How's it going over there? Nothing. You all right? Yes. Do you need anything? No. He watched as Tuffy joked into the phone. He had slipped into reservation talk, hard to understand and filled with dry, fatalistic humor.

"She's managed to keep Kyle in the house all day and Pete in the bunkhouse," Tuffy said as he hung up. "The cows were in the draws and fed up when it hit. She figures they're as good as they can be. One of their heifers calved. They got it dried off before its ears froze. It's up and sucking."

"Let's hope nobody on this place calves tonight."

Tuffy nodded and handed Ross the phone just as Stewart came into the kitchen. "Just checking on the neighbors," Ross explained. He put the phone to his ear. The hum was worse, but the dial tone still droned behind it. Ross dialed the Millers and it rang only once. Edith answered and handed the phone over to Cleve. "Is it storming over your way?" Ross joked.

"You bet your sweet ass. One nasty son of a bitch. How you doing?"

"We're all right. Tuffy's snowed in here with us."

"Us?" The connection was getting worse and Cleve had to yell.

Ross looked at Stewart, who seemed to have caught the mood of the evening and was stirring the fire. It would be too hard to explain to Cleve that Linda's brother was out for a visit. "Got a guy staying here for a while."

"Good," Cleve yelled. "A man can always use another hand."

"How about you?"

"Won't know until it quits. Maybe . . ."

The hum drowned out Cleve's voice. Ross looked at the phone. Tuffy and Stewart looked at him. He spoke loudly. "Can't hear you, Cleve." There was no audible answer and Ross hung up.

"He's a tough bastard," Tuffy said, then looked at the refrigerator. "Tougher than me. Don't you think it's time we got this over with. There's only seven of the little devils. Might as well drink them so we'll have plenty of motivation for digging out when the time comes."

"Best idea of the night," Stewart said. They each drank two beers as they talked, but that was not enough to stimulate any real conversation, and at ten thirty Stewart announced he was ready for bed. Tuffy took the last beer from the refrigerator, popped the top, took a sniff, and gulped down half of it. He moved to the window and sipped at the beer as he watched the snow whip past the window. "Well, go ahead and blow, you son of a bitch. Just go ahead and blow." He finished off the beer, crushed the can, and laid it on the table as he walked past Ross on his way to the couch.

Ross stoked the stove, then turned off the kitchen light so he could see out into the yard better. Nothing had changed except that the drifts were deeper. It had been snowing and blowing for twenty-four hours now. There were maybe twelve inches of snow, and the chill temperature was still far below zero. Ross sat down in a hard-backed chair in the darkened kitchen and scooted as close to the window as he could get. From there he imagined he could hear the wind killing calves. A week before he had considered moving the cows to the outer pasture. It would have been a terrible mistake. They were still close to the buildings, and he was thankful for that. It would make the feeding easier when the storm let up. It seemed possible that it would never let up, and for a moment panic rose in his throat. He tried to think what he could do. He thought about saddling a horse and riding out to check for new calves. But that, of course, was insane. There was really nothing that could be done.

He knew he was going to think about the calves before he actually did. He had had the same thoughts before, and he hated them. But sitting there in front of the window, feeling the cold through the pane of glass, he could not help himself. He began to wonder what it would be like to be born on a night like this, tried to imagine coming into a freezing, wind-ravaged world and living for only a few minutes, maybe less, unable to dry the wetness of the womb, feeling the warmth drain first from the extremities, then from the body cavity, until finally the core temperature began to fall. He imagined the first and last thing a calf born that night would see. Just the mother cow, nervous, trying to dry the slime of birth with her tongue, lowing gently, nudging with her nose and all the time clouds of warm breath vanishing in the wind-driven snow.

Ross had not seen it like this when he'd read Darwin all those years ago. It had seemed precise back then, mathematical. But he had known, even then, that he was insulated. Part of the decision to come to this place had been a desire to strip away that insulation, to escape what was artificial and become a participant in what was real. Well, he thought, this is real. He turned sideways in his chair and held one hand out toward the stove. The feel of wood heat was solid. He touched the icy pane of glass with his other hand, closed his eyes, and listened to the wind.

But memories would not leave him alone. There was something about one hot hand and one cold hand that made him think of 1970, the year he graduated from college, the year he was drafted into the army. He did not want to go and tried to tell his father. "It's a rotten war," his father had said. "As Bradys we're against it." He was in the warehouse getting tomato boxes ready to be filled for the trip to Philadelphia, but he stopped his work and looked at Ross. "But Bradys aren't cowards. If we're called, we serve."

Though Ross never saw combat, he had gone to his physical examination and been sworn in a month later at the Selective Service office in the town of West Chester. All during that time he had wondered what his father had meant about not being cowards. He still wondered.

He was thinking about cowardice and bravery that night because the storm frightened him. He couldn't help being afraid, couldn't help thinking about what it would be like to freeze to death, to walk in waist-deep snow until exhaustion pushed you down and the drifting snow smothered you. Did other people think about such things?

Ross brought his hand down from the window and moved closer to the stove. It was best to try not to think. He opened the stove door and stared into the yellow-orange coals.

▲

NINETEEN

Because of the sea breeze, Linda could see the San Gabriel Mountains for the first time in weeks. They were really quite impressive, she thought: a gray-blue wall of mountains looming over Los Angeles.

She could see both the mountains and the ocean from the deck of the apartment she rented in Hermosa Beach. It was seven o'clock in the evening, and she was eating a snack on the deck before making the drive to the Barowitz studio for the day's second practice. So far March had been hot, and the air of the inversion layer that plagued the city had been very still and humid. But this evening the breeze was cool from the ocean. The feel of that sea breeze against her face made her think of growing up in her parents' home only a half hour away, in Long Beach. Though she'd done some traveling and spent those years in South Dakota, it was hard to remember not always being right here between the mountains and the ocean.

She stirred the fruit in her bowl and thought about how she would soon be setting out across the country. The tour included nine cities in the western states, starting with San Francisco, Portland, and Seattle. They would make a large arc; ending with Albuquerque and Tucson before bringing the show back to LA. The city in the middle of the tour was Denver, and even though her life had lately been filled with excitement, the thought of performing in Denver, with Ross in the audience, rose above all that was in front of her. It would be so very nice to see him, so nice to show him how she could dance when she was at her best.

Linda stood up and faced the ocean, where the sun was beginning to touch the water and send its reflection toward the city. She was dressed in dark blue sweatpants and a USC Trojan sweatshirt. She wore the Mexican sandals her father had given her a year before, when he had taken the whole family down to Mazatlán over Hanukkah. He had insisted that everyone go. To keep the family close, he had said. It was the last place Stewart had wanted to be at that time of year, but he had gone along, and their father had been proved right. The family had had a wonderful time. They set up a cheap menorah in the living room of the condominium and remembered, most nights, to light the candles. The shammes refused to burn, and Linda's father proclaimed it fireproof. He used a Bic lighter to light the candles. There had been a lot of jokes, and the vacation had done what Linda knew it was partly intended to do: help her forget that she was spending the first Christmas in seven years away from Ross.

Now Linda laughed to think of Stewart and her father, neither very athletic, strapped under the bright-colored parachutes pulled around the bay by Mexican speedboats. She had laughed that day, too, while she sat on the beach comforting her mother, who refused to watch. Later, after her mother had gone back to the apartment, she had tried it herself. She could still remember the feeling of hanging over the beautiful blue bay, watching her father and Stewart becoming smaller and smaller as they waved instructions from the crowded beach. It had been quiet above the bay. The rope that connected her to the boat was only a gossamer thread from that height, and the human activity below became quickly insignificant. She thought it must be like that for the man-o'-war birds that sailed for hours high above the beaches. She thought how wonderful it would be to put that freedom in her dancing.

Her dancing. She had been daydreaming and now picked up her bowl, fork, and half-filled glass of iced tea on her way to the kitchen. She dumped them into the sink, turned to lock the sliding-glass doors, and picked up her gym bag on her way out. The apartment was small, but the garage that came with it was huge for Hermosa Beach. Its size had interested Stewart. Before he left for South Dakota, he had come over late one night and asked whether he could keep his car in her garage. It was a classic Jaguar, and he didn't want to leave it at his house while he was gone.

He mentioned without much enthusiasm that when he came back, he'd probably move on to one of several companies that wanted him. He'd take some of his best customers with him and of course keep the percentage in the company he had just quit. He had done this before, and now in addition to a high salary, he received dividends from half the long-distance companies in LA. Stewart was smart, but he could also be silly sometimes and was always cute enough to be completely irresistible to his older sister. But still she worried. The car in her garage reminded her that he was a long way from home.

When Linda pressed the mechanism to open the garage door, the overhead light came on, and the two cars were illuminated. Hers was an orange Honda Civic. It was a sensible car and she liked it, but it looked small and austere parked beside Stewart's yellow Jaguar. Linda shook her head. She was aware that her tastes had been influenced by her life with Ross, and she was glad. The Jaguar was some rare model. It seemed decadent. But she had to admit it was a beautiful car. Stewart had, of course, brought the car over for her to drive while he was out on his adventure. He had left the keys on the kitchen counter and told her to take it whenever she liked. So far she had resisted, but she felt her resolve slipping. She took one last look at the Jaguar, got into her Honda, and began to back out of the garage. She pushed the button to close the garage door and watched the door go down in front of Stewart's car.

▲

TWENTY

Ross sat in the darkness of his kitchen on the second night and listened to the blizzard. There would almost surely be dead calves, but he had worried all he was capable of worrying. Now his thoughts wandered in time: his years with Linda, college, and finally, growing up in Pennsylvania. He was aware that he had backed away from the fight in The Oasis the night before, and it reminded him of a day in his junior year of high school. It had been in a study hall on a Tuesday afternoon. He remembered it was a Tuesday because that was the day the football coach got the developed film back from Friday night's game. They had won the game, and Ross, who played defensive cornerback, felt that he had done well. So when he received a note saying the coach wanted to see him in his office in the gym, he had not been nervous about being chewed out.

The coach liked Ross and waved at a chair when he came through the door. The screen and projector were set up, and the coach had obviously been studying the film for signs of weakness and ways to improve the team for the games to come. It was a big high school, and football was taken seriously. On Wednesday all the players would get a score sheet telling them how well they had done in the last game. Ross could see some partly filled out score sheets on the table beside the projector.

"You played a pretty good game, Ross. You were heads up, read the offenses well, and that interception came just at the right time." The coach walked to the light switch. "You're smart, Ross. You've got a chance of being our defensive captain next year." The coach switched off the light. "But there's something in the film I'd like you to watch."

The room was only half-dark, and the coach handed Ross the projector control. "You know how to work this," he said. "Up is forward, down is reverse." He flipped the projector on. "This is an end sweep, where you come up and make the tackle. You made several tackles like this last Friday." The picture came into focus, and the play began to take shape in slow motion. "I'm going to leave and let you watch. Just play it back a couple times and watch yourself." He walked to the door as the opposing quarterback handed off the ball to the halfback. "Watch it very carefully," he said.

After the door closed, Ross watched the play develop. One guard had pulled and was already out in front of the halfback. The flanker was cracking back on the defensive end, and Ross was coming up to turn the play into the pursuing linebackers. The defensive end fought loose, and the pulling guard turned in to help the flanker. That left Ross in the open field with the halfback. Ross would never forget the way he, number twenty-one, had squared up on the halfback at the line of scrimmage. His shoulders were parallel, he did not go for the fake, and the halfback was stopped with only a yard gain. He reversed the film and watched again, this time at full speed. It looked good, right out of the play book, and he could not figure out why the coach wanted him to study it. He played it back again in slow motion, this time just from where they both committed themselves, and it struck him that something was not quite right. Something just at the instant of impact was wrong. Was this what the coach had wanted him to see? He played it over several times at that speed, then as slow as it would go. At the slowest speed the tiniest movements did not go unnoticed, and after three replays Ross realized what the coach had wanted him to see. It dawned on him that the coach had left the room so Ross would not be embarrassed. It had been a good pickup on the coach's part. Ross watched that split second before the tackle over and over but was not sure what it meant. It was a good tackle, and no one in the stands would have seen, but at the very last instant, when the tackler should have been driving hardest, number twenty-one had turned his head away.

Ross had played it over until it was imbedded in his memory. That split second was so much a part of his history that he could see it clearly twenty years later as he sat in the darkened kitchen listening to the freezing wind. He had no description for the way that memory made him feel. Sometimes the feeling was very real, sometimes it seemed imagined, but it was always present.

They had given Ross a month before he had to report to Fort Jackson for basic training. He thought he would raise hell that month, do all the things he'd always wanted to do. But in the end he hadn't been able to think of much to do. He'd gone home to help on his father's farm. It was not like a real farm. It was like a business set up on sixty acres, and it had always been assumed that Ross would run it when his father retired. But on the day that Ross remembered, there was no talk of taking over the farm. Instead, his father talked of his time in the navy. He had been an officer in the engine room of a frigate that spent much of the Second World War protecting convoys between England and the United States. Until that day Ross had known no more about his father's military service than that. But that day, perhaps in light of his son's uncertain future, his father had felt a need to talk. He had begun to tell war stories.

"There's no way to describe the feeling of being in the engine room of a warship thirty feet below the waterline and knowing perfectly well that you are being watched by

U-boats." They had cleaned the carburetor of one of the trac-
tors, and a hundred parts lay in perfect order on the workbench in front of them. Ross's father worked expertly with tiny
wrenches and screwdrivers to reassemble the carburetor.

"It was strictly against regulations not to have all hatches
secured, but I want you to know that I couldn't do it. When I
was on duty, the hatches to the deck were closed but never
locked. And I had an illegal radio down there, too. I listened
to the admiral talking to the other ships in the convoy." Ross
had never heard his father talk like this before, and his awkward help with the tiny springs and floats of the carburetor
became even slower as he listened.

"I had the third shift one night. We were a few hundred
miles off the coast of Iceland in the winter of 1943. Those
diesels were clanking away like always when I heard some
activity on the radio. Someone's sonar had picked up a U-boat
following us pretty close." Ross's father stopped assembling
the carburetor. "That wasn't so unusual. Those wolf packs followed us constantly. But this time the old man got to talking
to the captain of the destroyer we were assigned to escort, and
the next thing I hear they've sent one of the four escorts back
after the sub. It was crazy but they did it.

"It was about an hour before we heard the skipper of the
escort calling for help, saying he was hit. I checked the engines
to be sure we were ready because I figured the whole convoy
would be turning back to help, but they didn't. They sent the
other two escorts back, leaving only us protecting the destroyer.

"Everyone in that engine room was listening to the radio,
and no one could believe it. We were just kids, like you, Ross.
That U-boat was just waiting. Scared? We were so scared we
couldn't talk. Everybody's scared, Ross." He shook his head
and thought back. It was as if he were reliving the story. "And
sure as hell, another hour and the two escorts were calling for

help. In a way I was right there with those other engine crews, that Arctic water rushing in, hot oil and steam busting from the pipes, everybody screaming. Believe me, Ross, we were scared, 'cause we knew we would be ordered back next."

Then Ross's father went silent. It was as if Ross were not there in the gloom of the machine shop with him. He stood very still and wrestled with something in his mind. "But they never ordered us back," he said. "They did what they should have done when they first knew the U-boat was there. The whole convoy went back. I guess they were in a hurry to get to England. I guess that was it. Yes." Then he did something Ross had never known him to do. He turned to his son and put his arms around him and held him stiffly. For a few seconds, there in the dull light of the machine shop, they were frightened together.

There had been much more to say, but it was never said. Ross wanted to resent the assumption that he was afraid, but by then he wasn't sure. But from that day on he knew he could never make a life working with tiny springs spread out on that workbench. Though he was touched by his father's love, he never liked going into the machine shop again. Perhaps that was why he sold the farm as soon as he could and came to the prairie. There were other reasons, of course. And he hoped that all his reasons were not negative. He tried to think of the beauty. A clear sunrise would help, and he strained to see the dawn. The eastern sky was growing lighter. The night was nearly over, and that, at least, was good.

It was odd how it had worked out. Two years after that day in the machine shed his father was dead. In another year the truck farm would be sold and become part of his past. But in a way, he thought, the past is more a part of you than the future. He rubbed his face and could feel that his eyes were red. The light was pushing the darkness away. The fire was nearly out and the kitchen was cold. He squinted into the grayness to see whether the blizzard was over. He held his hands up to the window to cut his own reflection. Between the house and the barn there was only white. Nothing moved. Nothing seemed alive. Even the wind had died.

▲
TWENTY-ONE

Tuffy came into the kitchen just after first light and caught Ross squinting out the window. The coffee had already perked, and Ross had dug out a few old flannel shirts. He wore one over his regular shirt and was carefully wrapping his neck with a black silk scarf. Tuffy poured a cup of coffee and looked out the window, too.

"I'm going to ride out and see how the cows are doing," Ross said. "You coming?"

Tuffy sipped his coffee. "You bet your ass and all its fixtures."

Ten minutes later, wrapped in coveralls and scarves, they were in the barn pulling saddles and bridles down and carrying them to the two horses tied to the top rail of the corral. They had tossed some hay to the heifers who stood quietly nearby. None of them looked as if she would calve that day.

Tuffy saddled Bozo. The horse was seven years old and just in his prime. He adjusted the saddle carefully and talked to his old horse in hushed tones that were not meant for Ross to hear.

Ross's mare was a black named Lady. She was getting some age on her, and she was not as big as Bozo but she was tough like many mares, and her gait was much more pleasant than Bozo's pounding trot. Ross had ridden her since the second year he came to the ranch. She had taught him most of what he knew about working cattle from horseback, and he hated to see her getting old.

They led the horses out of the barn and made final adjustments. Though it was cold, there was no wind, and the sun promised to warm the day quickly. Some of the snowdrifts were impossible for the pickups to penetrate, and by midafternoon mud would make matters worse. Horses were not used every day on the edge of the Badlands, but on days like this there was nothing else that could move. Tuffy had already swung onto Bozo and Ross had tossed the reins up over Lady's head when Stewart came out of the house. He stood on the back porch wearing only a T-shirt and pants, and he squinted.

"Where you guys going?"

"We'll check the cattle first," Ross said. "Then we'll try to get some hay to them."

Stewart was squinting terribly, and Ross realized that it was not only the sunlight. Stewart was not wearing his glasses. He also was not wearing shoes and shifted his weight from one foot to the other. "When will you be back?"

"For lunch," Ross said. "Keep the fire going." Stewart nodded and waved. He hopped back into the house, and Ross and Tuffy pointed the horses toward the calving pasture.

The drifts were deep and hard. Ross knew he would be very lucky if they found all the cattle safe. The weakest would surely have given up. But Sweet Grass Creek had good protection. If the cattle had used the cottonwoods to their best advantage, they would have survived. If they had gone into a low place, where the wind could carry snow over them, they would have been smothered. It had happened to Ross four years before: he had lost four cows and five calves.

Six cows stood at the calving-pasture gate not far from where they had been fed two days before. They were fat, still a long way from calving. They were safe and only bellowed a frosty complaint at the riders who passed the haystacks and dismounted to dig the gate loose. Ross left the gate open. Today it would be easier to take the cattle to the hay than the hay to the cattle.

From the gate Ross and Tuffy split up. Ross, his fingers and toes already stinging with cold, rode to the top of the ridge, where most of the snow had blown clear. Tuffy backtracked to the six cows to see whether more were down in the draw.

Ross watched the trees along Sweet Grass Creek and finally saw a bunch of cows, ten of them, and three calves. At last count there were ten calves in the herd. Any that were born during the storm probably did not make it, so Ross would be very happy to count ten calves before the day was finished. He watched the little bunch and realized that they were moving toward the feeding ground, where the first six had been.

Somewhere there were seventy-three more cows and seven calves, but Ross could see nothing. He could not even see Tuffy, who was probably pushing Bozo through the drifts in the bottom of one of the smaller draws. It was understandable that a man and a horse could be difficult to see, but a herd of eighty cattle would be hard to hide unless it was covered with snow. He had heard of people losing their whole herd, buried alive, revealed only when the drifts melted days later. He took a deep breath and rubbed his face with a gloved hand. It was warming up. His fingers no longer hurt, and he pulled off the gloves as he scanned the draws. Lady moved nervously under him.

If the storm had killed his cattle, he was finished. He owed five hundred dollars on each of those cows, not to mention the land payment, and selling the calf crop was the only means of making the payments. Lady shifted under him again, and he jerked the reins to make her stand still while he searched the draw one more time. As soon as he jerked the reins, he cussed himself. It was not Lady's fault. She pranced a little more, anxious to be moving, and Ross gave up.

They went directly downhill and into the draw. Ross was beginning to feel the night of no sleep. He decided to ride the draw back toward the feeding ground, looking for tracks. He didn't know what else to do. But the snow in the draw was four feet deep. Lady had to gather herself and lunge at it to make any progress. She wanted to get back to the high ground, where the snow had blown away, but Ross forced her to continue to break the drifts in the hopes of finding a few more cows alive. By the time they had gone a quarter mile, they were both sweating, and the crust on the snow had begun to scrape the skin off Lady's legs.

They reached a turn in the draw where the bank was very high. The drift ahead was too deep. Ross would not ask Lady to try it. They were standing at the bottom of the draw staring at the drift when Ross saw what he had hoped he would not see. The brown and white leg of a Hereford calf protruded from the drift. He dismounted and brushed the snow away. It was a newborn calf, perhaps the one he had imagined the night before, with the dampness of birth frozen to a transparent glaze. A wave of fatigue swept over Ross, and he let himself slump into the snow with one hand holding Lady's reins and the other touching the dead calf.

He sat like that until he regained some strength and looked up. At first he thought Lady was watching him. Her ears were pointed, but her stare was focused over his head. He turned around and saw the mother of the dead calf standing in a cavern she had dug as the storm piled snow into the draw. She looked thin, and a trace of afterbirth still hung in a ribbon from under her tail. Her teats were swollen from the milk that was never sucked, and her eyes were dark and wild.

A four-foot wall of snow separated her from the dead calf, and Ross was careful not to frighten her as he broke it down with his legs. He tied Lady to a tree thirty feet away and moved slowly into the cow's cavern. He walked around the cow to get her started, and she watched him carefully. Once she acted as if she might come for him, but she was exhausted and finally moved out, only to stop and try, for what must have been the hundredth time, to revive the calf with her tongue. She lowed once, and Ross waved his arms and chased her up the bank. When he returned to Lady, he happened to look up into the tree to which the horse was tied. Two silvery sharp-tailed grouse sat quietly above. They turned their heads to look down at Ross and clucked to each other, and as if on cue, both began to preen.

When the cow reached higher ground, she lined out in front of Lady toward the haystacks. Only twice did she stop and bellow back toward the draw where her calf lay dead. After they had gone a quarter of a mile, she grew tired, and when she came to deeper snow, she would wait for Ross and Lady to ride around her and break the drift.

By the time they joined the other cattle on the feeding ground, Ross was exhausted. Tuffy was nowhere to be seen. Ross looked over what was left of his herd and felt sick. He was bone tired but he knew he had to go look for Tuffy. He turned Lady back toward the rough country and put her into a slow walk. The cattle started to follow him but stopped after only a hundred feet and began again to bellow.

Ross rode on, his head down. The bellowing continued, and he tried to block it out. He would feed them later; now he had to find Tuffy. Lady moved on but the bellowing did not stop. It intensified, and suddenly Ross realized that it was coming not only from behind him. There were cattle ahead of him. He looked up and saw Tuffy, his hat pulled low and his scarf covering his nose and mouth. He was pushing Bozo through the deep drifts of snow. Behind them a long string of cattle followed up and out of the draw.

Bozo's forelegs were bloody from the crusted snow, but he held his head high and arched his muscled neck. With every touch of Tuffy's spurs the big horse lowered his broad hind-quarters and lunged forward until the drifts stopped him. Then, like huge pistons, the powerful hind legs sent them forward again. Tuffy moved with the horse, helping him through the deepest of the drifts, and the cattle followed in their wake.

Ross counted them. They were all there, including the calves. The storm had claimed only the newborn. Ross fell in beside Tuffy, who lowered his scarf and laughed. "You want to leave them here," Tuffy asked, "or take them on in to the haystacks while we got our dicks swinging?"

Ross broke into a smile. "Take 'em in," he said.

▲
TWENTY-TWO

The blizzard forced the people of Harney into their homes and sealed them there. For an entire day and most of that night Karen Sorenson watched her husband pace and fidget. She knew what was on his mind; he had told her the evening before, when he got home from Rapid City, about some mining development. He impressed upon her that this was to be kept secret, then he drifted off into thought.

It wasn't uncommon for him to become preoccupied with business, but this time it was different. She attributed the difference to the storm. They had never been snowed in together when Larry was working on something big, and so his frustration at not being able to get to his office was laid bare for her to observe. When the storm intensified the next day, Karen saw that her husband was becoming nearly desperate. He would sit in a chair for a minute or so with a magazine open in his lap, then he would get to his feet, stretch, and move to a window, where he would stare for several minutes at the blizzard slanting from west to east. The telephone lines had been dead since early the first day, but every time Larry passed a phone, he would pick it up and listen for a dial tone.

He told her when they sat down for supper that he was missing a meeting with Cleve Miller. It was a silly thing to say because he said it like the storm was somehow his fault. Karen knew it was only frustration. "Cleve Miller is snowed in, too," she said. "You'll be free of this place tomorrow."

Then he looked up from his supper. "I'm sorry," he said.

He squeezed the bridge of his nose between his thumb and index finger. When he looked up again, his eyes had changed. They looked like the eyes of a younger Larry Sorenson. And the shy smile that had become so rare curled the corners of his mouth.

"It's just that I'm excited about the possibilities of this mining thing," he said. "It could make a difference, Karen."

"A difference in what?"

He smiled that old smile again. Twice in one night, Karen thought. "Jobs, Karen. This thing is big enough to make real work here in Harney. Change this place. The young people can stay here. They won't have to leave."

Then Karen knew what he was hinting at but was too proud to say. He was thinking that Loni would come back to live in Harney if it were more prosperous, thinking she had left because her hometown was a backwater. It was preposterous, and Karen felt sorry for her husband. Loni was married to a fine man in Minneapolis. She wasn't coming back. It was sad that Larry thought she might. But even sadder was the fact that he thought it was something as simple as economics that made her leave in the first place.

TWENTY-THREE

Ross and Tuffy checked and fed the heifers in the barn as soon as they got back. They were all right, though the melting snow from the roof was beginning to make a mess of the corral. The sun was hot, and Tuffy and Ross stripped off their coveralls as they unsaddled the horses at the hitching rail near the barn. By the time they reached the house, the snow drifts had softened, and the horses' legs that had been cut by the early morning crust were washed clean. Ross sprayed the cuts with Scarlet Oil before they turned the horses back into the corral. They were forking hay to them when Stewart came out of the house.

He had found some of Ross's work clothes, and though they were big for him, he looked much more at home. He still wore the hat he had arrived with, but its crisp lines and shiny band were gone. Had it not been for the dark glasses he wore, he could have been a hired man. "What happened?" he asked coming through knee-high wet snow.

"Lost a calf," Ross said. "That's all."

Stewart nodded. He obviously wasn't sure whether one calf was an acceptable loss. "I was worried."

"I'm still worried," Tuffy said. He had finished pitching hay over the corral rail and looked around the yard. Both his pickup and Ross's were covered with snow. "We might not get shoveled out of here until midnight. The Dust Buster might be closed by then."

137

"We better check on the Millers and Elizabeth before we leave the bench," Ross said.

"Right." Tuffy stabbed the pitchfork into the small stack of hay beside the corral. "That means we better get at it."

"I got to eat before we start pushing snow," Ross said.

Stewart said, "I thawed some hamburger, and there's coffee on the stove."

Ross and Tuffy looked at Stewart, who was proud of his foresight. "You know, Ross," Tuffy said, "you ought to think about putting this *schlockmeister* on full-time."

They were halfway to the house when they heard the sound of a diesel engine on the county road. "What is it?" Stewart asked.

"Snowplow," Ross answered without slowing his pace.

"Will they clear your driveway?"

"No way. They wouldn't even clear the bench road if it weren't for the missile silo. If anything, they'll push a bigger pile of snow into the driveway from the road."

"Missile silo?" Stewart asked. "What's a missile silo?" But neither Ross nor Tuffy paid any attention. They were concentrating on the thought of hot coffee and lunch.

For two hours after they had eaten the hamburger mixed with baked beans and sliced onions, they moved snow. Ross operated the tractor with the bucket on the front, and Tuffy and Stewart used scoop shovels on the drifts that covered the pickups. The snow was heavy, and the drifts shrank from their own weight. But the going was difficult. Stewart was good for only a few shovels without a rest. Tuffy laughed and told him it must be the altitude. But finally, just as the afternoon began to cool, Ross drove the tractor through the last drift and out onto the county road.

Earlier, they had tried to call the other ranches on the bench a couple times, but the lines were still out. Ross and Tuffy were anxious to check on their neighbors. They knew they might not have been as lucky as Ross. So by the time Ross returned from the road on the tractor, Tuffy had both pickups started and was ready to go.

Stewart rode with Ross, and Tuffy followed in his own pickup. The wrought-iron fence was still in Ross's truck. He planned to check on the neighbors, then deliver the fence to Tuffy's place. Tuffy intended to make sure the neighbors were all right, then go on to Milo for a beer. He had also started to think about Clyde. He hadn't been home for two days and knew that Clyde would be hungry. There was still some snow on the driveway, and they kept the pickups moving slowly but steadily until they turned onto the bench road. When the tires hit gravel, Ross shifted into third and accelerated as if he had just broken free.

"You've never seen this road in the daytime, have you?" Ross said.

"I don't even know where we are."

"The neighbors are Cleve and Edith Miller. Their driveway takes off about a mile ahead. Another two miles and we come to where Elizabeth Janis and her son, Kyle, live with old man Kiser and Pete Rienrick, the hired man. The next place is Tuffy's, and then it's nothing but Badlands and prairie until you get to Milo."

"I remember Milo," Stewart said.

"I'll bet you do."

Cleve's tractor was just pushing the last of the snow from his driveway. Ross slowed the pickup, and Stewart pointed out the window. "What's that?" The chrome letters of Cleve's sign jutted out of the snowbank that had been created by the plow. The faded red toolbox was just visible above the snow.

139

"Center of the Nation. Can't you read?"

Stewart looked at Ross. "No," he said. "That's the ugliest sign I've ever seen."

"Tourist attraction."

"No."

It was late afternoon and cooling off fast, but Cleve sat on the tractor in shirtsleeves. He raised his hand in greeting as the pickups halted. Cleve had shut the tractor down and turned in the steel seat to talk to Ross and Tuffy, who were getting out of their trucks. "Well," he said, "do you think we'll get any snow this spring?"

"Looks like you weathered things all right," Ross said.

"I can't believe it but haven't had any real problems that I know of. A few cows look pretty weak, but, hell, it'll be seventy degrees tomorrow. They'll make it. You?"

"Not bad. Cow lost a calf. Pretty lucky, really."

"You heard anything from Elizabeth?" Tuffy asked.

"Nope. Edith says I should head over that way before dark. But if you boys are going that way, I won't bother." Cleve looked at Stewart, who leaned against Ross's pickup. "That's your friend?"

"That's Linda's brother," Tuffy said.

Cleve looked at Ross. "Your Linda?"

Ross didn't know how to answer in a way Cleve would understand. He nodded and waved for Stewart to come meet the neighbor. The two shook hands through the hydraulic arms of the loader. "Brother-in-law, huh?" Cleve hadn't shaved and looked rough. But he was smiling, glad to meet someone new.

"We better get going," Tuffy said.

"What's your hurry?" Cleve smiled. "The Dust Buster burned down."

"What?"

Cleve pointed at Tuffy and everybody laughed.

"Not funny," Tuffy said. "Come on, I got to get away from this hillbilly."

Cleve started the tractor, and his laughter was drowned out by engine noise. "There's your missile silo," Ross said to Stewart. He pointed to a chain link fence fifty yards off in a pasture. The approach had been completely cleared of snow.

"There are missiles under there?"

"That's what they say." Stewart turned in his seat and looked out the rear window as they passed. When he turned around again, they were nearly to Elizabeth's driveway.

No one had been out to plow this driveway. Except for the dark fence posts lining it, it was indistinguishable from the rest of the landscape. They parked the pickups as far from the center of the road as they could and got out to talk it over.

"You feel like a half-mile walk through the snow?" Tuffy asked.

Ross was exhausted from the day's work and the nights without sleep. "Not really, but if they haven't had time to push their driveway clear, they might be having trouble back there."

"That's what I was thinking." Tuffy reached back into his pickup and brought out his gloves. "It won't be that bad. The drifts have shrunk a lot today."

They started down the driveway toward the house. In a few minutes they could see the tops of the cottonwoods, then the roof itself. No smoke trailed from the chimney, and both Ross and Tuffy recognized that as strange, though they said nothing. It was nearly dark, and the temperature was falling fast. It was not terribly cold yet, but it was cold enough to need a fire.

Tuffy and Stewart were panting pretty hard as they came into the area between the barn and the house. A dim light glowed in the house. They walked to the front porch and knocked. No one answered, so Tuffy pushed the door open, and they all stepped inside. The house was quiet. Tuffy called out as they stepped into the kitchen. There, his eyes fixed in a gentle stare, sat John Kiser. The kitchen was silent.

"Jesus," Stewart whispered.

"Hello, John," Tuffy said. "You remember Ross. This is his brother-in-law, Stewart." John showed no sign of recognition. The kitchen was silent again.

"Well," Tuffy said, "we're going to go help Elizabeth." The three backed out of the kitchen. "Take care," Tuffy said.

"Good-bye," said Ross.

A plowed trail led away from one of the machine sheds toward the creek below. Ross followed the trail with his eyes; where it disappeared over the hill, a finger of smoke twisted skyward against the setting sun. "What the hell?" Ross mumbled.

"Nothing down there to burn," Tuffy said. "Nothing down there but a dam." They looked at each other, glanced quickly around the place, then took a minute to think.

"They must be down there," Ross said. "Looks like they been coming back and forth." He pointed to the pickup tracks in the snow.

The smoke seemed to grow as they moved toward it. It came from very near the edge of the dam, and as they approached the pickup, the loader tractor that had made the trail and the figures of two men could be seen against a huge bonfire. Two tired horses were tied to the tailgate of the pickup. They stood hipshot with sweat dried on their necks and hindquarters. Pete was throwing cottonwood branches on the fire while Kyle, with a burlap sack from the pickup bed, rubbed the back of one of the six cows that lay prostrate on the snow beside the fire.

The three men rushed to help. "What the hell happened?" Ross said as he took a dry sack from the back of the pickup. Kyle and Pete jumped. Kyle's exhausted face broke into a smile, and Pete muttered a few swear words before he explained. "Goddamned cattle wandered in the storm. Took us till noon to find that ten of them went out on the ice." He pointed at the three-inch thick slabs of ice bobbing in the black water along with four dead cows. "Finally got these sons of bitches hauled out. Don't know if any of them will make it or not. Probably end up shooting 'em after all this." He reached into the front seat of the pickup and pulled out a rifle. Ross froze. This old man frightened him a little, even without a rifle. Pete swung the rifle around with his good hand and pointed at the six cows that lay motionless in a semicircle round the fire. They were slightly bloated, and their legs stuck out stiffly. One had a log chain wrapped around its hind legs. The chain was still attached to the tractor.

"Put the rifle back," Ross said. Pete balanced the rifle on his withered arm, then caught it by the barrel with his good hand and slid it back into the truck.

"Where you getting the wood?" Tuffy asked.

Kyle pointed. "The draw. Back there. Been dragging it up by horse. There's a chain saw down there."

Tuffy started for the horses. There were three empty bottles of liquor in the snow beside the pickup. A fourth bottle still held an inch of whiskey. "We gave each cow a good shot," Kyle said.

"They all had theirs?" Tuffy asked, picking up the whiskey bottle. Kyle nodded. "I'll haul some wood," Tuffy said and drained the bottle.

Pete tended the fire. Ross and Kyle rubbed the cattle and Stewart joined in. "Kyle? This is Stewart. Stewart, Kyle." They rubbed in silence until it dawned on Ross that Elizabeth was not there. "Your mom? Where is she?"

Kyle looked up surprised. "You didn't see her? I left her

at the barn a couple hours ago when we went to get the sacks. One of the heifers was close. She stayed to watch."

They pushed the sacks out of the pickup, and Ross backed the truck around and started toward the house. Now it was getting dark, and in the rearview mirror he could see Stewart and Kyle working on the cows with Pete in the background dancing around the fire like a Druid priest.

Ross had driven fifty yards up the trail when he saw that the rifle was with him in the front seat. It was dark in the pickup, and it seemed to hide there among the jumble of feed sacks and bailing twine. He stopped the truck and checked to be sure there was no shell in the chamber. He put the safety on and pointed the muzzle at the floorboards before he drove on.

There was a crack of light at the top of the barn door. Ross parked the pickup at the end of the emergency trail and started over the drifts toward the barn. He fell into step with whoever had made this trip before. The footprints in the snow were no doubt Elizabeth's. She had worn a path to the barn, where the two-year-old heifers were waiting to have their first calves.

Before Ross got to the door, he heard Elizabeth's voice. She was talking gently to one of the heifers. He pushed the door open and watched as she stroked a heifer's flank. The heifer was in the pen they used to deliver the calves who needed help, tied to a post against one wall. She could still swing her rear and kick, which is what she did as Ross watched. Elizabeth jumped out of the way of the hoof and bumped hard into the calf puller, which hung ready on the barn wall. When the heifer moved, Ross could see that she was very near having her calf. Her water had broken, and a nose was beginning to appear from the swollen vagina.

Elizabeth leaned against the wall and let the heifer calm down. Her coat hung on a nail, and she wore only boots, blue jeans, and a work shirt, the right sleeve of which was rolled to the shoulder. A strand of black hair had fallen across one eye, and she blew it away because her hands were covered with the fluids of birth. Ross had seldom before had the opportunity to look closely at Elizabeth. She always disappeared when he came around. But in the moment before he spoke, it struck him that she was prettier than most people thought.

"Let me help."

She spun at the sound and stepped back so that her back went flat against the wall. "It's me," Ross said. "Sorry." But Elizabeth's dark eyes still flashed from side to side. It was as if she were looking for a way to escape. There was panic in her face, and Ross thought he saw her shaking her head. "Looks like you could use a hand." He took a step back and that seemed to help.

"Does the calf have a leg back?"

Elizabeth nodded. "Both legs."

"We'll need to push it back in and get the legs coming first." Ross took off his coat and unbuttoned his shirt. Elizabeth did not move from the wall. "Have you tried that?" The black eyes were moving again. Ross decided not to notice and pulled his shirt off. "Have you tried that?" he said again as he moved toward the heifer.

Elizabeth's voice was hard to hear. "I'm not strong enough," she said.

"She's on the fight now. Let's tie a foot up so she can't kick. Do you have a rope?" Ross looked at the heifer, then reached out and touched her flank. When he turned, Elizabeth handed him a lariat. He made a small loop and sent it deftly at the heifer's rear left hoof. When she felt it hit, she stepped up and into the loop.

"You guys caught hell, didn't you?" Ross jerked the rope

tight and moved to the front of the heifer. He pulled the rope through the halter Elizabeth had made earlier from another lariat. "Those cows drifting onto that dam was bad luck." He pulled the rope, and the heifer's foot came up, making it impossible for her to kick. He started to tell Elizabeth to push the heifer against the wall, but she already had her shoulder against the rib cage.

The heifer was nearly immobile and didn't struggle as Ross pushed the head back. That made her push, and Ross leaned hard against the head until the contraction stopped. He pushed again, and slowly the calf went back into the womb. Now when the heifer contracted, Ross's arm was pinched hard. His face was against the heifer's hip, and he leaned with all his might. Elizabeth's face was against the heifer's ribs, and she leaned, too. Slowly Ross reached down into the warmness and found a leg. He brought it up with great difficulty and went back down for the other. When both legs were up under the calf's chin, Ross took the soft hooves in his hand and brought them forward. His upper arm emerged from the heifer, and he pulled hard. Finally he backed away, exhausted. "There," he said.

"Keep her against the wall," Elizabeth said. She took the calf puller from the wall and unfastened the chain. Her hands were large for a woman but smaller and more adept than Ross's. In seconds one end of the chain was fastened to the calf's legs and the other to the small winch on the calf puller. Elizabeth cranked gently, stopping often to reach inside and check that the head was coming properly. Finally the front feet appeared with the nose just above them. Ross could feel the heifer begin to help. She did not need to be held against the wall any longer. Elizabeth and the heifer worked together. Push and crank, push and crank until the shoulders passed the heifer's pelvis and the calf seemed to float the last two feet into the world.

Ross held it up by the hind legs as Elizabeth cleared its airway. It coughed and shook its slimy head. As soon as the heifer was turned loose, she spun to the new calf and began to lick it dry. Elizabeth and Ross backed out of the pen, dragging equipment and coiling lariats as they went. They stood for only a few minutes before they were rewarded by seeing the calf stagger to its feet and make its way to the heifer's teats to suck. They watched for a moment longer as they pulled on their coats, then stepped out into the night and looked up at a billion stars.

Elizabeth ran to the house to check on John. By the time she returned, Ross had the pickup turned around. They rode in silence toward the bonfire. Before they got there, they could see that two of the cows were already up and moving about. Two of the other four had their heads up looking at the fire that had been heaped magnificently high. They could see all four men standing by the fire as if they were telling stories. When they were still thirty yards from the fire, Ross felt that Elizabeth was looking at him. He knew she was going to speak before she did. "Thank you," she said. But when Ross looked, she had already turned away.

▲
TWENTY-FOUR

By the time Kyle Janis went to his bedroom to sleep on the night after the storm, the sun was beginning to backlight the buttes to the east of the house. The temperature had barely dipped below freezing during the night, and the day would surely make the draws run with melted snow. Kyle opened his window because it was always easier for him to sleep with fresh air pouring over him. But he was afraid he was too tired to fall asleep. As he stood at the window, a single meadowlark pierced the predawn with its spiraling song.

He and Stewart Bergman had stayed up all night rubbing cows with burlap sacks and tending the fire. The others had gone back to the house, but Stewart had stayed to help. Tuffy had dragged up an enormous pile of wood from along Cherry Creek, and once the sacks were soaked, there was nothing to do but hang them up to dry and feed the fire. At first there was not much real conversation. Stewart asked questions, but Kyle did not volunteer anything beyond simple answers. What year in school? Junior. Was he born here on this place? No, the hospital on the reservation. Was his father still alive? Don't know. Never knew him.

Stewart was talkative, not afraid to lay back in the firelight and jabber away about what was on his mind. He had known Kyle for only a few hours when he told him that this had been the most exciting two days of his life. Kyle couldn't believe that. Stewart said he lived in Los Angeles, a big city beside the ocean, and Kyle imagined he had fancy girlfriends, wore nice clothes, and drove a new and perfectly clean car. At first Kyle thought Stewart was kidding him or talking to him like people talk to babies, simplifying and glorifying everything. But as Stewart went on about how the storm had made him feel and how frightening but beautiful the morning had been, Kyle began to believe that he was telling the truth. "I've had more adventure in the past three days than I have in five years back home."

"It's not always like this."

"Maybe not, but this stuff is for real. I mean, hell, we been rubbing cows with burlap sacks."

"Big deal."

"You saved their lives."

"Not yet. Look at number sixty-two." Kyle pointed to the one cow that had not stood up. "She doesn't look too good." The cow's legs were stretched out in front of her, and she convulsed with tiny tremors.

Her condition hadn't changed for hours, but Stewart looked at her as if she had taken a turn for the worse. He stood up, threw more wood on the fire, and took a burlap sack from the makeshift drying rack. He continued to talk as he rubbed number sixty-two. "You plan to be a rancher?"

Kyle shrugged. "Don't know."

"Well, you like it, don't you?"

"Some of it."

"What's your favorite part? What are you best at? You got to do what you're best at."

"Saddle broncs."

"Saddle broncs?"

"I guess that's what I'm best at. How about you?"

Now Kyle was lying on his bed with the morning sun changing the light in his room so subtly that it was hard to notice. Other meadowlarks had joined that first one, and other birds, too. Kyle recognized a robin, a grackle. They would be standing on the snowdrifts waiting for the grass to be revealed and wondering why they had come back north so soon. He had gotten his boots and shirt off but had only unbuttoned the pants. He closed his eyes and saw Stewart wrestling with Kyle's question about what *he* was best at. Finally he had said something that Kyle did not understand. "I don't leave without the order in my hand," Stewart had said and shrugged. "A tremendous character trait in my line of work."

Kyle had looked away because he was embarrassed that he did not understand what Stewart was talking about. He had had that trouble with other people who lived far away, but he had never really cared whether he understood what those other people meant. It was too much trouble. But Stewart was different. He seemed happy about being out in the middle of the night trying to keep cows from dying of exposure, and Kyle liked that. He didn't want Stewart to know he was dumb.

In the end number sixty-two had to be shot. Pete, Ross, and Tuffy had come back out about five o'clock. They had slept for a few hours in the bunkhouse and had come out to relieve Kyle and Stewart. Pete looked at the four cows that had lain by the fire all night. He touched two of them gently, nodded his head to show that they were doing all right. He kicked the third cow, and she swayed to her feet. "Goldbrickin' old son of a bitch," he said. The cow bellowed and walked shakily into the night. But when he came to sixty-two, he shook his head. "Better put a stop to this," he said and pulled the rifle from the pickup. Ross turned away, but Stewart watched with awe as Pete raised the rifle with one hand and took the cow just behind the eye. Kyle wasn't sure what it was that Stewart had said. He didn't say it loudly, and perhaps it was another of those things that Kyle didn't understand. It sounded like "shalom."

▲
TWENTY-FIVE

By the time Tuffy left Elizabeth's place, water stood in the ditches along the county road, but the road itself was nearly dry. He thought about turning into his driveway as he passed but didn't want to fight the mud just to get to his house. He drove on to Milo and pulled up in front of the Dust Buster. There were three other pickups parked there, and Tuffy recognized them as belonging to guys from the reservation. It was the middle of the afternoon, but Tuffy knew there would be some low-level celebrating going on because the storm was over.

John Kills on Top sat at the bar with Rich Tapio. Tuffy knew that John had been down in New Mexico for the winter. He had obviously just gotten back and was getting caught up by talking to Rich, who knew everything about everybody. They had already had too much to drink. Ruth stood at the end of the bar looking at a VCR that Helen Eagle Bull held balanced on a bar stool. Ruth wiggled a couple wires at the back and shrugged. "Two cases," she said. Helen nodded, and Ruth carried the VCR behind the bar and put it with a coffeepot, a bicycle, a television, and three pairs of cowboy boots. Tuffy greeted John and Rich as he sat down on a stool near Helen. "How's it going?" he said to Helen.

"Good, Tuffy. Things are good. You?"

"Fine as frog hair."

Ruth came back carrying two cases of Old Milwaukee. She

handed them to Helen along with a pawn ticket. Helen smiled and struggled out the door.

"End of the month," Ruth said.

Tuffy nodded. "Checks in three days." He had his wallet out and held it open to show Ruth a few bills. "In the nick of time." Ruth had already pulled a can of Coors Light from the cooler. She took a five.

"You get any snow?" Ruth smiled as she popped the top and put it down in front of Tuffy.

"Just a skiff," Tuffy said. He held the beer reverently in front of him. "Just enough to give a man a thirst." He smelled the beer before he drank. "Sweet Jesus and Crazy Horse," he said.

In the background John Kills on Top was speaking. "So what do you hear from old Chief?"

Chief was Bill White Elk's nickname. He was a character from Porcupine who everyone knew. "Oh," Rich said. "Goddamn, Johnny boy. You didn't hear?" Tuffy and Ruth looked at each other. They were both listening. "Goddamn, Johnny boy. I hate to be the one to tell you." Rich was becoming very emotional, and Ruth made a face. "Goddamn, Johnny, I hate to say it, but old Chief is dead."

Tuffy was shocked, but Ruth made a face and shook her head. "He was in here this morning," she whispered and motioned behind her. "Hocked that coffeepot for a case of beer."

"Dead? Chief dead?"

"Fuckin'-A, Johnny. Hit by a cattle truck a month ago. Right in front of my house."

Tuffy drained his beer. Now he knew what was going on. Rich had a dog named Chief, a worthless hound that was always lying in the road in front of the Tapio place. Tuffy crinkled his beer can and held it up so that Ruth could see he needed another. John and Rich went on lamenting the death of Chief.

"He was a good son of a bitch," John said.

"Best friend I ever had," Rich said.

"Buy those guys a beer," Tuffy said.

Ruth took them each a beer and Tuffy sipped his. "It tastes even better when you're deprived of it for a few days." Two days without a beer had actually been a little tough, and that bothered Tuffy. But even without beer it had been a wonderful few days. The best of the winter, Tuffy thought. He was sorry that Elizabeth had had bad luck and hoped her losses wouldn't be too rough on her shaky hold on the ranch, but he had enjoyed being helpful. He finished off his second beer and thought how he loved living on the bench. He'd never lived any place else, and he couldn't imagine it. If it just weren't so damn lonely, he thought. Then he remembered Clyde. He'd be waiting.

John and Rich were calling to him. "Thanks, man."

"No problem."

"Jesus, too bad about Chief, huh?"

"Yeah," Tuffy said, "bad break."

"You need another one?" Ruth asked.

Tuffy started to say yes, then changed his mind. "No, I got to get home." He was pretty sure he had at least a case of beer in the refrigerator, but he figured he'd better get more. "Give me a case to go."

"You'll be mud up to your ass."

Tuffy shrugged and emptied his billfold on the bar. Ruth pushed the beer across the bar to him and took all his money but two dollars. He stuffed the two dollars in his shirt pocket and buttoned the flap. "Check's in three days," he said.

"Your credit's good."

Tuffy saluted Ruth and turned from the bar. The last thing he heard was Rich and John talking in increasingly sad and drunken tones.

"Did he suffer?" John asked.

153

"No," Rich said. "He was just sitting in the road licking his nuts. He never felt a thing."

Clyde yowled and rubbed against the table leg when Tuffy came into the kitchen. In between the yowls his throaty purr gave away his joy. He fell on his side and rolled at Tuffy's feet. "Glad to see you, too," Tuffy said. He walked to the refrigerator and reached up to get Clyde's empty bowl. "Just as I suspected; you don't care about me. You're just hungry."

Clyde was on top of the refrigerator, purring and pacing. "Hold on," Tuffy said. He took a can of cat food from the cupboard and opened it. Clyde's purring had reached fever pitch. "Yeah, yeah," Tuffy said. He dumped the cat food into the dish. "Jesus. Smells like canned garbage." Clyde had jumped down to the counter, had his head in the dish, and was wolfing down the food before Tuffy could get it back to the top of the refrigerator. "Your manners are deteriorating," Tuffy said and left the dish on the counter.

The two nights Tuffy had spent at Ross's he had used Ross's toothbrush. The next night he had slept on Pete's bunkhouse floor and hadn't been able to find a toothbrush. He was not sure he would have used Pete's toothbrush if he had found it. At any rate, he had missed brushing his teeth and now headed for the bathroom. It was good to be home. It wasn't much, but home was home, and he couldn't think of any place he wanted to be more. He would brush his teeth, then sit in front of the television and have a few beers. It had been a tough four days.

But his toothbrush was gone. There was no sense looking for it. He knew the pack rat had it tucked away in his tangled nest of prickly pear at the bottom of the old gasoline tank. Tuffy's first impulse was to scream, but he didn't. What, after all, would be the use? He stayed calm, put a little toothpaste on his index finger, and brushed as best he could. By the time he came back to the kitchen, Clyde had finished his meal and was sitting on the kitchen table methodically washing his paws and face.

Tuffy took a beer from the refrigerator, popped the top, and stood staring at Clyde. He was about to say something about how it took a lot of nerve for the cat to clean itself in front of him after he had allowed a pack rat to steal his toothbrush when there was a noise under the sink. Tuffy's head came up and Clyde froze, one partially washed paw held rigid in front of his face. The noise came again: a rustle of paper, a scratching of tiny claws against plastic. The pack rat was in the trash can.

Tuffy looked at Clyde and Clyde looked back. Tuffy took a sip of beer and nodded at the cat. He moved toward the cupboard under the sink. Clyde was in a perfect position. If Tuffy could jerk the door open and tip the trash can onto the floor, the rat would have to make its escape through the hallway door. He'd have to run right under Clyde, an easy pounce from the kitchen table, a quick kill.

It's hard to tiptoe in cowboy boots but Tuffy managed. The scratching sounded again as Tuffy took one last sip of beer and set the can down gently on the edge of the sink. He worked his elbows in space to ensure ease of movement, then reached down and took hold of the cupboard handle. Clyde had crouched, his ears pointed forward and his eyes black with concentration. Tuffy looked back, nodded to Clyde, then jerked the door open. But before he tipped the trash can onto the floor, he saw that the rat was trapped. It had crawled into the trash can and couldn't get out. It ran under a piece of trash at the bottom of the can. Tuffy smiled.

"Ah hah," he said, picked up the trash can, and moved it out onto the floor, just under Clyde.

"You're a prisoner," he said. "For high crimes against the state, I sentence you to death by Clyde." He reached over and

155

stroked Clyde's head, but the cat was intent on the faint scratching noise in the trash can.

"Reprieve?" Tuffy asked. "Certainly. But first you must return," he began counting on his fingers, "my truck keys, the soap, about five ballpoint pens, the pliers with the blue plastic handles, the stapler, the package of flashlight batteries, the comb, the pocketknife, and my toothbrush." Tuffy waited for a moment, as if the rat might speak. "Your refusal leaves me no alternative," he said. He turned to Clyde and tipped over the trash can.

The pack rat came tumbling out, blinking and disoriented. He was a big one, nearly as big as Clyde. He stood for an instant appraising the situation. Tuffy blocked his path back under the sink, and so the rat turned, as Tuffy had planned, and scurried for the hallway door. He ran right under Clyde. But there was no pounce. Clyde watched intently, tail flipping like a metronome, but he never left the table. The rat disappeared down the hallway.

"Jee-sus Christ!" Tuffy bellowed. "Talk about blowing a chance for glory. What the hell is your problem?" He was down on his knees in the trash, his face only a few inches from Clyde's.

"What is it?" he said. "You're pissed 'cause I left you alone? I'm sorry." Clyde was sitting up now looking at Tuffy. "We got to get that rat." Clyde looked away. "Listen up, feline." Tuffy tapped the cat on the chest. "This is important."

▲
TWENTY-SIX

Two days later, when Ross and Stewart brought Tuffy's wrought-iron fence over, the mud in the driveway was nearly dry. Water still stood in the ditches, and there were some piles of snow left where the drifts had been. They pulled up beside Tuffy's pickup with the idea of transferring the sections of fence from their pickup to his.

On the way to the house Ross noticed only one set of tracks in the driveway. Tuffy hadn't been off the place since he got back from Elizabeth's. They stood on the back steps and knocked. There was no answer, so Ross yelled hello and they went in. Clyde slipped out as they entered.

The kitchen was a mess. There were empty beer cans on the counters, the table, and crushed flat on the floor. The trash can had been righted but stood in the center of the floor, surrounded by pine planks that formed an enclosure with an opening that led into a tunnel of planks disappearing into the hallway. Ross had seen this sort of thing before, and he shook his head. He wished that Stewart weren't there, and he considered just backing out of the house and leaving Tuffy by himself. But he knew from experience that Tuffy might need help. Ross turned to Stewart, who was looking at the crude maze. "Wait here," Ross said. "I'll see if he's in his bedroom."

Ross stepped over the wooden tunnel and followed it down the hall, where it opened into another enclosure about three feet across, just outside Tuffy's room. He couldn't imagine what Tuffy had been up to until he saw a huge piece of moldy cheese in the center of the enclosure. The structure was some sort of trap.

Tuffy's bedroom smelled of sweat, stale clothes, and vomit. Tuffy was collapsed on the bed, fully clothed with a pistol strapped to his waist. There were more beer cans scattered around the room. An electric space heater glowed blue in the corner. Ross moved to the edge of the bed and gently pulled the pistol from the holster. It was a .45 automatic, very much like the one Ross had learned to shoot in boot camp at Fort Jackson. He'd qualified with the .45 but never liked it much. He held the pistol with two fingers and looked around for a place to hide it. Finally he opened a drawer on the dresser and laid it on some of Tuffy's socks. Then he covered it with more socks. When he turned, Stewart was standing in the doorway.

Ross thought he would have to explain, but Stewart didn't seem surprised. "Come on," he said, "let's get those clothes off him and get him cleaned up."

Ross nodded. "Easy. He can be touchy."

Tuffy complained when they pulled his boots off. "Fuck off, you guys." And when they persisted, he jerked his arm away from Ross and glared at them as if they were strangers.

"You're a mess," Stewart said calmly. "Let us help you."

"Go fuck yourself, Jew boy."

"Come on, Tuffy." Ross held his arm but Tuffy was looking at Stewart. Stewart did not lower his eyes. They stared at each other for a moment, and then Tuffy seemed to give up. By the time they had stripped his shirt off, he was crying.

He cried through his shower, then dried himself and pulled on a clean pair of pants. Ross and Stewart had already picked up the kitchen and were started on the bedroom. Tuffy stood watching them, no shirt on and his hair wet. He was still drunk but sobering and now looked very ashamed. He started to cry again as he pitched in to straighten the room. "There is a pack rat," he tried to explain, but his voice cracked, and he went silent for a minute. "I used to be a pretty good cowboy," he said. "A pretty good cowboy," he said. "A pretty good cowboy."

No one spoke for a long time. Then, "We brought your fence," Ross said.

"Is it like this with you," Tuffy said, "since Linda's gone?"

Stewart looked at Ross. Ross spoke softly. "I know how it is," he said. Tuffy nodded but did not look up. "We'll put your fence in the back of your pickup."

Tuffy continued to nod, and the other two moved to leave him alone. But they stopped and looked back when they heard him call out. "Stewart?" He was holding the high-school yearbook and did not look up. "Sorry," Tuffy said. "I know what it's like. I'm sorry."

▲

PART FOUR

▲

TWENTY-SEVEN

The first day the road between Red Shirt and the bench became passable was a Saturday, and Tracy and Louis brought the kids up for the day. They hadn't had as much snow at Red Shirt, and Louis had been able to get a day off. Usually Elizabeth did not like having Louis around, but with the mud and more calves coming every day, she was thankful he was there to help. But having Tracy and the kids there meant that Elizabeth had to stay close to the house. If she went about her chores in the usual way, she would have to leave Tracy in the house with the kids and John, and Tracy would take offense. Tracy liked having someone to chatter to. Mostly it was about herself, Louis, and the kids. Hearing about her perfect family tired Elizabeth, who believed that Tracy felt sorry for her. Elizabeth couldn't help thinking that Tracy thought Elizabeth's life was a mess.

But it wasn't like that. Elizabeth could never tell her sister the truth about either of their lives. There was no point. She didn't feel that she had to defend herself, and there was no sense hurting Tracy. Her sister had inherited all the good features from their mother except one. She was not kind. It wasn't her fault. It was just that she had a need to be seen as a little better than everyone else. It was important to her and Elizabeth didn't care. After John Kiser's accident they had found a paper in his safe-deposit box that said the ranch belonged to Elizabeth. Even if it was heavily mortgaged, it was something. You could never tell what would happen. Things always

163

worked out. Elizabeth believed that. She would just keep doing the best she could. She would let her sister believe whatever she wanted.

But after several hours of talking with Tracy and the kids running in and out, Elizabeth had to get away. The mail was delivered about eleven o'clock on Saturdays, and she told Tracy she was going to walk out to the road to pick it up. Tracy offered to drive her out in Louis's new pickup, but Elizabeth said no. It was a beautiful day and she'd rather walk.

There was a lot of talk about stopping Saturday mail delivery, but they hadn't yet and Elizabeth was glad. It gave her an excuse to get out of the house and take in the fresh April air. This time Elizabeth was sure that spring had arrived. The meadowlarks had come back in force just after the snow. She had seen a male towhee in the budding lilac bush that morning, and robins flipped along the driveway ahead of her.

As she walked, she could see Pete and Kyle riding the ridge to the south with a cow and calf in front of them. It reminded her that she would have to get the branding arranged soon. They put the cattle out to summer pasture about the fifteenth of May. The calves had to be branded by then, the cows vaccinated and ear-tagged. Branding was a good time when you had enough people to do the work. Usually everyone on the bench helped out, so it was more like a party than work. But she had been to brandings that were poorly organized, with too few people, and they were disasters. She made a mental note to start planning the branding in the next week or two.

She was moving away from the house and buildings when she heard Louis yell at one of the kids. The sound made her shudder, and she hurried down the driveway. Suddenly she experienced an unexplainable rush of happiness. She found herself walking faster toward the mailbox and smiling. Her mood made her think of when she was a child on the reservation: it was the happiest time in her life. She had walked to the mailbox for her mother. Perhaps that was it. Perhaps it was the thought of her mother that made her happy. Now that winter was over, she would have to go down to Rosebud to visit. She should go more often, but it was not as if her mother needed her. She always seemed so content, at peace with her life there in the tiny cabin with her sisters. The old ladies were happy together, and Elizabeth knew it was because they were able to close their eyes to each other's faults. That had been an example she had tried to follow. She knew how hard it was.

The thought of the independent old ladies made her smile, but she had been wrong. Today her mood came from some other source. She stopped in the road and looked around. What was making her feel this way? The mailbox? Could there be something important in the mailbox? No. There was never good news in the mailbox. It was something else. She walked on, looking ahead at the road and the buttes beyond. She concentrated on what was happening inside her. Her mother would know what the feeling meant. She would be able to tell what was going to happen.

Elizabeth walked slowly to the middle of the gravel road, toward the mailbox. She looked north and south, forty-two miles to Harney, sixteen to Milo, then walked the final ten feet to the bent silver mailbox.

Inside she found *The Weekly Shopper;* a newsletter from one of the U.S. senators; *The Highliner,* a newspaper from the Rural Electic Association; and a letter from the First Bank of Harney. She held the letter up as if she might be able to see through the envelope. Seeing her name on official letters frightened her. She folded it into the newspapers and squeezed the bundle tightly. Then there was the vibration and sound of an approaching vehicle. She tucked the mail under her arm and moved quickly across the road and down the driveway. There was no place to get out of sight for fifty yards.

She moved as fast as she could without running. The vehicle was coming from the direction of Milo and moving fast enough that reaching the cottonwoods before it came into sight would be close. Elizabeth kept her head down and walked on. When she reached the trees, she stepped among them and felt the relief of her own disappearance. When Ross Brady's pickup appeared on the county road, she knew exactly why she had been drawn to the end of her driveway, and it frightened her, but she could not bring herself to step from the shelter of the cottonwoods and into the open as the pickup moved past.

▲

TWENTY-EIGHT

Larry Sorenson and Cleve Miller talked it out in the Enchanted Forest. They spent nearly an hour in the snack bar near Hansel and Gretel's garden. The Enchanted Forest was closed for the season, and there was no possibility that they would be overheard, but still they talked in hushed tones. Cleve was of course in, but neither he nor Sorenson thought it was a good idea for him to be directly involved. Sorenson had already written Elizabeth Janis informing her that her loan was in default. That would give them two of the ranches, enough to make the deal happen.

Cleve immediately grasped the importance of what Sorenson was saying. He rubbed his face with his big hands as Sorenson spoke. He nodded when Sorenson talked of the possible benefits to the community: the increased business, the new jobs. Sorenson talked on about full-time, year-around employment for the people of Harney, but all the while Cleve was putting figures together in his head, trying to decide how much he could ask for his ranch and how much he'd have left after he paid off the bank on the bad cattle deal.

"Of course, it's not completely altruistic," Sorenson said. "The bank will realize a tremendous profit on the resale of the Kiser place, and the value of your land will increase sixfold."

Cleve nodded. It was an answer to his prayers. God had heard him and was trying to help. No out-of-state bankers

167

would be foreclosing on him if this deal came through. They'd be coming asking if he needed more money.

"But it's not a sure thing," Sorenson said. "This needs to be thought out carefully. We need to get our ducks in a row before any of it slips out. Speculation could be a very bad thing."

Cleve's eyes were focused on something far away, and it made Sorenson wonder what he was thinking. "It has to stay quiet," Sorenson said. "If word gets out, those ranches on the bench could get refinanced and bump First of Harney out of the picture. Any bank in America would jump at the chance."

"Any bank anywhere," Cleve said.

Sorenson was standing then. "Come on; let's walk."

They pushed open the door of the snack bar and stepped into the evening air. The Enchanted Forest was all around them. Hansel and Gretel's garden, where tulips would soon pop up between the slabs of petrified wood, was to their left. The quartz and crystals in the rock sparkled as they moved on the Enchanted Walk toward the Pirates' Hideaway, a series of caves built of petrified wood where kids could play as their parents browsed the gift shop. The night was pleasant. Snowdrifts inside the walls of the Enchanted Forest had been minimal, and only a few puddles of water remained. They walked on, past the Oasis and the Castles.

"To tell the truth," Sorenson said, "I think it would be best to lock that whole area."

"Buy it?" Cleve shook his head. Larry was just a small-time banker. The only thing he had in common with the world bankers who controlled everything was the name. But sometimes he said things that made Cleve wonder. "Buy them out? Just like that?"

"If necessary, yes. The Indian woman is way behind with her loan. If we're diplomatic, we could get it without even going through a foreclosure. I don't know about Ross Brady; only met him once. I know he had his trouble with the army, but still he seems like a reasonable sort. And the other Indian, Martinez, I don't know at all."

"I know him," Cleve said. "He's a good kid but as hard up as any Indian. You might get the whole place for a pickup load of booze." They were passing the Tower of London. It was the largest structure within the walls of the Enchanted Forest. The bottom floor was fifteen feet in diameter and had bars on the windows and door. The Forest's Keystone Cops spent all summer locking squealing children into the tower. It was a very popular feature.

They paused on Fishing Bridge, where in a couple months children could fish for hatchery trout. The pool below the bridge had no water in it yet, but Sorenson and Cleve leaned over the rail side by side and looked down as if there were a clear, cold mountain stream below them. Neither talked. It was a beautiful night and they were enjoying it.

Before they left the Enchanted Forest, Cleve turned solemnly to Sorenson. "You know this isn't going to be easy," he said.

Sorenson smiled and patted Cleve's back. "Worthwhile things seldom are."

"You couldn't have said it better," Cleve said. "There's a lot of evil out there. And every bit of it will be working against us."

Cleve Miller sat beside his wife in the front of the Good Shepherd Lutheran Church. He had noticed Larry Sorenson come in just before the processional. Karen was not with him, and Cleve thought that was a shame.

The sermon was taken from the Thirteenth Psalm:

How long, O Lord? Will you forget me forever?
How long will you hide your face from me? . . .
Look on me and answer, O Lord my God. . . .

Cleve Miller listened closely to the new, young preacher
from Minneapolis and believed that he understood what he
was getting at, though he had a hard time believing that a
privileged kid like him could know much about being forgotten by anyone. Sunday mornings often made Cleve depressed,
and this morning was no exception. Edith nodded her head in
the pew beside him as the preacher spoke. She had more faith,
Cleve thought. She had the real stuff, the kind of faith that
could carry her through. She made things come true, made it
all work out in the end. Cleve couldn't see his way clear to
being always positive.

But he had studied what was really going on in the world.
Of course, he couldn't tell people what was happening,
couldn't tell them about Satan's conspiracy, because they
would call him crazy. That was all part of the plan. So he had
to keep what he'd learned from the Bible and his secret litera-
ture to himself. A chill ran down his back. It was difficult knowing what he knew and having no one to share it with.
Especially on Sundays. In a way he envied Edith and all the
other members of the church. It was certainly easier just to
have faith.

He alone knew why everything in their lives turned to
shit. Then he felt bad for thinking a swear word during church.
But it was true. Maybe it was God hiding his face. Cleve didn't
really know about that. But he did know that he'd worked all
his life, quit drinking, never chased women, never stolen, or
done much that was mean, and still he had nothing. Sitting in
that pew thinking about it made him mad. Being mad in the
Lord's house made him ashamed. He crossed his arms and
tried to concentrate on what was being said. The young

preacher was asking everyone to pray for the members of the congregation who were in the hospital. Carey Adams had had a baby. Ivan Thompson was in for tests. Emily Brunick had cancer. It could be worse, Cleve thought.

When he was supposed to be praying, Cleve peeked over at Edith. Her eyes were closed tight, and he could see the muscles of her jaw moving as if she were talking tough to the Lord. Cleve turned his head, opened both eyes, and looked full on at his wife. He glanced around the church. Everyone's head was bowed; all eyes were closed. He looked back at his wife and was suddenly overcome with love for her. In an instant a hundred moments of their life together flew through his mind: their first date in his father's Model A, the wedding, the honeymoon, the children, the arguments, the quiet times. It struck him that he had not done enough for Edith and that she loved him anyway. What if she got cancer, like Emily Brunick? Fear crashed down on him and he lowered his head. But the prayer was over. When the collection plate came around, Cleve emptied his pockets, and he felt relief when he heard the high chords of the recessional.

As the congregation moved from the church into the warm April sunlight, Cleve's hand brushed his wife's. It occurred to him that they could hold hands on a beautiful day like this, that there would be nothing wrong with it. But he didn't take Edith's hand, and she did not even notice that their hands had touched. They filed out past the young preacher, and Cleve took his hand instead. "It was a nice sermon," he said.

Edith shook the preacher's hand, too, then they started to cut across the lawn toward their pickup. Cleve was looking down, noticing that the grass was turning green near its roots, when he heard someone call his name. When he turned, Larry Sorenson was motioning for him to come over. He stood under an ash tree whose buds were just beginning to open.

▲
TWENTY-NINE

The letter from the First Bank of Harney lay unopened on Elizabeth's dresser for two days. The first day Elizabeth was able to ignore it. She didn't go into her bedroom at all during the day, and when she went to bed, she undressed in the dark so that she wouldn't have to see the letter. But the next morning she woke up with the same feeling as when someone is watching you sleep. When she opened her eyes, the envelope was the first thing she saw. Its whiteness seemed to glow in the first light of morning, and she rolled away from it, bringing the blanket up under her chin and staring at the pale green wall until she could stand it no longer. She jumped from the bed and scooped her clothes from the back of the chair as she streaked for the bathroom.

All the next day as she helped Pete sort off the cows that had not calved yet, her mind wandered to the letter. But she wouldn't let herself think about it. Kyle had not wanted to go to school again that morning, but she had insisted. She wanted very much for him to graduate from high school. She knew that he was partly right when he said graduation didn't really matter, that he already knew more than he would ever use. But he was not completely right. The more education he had, the better. You could never tell what was going to happen. Look at Ross Brady. He didn't need all his education, but it made him special anyway. She wanted to tell Kyle that, but she never could. Instead she argued with him almost every day. She knew she was right, but as she helped with the sorting, she wondered whether the real reason she had made Kyle go to school that day was so she would have to help Pete. She wondered whether she had used it as an excuse to stay outside of the house the whole day and not have to open the letter.

They broke for lunch and walked side by side to the back porch to take off their muddy coveralls. Pete had been talking to himself as they sorted cattle, but it didn't bother Elizabeth. It was usual for many people to mutter as they evaluated udders and tried to get cattle to go in a particular direction. But as they sat on the porch steps and pushed one boot and overshoe off with the toe of the other, Pete jabbered away to someone named Oscar. "There's twenty-five head there," Pete said. "Goddamn it, Oscar, John told you that."

Elizabeth didn't know who Oscar was, but John was probably John Kiser. It had been a long time since John's accident, and it had been hard for everyone. But for Pete the loss of his old friend had made him sink further into the world of the dead. She looked down at Pete as she started into the house. He threw his boot down and spoke to thin air, his eyes squinting and his index finger pointing. "Now I told you that. Damned right."

"Come on," Elizabeth said. "Just soup and sandwiches. But the soup's hot."

She smiled at John, who sat looking out the kitchen window, but her smile disappeared as her eyes came to her bedroom door. She would not let the letter take over her mind. She spun toward the stove and went to work. She fed John first, pushing the pieces of sandwich into his mouth and waiting for him to chew. He ate to the sound of percolating coffee. Pete slurped his soup and kept saying how good it was.

When John was finished, Elizabeth brought Pete a second bowl of soup. Then suddenly she could stand it no longer. She put the bowl down in front of Pete and walked across the kitchen and into the bedroom. She took the letter from the dresser and held it up with both hands. She read the address as if to make sure it was for her, then neatly tore the end off, blew into the envelope, and dumped the letter out into her hand.

She unfolded the letter and stared at it without reading. This paper, she thought, where did it get its power? Little ink marks on a piece of white paper. She wanted to laugh at it or take it to the window and let it fly away, but she couldn't. It frightened her too much. The bank logo was in the upper left-hand corner, and she read it first as if the message were hidden in the design or in the slogan, "PARTNERS IN PROGRESS." She read on; her name and address again—why? From Larry Sorenson—who was that? Her name again. Then dates and figures, percentages, and a big number at the bottom. It was what she thought. She would have to go into the bank and talk to a man. Tears of frustration tried to get out. That was silly. It would do no good. She folded the letter carefully and slid it back into the envelope. Then she crossed her arms in front of her, lowered her head, and thought.

Pete was putting his dishes into the sink when Elizabeth appeared from the bedroom. "Good," Pete said and smiled. Two cups of coffee steamed at the table. "Have you a sit down." Pete waved to the table. "Only a few more to sort off. Easy afternoon."

Elizabeth sat down and picked up the coffee with both hands. It was warm outside and the house was comfortable, but still the hot coffee felt good in her hands. "Can you finish up by yourself?" she asked.

"S'pose," Pete said.

"And keep an eye on John?"

"S'pose."

"I think I'll drive down to Rosebud to see Mom."

"Agnes? Well, say hi to old Agnes." He slurped his coffee.

"Hell, I haven't seen Agnes for a year. She still livin' with those other old ladies?"

"Yes."

"Well, say hi to them all."

Pete was more cheerful than he had been for a long time, but then he came and went quickly these days. Elizabeth blew gently into her coffee; the steam came back into her eyes and moistened her forehead. "You won't need the pickup?"

"No. I'll finish sortin', then ride the main bunch. Don't need no pickup for that."

"I might not get back for suppertime. Tell Kyle I went to Mom's. There's a roast cooking now; maybe you could turn down the heat when you get back."

"We can handle it," Pete said. He finished his coffee. "Don't worry about us." He stood up and glared to his left. "Right, Ivan? Hell, yes. We can take care of ourselves. Can't we?" He turned back to Elizabeth and nodded his head. "See there? We can handle it." He slapped his knee and stepped into the mud room off the kitchen.

Elizabeth could hear him talking as he pulled on his coveralls and boots. She moved to the sink with the two cups and through the window watched Pete walking toward the corrals. He continued to talk, gesturing left and right as if he were giving a tour of the ranch. He pointed out the barn, the machine shed, the cattle standing in the corral, and then Dancer, who watched him from near the barn. Pete stopped, talked to his imaginary friend in earnest, motioning to the colt twice more. Finally he began nodding his head, and he, presumably with his companion, walked on to the corral, where the cows stood staring at him with great interest.

* * *

175

The drive down through the reservation was one of Elizabeth's favorites. It was a little faster to go by way of Interior, but Elizabeth liked the country better to the southeast, so she usually took the gravel that left the county road just past Milo and wound its way to Potato Creek. At first the land was rough and eroded like the land in the Badlands National Monument to the north, but by the time you reached the White River, the native grass had become stronger and grew in lush sod on the valleys and benches.

This was a long way off the beaten track, the heart of Pine Ridge. And it was beautiful, with very few fences and, on the high places, the pine trees that gave the reservation its name. Elizabeth had heard well-meaning whites talking about how the pioneers had taken all the good land and left the worst for the Sioux. She smiled to think of her friends who let that little misconception go uncorrected. It was nice that the beauty of the Pine Ridge and Rosebud reservations was a well-kept secret. It pretty much assured Elizabeth of a hundred miles of driving without worrying about much traffic.

In fact, she had made the trip from the bench to the old family house near Parmelee several times without passing another car. She always saw lots of cars in the communities of Wanblee, Longvalley, and Norris, but mostly they were junkers that hadn't run for years. There was no alcohol sold on the reservations, so the roads that led to "border" towns like Milo were often traveled by people on liquor runs. When Elizabeth did pass a car, she did it carefully. She could name thirty people she'd known personally who had been killed on these seldom-traveled roads.

But there was no use thinking about that. If you worried about everything that could hurt you, you would stay in bed all day with the covers pulled over your head. You had to think about the good things, like the way the cottonwood trees were leafing out along Bear in the Lodge Creek or the very white small clouds that looked as if they were painted on the very blue sky. You couldn't think about embossed letterheads from banks. You had to think about three old sisters who lived now in the small, square house where Elizabeth was born.

The old men of both reservations called them the Bad Wound girls. Rachel was the oldest, Sarah the middle, and Elizabeth's mother, Agnes, was at sixty-eight, the baby. Between them they had twelve children. At last count there were thirty-six grandchildren, though many of the children had not been heard from for a long time, and so that figure was probably much larger. Elizabeth had two older brothers whom she had not seen for five or six years. One had gone down to New Mexico with his wife and not been heard from again. The other one had been in and out of trouble, had robbed a man in Rapid City when the twins were babies, and had done some time in Sioux Falls. Elizabeth didn't know what became of him after he got out, but the rumor was that he had gone up again. Agnes probably knew, but Elizabeth knew she didn't want to talk about it.

The road to the house was still muddy. It had not been graded in a long time, and the ruts were deep and, in some places, filled with water. Elizabeth pushed the transmission lever into four-wheel drive and eased through the puddles. In three weeks the road would be hard as granite and rattle the rivets from a pickup frame, but today it was soft and warm as if moisture were oozing from somewhere deep inside the earth itself. It felt like home to slide down this road with mud squishing beneath the tires, and Elizabeth recalled little scenes from her childhood: her father being bucked off a horse in the front yard, a deer being skinned as it hung from the cottonwood in the front yard, her mother sitting in the shade house on a hot summer day making a star quilt.

Though they had older brothers, Elizabeth and Tracy were raised mostly with just each other for playmates because the boys were already teenagers when they were born. Her mother was fond of saying, "The twins took us by surprise." They had played in mud like this beside the pink government house, and for the first six years of their life it was their whole world. It was an isolated place, and until they went away to the Catholic boarding school, the twins did not see many people. Elizabeth remembered the horror of that first year of grade school, away from their parents, how they cried for days at a time between the holidays, when they could come home. She remembered how the two Janis girls huddled together in their room waiting for the day that their father, big, handsome Charley Janis, would come to pick them up. They longed to see Charley's old pickup pull into the parking lot and to hear him laugh as they broke past the nuns to meet him. He would scoop them up into his hard arms, and they would smell his hair and tobacco. They hated the boarding school and were happy when they were allowed to go to the public high school in Harney.

When the house came into sight, Elizabeth felt the same way she had coming home on those holidays. Her jaw quivered, and she smiled when she saw Charley's old pickup, stationary for years now and cannibalized down to body and frame. It was up on three wooden blocks near the corral where he had kept horses he was breaking. The corral was tumbling down, and grass was beginning to lick at the running boards of the old truck. There were more cars scattered around the place, but Elizabeth knew that most were lacking some important ingredient that would make them mobile. The big Buick that the Bad Wound girls had used most recently to bring in supplies was parked in front of the gate. The gate was wired shut, and there was a green Ford Pinto with splotches of gray primer parked beside the Buick. Elizabeth assumed relatives were visiting a grandma.

She was making her way through the mud to the gate

when a small brown face framed in black braids appeared at the corner of the house. It was a little girl wearing a print dress and rubber boots that were too big for her. This shy, black-eyed creature was one of Elizabeth's nieces, but she could not place the face. They grew so fast, she thought. Then, startled, she wondered whether she had lost twenty-five years and was looking at herself. But the door opened, and her cousin Kim stepped out in time to reassure her that this little girl was Beverly.

Kim squealed and thundered down the steps to meet Elizabeth. They threw their arms around each other and began a dance of greeting on the front walk. A heavyset old lady appeared at the door, and then two more. In a moment there was a cluster of five women, jabbering in two different languages, clinging to each other in the front yard of Agnes Janis's house. The little girl, Beverly, watched this with huge, dark eyes, then she streaked from the corner of the house. She made directly for the mass of women with her arms spread. She hit, hugged, and stuck to one of the ample backsides that blocked her way to the center of whatever was happening.

The inside of the house was very much the way it had always been, except that now Rachel and Sarah slept in the room that had been the twins'. Agnes still slept in the bedroom she had used before Charley's fatal crash. Kim was sleeping on the couch, and Beverly on the floor. This, Sarah secretly assured Elizabeth, was temporary. "Just until that worthless husband of hers straightens up." Sarah frowned. "You know what it's like. Living with a white man, I mean."

"Not really," Elizabeth said.

Sarah thought for a moment, then agreed. "John Kiser was a little different. He must have had some Indian in him somewhere."

Both Elizabeth's aunts had known John Kiser, and she suspected they might have had a crush on him. It made her smile to see Sarah's eyes sparkle. "I just live there, Aunt Sarah. He has always been a little old for me."

Sarah nodded and winked. "Right."

Elizabeth had always been teased about Kyle's "virgin birth," and some people believed that John Kiser was his father. But nobody who knew John or Elizabeth really thought that. Elizabeth didn't mind the teasing from her family. At least it kept them from asking who Kyle's father really was. Elizabeth tried never to think about that. It had been a terrible event in her life. After Kyle came, she was so ashamed and frightened that she had run from this place straight to John Kiser's place on the bench. This was before she learned that the pain and fear went away if she simply stopped thinking about it.

Elizabeth talked to her aunts and cousin but tried to catch her mother's eye as the older woman worked at the sink. She could not stay long and wanted desperately to talk to Agnes. Finally her mother nodded to show that she understood. "Rachel," she said, "could you finish cutting these carrots?"

They stepped out into the front yard. The sun was low, and it was beginning to cool off. "Walk with me to the barn," Agnes said. But Elizabeth shook her head. She had not been in that barn for eighteen years, and the thought of it made her shudder.

"We can talk here."

"I have to sit down," Agnes said. "I'm too old."

They went to the shade house, where there were a couple hard-backed wooden chairs and a table. The pine boughs that were laid across the rafters had lost most of their needles during the winter. They would have to be replaced before the summer sun began to heat up. The legs of the chairs had sunk into the earth, and Agnes had to pull hard on hers before she could move it so they could face the sunset together.

They watched the western sky for a moment before Agnes turned and brushed a strand of black hair back away from her daughter's face. "You were always my beautiful girl."

"Mother." Elizabeth shook her head partly from embarrassment but mostly because everyone knew that Tracy was the beautiful one.

"I don't mean in looks," Agnes said. "In the heart. You are the beautiful one, the thoughtful one, the sensitive one." She brushed the hair back again. "Why have you never found a man? They can be very nice, you know." Elizabeth looked up and saw in her mother's eye the same sparkle she had seen earlier in her aunt's. The Bad Wound girls, she thought and shook her head.

"I've got a problem, Mom."

Agnes nodded. "Yes," she said. "And what would that be?"

Elizabeth dug into her pocket and pulled out the letter from the First Bank of Harney. She handed it to Agnes with a shrug. The older woman took the envelope from her daughter and removed the letter. Her glasses hung from her neck on a chain and she raised and looked through them but did not put them on. Her lips moved as she read.

"They are trying to take the ranch that John Kiser gave me," Elizabeth said after her mother finished reading.

"I can't tell that from this paper. But it was never your ranch anyway. It was never John's either. He would be the first to say that these ranches never really belong to anyone."

"Then it doesn't belong to the bank either," Elizabeth said.

Agnes nodded. "That's true," she said, "but this is whiteman business."

"Should I go into the bank when it says?"

"It probably won't do you any good, but if you do, talk to a white man first. Let him explain what this thing says so you'll be ready."

"You think I should get a lawyer?"

"Any white man. They understand this kind of thing. They can tell you if you have any rights in it."

They sat quietly for several minutes. The sun was cut in half by the pine-covered butte to the west. "When did you last pray?" Agnes asked without looking at her daughter.

Elizabeth shook her head. "It's been a long time."

"Shame on you." Agnes stood up. "Maybe that would be a good place for you to start. A Yuwipi would be better, but there is no time for that." She reached out and took Elizabeth's hand from her lap. "Come on. We'll pray before you have to go home."

The house was beginning to smell like supper. Beverly lay on the floor and watched "Sesame Street." Rachel, Sarah, and Kim made jokes as they bustled around the kitchen. Agnes stepped into the middle of the supper preparations. "We have to pray," she said. "Elizabeth needs to get home." Everyone looked up from what she was doing. "Go on, Rachel," Agnes said, "get the pipe."

Beverly turned off the television. She was too young to participate but loved to watch. She went to her place on the floor beside the couch and sat cross-legged and wide-eyed as the adults finished what they were doing and came to the living room. Though anyone in the family could handle the pipe, Rachel was a medicine woman, so when she was present, she presided over the prayers. The pipe was kept in the cupboard beside the refrigerator, wrapped in a piece of red felt. The bowl had its own felt sack, and Rachel handled it with particular care. She carried it gently into the living room along with a braid of sweet grass, which she handed to Kim, whom she knew smoked cigarettes and so would have a lighter.

"That's one of the bad deals," Rachel said. "Nobody smokes any more. It's hard to find people with matches."

"They all died of lung cancer," Kim said as smoke began to curl from the sweet-grass braid.

"Are any of us on our moon?" Sarah asked.

Agnes whispered to Elizabeth. "She always says that. She hasn't had a period for ten years." Sarah looked at them sharply. Agnes kept a straight face, but Elizabeth had to turn away.

Kim handed the braid to Rachel, who let the smoke cleanse the pipe before she put it together. She also passed the mixture of tobacco and red willow through the smoke before she began to pack it into the bowl. As she worked to prepare the pipe, Elizabeth looked around the circle. Everyone was serious. They looked different now, ancient and wise. Even Beverly looked wise. She watched her great-aunt, the oldest of the sisters, and understood perfectly. The sweet-grass smoke swirled around Rachel's head and mixed with her silver hair. Her face had become older and proud. She moved with grace and purpose, and although she spoke in Lakota, Elizabeth understood the words.

The old woman pointed the pipe in the four directions and asked the winds to come into the pipe and help them pray; then she pointed it to the sky and asked the spotted Eagle to carry their prayers to heaven. And before she smoked and sent the pipe to the next person, she pointed it to Earth, because Earth is the birthplace of everything that is good. "All my relations," the old woman said.

▲
THIRTY

Tuffy, Kyle, and Stewart sat in Tuffy's overloaded pickup as it bounced slowly across the pasture. The wrought-iron fence clattered in the back, along with wooden posts, shovels, augers, and a bushel basket filled with hand tools, wire, and nails. They were on their way to the little hill in the center of the ranch where Tuffy's parents were buried. He had enlisted Kyle and Stewart to help him erect the fence around the family cemetery.

The wind was warm but thirty miles an hour. The ground was drying fast, and the grass was greening up but still very short. "Another week of this, and we'll be praying for more moisture," Tuffy said. "She'll dry out like a cow chip in a microwave."

He had just told the boys that today he was delivering on a promise he had made to his mother and father. They wanted to be buried on the ranch that they had worked their whole lives to pay off. "Mom wanted a fence because she was Catholic and she said real graveyards had fences," Tuffy said. "Dad wanted one because he couldn't stand the thought of cows rubbing on his gravestone."

"You mean you can be buried out here?" Stewart asked. He was sitting in the middle and moved his hand to indicate miles of treeless prairie stretched out in front of them. "Isn't there a law out here about being buried in a legitimate cemetery?"

"Spoken like a true white eyes, right Kyle?" Tuffy shook

184

his head. "This whole place is a cemetery. Always was." They were at the bottom of the hill. "But, yeah, they had to get some damned permit for a family graveyard. One of the rules is that family graveyards have to have fences around them."

"So the cattle won't rub the headstones over?" Kyle asked.

"Don't know for sure," Tuffy said. "Probably because the governor is a Catholic."

Tuffy stopped the pickup and shifted it into low range. "Hope everything stays in," he said and pointed the pickup directly up the hill.

The truck roared, but because of the low gear ratio it barely moved. The wheels didn't spin at all. The pickup marched to the top of the hill and came to a stop beside the graves of Tuffy's parents. To the southwest for as far as they could see, bare, eroded buttes lined the edge of a tear that exposed, in layers of brown, red, and yellow, the entrails of the earth. It was a view of the Badlands that froze them in their seats.

Tuffy and Kyle left Stewart staring from the middle of the pickup seat. The strong wind rocked the truck, but Stewart didn't move until he felt Tuffy and Kyle begin to pull the sections of fence from the back.

The hill was larger than it had appeared from below. The twenty-foot plot that the fence would surround was only a quarter of the hilltop. They began by setting four wooden posts at the corners. Tuffy measured the fence, then transferred the measurements to the ground. He looked at his parents' graves and stepped back to imagine how things would look when the fence was up. "I go right there," he said, indicating a piece of sod to the west of his mother.

Kyle pointed to the large area to the east. "Who goes there?"

"Kids," Tuffy said. "Unborn, illegitimate kids. Could be this graveyard will have to be expanded."

Tuffy turned over one shovelful of dirt to mark the corner of the proposed cemetery fence. "Unbe-fuckin'-lievable," he said as he banged the last shovelful of dirt from the shovel. "We get three feet of snow, and a week later the ground is hard as striped hooves on a spotted horse."

Kyle had started on the first hole with the clamshell digger. "Don't go wishing more rain on us," he said and slammed the digger down for another bite.

"Bring me that auger, would you Stewart?" Tuffy pointed to the back of the pickup. "You'll be praying for a turd floater come July," Tuffy said.

"I'll be in Arizona before July," Kyle responded.

Stewart was looking at the tools in the pickup. The wind had made his glasses slip down. He pushed them back up his nose. "OK," he said. "Which one's the auger?"

"Arizona?" Tuffy said as he walked toward Stewart. "What would you do in Arizona?" He reached into the pickup bed and pulled out a four-foot-long tee made of pipe with two spoonlike blades welded on the end. He held it up in front of Stewart. "Auger," he said. "Well? What would you do in Arizona?"

"Ride."

"Ride?"

Now they were both digging at the corners of the cemetery and shouting over the graves of Tuffy's parents because of the wind. Stewart didn't know how to help.

"You mean rodeo?" Tuffy yelled.

Kyle nodded. He had become shy in the face of Tuffy's questions. Stewart took up the shovel and went to one of the other corners. "IRCA?" Tuffy asked.

Kyle didn't answer. Stewart started to dig where Tuffy had taken out the first shovelful of dirt. "What's IRCA?" he yelled.

"Indian Rodeo Cowboys' Association," Tuffy said to Stewart. Then, to Kyle, "You're just a kid."

"I'm seventeen."

Tuffy didn't respond. He twisted the auger into the ground. Kyle jabbed with the clamshell, and Stewart wrestled a couple more shovelfuls from his hole.

Kyle's hole reached four feet first, and he moved to the fourth corner. When Tuffy finished his, he brought the auger to Stewart. "You're about as far as you're going to get with a shovel," he said, then went to the pickup and dragged out an eight-foot wooden post.

Stewart put the auger into his shallow hole and began to twist it the way Tuffy had. The two spoons cut at the bottom and sides of the hole, and soon a half a cubic foot of earth was packed between the spoons. Stewart pulled the auger out, emptied it, put it back down into the hole, and began twisting again. The hole was becoming neat and straight. "Amazing," Stewart said to himself. But Tuffy was carrying a post to another hole and heard him.

"You keep this up, Stewart, and we really are going to put you on full-time. How long you staying, anyway?"

Stewart emptied the auger again. He looked intently at the sharp spoons. He marveled at the simplicity and efficiency of the thing. "Don't know," he said. "A while, though. Maybe long enough to see a turd floater." He smiled and began twisting the auger.

They took turns tamping the posts. Tuffy was fussy about this procedure. He claimed that if the moon were right, you didn't have to tamp posts at all; just throw the dirt back in, and they'd be solid forever. But the moon wasn't right, so they tamped after every shovelful. When the posts were solid, they dragged the sections of fence out and lag-screwed them into the wood. The wind dropped off, and the shadows of the buttes to the west began to stretch across the Badlands. The three stepped back to have a look at their work.

The black wrought-iron fence looked as if it had been there forever. It looked as solid as the two gravestones that stood up, casting shadows along with the fence, in the middle of a prairie that was now more special and separate from all the rest.

"Gorgeous," Stewart said.

Kyle nodded. "Not bad."

Tuffy said nothing but looked at the gravestones for a moment longer than the other two, who had begun putting the tools into the pickup.

They took Kyle home first. Just before Tuffy stopped in front of the house, he turned and looked past Stewart. "That circuit starts soon," he said to Kyle. "Before school's out."

Kyle nodded. "First rodeo's in Rapid. Indoors."

"Your mom know?"

Kyle's door popped open a crack. He shook his head. "Not yet," he said.

Stewart and Tuffy drove in silence out to the county road, past the missile silo and Cleve Miller's sign. "You're not drinking beer tonight?" Stewart asked.

"No," Tuffy said. "I kind of overtrained the other night. Thought I'd lay off."

They drove for a half-mile in silence, and both felt uncomfortable. There was no need for it, Stewart thought. "You were having a tough night," he said. "We all have them."

It was dark now, and Stewart watched Tuffy nod in the green dashboard light. "Memories?" Stewart asked.

Gravel popped from under the tires. "Sure. Remembering is what nights like that are all about."

"A woman, I'll bet."

"A girl, really. But it was a long time ago." The dash lights let Stewart see that Tuffy was smiling. "It's like a badger," he said. "I don't notice it until I step on it in the dark." There was more popping of gravel. A mule-deer doe stood alertly at the roadside watching them pass, and out of their vision a great horned owl sailed ghostlike at the edge of the headlights' beam.

▲
THIRTY-ONE

The bus would leave at seven thirty the next day and drive straight through to San Francisco. Linda lay on the floor of the LA studio, stretching in preparation for the last rehearsal before the tour began. She had already worked on her ankles, feet, neck, and lower back. Now she lay on her back, knees bent and the bottoms of her feet flat together. Her groin muscles slowly relaxed and let her knees fall farther apart. The ceiling of the studio was metal, stamped out in two-foot squares divided into four triangles with a stylized flower in each. Linda concentrated on the center of one square and reached down to feel the tightness in her thighs. She gently pushed her legs another inch apart.

Sometimes when she lay on the floor like this, she thought about men. Usually it was no one in particular, and although her thoughts were often sensual, they were seldom sexual. There was a unisex quality to the dance company. Of the other four members who were going on the tour, there were two men. One of the routines involved Linda dancing with Jonathan, each matching the other's movements exactly, their bodies touching from chest to knee. They had perfected the moves so that there was never any distance between them, but their relationship was still professional. Linda had learned to know and work with the bulges and bumps of Jonathan's body. Only when she tried did she think of him as anything but a dancer. He probably thinks the same about her, she thought as she rolled up onto her knees, then leaned back to stretch the tops of her thighs.

Then she could see the other members of the company, each on his or her own section of floor working on a particular set of muscles. Linda forced herself to look at Jonathan and to notice how graceful he was. She wondered whether he was gay. Could Ricardo, the other male dancer, be his lover? Linda watched them but could tell nothing. She would know by the time the tour got to Portland, she thought. If they weren't, would one of them make a pass at her? In a way it would be nice if one did. But would she sleep with him if he did? Why was she thinking about this? She stood up, put her feet together, and with knees straight put her palms on the floor. She counted to fifteen, then went to the exercise bar, hooked her left heel over it, and laid her chest on her thigh and her head on her knee.

She had not made love to a man since she left South Dakota. It was not particularly that she was staying true to Ross: they were both realists. She just had not felt the need. She supposed that dancing had kept her too busy. But today men were on her mind. Her situation was ridiculous, and she knew that even though there was no real pressure to do so, it should be resolved. Her father was right; it was not a good way to live. If Ross was going to stay on the ranch, then they should get divorced. She knew Ross could never get the money he had invested back if he sold the place, that they had made a mistake, and now Ross was economically trapped. And she felt some guilt; after all, she had gone along with the whole silly plan. She had been just a kid, but that was no excuse. Maybe it had all been foolishness, but she had believed that Ross's survival depended on the remoteness they'd found on the ranch.

Now she wasn't so sure. The world was different. It didn't

seem like such a bad place, and self-imposed exile had ceased to make sense to her. Linda brought her left leg down from the exercise bar and raised her right. She felt her nipple brush against her thigh as she stretched her head down to touch her knee. The nipple became erect. It embarrassed her though no one could see.

He had been so attractive: handsome, intelligent, experienced. She straightened up, brought her right leg down, and began to swing her torso from side to side. She did not want to think of those nights back in 1976 when they had lain in each other's arms and Ross had taught her about love. She didn't want to think of the helpless feeling she got when she would wake and find that he was still awake, staring at the ceiling, his face glistening with tears.

Yes. Ross was in peril in those days, and from that standpoint perhaps the ranch had been a good idea. But she had never believed him when he said that he had dreamed of that very ranch since he was a boy, that he had recognized it when they drove out to Sweet Grass Creek for the first time. She had always thought that Ross was being overly romantic, as he was prone to be. And now she believed Ross was rethinking it. She had talked to Stewart, who was full of excitement about a spring blizzard they had had, and he said Ross seemed fine. Perhaps seven years had been enough penance and when she saw him in Denver, he would be ready to leave that part of his life behind.

Linda's thoughts jumped ahead to Denver. He had agreed to come that far. It could be a new beginning. But there were several performances before then, and Linda wanted to be at her best. As Anita Barowitz clapped her hands to get the practice underway, Linda rolled her shoulders to loosen the center of her back and promised herself that she would not let thoughts of Ross break her concentration again. She walked to the center of the practice floor, where Jonathan waited. She draped her body along the contour of his rigid leg and torso, then wrapped her arms and hands around his face, looked into his eyes, and froze. In the real performance they would be in total darkness. The lights would come up gradually along with the gentle roll of the timpani.

THIRTY-TWO

▲

Tuffy didn't want to go home after dropping off Stewart. It was dark by then, and he drove slowly back toward his place. He wanted to stay at Ross's, but he'd spent a lot of time there lately, and he didn't want to wear out his welcome. He thought about going out to Milo but knew that nothing good would come of it. When the bench road curved as it came to the Millers', Tuffy continued to turn and headed down-country along Cleve and Edith's driveway.

The night was the warmest of the spring so far, and Tuffy rode with his window down, trying to think of a good reason for stopping in on the Millers. He had checked the combine behind his house, and it looked as if it had the bearings that Cleve had asked about. He could pretend that he'd come to tell Cleve that. But it was the kind of thing that most people would use the telephone to do. It was a strange time to show up at anyone's house uninvited. Edith would think that he'd come over to mooch a meal.

The whole house was lit up, and through the window Tuffy saw Edith moving around the kitchen. He sat in his pickup, watched, and tried to decide whether he should knock on the door. The house looked very bright and warm, and the night felt as if it was cooling off. Tuffy had almost decided to turn around and go home when there was a hard whack on the side of his pickup. Tuffy jumped in the seat.

"What the hell's going on here?" Cleve said. He had been

in the barn and sneaked up on Tuffy. Cleve was laughing at the start he'd given him.

"Real funny," Tuffy said. "Heart attacks are hilarious."

"What are you doing?" Cleve asked, unimpressed with Tuffy's complaint.

"Just finished putting a fence around the family grave-yard."

"Just in time. How's that heart?" Cleve laughed again. "Come on in. Edith'll have chow on the table."

Tuffy put up only mild resistance. He was glad to be able to have supper with the Millers and went out of his way to be nice to Edith.

It was a modest meal, beef, potatoes, and string beans, all home-raised.

"This is about the best supper I've had in months," Tuffy said.

"Am I supposed to take that as a compliment?" Edith was joking. At least Tuffy thought she was joking.

"It is good, Edith," Cleve said. "It's a fine meal. We should all be thankful. Have more spuds, Tuffy."

Tuffy took more potatoes and Edith passed the gravy. "Have some more meat, too," she said. "No sense having to put away leftovers."

Tuffy filled his plate again.

"Now, what's this about a fence for your bone yard?" Cleve said.

"Picked it up in Rapid. It's one of those fancy jobs. Be-longed to the Catholic church."

"If it belonged to the Catholics, I'll bet it wasn't cheap."

Tuffy shrugged. "I got it reasonable," he said. "We kinda schmoozed them out of it."

"You what?" Edith asked.

"Schmoozed. Sweet-talked them on the price. Me and Ross and Stewart."

"Now, this Stewart," Cleve said. "He's Linda's brother. Where's he from?"

"LA," Tuffy said. He was nearly done with his second helping. "He's a *schlockmeister* out there."

"A what?" Edith asked again.

"Are these Indian words?" Cleve said.

"No," Tuffy said. "Jew words."

"What?"

"Jew words. Stewart is Jewish."

The room fell silent. Cleve stared at Tuffy but could not speak. Edith began to fuss with dirty dishes. The silence buzzed in Tuffy's ears. He smiled and looked from Edith to Cleve.

Finally Edith spoke. "Well, if he's the young man I saw go by with that Ross Brady. He looked very nice. He didn't look Jewish at all."

"Hell, no." Tuffy said. "He looks like Dustin Hoffman. He's a good guy."

Cleve still said nothing. "Why, I'm sure he is," Edith said.

"Finest kind," Tuffy said. He nodded his head and looked to Cleve. "Not too bad at setting fence posts either."

Edith was clearing the table. "I don't know," she said. "But how about dessert?" Tuffy handed her his plate and smiled. The plate was clean. "You have room, don't you, Tuffy?"

"You bet."

Cleve had stood up. Now he rubbed his face and smiled. "It's pretty warm out," he said. "And I got a couple cigars. Maybe we could have our dessert on the porch." Cigars were an extravagance for the Millers.

"Well, it's not summer," Edith said.

"Warm enough," Cleve said. He looked at Tuffy, who shrugged. "We'll have our dessert on the porch."

The cigars were big and black. They tasted great. But

Tuffy liked the peach cobbler even better. Edith would not join them. She said they were a couple of polar bears. Cleve sat in his chair and looked at the sky. There were thousands of stars and a quarter-moon. Tuffy watched him and wondered what he was thinking. "Nice, isn't it," Tuffy said.

Cleve nodded his head. "Yeah," he said, "it's nice."

"Best part of this country is the sky."

"You might be right," Cleve said. "Too bad you can't pay bills with stars."

Tuffy laughed. "Your bills get paid." Then he thought he shouldn't have said that, that it might make Cleve mad.

But Cleve nodded. "Month by month," he said. "But do you know, in thirty years we haven't saved a thing?" Cleve's voice was wistful. Suddenly he seemed calm.

"You got everything you need," Tuffy said.

"Yeah, but it would be nice to buy something special."

"Like what?

"I don't know. A trip someplace, a new car."

"Who needs a new car? You've got that big old Ford in the shed."

Cleve smiled. He was proud of that car. "Well," he said, "just a little in the bank so a fella wouldn't have to work forever."

Tuffy couldn't help himself. "We got plenty," he said.

"That talk's easy for you," Cleve said. "You aren't trying to figure a way to retire."

"I already retired."

"How do you like living on starlight?" Cleve laughed but Tuffy only shrugged.

By the time the cigars were finished, both men were shivering. Tuffy did not want to go home, but he knew it was time. He told Cleve about the bearings for the combine, and Cleve asked a question about how they were attached to the shaft. Tuffy couldn't answer the question.

"I'll just have to come over," Cleve said. He said it the way you say something that ends a conversation, and Tuffy knew that now he had to go.

"Any time," Tuffy said as he got to his feet. He stood on the porch and looked for the moon. It was partially hidden by the cottonwoods that surrounded the Miller place. "Stop by any time."

He stepped off the porch and into the darkness. In a minute he was moving along the road again. He still didn't want to go home. But he felt better. The cigar had relaxed him, and his stomach felt full and warm.

▲

THIRTY-THREE

It was dark by the time Elizabeth reached Milo and turned north on the bench road. She drove slowly, still trying to decide what she should do, when she came to Tuffy's driveway. She did not plan to pull in, but when she saw the owl float across in front of her, she stopped dead in the road, watched until she knew it was heading for Tuffy's house, then quickly turned onto the driveway. She drove fast, but the owl vanished before she came to Tuffy's.

She stopped the pickup and jumped out, slamming the door as she started up the walk to the back door. Her hope was to frighten the owl if it was still around. But halfway up the walk she thought that she might be too late. Her hand hesitated at the back door, but she screwed up her courage and burst into the house.

Tuffy sat at the kitchen table in his underwear. "Jesus," he shouted as he jumped up trying to cover himself. Finally he gave up and ran down the hall. "What the hell are you doing?" he called from the bathroom.

Elizabeth stood in the kitchen with her hands over her mouth. She was embarrassed but couldn't keep from laughing. "I thought you were dead," she said when Tuffy came back pulling on his clothes.

"Well, I'm not," Tuffy said.

"I saw an owl," Elizabeth said.

"Yeah," Tuffy said. "They live out there in nature, you know."

"I've been down with my relatives all day."

"Ah," Tuffy said, "the old mumbo jumbo about the owl being an omen of death." Elizabeth smiled and nodded. "You been smoking those heathen pipes?"

"Willow bark and tobacco only."

"Well, I'm alive. Here, pinch me so I'm sure." He held out his arm, and Elizabeth pinched him pretty hard.

"I'm alive," Tuffy said. "And, boy, am I thirsty." He reached out and rubbed Elizabeth's head as if she were a child. "Come on, have one with me."

"I can't. I have things to do yet tonight."

"It's late," Tuffy said as he got a beer out of the refrigerator.

"But I have to go."

"Sure, barge in here on a man relaxing in his underwear. Scare him to death, then leave him for someone else."

"I have to go."

"You're going down to see Ross, aren't you?"

As soon as Tuffy said it, Elizabeth knew that he was right. "No," she said. "Don't be ridiculous."

"It's all right." He rubbed her head again.

She turned, embarrassed, and walked outside. Tuffy followed, and they both looked at the sky. "I really was worried about you," Elizabeth said.

"You shouldn't believe all that redskin mumbo jumbo."

"You believe it, too."

Tuffy shrugged. "Thanks for being worried."

Elizabeth looked at him, and for an instant he thought she might kiss him. It felt good to think that, but she didn't kiss him. "You, too," she said.

"You take care."

Elizabeth got to her driveway just before ten o'clock, but she did not turn. She drove on past the Millers', the Center of the Nation, the missile silo, and finally turned into Ross Brady's driveway. Her mother had said it took a white man to understand these things. If anyone would know and still not take advantage of her, it would be Ross Brady.

She had not seen an electric light since she left Tuffy's, so the yard light that first appeared as she dropped down into the Sweet Grass Creek drainage seemed odd. Another hundred yards and a light from the house spilled onto the new grass in front of Ross's house. She had been there only two or three times since Ross and Linda bought the place. Never since Linda went away. As the pickup clattered over the cattle guard, Elizabeth began to lose her nerve. But it was too late; her headlights had already swung over the house, and someone had moved to the window. She cursed herself for being so silly, but it would look even worse to turn around now. The porch light came on as she let the pickup roll to a stop, but she did not get out until Ross appeared on the front step.

He wore no boots, only a T-shirt and jeans. He stared into the dark at the pickup he couldn't place. The blue flicker of the television told Elizabeth that he had been watching the ten o'clock weather. She had heard it on the car radio: chance of rain, northwest wind at fifteen, highs in the sixties. Spring, she thought. She would have to get ready to brand. But Ross was coming off the porch, and she had to force herself to get out of the pickup and meet him. The inside light came on, and she hurried to shut the door behind her. She stood in the dark and watched Ross moving gingerly across the gravel of the driveway.

"Elizabeth?" He was close enough now to see for sure that it was she. "Is everything all right?"

"Yes." Elizabeth spoke too fast. She knew she sounded silly and frightened.

"Well, come on," Ross said. "Come on in the house." He motioned for her to come.

As she pushed away from the pickup, she checked her

back pocket to be sure the letter was there. It was folded and crumpled tight against her buttocks, and it struck her that Ross might think she had treated it disrespectfully. But it was too late to worry about that. She was beside Ross then. He smiled and she pulled up short. "Good to see you," he said. "Come on in."

But when he turned, his foot came down on a sharp rock, and he stumbled. Elizabeth caught his left arm before she could stop herself. The biceps were bigger and harder than she had expected.

"Goddamn," Ross said and held her hand against his left arm with his right hand. "Clumsy son of a gun." He got both feet under him and looked up. They were very close, and in the light from the porch Elizabeth could see that his eyes were green. She pulled back, but he still held her hand. "Thanks," he said and let the hand slip from his arm.

She stepped back and did not move. "You should wear boots," she said. It was all she could think to say.

"Yeah, yeah," Ross was saying as he hobbled toward the porch, "or grow hooves like everything else around here."

Now she was following him. He held his arms out for balance and tiptoed the last few feet to the porch. When he turned back toward her, he nearly caught her smiling.

"Stewart and I were having a beer. Could I talk you into one?"

Elizabeth nodded. "Sure," she said. "A beer would taste good."

Stewart had come to the door just in time to hear her agree to a beer. "All right," he said. "A girl. Let's party down."

Elizabeth lowered her eyes as she moved through the door, but both Ross and Stewart could see it was more to hide a broadening smile than because she was embarrassed.

They sat at the kitchen table and Elizabeth took the letter from her back pocket. She held it for a moment, then as Ross handed her a can of beer, she gave him the letter. "I was wondering," she said, "if you could help me with this."

The envelope was folded in half and bent concave from the day in Elizabeth's pocket, but Ross recognized the logo and slogan in the upper left-hand corner. He had received many envelopes like it over the years. Stewart had been watching and felt he might be intruding. "You want me to leave?" he asked Elizabeth.

"It doesn't matter," she said. "You look, too, if you want."

Ross read the letter and handed it to Stewart. "Sorenson just wants you to come in and talk about your loan. They do that all the time."

"He wants to take the ranch away."

"No. It says you're a few payments behind. Everybody's a few payments behind. They'll just make a plan for you to catch up."

"I think he wants the ranch."

"The last thing any banker wants is a ranch. They know a crummy investment when they see one. It's their business. They just want you to make some payments. That's how they make their money. They aren't ranchers."

Stewart finished reading the letter and handed it back to Elizabeth. "Ross is right. Bankers do this stuff all the time. They get bored and send out letters like this."

"It says foreclosure."

"They always say things like that," Stewart said. "It's just a threat. Ross is right. They don't want your ranch. They want you to keep making payments. Besides, if this state is anything like California, it would take them a couple years to foreclose."

"Relax," Ross said.

"I can't," Elizabeth said. "I have a bad feeling. John Kiser gave the ranch to me. He still owed a lot of money on it, but he expects me to make the payments. I'm afraid they'll take it, and I will have let John down."

"They're not going to take it away," Ross said. "You're not going to let down old John."

"But it says I have to go in and talk."

"Look," Ross said, "I'll go with you."

"OK," Elizabeth said quickly, then looked away.

Ross was surprised. "OK." He raised his beer. "OK."

"OK," Stewart said, "drink up."

Ross slipped on his boots before he walked Elizabeth to her pickup. She said she had to go just as Ross and Stewart opened another beer. Stewart had tried to talk her into staying for one more, but Ross felt her first can of beer and knew that she hadn't even finished that one. She was nervous and clearly wanted out of the house.

Once outside she seemed to calm down but still moved steadily toward her pickup. She glanced at the sky when Ross pointed out Orion, but she didn't stop. "Hey," Ross said, "what's the big hurry?"

"I need to be home. I wasn't home for supper."

"Too late now."

She made it to the pickup and leaned against the fender with one finger hooked in the door handle. She glanced at Ross, then looked away. "When can you go to town?"

"Not tomorrow," Ross said. "How about Thursday?"

"There's a rodeo in Rapid City on Thursday. Kyle's going to ride. I have to be there."

"We could do it on Friday then."

"Good."

"On one condition," Ross said.

She looked at him with a set jaw. "What?"

"That you let Stewart and me take you to the rodeo."

She did not look away, and she didn't speak for what seemed like a long time. "OK," she said. "We'll have to leave by five o'clock."

Ross smiled. "We'll be there." But she was already in the

pickup. The engine came alive, and the lights beamed out into the night, spoiling the view of the sky.

Elizabeth did not look to the side as she pulled away. She left Ross standing in his driveway. He stared at the pickup's taillights until they climbed out of the low place that gave the house shelter from the wind. Then there was just the yard light and the dull, blue flicker of the television through the window. In a moment even the sound of Elizabeth's pickup was gone, and the night became deadly calm. Ross folded his arms and looked up at Orion, who was moving up from the southeast toward his apex for that time of year. In another hour or so he'd be as high as he was going to get, Ross thought. It would be nice to watch until then, to dig a sleeping bag out and lie on his back and watch for meteorites.

But it would be cold by morning, and Stewart would think he was crazy. Ross looked down at the eerie blue light from the television. He wondered whether Linda had already told Stewart that he was crazy. If she had, Stewart didn't seem to care. Ross considered inviting Stewart out to watch for meteorites but decided against it. He'd just spend a couple more minutes out there by himself, then go in and catch the end of "The Tonight Show."

▲
THIRTY-FOUR

Tuffy found a couple cardboard boxes in the barn and cut them into strips eighteen inches wide. There was a half carton of staples that happened to be the size that fit the staple gun he found in the five-gallon bucket under the workbench. Clyde sat on the porch rail and watched him wrestle the cardboard into the house.

Tuffy stapled the cardboard strips across the doorways in the hall so that once the pack rat left the kitchen, it would have to keep going until it got to the bathroom. All the holes and hiding places in the bathroom had been sealed off so that if the rat ever went in, it would have no way out, except past Tuffy and his .45-caliber Colt.

A mason-jar lid, heaped with a glob of peanut butter, was placed three feet from the open cupboard under the sink. With his last staple Tuffy attached six feet of string to the cupboard door and sat quietly at the table, where he had left a six-pack of Coors Light. Clyde had come in by then and together they waited.

It was a perfect day for this sort of thing; a fifteen-mile-per-hour wind from the northwest and a chill to the air that might mean a little rain. It was a day for inside work, if you had any, for two reasons. First, it was nasty in the wind; but second, it was the kind of day that made you know spring was coming fast. If the rain did come, it would be a spring shower, which would give the grass a shot of growth. For most people there wouldn't be much time to spend inside until next fall. Soon it would be time to brand the calves and put the cows out to summer pasture. It was a perfect day to sit inside, sip beer, and wait for the pack rat to show up. Of course, the weather and the cattle prices didn't mean much to Tuffy anymore. He'd rent his place out to someone to run their cows again that summer. He could stay in his kitchen all summer if he liked.

But he wouldn't. He'd go borrow Bozo back from Ross and ride out through the breaks and look at the cattle that were being run on the place. He'd ride out to the edge of the reservation and spend some time among the crumbling buttes. He'd watch the summer sun splashing color back at him off the clouds that would hang in the west. He'd look for coyotes or broods of grouse. Then he'd come back to this kitchen and spend the night alone. He'd sit like this and sip on the beer without moving any more than was necessary. The only difference was that now he watched the cupboard under the sink. Clyde sat near the beer cans on the table and watched, too. He seemed to be taking this all very seriously, never moving his eyes from the cupboard, even when Tuffy glanced at him.

"I'm giving you one more chance," Tuffy whispered. "When I pull that door shut, he's as good as trapped in the bathroom. It's his only option. Then he's all yours."

They sat like that for over an hour. Tuffy never took his eyes off the spot where he expected the pack rat would appear, but his mind moved from one point in time to another. He thought first of Loni Sorenson. The image in Tuffy's mind was not of the twenty-nine-year-old ex–Miss South Dakota who was married now to a fancy attorney in Minneapolis. It was not of the beautiful high-school senior who the day after graduation loaded up her car and drove to the university to begin her college career as soon as possible. What Tuffy Martinez saw when he thought of Loni Sorenson was a tall, slightly awkward teenage girl with high Swedish cheekbones, blond hair, and a curious smile for the half-breed star of the high-school football team. But that was a very long time ago. He was sure that Loni had forgotten him, so he made his mind move on as he waited for the pack rat to appear.

He thought naturally of horses, rodeos, and jackpot ropings, where he had made a little money from time to time. But as always his mind stopped rendering up vivid pictures and stopped on a frame of vague landscape: nothing recognizable, more buttes, draws, chokecherry bushes, and the impression that living things would be visible if the picture were more clear. He was watching that scene, superimposed on the reality of his own kitchen, when he heard something move under the sink. Clyde's ears swiveled slightly, and his eyes became dark and deep. They waited. Another faint scratching sound. Silence. No one moved. Tuffy stopped breathing, and suddenly the pack rat was there, standing at the edge of the cupboard, sniffing at the peanut butter as if there was no reason to be afraid. Tuffy wanted to take up a little slack in the string that was stapled to the door but didn't dare.

The pack rat seemed at ease. He looked left, then looked right, letting his soft doe eyes linger on Tuffy and Clyde. It was the first time that Tuffy had ever had a really good look at a live pack rat, and he was taken by how gentle it appeared. It wasn't at all like a real rat. It's fur was long and silky, tan on the back and white underneath. It's head was large, with round ears, and its tail was bushy as a chipmunk's. The whole animal was perhaps three quarters the size of Clyde, and it sat up on its hind legs to groom its whiskers with a front paw. After smoothing back its whiskers, it dropped down on all fours and looked intently at the peanut butter in the center of the kitchen floor. It was ready to move away from the cupboard, and Tuffy and Clyde tensed with anticipation.

But just before the pack rat stepped from the cupboard, the telephone rang. The pack rat shot back into the cupboard, and Tuffy banged the table with his fist. "Snake shit!" he yelled. Clyde ducked and looked at Tuffy in terror. It took him a moment to realize that the anger was not directed at him, but he jumped down and slunk into the other room to be safe. The phone rang again. Tuffy shook his head and rubbed his face. He popped the top on another can of beer before he reached for the receiver, picking it up just after the third ring. "Hello."

"Theodore Martinez?"

"You got him."

"I'm glad I caught you. This is Larry Sorenson at the First Bank of Harney." Tuffy could not respond. "I'm the president up here." Of course, Tuffy knew that. "I don't think we've ever met."

That wasn't exactly true but Tuffy nodded into the phone. "No," he said.

"How are things out your way?"

"Fine."

"Sure is nice to have all this moisture, isn't it? Looks like we might get some more. Rain this time." Sorenson laughed.

"Yeah," Tuffy said.

"Mr. Martinez, something has come across my desk that I think you might be very interested in knowing about."

"Like what?"

"I'd rather not discuss it over the telephone." Sorenson waited as if expecting Tuffy to say something. When he didn't, he went on. "Perhaps we could get together."

"What's it about?"

"Well," Sorenson paused. He thought for a moment. "Someone has contacted me about buying some land in the area, and I thought you might be interested in selling your ranch. The price would be generous."

"No," Tuffy said.

"Very generous."

"No. This place isn't for sale."

Sorenson spoke deliberately. "I don't think you should dismiss this, Mr. Martinez."

"It's my land. It was given to me by my parents. It's not for sale."

"As you know, no land has sold in this country for years. It's an opportunity. This offer would allow you to earn interest on the proceeds and make much more than you are making now by owning the land."

"Nobody should own land just to make money off it." Tuffy was getting upset. He wanted to hang up, but he couldn't. He heard himself talking angrily. This was Loni's father. He should not blow up. But he couldn't be quiet and listen. "There's only one reason to own this Badlands ranch," he said.

Sorenson was not going to lose his temper. "And what reason is that?" he asked evenly.

"To keep assholes like you from getting it." Tuffy couldn't believe he was saying this to the president of the bank.

Sorenson chuckled, and Tuffy realized that he had taken what he had said as a joke. "You might well have a point," Sorenson said. "I'm certainly not a rancher. But let's do get together. I'm sure when you hear what I have to say, you'll understand that this is a true opportunity."

Sorenson didn't realize that Tuffy had insulted him, and for an instant Tuffy wasn't sure he had. But then he was frightened. He should never have talked to this man like that. Sorenson had power and could change lives just by what he said. Tuffy had seen him do it. "Give it some thought," Sorenson was saying. "I'll call you in a couple days. You think about it. Can't hurt to talk."

Now Tuffy had lost his nerve.

"I'll call you," Sorenson said again.

"Sure," Tuffy mumbled into the phone.

"Excellent," Sorenson said. He said it as if he had never

heard what Tuffy had said, and now Tuffy was thankful. It was as if Sorenson had forgiven him.

"Sure," he said again.

Tuffy sat at the kitchen table for a long time after he hung up the telephone. He sat long enough for Clyde to forget his fright and jump back on the table beside the last can of beer. Tuffy thought his mind would be full, but nothing came, not even the fuzzy picture of the Badlands. He felt a little sick to his stomach. It had been a very bad day, and the only thing that might make him feel better was a hot shower. But then he reached out and took the last can of beer and popped the top. It tasted like malt. He couldn't remember for sure, but he thought there was another six-pack in the refrigerator.

▲
THIRTY-FIVE

All that day before they picked up Elizabeth to go to the rodeo in Rapid City, Ross thought about Linda. It had to do somehow with Stewart being around. He found himself noticing little things about Stewart that reminded him of Linda: a particular phrase, the shape of his jaw. That made sense. But his thinking about Linda also had to do with Elizabeth, and that puzzled Ross. Something was making him uneasy about going to the rodeo with her. When he pictured her riding in the pickup between Stewart and him, he knew what was bothering him, and he smiled at himself. It would be a little like going on a date with your brother-in-law for a chaperon. But that was silly. Elizabeth was the shy neighbor woman, she could never threaten his relationship with Linda.

But something was threatening that relationship. Linda was never coming back and Ross knew it. He tried once to talk to Stewart about it, but Stewart only shrugged. He didn't want to verbalize what was clear to everyone. The only real questions were, How long was Ross going to continue hiding out on these plains? And would Linda take him back when he gave up? Stewart realized Ross was not ready to talk about that yet.

Ross had showered first, and now he could hear Stewart singing in the bathroom. This would be Stewart's first rodeo. He was excited in a way that seemed incongruous with his experience. Here was a guy who never missed a Laker's or a Ram's game, had gone to the Indianapolis 500 several times, and had even been to the Kentucky Derby, grandstand seats—

no infield for Stewart. Yet he had been giddy all day about the small-time rodeo.

"This isn't the national finals," Ross said when Stewart came into the kitchen.

"Well, hell," Stewart said. "Neighbor Kyle's ridin', ain't he?" He was dressed in the same clothes he had worn when he came off the airplane two weeks before. They had been used hard and washed several times. They looked a lot better on him now than they had.

"Come on, cowboy. I think you're ready." Ross took their hats from a rack near the door and plunked Stewart's on his head. He looked at him for a moment before opening the door. "Not bad," he said. "If you keep your mouth shut, there's a chance you won't get beat up."

Stewart had insisted that they sweep out the pickup and hose most of the mud off. He wanted to wash and wax it. He had even asked whether Ross had any Turtle Wax. "Turtle Wax?" Ross had asked.

"Yeah, you know. Shine 'er up a little bit."

"No Turtle Wax," Ross had said. "Just hose it down. I don't want you spoiling my pickup. If it gets used to that sort of treatment, it might follow you back to California."

But as they walked across the yard toward the pickup in the afternoon light, Ross had to admit that it looked pretty good. There was the old saying about a car running better when it was clean. Ross's father had said that a lot, but Ross hadn't thought of it for years. When he slid behind the steering wheel and turned the key, he half-expected not to hear the blown muffler or the clatter of the bad lifter. But the engine sounded the same as always.

Pete Rienrick was brushing Barney when they pulled up between the house and barn. Dancer, his winter coat now completely shed for the summer and looking sleek, stood in his corral with his head over the top rail and watched. Pete grumbled to himself and waved to them as if he wanted them to go away. They paid little attention.

Elizabeth was waiting for them on the porch swing. As soon as she stood up, the tangle of feelings descended on Ross again. She was dressed in tight blue jeans and a loose white blouse. The jeans were tucked into powder-blue boots with dark blue stitching. Her black hair was braided into two thick plaits and tied with thin blue ribbons that matched the boots. She smiled as she came off the porch but did not make eye contact. Ross had never seen her like this. She was still raw-boned and plain, but the girlish touches illuminated something in her that Ross had never before noticed.

"You're a fox!" Stewart said as he jumped out to let her slide in. He clapped his hands. "We rodeoin' tonight," he said.

Elizabeth tried not to laugh at him but didn't stop smiling. She kept her eyes on the dashboard in front of her, and Ross was able to watch her closely in profile. Her skin was a rich brown, and beneath the braids long, dangling porcupine-quill earrings lay softly against her neck.

"Let's get this show on the road," Stewart said.

The engine was still running, but the transmission was in neutral, and the gear shift was against Elizabeth's knee. Ross reached for it slowly, and Elizabeth glanced up briefly before she moved her leg. Ross tried to catch her eye, but he was too late. Elizabeth was looking at the dashboard, but the smile was still there. "Right," Ross said as he popped it into first. "Let's get this show on the road."

When they passed Tuffy's place, Elizabeth explained that Kyle had ridden into Rapid with him. It had been Tuffy's idea. He said he wanted to give Kyle a few pointers. Ross got a laugh out of that because everyone knew that Kyle was twice the bronc rider that Tuffy had ever been. Roping and bulldogging were a different story, but when it came to saddle broncs, Kyle was a star.

Stewart insisted on stopping at the Dust Buster for a six-pack.

"You been spending too much time with Tuffy," Ross said.

"Just trying to be western," Stewart said. "Come on. Say hi to Ruth."

Ross and Elizabeth glanced at each other. Elizabeth shrugged. "Why not?" said Ross. "We have time."

They walked across the parking lot, past two reservation jalopies. Neither car had a valid license plate, but both had bumper stickers: CUSTER DIED FOR YOUR SINS and SHIT HAPPENS.

"This must be the Kyle Janis fan club," Ruth said as they came through the door. Three old Indians sat at the bar and turned to stare. "Where are Tracy and Louis?"

"They're going to meet us there," Elizabeth said.

"Give us one, two, three Coors Lights," Stewart said. He laid a twenty on the bar.

"Should be a good rodeo," Ruth said over her shoulder. "This early one brings all the big guns. Two Bears, Clifford, Her Many Horses—all the big skins come to this one. The stock is Sutton's. I hear the bulls are bad."

"Bad bulls," one of the old men at the bar said.

"You nervous about Kyle?" Ruth asked Elizabeth as she put the beers down and picked up Stewart's twenty.

"A little," Elizabeth said.

Ruth reached out and patted her hand. "I know how it is. I have a son, too, you know. Older, of course, but he did every dumb thing a boy can do. It's hard on a mother."

"Don't worry about Kyle," Stewart said.

"Yeah," said Ross. "He's the best I've ever seen."

"But this is the big time," Elizabeth said. "Tough horses, big money."

"He can handle it," Ross said.

Ruth reached out again and touched Elizabeth's hand.

"They grow up," she said. "Like kittens and puppies they get to be something else."

The civic center in Rapid City is a huge, new building. It is brick with long angular lines, and it is situated, along with one of the city's high schools, in the flood plain of Rapid Creek. Both these buildings are really too nice for the town of Rapid City, but in June of 1972 the hills to the west of Rapid received fifteen inches of rain in a five-hour period. The resulting flood killed 237 people and swept away a half billion dollars' worth of property. Many of the buildings that were destroyed were old, and there are those who say that the federal money that poured into Rapid City on the heels of the flood was the best thing that ever happened to the town.

Now Rapid Creek winds scenically through a seven-mile-long public park that is the backbone of the town. The flood plain has remained fairly clear of buildings, except for the public buildings in the center. The townspeople have been assured that these buildings will withstand any flooding that might occur.

But at the neglected east end of the park, where the joggers and bicyclists seldom go, the old Sioux men and women who live under the bridges laugh at the idea of trying to resist the power of an angry river. They pass bottles back and forth and talk about Wakinyan Oyate, the Thunder Beings, who must certainly be amused by those petty piles of brick in the center of a petty little town on the edge of the sacred hills. Except for the whiskey, the world of the white man avoids the shadows under these bridges. Here the names have not been Anglicized: they are famous names like Pretty Shield, Plenty Wolf, Red Cloud, Kills on Horseback, Yellow Boy, Afraid of Hawk, Black Elk. They tell old stories and laugh. They pass the bottle. They pass the time. They try to figure a way to get into the civic center to see the Indian rodeo.

Inside the civic center the young, strong Indians of all nations get their gear, heads, and hearts in shape for the contest to come. This was the first rodeo of the season, the beginning of the great western road trip that would take these young men to thirty cities in the Rockies and the West Coast. They joked as they worked, but this was serious business. It was important that everything be right. They wrapped the hocks of their roping ponies, oiled the cinches, polished the bells braided into their bull ropes, and sat on the ground in their bucking saddles to recheck the stirrup length.

Tuffy stood above Kyle as he rocked back and forth to simulate a ride. Tuffy remembered when he was Kyle's age and had a chance to go on the circuit calf roping and bulldogging. He'd been a damned good cowboy, and for the life of him he couldn't figure out what had happened. One day it was all in front of him; the next day it was gone. He'd never competed after high school. All of the thrill and the challenge had just stopped for him, but he could see it again in the set of Kyle's jaw and the nervous smile when Kyle looked up at him.

"You're as ready as you'll ever be," Tuffy said.

Delbert Benson, a part-Sioux from the Standing Rock Reservation, kicked Kyle playfully on the hip. "You lookin' good for a skin," he said. He was a young hot shot like Kyle, a roper who was supposed to have one of the best horses around. It made Tuffy a little jealous to think of this kid owning a really good roping horse.

"You don't look so bad yourself for a calf choker," Kyle said. They continued to joke, and Tuffy began to feel that he was intruding. The area was filling with cowboy hats. The

Indian princesses and rodeo queens were checking their makeup in hand mirrors for the grand entry. Horses were being saddled, banners unrolled. Tuffy wanted to wish Kyle and Delbert luck, but now the bareback horses were being run into the chutes, and the two boys went to watch them.

Tuffy found his way into the arena. He had talked to Louis and knew that he and Tracy were sitting low on the west side. He figured the rest of the crew would be there, too. But before he went to find them, he got in line for beer. The line was long and the wait unreasonable, so when it was his turn, he ordered eight cups of Bud. That was all he could carry. He figured someone would drink them before they got warm.

Louis and Tracy looked as if they had been drinking all the way up from Red Shirt. Louis was loud, which meant he had already had his limit, and Tracy's speech had the sharp edge to it that could easily become bitchy. But for now they were having a great time. Louis jumped to his feet to help Tuffy with the beer just as the rodeo announcer rode from the chute area with his portable microphone to announce the grand entry. In came every saddle horse on the grounds, the queens, the pickup men, saddle clubs, a group from Rosebud riding bareback, painted and dressed in breechcloths and feathers. Around and around they went until the spectators could feel the wind they created. Ross, Elizabeth, and Stewart found the others just as the riders pulled up in the dusty arena to face the flag. A semifamous local singer sang the national anthem in reasonable sync with a scratchy recording. When it was over, a few in the crowd cheered; the grand entry reversed; a hat or two flew into the air. Stewart was introduced to Tracy and Louis. Ross nodded to everyone, and Tracy looked very hard at Elizabeth. At the instant the crowd quieted down in antici- pation of the first bareback ride, Tracy turned to her sister. "My," she said, "aren't we gussied up?"

Then the first bronc broke from the chute. Pickup riders

mounted on big bay geldings followed slightly behind the bronc. The rider fell off quickly, landing hard in the dust long before the bell sounded that would have qualified the ride.

The announcer kept his leopard-spotted Appaloosa out of the way of the action, but his voice was always center stage. "A lot of these cowboys will be packing up tonight to drive to Salt Lake City," he said. "And they better drive fast because that rodeo starts in less than forty-eight hours."

Ross poked Tuffy. "So what you been up to?"

Tuffy finished his beer. "Nothing. Trying to kill a damned pack rat. Talking to the banker on the phone."

"Banker? You aren't getting back in the cattle business, are you?"

Stewart sat on the other side of Tuffy and turned with interest. "Hell, no," Tuffy said. "When I call, all the bankers are out. This son of a bitch called me. Says he can sell my place."

"Who called?" Ross asked.

Now Stewart was paying close attention. He watched Tuffy roll his tongue inside his cheek as if he had trouble remembering. Elizabeth was on the other side of Ross and was not listening to the conversation. But when Tuffy finally spoke, her face jerked up, and she looked at Tuffy as if she wanted to reach out to him. "Larry Sorenson," he said.

"He called you?" Ross said. "You been trying to sell your place? You had dealings with him?"

"Place isn't for sale," Tuffy said. "Only talked to the man once before in my life." Tuffy looked down at his empty cup. Beyond him Stewart could see that Elizabeth had to force herself to look away.

"I'm a little nervous," Elizabeth announced. "Think I'll take a break."

When she stood up, Louis shouted at her. "Hey, good looking," he said. "I'm out of whiskey. Bring some beer after you pee." He laughed and turned to the other men for approval. He got none, and Tracy stood to go with Elizabeth. They squeezed out and made their way up the stairs.

The line for the women's restroom was not long. The twins stood together, with Elizabeth leaning against the wall. None of the cowboys who glanced their way from the beer stand would have taken them for twins. Tracy was petite, shapely, and graceful. Her bright eyes darted back and forth, trying to catch the cowboys staring.

Once inside, Tracy looked at Elizabeth and said, "Those jeans are plenty tight."

They were no tighter than Tracy's but Elizabeth nodded. This was something that Tracy could not help. Though there was no reason for her to be jealous of Elizabeth, she always was. No one would look at Elizabeth when Tracy was around. At least no one in his right mind and sober.

"I suppose it makes you feel better to make yourself a little more attractive," Tracy said.

"I like to look nice," Elizabeth said.

"Well, with your life, I can understand that. I don't know how you can stand it. When was the last time you had a date?"

"I've never had a date, Tracy. You know that." The person in front of Tracy disappeared into the stall. She was next and stood for a moment without speaking. She was trying not to say what Elizabeth knew was coming. But the beer drove her on.

"Maybe not official," Tracy said. "But, come on, you obviously know a little more about men than you've ever told anyone." She laughed out loud as the door to her stall opened. "I didn't think you took that boarding-school stuff about immaculate conception seriously."

"Leave it, Tracy."

"Don't be so touchy," Tracy said as she stepped into the stall. "You'd feel better if you'd talk about it."

The door closed in Elizabeth's face. The anger rose in her and she closed her eyes. It was a trick she had learned years before. She repeated what old John Kiser had told her to tell herself. "She's only a human," Elizabeth whispered to herself. "Only a human."

Elizabeth brought four beers back to the seats with her. Tracy was there already and acted as if nothing had happened. The saddle bronc event had already begun. The first rider had scored a sixty-eight. This was the ride to beat.

"Get sat down, Mother," Tuffy said. "Your boy drew Psycho. He'll be coming out of chute three, last ride in the go around." Everyone looked at her and suddenly she felt weak.

She sat down quietly, and as hands took the beers from the cardboard tray, a long-haired rider on a buckskin bronc burst from chute four. The horse ran hard for thirty feet, then planted his front feet, ducked his head, and pitched his hindquarters high off the ground. Its feet went out behind, and they could hear the rider grunt as he battled to keep the horse under him. His hat flew off, but he rode the buckskin for two more jumps before he lost a stirrup and his rhythm went to pieces. By the time he was shaken loose, he was completely off balance and landed hard, a full two seconds before the bell.

"Pay him off," the announcer said, and the crowd began to applaud. "That's all that young cowboy will be taking home with him, and I'm sure he thanks you." The boy raised an arm in an attempt to wave, but it was easy to tell that he was hurting. He hobbled over to pick up his hat. The applause had stopped long before he arrived back at the chutes.

The next rider was Jay Pinto from New Mexico. He had been on the circuit for years, and the crowd knew him. Everyone watched as he settled down onto a black bronc named Satan. "Now, here's a rider that is capable of a very high score," the announcer said. "And he's drawn the kind of horse that will give him the opportunity."

Satan came out bucking straight. Pinto was right with him, spurring easily and bringing his heels high on Satan's neck. When the bronc broke his pattern and jumped left, Pinto was ready. Two jumps in that direction, then back to the right, and only once did a spur miss its mark.

"Nice," Tuffy mumbled to himself. "Nice ride."

The bell sounded, and the pickup riders rushed in to pluck Pinto from Satan's back. The crowd was cheering. Stewart stood and yelled. He surprised the others when he put two fingers in his mouth and let loose an ear-piercing whistle. "Sit down," Ross said. "Here comes Kyle."

"Now here's a South Dakota kid," the announcer was saying; "Kyle Janis from down on the edge of Pine Ridge. He's been cleaning up in the local rodeos down there. He's come to town to show us what he's got." There was a pause as Pinto's score was relayed to the announcer. "And he's going to have to show us a lot to get in the money tonight. Seventy-six points for Jay Pinto on Satan."

The crowd roared. They whooped and hollered and did not pay much attention to Kyle, who was trying to settle down into the chute on the back of Psycho. It seemed to Elizabeth that she was the only one watching as the horse, still in the chute, boiled up under her son. Kyle, with a foot on the rail on either side of the horse, raised up and let Psycho calm down. He looked very small, there above the sixteen-hundred-pound horse, but he was calm and eased back down. He planted himself in the saddle, took a firm grip on the rope, pulled his black hat down tight, and nodded to let him out.

Psycho had already taken three hard jumps, and Kyle's spurs had not yet come down below the horse's withers when the crowd realized there was one more competitor. The cheering trailed off as they turned to watch this young Indian boy lay out on the rump of the squealing sorrel horse. His left hand was held high and graceful, and when Psycho started to buck,

Kyle began to spur. He spurred in perfect rhythm: high on the shoulder when Psycho's front feet touched the ground, deep in the flanks when the hind legs came under them for another lunge. The cheering began to pick up again, but this time it was for the kid from Pine Ridge.

Stewart was on his feet, his hands rolled into fists. "Ride that son of a bitch!"

When Psycho started to spin, everyone stood. When he reversed the spin and Kyle did not miss a beat, the cheer was deafening. But because they were standing side by side, Ross could hear Tuffy talking softly to himself. "Stay with him," Tuffy said. "Stay with him. Stay with him."

Just before the bell that would give Kyle the high score of the day, Psycho sunfished. He gathered himself and came high off the ground, squealing and curving his body as if he might touch his head to his tail. He did it several times, tremendous jumps, and at the very top of the jump Kyle let his free hand go that much higher. When the pickup men raced in to pull him onto their horses, they had to pull him down. Psycho bucked on, but Kyle was set down easily in the center of the arena. The crowd screamed, and for a minute Ross thought Kyle might take his hat off and give them a wave. But of course he was too shy. He moved quickly back toward the chutes.

The people around Ross were still going wild. Louis pounded his hands together, Stewart whistled, and Elizabeth and Tracy embraced. Ross looked around for Tuffy, but he was gone. When he looked above them, he thought he saw a hat like Tuffy's disappear beneath the exit sign. Then someone was turning him around. When he completed the turn, Elizabeth was there. She looked directly into his eyes with a huge smile, her eyes wet from crying. He started to say something but never got the chance. She threw her arms around his neck and hugged him. When she pulled back, her face was filled with surprise and embarrassment. She swiveled away and began clapping her hands as if she could still see Kyle high in the air above Psycho.

Tuffy had six dollars in his pocket, and he spent two of them on a couple more beers as he passed the refreshment stand. He walked the hall below the seats of the civic center and listened to the announcer giving background as they readied the arena for the bull riding. They always saved bull riding for last so no one would leave early. Tuffy didn't really care for it. It was the only event whose origins were not found on a working cattle ranch. It was a dangerous kind of show, more a test of strength than skill.

The sounds of the rodeo seemed far away, and if he listened hard, Tuffy could hear the sound of his boots, hollow against the polished floor. He walked down a flight of stairs to the glass doors that looked onto the parking lot. There were hundreds of shiny cars. The Hilton and Alex Johnson hotels, along with a tall bank building, towered over everything. They said there was a restaurant at the top of the bank building. Tuffy could see dim lights in the highest windows. He imagined candles burning on tables with stiff white tablecloths, but he really didn't believe there was a restaurant up there. He stared at the building for a long time. If there was a restaurant up there, he thought, they had a hell of view of a lot of country. He wondered whether they'd be able to see his little ranch, fifty miles east, from up there.

Tuffy finished his first beer and walked to the parking lot. It was cool and quiet except for the cars passing on the road. When he looked away from the streetlights, he could see lots of stars, but not as many as he was used to. There was a trash can beside the door, and he tossed the empty cup into it. It was nicer out here than inside the building, and he began to walk along the side of the high brick wall of the civic center. Rapid

Creek was behind him now, and he thought he could hear it moving over the rocks in its bed.

In a minute he was behind the building. The pickups, horse trailers, and RVs of the cowboys were parked on the back lot as if it were an old-time campsite. The semitrailers that had hauled the rodeo stock were lined up ready to start taking the horses and bulls away. They, too, would have another rodeo to get to. Here and there groups of cowboys drank beer and joked as they packed their gear. Tuffy sipped the second beer and walked slowly among the vehicles. He heard Kyle swear in the dark behind one of the big trucks. This might be a good time to tell him what a good job he had done.

When Tuffy came around the truck, he saw Kyle and Delbert leaning over the hood of Delbert's old pickup. A one-horse trailer was hitched to the bumper, and Tuffy recognized the flaxen tail of Delbert's roping horse. There was more swearing, and Tuffy saw light reflect off a chrome wrench in one of the boy's hands. Delbert was obviously trying to get his pickup running well enough to get on the road for that rodeo in Salt Lake. There was an air of haste to the way they worked, and Tuffy knew, even before he walked up alongside the pickup and saw Kyle's bucking saddle and battered suitcase in the bed, that Kyle was going with him.

"Problems?" Tuffy asked.

The boys jumped at the sound of his voice, but Delbert regained his composure quickly. "Goddamned distributor or something." Tuffy moved closer and saw that they had a very dim flashlight pointed at the side of the engine block.

"Where you going?"

"Salt Lake," Kyle said.

Delbert stuck up for him. "He's going to show them dumb-fuck Mormons that Indians are good for something besides targets."

"What about school? You don't get out for another six weeks."

"I won't be gone forever. I'll make it up."

"You tell your mom?"

Kyle had been looking at Tuffy, but now he looked away. "No." Tuffy continued to look at him even though Kyle's eyes were on the ground. "Who's going to help her get those calves branded?" Tuffy said. But Kyle wasn't answering.

Delbert was feeling uncomfortable. He wanted the subject changed. "Damned distributor," he said softly.

Finally Kyle looked up. "Hell, Tuffy, I made eight hundred dollars tonight. Where can I make eight hundred dollars around here?" Tuffy didn't answer. "I can ride those broncs. You hear those people cheering? Nobody's ever cheered for me at Harney High School. I'm just another damned skin out there."

Now it was Tuffy who looked away. His eyes found the bank building again. He could still see the dim lights from the top-floor windows.

"He's good," Delbert said. His voice was no longer that of the tough young cowboy. He was talking Indian now. "He's really good, Tuffy."

Tuffy nodded and turned back to the boys. "You'll never get to Salt Lake in this piece of shit." He waved at the pickup. "You'll be spending that prize money on parts or bus fare home." He stepped to the hood and looked in. The flashlight was weak, but he picked it up and shone it on the distributor. He followed the spark-plug wires out of the distributor to each plug. "There," he said. He pointed the light at one of the wires. It was burned nearly in half. "They're probably all bad. This thing ain't going anywhere." Delbert took the flashlight from Tuffy. "And the rodeo is going to be over in a few minutes. Your mom'll be out here to congratulate you." The boys looked at the wire. Kyle reached down to touch it and it came apart.

"Shit," Delbert said.

"Tuffy's right," Kyle said. "If this one's this bad, probably none of them are any good." Kyle turned back to Tuffy, but he was gone.

"We're fucked," Delbert said.

"I'm fucked," Kyle said. "You can get new spark-plug wires in the morning and head for Salt Lake. This was my only chance."

They stood in silence. On the other side of the big truck people were moving out, heading for the next stop on the circuit, going places where good things might happen. The rodeo was over; Ross, Stewart, Tracy, Louis, and Elizabeth would soon be looking for him. "I'm sorry," Delbert said.

The two boys were looking at each other when a pickup came up alongside theirs. It was Tuffy. "Does the hitch on that horse trailer of yours take a two-inch ball?"

Delbert looked at him and nodded.

"Well, let's get the son of a bitch switched over. You skins'll never get to Salt Lake standing here pissing and moaning."

They quickly unloaded the horse, moved the trailer, hitched it to Tuffy's pickup, and threw the saddles and blankets into the back. "Now keep an eye on the oil," Tuffy said as he leaned on the window near Kyle. "You know which road to take?"

Kyle nodded. His face was only inches away from Tuffy's. His jaw quivered and his eyes blinked. "You take care of yourselves," Tuffy said. He pointed to both of them to show he meant it. "Stay away from the booze and the dope the best you can." He dug into his pocket and brought out the four crumpled dollar bills and pushed them into Kyle's hand. "Make 'em know where Pine Ridge is," he said. People were streaming from the arena. "Now, go on," Tuffy said. "Give 'em hell."

They pulled away with a whoop for the real world that lay

227

ahead. But as they bumped out of the parking lot and began
the turn that would lead them to the interstate highway, Kyle
looked back to see Tuffy standing beside Delbert's useless
pickup. He was motionless, but just as the boys moved out of
sight, he turned and ambled away from the parking lot, away
from the frenzy of post-rodeo activity. He walked slowly, with
his head down, toward Rapid Creek, toward the east end of
town, toward the neglected part of the park and the bridges,
where he was sure to find someone he knew.

▲

THIRTY-SIX

Linda called early the next morning from Seattle. The tour was fabulous, she would be in Denver in a week, and she couldn't wait to see Ross. She talked with Stewart, too, teased him about becoming a cowboy and told him that before she left LA, several people had called, two wanting to know whether he was planning to start up a new long-distance company and the other wanting to know whether his Jaguar was for sale. Linda had taken down names and telephone numbers, but when she asked Stewart whether he wanted the numbers, he said no.

But he did want to tell her about the rodeo, and about how the land was greening up, and the way the gumbo soil had turned from an ocean of sticky mud to crumbly white clods as hard as stone. "The cattle go out to summer pasture in a month. Ross says we'll need a rain before then, or there won't be enough grass for them to eat. Can you believe that cows eat nothing but grass?"

"I know all about that, Stewart."

"Sorry. It's just that I can't believe they eat just grass."

"Look, Stewart, is Ross standing right there?"

Ross was in the kitchen, sitting at the table pulling on his boots. "He's just in the other room. You want to talk to him again?"

"No," Linda said. "I just wanted to know if you could talk."

Stewart became serious. "Sure," he said and turned his back toward Ross.

"How is he?"

"OK. He seems fine."

"Has he said anything about leaving that place?"

"You mean the ranch?"

"Yes. Has he said anything about coming to LA?"

"I think he misses you, but he hasn't said anything about leaving. It's really kind of nice out here."

"Stewart, you're on vacation. It's like a dude ranch to you. How would you like to live there?"

Stewart nodded. "You've got a point." He looked over his shoulder at Ross. He was standing up, stamping his left foot as if the boot didn't fit quite right.

"It's just that Ross has wasted so much of his life." It was unusual for Linda to let her frustration show. "And I wasted a few years myself. Stewart, I can't tell you how good it feels to be dancing." Her mood had swung. "You'll be heading home soon. Drive down to Denver with Ross, and we'll put you on the airplane there. We can have dinner. You can watch me dance."

Stewart's thoughts were still with what Linda had said about people wasting their lives. He fought against the edge of the sadness he felt by making a joke. "Sure, I could just sleep on the floor of your hotel room."

"Right." Linda laughed. "I don't think we'll be looking for a chaperon."

"No," Stewart said, "I don't imagine you will." He was watching Ross standing at the window in the other room. "Look, Ross is ready to go feed the cows. I've got to run. I'll think about riding down to Denver with him."

"Good. It would be great to meet you in the Mile High City. The Brown Palace for dinner."

"Sounds better than Red Baron pizzas at the Dust Buster."

"You've met Tuffy."

"Best of pals."

230

"Stewart? Seriously now, take care."

"You got it, Sis."

Stewart hung up but remained looking down at the phone. He couldn't shake the idea of wasting your life. What did that mean? What wasn't a waste?

"Hey," Ross called, "Let's move it. We've got a beautiful spring day and hungry cows."

They hustled across the yard toward the flatbed pickup. "Only another week or so of this," Ross said. "The grass is growing good."

They jumped into the pickup, moving old feed sacks and beer and pop cans out of their way. It hadn't frozen at night for over a week, and so the tractor with the grapple fork had been left out by the stacks. By now they had the routine down: Ross ran the tractor, and Stewart drove the pickup. Once they got to the feeding ground, they put the pickup in low gear and let it idle across the field as they pitched the hay off. They were feeding less hay every day because the cows were starting to eat the new grass. That was a good thing, because the stacks were dwindling. Ross figured it was going to work out about right: they'd be out of hay just when the cows switched completely to grass. His main worries now were getting the calves branded and whether or not there would be enough rain to get a hay crop for next year.

Stewart had become proficient with a pitchfork. At first he could not figure out how the layers of hay went together. He had pulled much harder than Ross and still came up with less hay. But now he could look at the stack on the back of the pickup and know that if he sunk the tines in a certain way, he would come up with an enormous flat layer of hay that would bend the pitchfork handle when he picked it up.

They pitched the first half of the load in silence, both men taking pride in the way they were moving the hay. But as the stack shrunk, Linda's talk about wasting time came back to Stewart. It seemed a proper thing to talk about as they worked.

"Did you ever think," Stewart began, "that you'd wasted part of your life?"

Ross knew immediately that this discussion had started with something Linda had told Stewart on the telephone. "Sure," Ross said. "Don't we all wonder if what we're doing is worthwhile?"

Stewart nodded and sank the tines into the hay at just the right angle. It was going to be a good forkful. When he lifted, he found it was perfect, about all he could manage. "Yeah, but wouldn't it be a shame if a guy's whole life amounted to nothing?"

Ross sank his fork into the hay, left it there, and spread his arms. "To find," he said, "that, when it was time to die, you had not lived?" Ross laughed.

But Stewart nodded and shrugged. "Something like that."

"Your sister started this."

"She did."

"Keep talking," Ross said. "But keep pitching hay, too."

"She said she'd wasted a lot of time."

"My fault," Ross said. "It was a mistake for her to come here. I should never have asked her."

"A mistake for her," Stewart said. "What about you? She said you'd wasted time, too."

Ross pitched a couple more forkfuls before he answered. Maybe it was true that he'd wasted a great portion of his life. There were the years in Canada and now the years on the plains, pitching hay to cows that raised calves that barely paid the bills when they were sold. "I've wasted some," Ross said. "Maybe I've wasted it all. Who knows?"

* * *

Elizabeth sat in her pickup waiting for Ross and Stewart to come back from feeding the cows. She could see them bouncing slowly toward the buildings but was sure they had not noticed her. She was supposed to pick them up on her way into Harney for her meeting with Sorenson, but she was two hours early. She had had a rough night. It was the dream of being raped, and as soon as she woke up fighting her own sheets, she knew that something was wrong.

At first she thought it might just be that she was worried about talking to the banker. But as she lay in the dark, she came to know that it was something more. It was very late, morning really, but she got out of her bed and moved slowly down the hall to Kyle's room. She had missed him after the rodeo and figured he was doing some celebrating and would be home late. But before she pushed the door open, she knew the bed would be empty.

She could not go back to sleep, and at eight o'clock, just when she was about to call someone—her mother, Aunt Rachel, perhaps Ross—the telephone went off in her hand. It was Kyle, calling from Rock Springs, Wyoming. He was safe, and Elizabeth surprised herself by whispering a prayer of thanks to Wakantanka as she listened to him try to explain. He talked about how he hated school and how he thought he had a chance to do well on the rodeo circuit. He mumbled and stammered like a child, but Elizabeth recognized, in the silly, impossibly hopeful things he said, that he was becoming a man. In the end there had been nothing for her to say except to be careful. When she hung up, she imagined him leaping from the phone booth outside a truck stop in Rock Springs with a squeal of joy. Freedom, she thought; they will do anything for freedom. But she sat by the telephone and grieved. It would do her no good, of course. But it was a sort of duty.

Later she tried to help Pete with the chores. She told him that Kyle was gone, and he grumbled, but no worse than usual.

Finally she let him finish up and went back into the house to get ready for the appointment with Sorenson. There was still a lot of time, but she had begun to want to see Ross. She had tried to deny it now for days, but what was the use? She washed her face, changed her clothes, and braided her hair.

A golden breasted meadowlark stood on every other fence post. She saw her first plover of the year not far from the entrance to the missile silo. It too stood on a fence post and let loose its eerie call as Elizabeth pulled near. It seemed to stand on its tiptoes and with the sun behind it could be seen in silhouette only. Behind it was the chain link fence of the missile compound. The plover's long, thin neck blended with the background of wires and antennae that sprang from the earth inside the enclosure. But when the plover lifted off the post with its stiff, pterodactyl wings, it was impossible to confuse it with anything else. It fluttered easily out into Cleve Miller's alfalfa field and stood watching Elizabeth with only its head above the vegetation. It stayed there until the pickup moved on. Elizabeth was fifty yards down the road, almost to Ross's driveway, when in the rearview mirror she saw the plover fly back to its fence post and position itself above what it was claiming as its territory.

Now Elizabeth sat in the pickup and watched Ross and Stewart pull into the yard. When they saw her, they were clearly surprised. Ross glanced at his watch as he pulled the pickup into the shed, and Elizabeth wished she had not come early. She wished Kyle was at home, helping Pete as usual. She wished she had not asked Ross to go with her to the bank. She wished with all her heart that it was all just another bad dream and that Sorenson had never written her a letter. For an instant Ross and Stewart disappeared in the shadows of the shed, and Elizabeth felt the impulse to drive away, to go back down to her mother's house on the reservation and never return. But then Ross was coming toward her from the shed, slapping his work gloves against his thigh. Stewart had just appeared from the shed when Ross stepped up to the window.

His hat was pushed back, and his face was dirty where sweat had collected hay dust and then dried. "Hi, Liz. Didn't expect you so early."

Liz. No one had called her that since she was a little girl. She looked up at him and knew she was going to cry.

When Ross saw how full her eyes were, he looked up and called to Stewart. "Hey," he said. "Do me a favor. Go feed those two heifers and make sure their calves have sucked." He jerked his head toward the barn, and Stewart caught on.

"Sure," he said, waving and altering his course.

Ross waited until he disappeared into the barn, then opened the door of Elizabeth's pickup and touched her shoulder. "Come on," he said. "Let's walk."

They moved away from the buildings and down toward the budding ash trees along Sweet Grass Creek. They didn't speak. They walked down the bank and jumped the tiny trickle of water that was the beginning of the creek. On the other side the snowberry bushes were starting to leaf out. There were no flowers on them yet, but farther up the choke-cherry blossoms showed a fringe of white and a promise of August's tart black fruit. They stopped beside the chokecherries, and Elizabeth told Ross about Kyle. Once she began, she talked on about how it was really no surprise, how it had to happen. Then, without Ross urging her, she told him about John Kiser, how he had been different, a throwback or ahead of his time, and how he had been able to ease her troubles by talking to her about how things fit together. She told him how John used to see what things had in common, how they differed, and how it didn't bother him either way. She told Ross that everything had been understandable before his accident and that now it was all beginning to twist around and jumble in her mind.

She went on to say that she felt very bad about what might happen with Sorenson. When Ross thought that she had said enough, he reached out and took her hand. She continued to talk, and he touched a finger to her lips. Her eyes looked frightened but she did not pull away. Ross looked directly into her eyes and smiled. "Come with me," he said.

They moved westward, still above Sweet Grass Creek, and walked through ankle-high porcupine grass that was turning deep green near its roots. They continued along the creek for five minutes, and Ross did not let go of her hand until they came to a side draw and had to descend the steep bank. They moved across the draw's bottom, past the buffalo-berry bushes, and up the other side. Ross whispered for Elizabeth to be quiet as they came to the top of the rise. They dropped to their hands and knees and crawled the last twenty feet. The wind was in their faces, and before they got to the top, it carried a wonderful drumming sound to them. The drumming was joined by what sounded like miniature turkey gobbles. When they had crawled far enough, they laid their heads in the greening grass and peeked through it at the dance of the sharp-tailed grouse.

It was a dancing ground that Ross had discovered the first year on the place. But the grouse had probably danced there for years, perhaps for centuries. These ten or twelve chicken-sized birds were all males. They sat in the grass with their short, pointed tails in the air and watched the bird on the next two-foot area of sod. Occasionally two would stand up, stamp their feet furiously, making the impossibly loud drumming sound, and run at each other. But they seldom came to blows. They stopped with their beaks an inch apart or jumped eighteen inches in the air, releasing the cackling sound that Ross and Elizabeth had heard as they crept to the top of the hill.

The birds took the defense of their symbolic little territories very seriously, one bird sometimes running first one way and then the other to fend off two invaders that never crossed the imaginary line. Ross and Elizabeth lay in the grass and tried their best to hold back laughter. Occasionally a bird would hear them but not know where the sound was coming from. Everything would stop and all the birds would freeze, their round, dark eyes alert for danger. In a minute they would resume spreading their tails and wings and spinning with their floating stutter steps in an effort to attract the attention of any female that might fly in to see what the fuss was about.

When a female did fly in, the group of males burst into a flurry of activity. But each bird was still restrained by invisible barriers. The female walked among them indifferently, scratching at the dirt here, pecking at an insect there, as the males jumped and cackled in her wake. Finally she chose a mate. She stood on his piece of turf and bowed her head. Though the other birds went on dancing, the chosen bird stopped and bowed also. Their beaks almost touched, and the female exploded into flight with the male close behind. Elizabeth followed their flight to the left and found herself looking into Ross's eyes.

His eyes were very close, and Elizabeth knew that they would kiss. She had kissed boys before, but never a man. She was frightened but didn't stop. It seemed to take forever for their lips to meet. There was the sound of the grouse in front of them, the smell of the new grass below, and all the blue sky in the world above. Finally there was the warm, moist tenderness of Ross. They held their lips together for only an instant, but neither pulled away. They kept their faces close, so close that it was impossible to focus. It made everything seem unreal and Elizabeth felt safe.

▲

PART FIVE

▲

THIRTY-SEVEN

The appointment was for eleven thirty, and Elizabeth, Ross, and Stewart got to town a half hour early. Tourist season was still a few weeks away, but the town was gearing up to host the tens of thousands of people who would soon be stopping off on their way to the Black Hills, Montana, or Yellowstone National Park. The hope was that they would all spend a few dollars in Harney.

Usually Ross would have stopped at the Badlands Café, but since the Enchanted Forest was open for the season and Stewart hadn't seen it, they decided to have a cup of coffee there while they waited for the meeting.

They entered between the snack bar and the gift shop. Already college kids with clean, scrubbed faces scurried about, stocking shelves and learning the jobs they would perform throughout the summer. They wore name tags—"Hi! I'm Stephanie from Findlay, Ohio"—and smiled at everyone who came through the door. Elizabeth, Stewart, and Ross got particularly prompt attention in the snack bar because the waiters and waitresses had been given strict orders to treat the locals well. At least two of these people were certainly locals. Ross looked like what the college kids had imagined a cowboy to look like, and Elizabeth was obviously a real Indian.

They sat at a booth sipping coffee. There were only a few tourists in the café; they wouldn't start arriving in force until after Memorial Day. One couple ate quietly in the corner; an old couple inspected the oil paintings on the wall. The pictures were by local artists. One was of a group of cowboys singing beside campfires; another was a buffalo being chased by Sioux warriors. There were oils of pheasants flying over cornfields. They were all for sale, and the old couple looked carefully at the prices of each but bought nothing.

Elizabeth was nervous and let her coffee get cold. They still had twenty minutes, so they crossed the hall to the gift shop, and Stewart wandered off between a rack of greeting cards and a wall filled with T-shirts with scenes from the Badlands silk-screened on them. He came back carrying a wooden tomahawk with brightly dyed chicken feathers tied to a thong attached to the handle. The feathers were blue and yellow, and the wooden blade of the tomahawk was painted with a few drops of blood. Stewart held it up and smiled. "A memento," he said.

They walked out into the Enchanted Forest, passed the Pirates' Hideaway, the Oasis, and the Castles and stopped at the Tower of London. Stewart touched the huge pieces of petrified wood in the wall of the tower. "Is this stuff really wood?"

"It was," Ross said, "about a million years ago. There's lots of it out in the Badlands."

"You can just go out there and pick it up?"

"Not anymore. Everything in the park is protected now. They moved this stuff in years ago."

"I'll be damned," Stewart said. He tapped the side of the Tower of London with his new tomahawk, then slapped it with his hand to test its strength. "This thing must weigh a hundred tons." He peered into the darkness beyond the iron bars. "I'll be damned," he said again.

Elizabeth had walked on. She stood on Fishing Bridge, not far from the exit, and looked down into the water. There were no fish yet.

"They put fish in here for kids to catch," Ross said to Stewart.

"What kind of fish?"

"Beats me," Ross said. "Elizabeth, do you know what kind of fish?"

Elizabeth shook her head. "Let's get out of here," she said. "This place gives me the creeps."

They walked past Bronco Barney's Ice Cream Store, crossed Second Street, and moved on to the First Bank of Harney. Elizabeth hesitated under the time-and-temperature sign, but Ross took her arm gently and guided her into the bank. He didn't like going into the bank much better than Elizabeth did. He had been a payment behind once or twice himself and knew it did no good to put off the bank. They went to one of the tellers and asked to see Mr. Sorenson. She pointed toward some chairs along a wall and said she'd tell him they were waiting.

Ross watched the office door and saw Sorenson's smile fade when he came out and found Elizabeth sitting with two men. He hesitated, but when he saw that Ross was watching him, he smiled again and came forward.

"Miss Janis?" Elizabeth stood up and thrust her hand out. "I'm Larry Sorenson," he said. "I don't believe we've ever really met. I think one of the junior officers has talked to you in the past." He turned to Ross and Stewart. "And I don't believe I know you."

"Stewart Bergman," Stewart said, tucking the tomahawk under his arm and shaking Sorenson's hand. "Pleased to meet you."

"We've met," Ross said. "I'm Ross Brady."

Sorenson's eyes narrowed for an instant, then he smiled. "Certainly," he said. "I believe I've seen your file."

"We're here with Elizabeth."

"Oh," Sorenson said. He turned to Stewart. "Are you representing her?"

Stewart shook his head. "No. I'm just along for the ride." Stewart made a point of looking Sorenson in the eyes. "Does she need representation?" he asked.

Sorenson met his stare, glanced at the tomahawk, then smiled. "Of course not. We just need to straighten a few things out." He turned to Ross. "And you, Mr. Brady, are you here in an official capacity?"

Ross shook his head and looked at Elizabeth, who had not been able to look at Sorenson yet. "Just a friend," Ross said. He saw Elizabeth's eyes dart back and forth across the floor, but she did not look up. "A close friend," he said.

Sorenson smiled even wider. "Of course," he said. "Well, Miss Janis, would you like to step into my office?" He glanced back at Ross and Stewart. "You fellows can just have a seat." Now Elizabeth looked at Ross. Her eyes were big, and her mouth was slightly open as if she might speak.

Ross shook his head. "No," he said. "You don't understand. I came to sit in on the meeting."

Sorenson's eyebrows came up. "Me, too," said Stewart, who looked again directly into Sorenson's eyes. Sorenson returned the look, then looked to Ross and let out a little laugh.

"Of course," he said. "If Miss Janis doesn't mind. Step right in." He waved for them to walk in front of him. "Certainly, certainly. Come right in."

They took chairs across the desk from Sorenson. "The purpose of having you come in, Miss Janis, is to talk about your deficient payments." He shuffled through papers on his desk as if he didn't know where the files were. He took Elizabeth's folder from the top and quickly covered Ross's with another sheet of paper. "We need to work out a way, Miss Janis, for you to take care of the outstanding interest and principal on the note that you assumed from John Kiser." He took a piece of paper from the folder and handed it across to Elizabeth. She looked at it and handed it on to Ross.

"The way things stand right now, you are in default. There hasn't been a payment made for three years."

"The calves sold cheap," Elizabeth said. Her voice was sharp, and Ross realized that she was not only afraid of Sorenson; the tone of her voice told him that she disliked him as well.

"It's true," Ross said. "The last few years prices have been way down." He passed the paper to Stewart, who took it anxiously and ran his index finger quickly down a column of figures.

"I realize that," Sorenson said. "But this is a business. We have rules. Things go bad for us, too."

"But everyone has had it tough," Elizabeth said. "Why pick on me?"

"I'm not picking on you, Miss Janis. I am reviewing all loans that are deficient. That's part of my job." Ross watched to see whether Sorenson would look up at him, but he didn't. "I asked you in here today to talk. To begin to work something out. There are things that can be done, and we don't have to decide anything today."

Elizabeth was gaining courage. "Like what?" she said. Sorenson shrugged. "You want the place, don't you?"

"That's only one possibility. Perhaps we can restructure your loan." He fumbled with some papers. "How did your calving go this year?" That caught everyone off guard. Could Sorenson know about the cattle that were lost in the dam?

"She did fine," Ross said.

Stewart laid the piece of paper back on Sorenson's desk. "She owes you a little more than forty thousand dollars?"

Sorenson looked at the paper. "About. There's a couple hundred more in accrued interest that doesn't show here."

"Forty thousand is the entire loan?" Stewart shook his head.

The money talk seemed to upset Elizabeth even more. She stammered before she began to speak. "You called Tuffy. You're picking on me just like you're picking on Tuffy."

"Tuffy?"

"Tuffy Martinez."

Sorenson squirmed but answered pleasantly. "I don't even know Mr. Martinez."

"I think you do," Elizabeth said. "You just don't remember. He was just a kid. You called him an ignorant mongrel. I was there. In the school yard."

Sorenson stared at her, and time hung still as the incident came vividly into his mind. It was when Loni was a freshman in high school. They had just had a new refrigerator delivered to their house, and he had come to the school to speak with the shop teacher about doing some wiring for a more convenient electrical outlet. He was sweating from the heat, and the school yard was filled with kids. He walked through them toward the school and was not thinking about anything except getting that new refrigerator working when he came around the corner and there was his daughter in a pretty yellow dress leaning against the building, smiling broadly, and talking to an Indian boy. The boy's hand was on her shoulder, and before he could think, he grabbed her arm and jerked her harder than he should have. He remembered pulling her across the playground with the Indian boy following helplessly behind. The other children moved out of their way, and Loni cried. He planned to put her in the pickup, but the front seat was filled with tools. There was no place for her except the bed of the pickup. He shook her once more and lifted her into the pickup bed. He made her sit in the discarded cardboard refrigerator box.

Now, nearly fifteen years later, he remembered the way she had looked sitting there: a beautiful young girl in a yellow dress, crushed, humiliated, and crying, her head against her knees. It must have been then that he spun and came face-to-face with the boy. It was very possible that he said something to him. If so, he was sorry. But that was not the only thing he was sorry about that day.

"I'm not sure what you're talking about," he sputtered. "You are a little upset. Let me assure you that this bank is here to serve you. We're not singling anyone out."

Stewart leaned against the desk. "Then you've got no specific action in mind."

Sorenson shook his head. "We'll work something out." He put his hands together and smiled. "Let me do some thinking. I'll give you a call." He stood up. "Try not to be upset. There's always a reasonable solution."

Sorenson walked them to the front door of the bank and made a point of shaking their hands before they stepped out into the street. When they were gone, he returned to his office and shut the door. His hands trembled, and he sat for several minutes before picking up the telephone and dialing Cleve Miller's number from memory.

▲
THIRTY-EIGHT

It came as no surprise to Cleve Miller that Elizabeth Janis lost her temper and that Ross Brady and another man had come with her. He was a little surprised that Tuffy had treated Sorenson so badly. That didn't make sense to Cleve, and he wondered whether there was something he didn't know. He would have bet Tuffy would have jumped at a chance to get out of that place. He wanted to drive over and ask Tuffy what was going on, but Sorenson thought it might still work out. Cleve hoped Sorenson was doing his best. Larry Sorenson was a good man and a close friend, but he was naive. It was true that his bank was small, local, and, to some extent, insulated from the forces that controlled world finance, but still he should know that those forces could not let them put together a land deal of this size without opposition. Cleve was sure that Sorenson had no idea he was dealing with the power that threatened to drive Christendom into economic and spiritual ruin.

This is what Cleve thought about as he walked around his family's old homestead. For some reason he had not driven his pickup. When he left the modular house, he had walked straight to the shed where the Ford Crown Victoria was stored. He had driven it in spite of the fact that he had to come across a pasture. Now it was parked behind the crumbling house, near the machine shed. Cleve walked along the driveway that surrounded the house. The years of vacancy were obvious: the yard gate hung on one hinge, the Kentucky bluegrass had been crowded out by native grass, the siding was buckled, and an upstairs window had somehow been broken. In the early seventies there had been a chance to sell the place. The cattle market was high and people had been optimistic. Time had proved that those years had been a wonderful time to sell and a terrible time to buy. Cleve was ashamed that he had not seen the crash coming. Had he sold, his life would have been different. He would have never seen his assets sink the way they had, never gotten caught holding the bag on a cattle deal gone bad.

The gate balanced on its hinge and looked as though it could fall at any moment. Cleve walked through without touching it and moved slowly to the porch. For an instant he thought he might go inside but decided against it. What he wanted to do was sit on the porch with his feet on the first step. He remembered sitting like that as a child, staring out at the desolate landscape and thinking of things that were important to him.

Now he could not remember what those things were. Instead he thought about Sorenson and how important it was that they should be successful. He had never been an impatient man; he had believed in letting others make their own mistakes, but if it came to a test, it could be that Sorenson would not have the courage to do what was needed. It seemed an odd quirk of fate that Cleve's whole life could depend on Larry Sorenson's courage. He knew he could not let Larry bungle it. He would help Larry with his courage. He would do whatever he had to do, anything, to see that his land was sold. The alternative was bankruptcy, and even thinking the word made Cleve lower his eyes and bow his head.

Cleve knew what was happening even if Larry didn't. He wished there was something he could say to make other decent people see that the struggle was really not with little, insignificant daily matters. He wished there was something he could say to make them see that the danger from Satan was real and that they needed to stiffen their backbones and hold on until Jesus returned. But he was not one to proselytize. He believed every man must come to know these things on his own.

There was a scratching sound above him, and he froze until he heard the flapping of wings. A huge black crow sailed out from above the porch roof and cawed twice. The noise was echoed from somewhere in the house, and Cleve knew the birds were using the broken window on the second story and building a nest in the house. He did not move but watched the crow fly down to the driveway and pick up a stick in its beak. The crow was only thirty yards from Cleve, but it did not notice him. Cleve was able to see how black it was. It strutted on stiff legs and moved the stick so it would be easy to carry. The bird seemed proud of its blackness and flew back to the broken window.

Cleve remained sitting and listened to more cawing and scratching from above, and at that moment it came to him that he could not let the mining plan fail. He stood up slowly and moved into the side yard. There was a weariness in his walk, a certain resignation that there was a job to be done.

In the trunk of his car, beneath a blanket, he found his old pump shotgun. He pushed twelve-gauge shells into the magazine as he returned to the yard. There were always unpleasant jobs to be done, he thought as he scooped up a handful of pebbles from a neglected flower bed. But there was survival to consider. He threw the pebbles against the siding of the second story. Human survival. The shotgun was already leveled at the window when the crows came scrambling through the broken pane.

THIRTY-NINE

The performance in Portland went beautifully. It was sponsored by the local arts council, and even though the facility was only a high-school auditorium, the audience was very responsive; they sighed at the right times and caught their collective breath when Jonathan and Linda hoped they would. When it was over, they stood and cheered. There had even been a couple of whistles.

The work was one of Anita Barowitz's new pieces. Anita was featured and Linda was the other female dancer. Jonathan was the sole male and spun between the two women dressed in the costume of a dockworker. Linda loved the piece. It was filled with the spirit of jazz. Everything was built around syncopation, with Anita playing the part of the wise, and finally irresistible, woman and Linda mimicking the motions of a workaday life. Jonathan's character was the loser in the play, and the dance ended in a closely choreographed segment with soft spotlights on the two women.

It was the kind of performance that Linda had dreamed of ever since she started dancing seriously in Vancouver. Anita had been wonderful, and Jonathan danced with a passion that had been contagious. Linda thought she had responded to the energy on the stage and had danced better than she ever had before.

As she sat at her dressing table, set up makeshift in the girls' locker room, she thought that her life was once again on track. Anita had stepped into the hall to talk with a reporter.

Linda sat in the locker room alone. It amused her to think that there was something to being in this high school that made sense. The last time she could remember feeling as if she understood what was happening in her life was when she was a senior at Hamilton High in West LA. She wondered just what it was that made this night seem so good. There should be some guilt about Ross, about leaving him to deal with the mistakes they had made together. She should feel somehow bad about the things that were happening in her life. She should worry that she was not living up to the commitment she had made. But that commitment had grown beyond her young expectations and finally had become more than she could manage.

She left the ranch for this. She looked around the locker room. Could it be that people come with places already in their blood? She didn't want to believe that. But there was Ross, part of a place. And here she was, part of another place. Certainly what they felt for each other was stronger; certainly what people found in a place was temporary, and what they found in each other was permanent.

But the excitement of the tour, the sound of those Portland Arts Council members cheering beyond the stage lights, continued to rise in Linda's consciousness. If there was guilt about another part of her life, it was overshadowed by what was happening now.

▲
FORTY

Tuffy arrived back at his place in the middle of the afternoon. He had caught a ride from Rapid City with Johnny Yellow Boy, who dropped him off at his mailbox. They had stopped at the Dust Buster at about ten o'clock, so the entire trip took almost seven hours. By the time Tuffy got home, he was well on his way to being drunk.

The first thing he did was go into the house and feed Clyde. The cat meowed loudly as Tuffy searched for the can opener. It was not on the nail where it usually hung. It was not in the sink. Clyde continued to yowl, and finally Tuffy gave up and went to the toolbox on the porch. He took the tin snips from the top drawer, and he put the edge of the can between the blades. By placing one handle of the snips on the floor and stomping on the other, he was able to cut a corner off the can of cat food. He held his face away from the fumes as he spooned the food into a dish he found in the sink.

On his way to the shed to check on the motorcycle, it hit him like a two-by-four. He changed his course and went to the filler pipe of the underground gasoline tank. By holding his head just right, so the sunlight would go down the hole just over his left ear, he was able to see the can opener in the center of the enormous mass of bailing twine, cactus, horse turds, and wire. "Well," Tuffy said, still peering down the filler pipe, "serves the silly son of a bitch right. I ought to let him see if he can gnaw those cans open."

Something had to be done about that rat, Tuffy thought as

he walked to the shed. He slid open the door, and it caught on the rail where the carriage bolts had pulled out of the wall. Someday he'd fix that, but for now he needed to make sure the Harley was running at full power. It looked as if it was going to be his only means of getting around until Kyle got back from wherever they were going.

There were sparrow droppings on the seat again, and Tuffy wiped them off with his shirtsleeve. It crossed his mind again that Clyde should be controlling the sparrows in the building, but he didn't dwell on it. He pushed the Harley out into the sunshine and saddled up. He had kicked it only once when a car pulled into the driveway.

It had been a long time since a car had come down the driveway. This car was big and shiny and looked very out of place. About the only other people besides Ross, Elizabeth, or Cleve to come down the driveway were the Jehovah's Witnesses, and this was too nice a car for them. Tuffy had been poised above the Harley, ready to kick it again, when he first saw the car. He sat down on the seat and watched the big Ford approach. When the car was still a hundred feet away, he recognized it.

It was Cleve Miller. He smiled and raised his hand in a wave. Tuffy nodded to Cleve as Cleve stopped the Crown Victoria beside the Harley.

"Afternoon, Tuffy," Cleve said as he turned the car off. "Wonderful day, isn't it?"

Tuffy looked around. There was a green hue to the hillsides. The trees were beginning to bud. "Yep," he said. "They could all be like this one. Suit me fine."

"Came over to take a look at that bearing," Cleve said.

Tuffy climbed off the bike. "Over there," he said.

Cleve smiled as he slid from the car. He looked in the direction Tuffy indicated. "That's a Gleaner, all right. Best Allis-Chalmers ever built. Same model as mine, looks like."

They walked to the combine and Cleve slid underneath. "Yep," he said. "That's the one. You got some sockets?"

Tuffy's shop was a mess, most of the tools lost. He had no idea where to look for the sockets they would need to remove the bearing. "No," Tuffy said. "It would take longer to find them than to drive back to your place for a set."

Cleve crawled out from under the combine shaking his head. He was disappointed in Tuffy. His face showed it. "Damn, Tuffy, you got to get some pride." He stood and looked at Tuffy as if he were thinking about something very different from the combine. Finally he put his big arm around Tuffy's shoulder. They started back toward the Harley and the car. There was something different with Cleve, and Tuffy didn't like it.

"Must be hell," Cleve said. "Living like this. Alone, I mean."

"I got Clyde." Tuffy tried to joke but felt uncomfortable.

Cleve had been looking around at the deteriorating buildings. When he heard Tuffy's reply, he looked at him and shook his head again. But Tuffy wasn't looking at him. He swung his leg over the motorcycle seat, folded his arms, and looked down at the ground.

Cleve walked a few yards toward the house and looked up at the roof. Some of the shingles curled up, and the rain gutters were broken down where they were filled with leaves from the cottonwood trees. Suddenly Tuffy wanted Cleve off his place, but he didn't know how to tell him. Cleve was older but stout and burly. Tuffy supposed he could still throw him off if it came to that, but he knew it never would.

"What do you want, Cleve?" Tuffy said.

Cleve spun around as if Tuffy had said something pleasant. "Just the bearing. I'll come back for it one of these days." Then, moving a few steps closer and becoming serious, "It's been rough, hasn't it, Tuffy?" Tuffy looked down again. "Been real hard, I'd say," Cleve said and came even closer. "Everything you try turns to shit, don't it?"

Tuffy didn't like this. Cleve was acting strangely, and for a moment Tuffy wondered whether he had gone back to drinking. "What are you saying?"

"Nothing. Nothing. Just that I've known you for a long time and know you're the kind of guy who knows a good thing when he sees it. Remember, Tuffy, the meek are going to inherit, and the Lord sets prisoners free." This sounded more like Cleve but still Tuffy was nervous. Cleve saw this, smiled broadly, and patted Tuffy's back. "You deserve a break. You aren't going to have to live in no shit hole like this." He waved his arm around to take in Tuffy's whole place, the pastures and the hills beyond. "Don't let your Indian pride get in the way of good sense."

"What the fuck are you talking about, Cleve?"

Cleve smiled and shrugged. He patted Tuffy's shoulder this time. "The Lord works in mysterious ways," he said. Then his eyes narrowed, and he reached out and gripped Tuffy's shoulder. "This country is going to change. And we're not as dumb as they think we are." He winked. "The reasonable ones will get their share." Cleve was no longer talking to Tuffy. "We're as good as they are," he said, then looked back to Tuffy. "Hell," he said, "we're better." He smiled his old smile and laughed.

Cleve turned and opened the door on the Ford. Once he was inside with the engine running, he turned to Tuffy, who still sat a few feet away on the Harley. "I'll be back for that bearing," he said and acted as if he might say something more, but he didn't. He only smiled as the car began to move up the driveway, and Tuffy thought for a moment before he rose up and kicked the starter sharply. He kicked twice more, and the Harley began to pop deep in its engine block. After a few seconds Tuffy shifted into first and headed up the driveway after the Ford. He wanted to stop Cleve, ask him what he meant. But when he came to the bench road, he lost his desire. He wanted to turn the other way, toward the Dust Buster, where his credit was always good.

But he shouldn't do that either, and so he turned the Harley slowly and headed back down his driveway. He had gone two hundred yards toward his house when he noticed something unusual on a fence post. It was a post he passed almost every day, but today, in the afternoon light, it looked different. The Harley popped as it was downshifted and nearly came to a stop. But Tuffy let it roll on toward the fence post.

It was an owl, standing as if it were an extension of the post, out in the light of day, its brown mottled feathers puffed out and its ears alert and pointing skyward. The yellow eyes were as large as quarters and stared at Tuffy as he dragged his feet to stop the Harley. The owl moved its head from side to side, then up and down. It let out a deep hoot, spread its huge wings, and without another sound, lifted off the post.

The wings almost touched Tuffy as the owl passed over his head and turned toward the house. It flew as if suspended on a puppeteer's strings, stiffly, silently, in a circle around the house. Sweat formed on Tuffy's face as he watched. His hands trembled on the handlebars.

When the owl was gone, he glanced at his watch. If he hurried, there would be time to get to Rapid City yet that day. He turned the Harley around once more and cracked the throttle. He pulled onto the bench road going thirty-five miles per hour and shifted into fourth gear. When he accelerated, the Harley leapt forward, and the front wheel nearly came off the ground.

▲
FORTY-ONE

Ross was caught up with the work around his place, but Elizabeth was behind with hers. There were three cows yet to calf, and it was hardly worth riding through the cattle every day just for them. They needed to be cut out of the herd and brought back to the barn. Since all the heifers with their calves had been turned out with the older cows, those last three cows needed to be put in the barn, where they'd be easier to watch. The haying equipment would have to be tuned up before long, and there were also fences to fix before the cattle could be turned out in the summer pasture.

Elizabeth ran down the list of chores. With Kyle gone, it was just Elizabeth and Pete. Without help they'd never get caught up before branding time, and so Ross and Stewart agreed to give her a hand for the afternoon.

Pete was throwing tools into the back of a pickup when they arrived, and Stewart volunteered to help him with the fencing. Pete muttered when he heard this but accepted the offer. He knew very well that having Stewart along would save him a lot of walking back and forth along the draws, where the weight of winter snow had broken barbed wire and pushed the steel posts an extra foot into the ground.

"We'll bring those three cows in," Elizabeth said.

Ross nodded and called to Stewart, who was just climbing into the pickup with Pete. "Take these," he said and took a pair of gloves from the dash of his pickup. He tossed them, and they hit Stewart in the chest and dropped into his hands. "You'll need them," Ross said.

Pete revved the engine. "Let's move it," he said out loud. Then mostly to himself, "Goddamned wire will rust away before we get there. Goddamned cows will all die of old age."

Ross followed Elizabeth to the tack room. It was very neat, with four saddles along one wall. A pair of saddle blankets lay over each saddle, and above hung a dozen headstalls, lead ropes, and bridles. On the other wall hung curry combs, lariats, riding slickers, spare reins, and girths. Elizabeth pointed to a saddle. "Might as well use Kyle's," she said. She took her own saddle and blankets from the rack, hefting them on her hip, then removed two bridles. Ross watched her move toward the door as he picked up Kyle's saddle. She had no problem with the load and, once outside, swung the saddle neatly over the hitching rail with a perfect twist of her hip.

Four geldings paced in the corral next to the barn: a sorrel, a gray, a bay, and a black. The bay was a big horse but looked played out. "Pete's been riding him all spring," Elizabeth said. "Take the sorrel; that's Jake."

"I like the black," Ross said. He stretched his hand out, and the shiny black horse moved his nose away but didn't move his feet.

"You would," Elizabeth said. "Everyone likes Dancer. But nobody's ridden him for years." She reached out, and Dancer let her rub his forehead. "He's the horse that fell with John." The other horses were crowding in around them. "I should have gotten rid of him," Elizabeth said. "But I like him." She rubbed his cheek and spoke to the horse. "And you're so damned good looking, aren't you, boy?"

"He is that," Ross said. He took the bridle from Elizabeth and began to slide it over Jake's head but couldn't stop looking at Dancer. The horse stood back, a little shy of the bridles but curious. His eyes were large and round and did not turn from Ross's stare. "Good looking," Ross said in a whisper. "He is that."

It was easy to see where Kyle got his riding ability. Elizabeth rode the gray by the name of Jinx effortlessly. She had a way of pulling one foot from the stirrup and turning so that she was standing in the other stirrup with only her thigh in the saddle. She rode like that and talked to Ross, who rode beside her. She could have been leaning against a barn for all the movement of the horse bothered her. She held the reins in one hand and gestured to the hills and draws with the other as she talked. Even when a meadowlark flew up at Jinx's feet and the horse jumped a couple feet sideways, she did not grab for the saddle horn or lunge for the stirrup. She kept right on telling Ross about the badger that would sit with her below his ridge, and she reached down and patted Jinx's neck with her free hand.

Ross had never known her to talk so much. She talked constantly until they came to a gate into the pasture where the cows were. Even as Ross opened the gate and led Jake through with Elizabeth and Jinx behind, she talked. Mostly it was about the ranch; little things like the weather and all the work that was ahead of them. There was some nervousness in her voice, and Ross knew that one of the reasons for all the small talk was to keep from talking about Kyle, or Sorenson, or about when they had kissed. Once through the gate they split up, looking for ear-tag numbers sixty-five, eighty-two, and ninety-one, and Ross was able to think about their kiss.

It had been sweet and exciting, and at that instant Ross had wanted it very much. But now, as he rode down through a draw filled with white chokecherry blossoms, he felt it was a selfish thing to do. He was sure that Elizabeth had wanted him to kiss her, but he knew that he was the one in control of the situation. He was afraid that he had taken advantage of her loneliness. In a week Linda would be in Denver. They had a lot to straighten out, and that was what he should be thinking about. When compared with Linda, Elizabeth was plain. But why compare the two? It wasn't fair. Ross kicked Jake into a lope as they came out of the draw. There were some cattle on the hillside ahead. Elizabeth had enough problems, he thought. He should be ashamed of himself.

The rest of the cows paid no attention to Ross, but eighty-two raised her head, stopped chewing, and watched him closely as he circled on the uphill side. She had not had her calf. She was big and round with a swollen udder and teats showing no sign of having been sucked. Jake worked down the hill easily and eighty-two's suspicions were confirmed. She raised her head higher and began to shuffle away. By the time she broke from the group, her tail was high, and she trotted for the draw that Ross had just ridden through. That was the right general direction, so Ross and Jake followed her until she got to the trees, then he turned back up the hill, loping for the highest spot to see whether Elizabeth had found the other two cows.

When they reached the top of the hill, Ross could see several bunches of cows and, in the southernmost corner of the pasture, the splash of red and white where a single cow lay just beyond several small hills and nearly out of sight in a patch of snowberry. Elizabeth and Jinx had cut a cow away from one of the bunches. She ran ahead of them the same way eighty-two had run, high at both ends and looking over her shoulder. Ross looked down into the draw to be sure that eighty-two was still there. She was sneaking up the draw, thinking that Ross was the only rider in the pasture and that she might escape. But she was on a collision course with Elizabeth, and so Ross rode down to help drive her cow.

He came down the hill in a slow lope and fell in beside her. The cow ahead of her was number ninety-one. "I got eighty-two in the draw up ahead," he said. "You see sixty-five?"

"She's not back there," Elizabeth answered. She twisted in the saddle and pointed behind.

"There's a cow off by herself to the south," Ross said.

"Maybe," Elizabeth said. "Let's get these two out of this pasture first."

Ross nodded and turned Jake to ride behind Elizabeth. He loped toward the draw and met eighty-two as she tried to slip behind them. She stood still as a mule deer in the brush, but she was much too big and the wrong color to fool anyone. Ross waved his hat at her and pointed Jake into the brush. Eighty-two spun and started out of the draw. When she popped out, she ran into Elizabeth and ninety-one. It was clear that she was caught. She fell in beside the other cow and lined out for the gate and barn beyond.

Ross and Elizabeth took them as far as the gate, closing it behind them so they wouldn't go back with the herd. When they brought sixty-five through, they'd pick up the other two and take them all to the barn at the same time. "Now where'd you see this other cow?" Elizabeth asked.

Ross couldn't help smiling at her as she swung into the saddle. "South," he said. "There's a few little hills. She's in the brush a quarter mile farther south."

"I know the spot," she said. "What are you smiling at?"

Ross shook his head and turned his smile away. "Nothing," he said. He touched Jake's ribs with the spurs, and away they went in a trot. Elizabeth kicked Jinx and came up beside them.

"No," she said. "What's so funny?" Now she was smiling, too.

When Ross looked at her, he almost laughed. "Nothing," he said and urged Jake into a lope. Jinx and Elizabeth went into a lope, too, and soon they were running.

They raced across the flat where the cattle had been fed all winter and toward the cottonwoods along Cherry Cheek. Ross was slightly ahead when they came to one place where the ground began to fall away. He pulled up, ready to stop this nonsense, but Elizabeth shot past him and into the rough country and trees. She was flattened out on Jinx's neck with her spurs against his ribs, the reins loose. "Jesus," Ross said and cracked the ends of his reins down along Jake's shoulder. They caught Elizabeth just as she began to pull Jinx up at the edge of the creek. Ross could hear her laughing as he rushed past at a full gallop.

The air was filled with water spray and the hollow sound of horseshoes against river rock. Ross and Jake were halfway up the other bank in two leaps with Elizabeth and Jinx right behind, but Jake slipped at the top and went down on his knees. Ross stayed in the saddle, but by the time Jake regained his footing, Elizabeth was ahead and running hard for the hills where Ross had seen the cow. She disappeared behind the first hill, and Ross stopped spurring Jake. It was a lost cause.

When he came around the hill at a walk, Elizabeth was already off her horse. She knelt beside a newborn calf that lay curled and motionless in the snowberry brush. The cow, number sixty-five, stood twenty yards away and lowed nervously. The horses and Ross were breathing hard; Elizabeth pretended not to be. She looked at Ross over her shoulder. "Where you been?"

"You're crazy," Ross said.

"You're just a sore loser. Get off that pony and come see my newest calf."

Ross jumped down and stood holding Jake's reins. "Will this nag run away?"

"Of course not," Elizabeth said. "All our horses ground-tie perfectly." She motioned toward Jinx, who stood unattended twenty feet away, chewing at the new grass and trying to catch

263

his breath. Ross shrugged and let the reins drop. He walked up behind Elizabeth and looked down at the calf.

His father had been an Angus. He was colored just like his Hereford mother, except black where she was red. His face was the purest white, his black hair glistened in the warm sun, and he moved nothing. He was no more than twenty-four hours old, and at this stage his only real defense, other than his mother, was an ability to remain absolutely still. Ross knelt down beside Elizabeth and rubbed the calf's head. He did not move. Even his long eyelashes remained motionless. "He's a dandy," Ross said.

Elizabeth nodded. "Guess sixty-five can stay out here," she said.

"Guess so," Ross said. He watched her looking down at the calf. "Listen," he said. "About this morning." Her eyes closed for an instant, then came open again and focused on the calf as she began to stroke its head. "I'm sorry."

"I'm not."

"Look, I'm still married."

"She won't be coming back."

"No. I don't suppose she will."

"Will you be leaving?"

Now it was Ross's turn to look down. "I don't know," he said.

Elizabeth gave the calf one last pet. "Well," she said as she stood up, "I hope not." She turned to the horses, then back to Ross with a puckish grin.

"Now, what's so funny?" Ross said. He followed her glance and saw just the rear ends of the horses as they disappeared around the first hill. Chasing them would be the worst thing. Ross and Elizabeth watched to see whether they would come out from behind the hill on the slope heading toward home. They did, gaining speed, their tails high and their heads held out at funny angles to keep the reins out from under their hooves. They disappeared in the cottonwoods of Cherry Creek and reappeared going up the other side, running flat out.

"Perfectly trained, huh." Ross stood with his arms folded watching the horses run.

Elizabeth was laughing. "They'll be waiting for us at the gate."

"Only because it's shut."

"Come on," Elizabeth said. "Don't be so ornery. You're just mad because now you have to walk me home." Ross refused to look at her. "Don't worry. I won't make you hold my hand if you don't want to."

Finally he cracked. "OK. Let's get going." He began to walk and Elizabeth came up beside him. She slipped her left arm through his right so that her hand rested on his forearm. They walked stiffly for several steps. Then Ross slid his hand down and took Elizabeth's. They did not look at each other, but the fingers intertwined and held.

▲

FORTY-TWO

It was five thirty when Tuffy got to Rapid City. The traffic on the downtown street was bad, but he kept the Harley moving as fast as he could. He had felt sick a half hour before as he came out of the rough country just east of the junction of the Cheyenne River and Rapid Creek, but the cold wind from traveling seventy miles per hour had made him feel better. He was not as frightened as he had been, but there was still a chill at the back of his neck.

He pulled up in front of a brick building on the west side of town. The sign said PHILIP BORDEAUX, ATTORNEY-AT-LAW. Philip was a cousin whom Tuffy had grown up with. He was the smart cousin, the one who did well in school and got a scholarship to college. Tuffy had seen Phil only a few times since he graduated from law school.

There was a parking place between two cars in front of the office, and Tuffy backed the Harley in until its back wheel touched the curb. He was sliding off the cycle and trying to get his wild hair to lie flat when a tall, good-looking Indian in a three-piece suit came out of the building. The man started to lock the door behind him. His hair was long and tied in a pony tail. It was Tuffy's cousin Phil.

Tuffy stepped up behind his cousin and tapped him on the shoulder. Phil turned and stepped back. At first he didn't recognize Tuffy.

"It's me," Tuffy said, "your relation."

"Tuffy?"

"Yeah, Phil. It's me."

Phil's eyes narrowed. "What is it? Are you OK?"

"Yeah, I'm OK. But I need to talk."

The keys were still in the door, and Phil twisted them and pushed the door open. "Sure, Tuffy. Go on in. Take a chair. Relax."

▲

FORTY-THREE

For some people spring is heralded by the return of robins, the bursting of plum blossoms in the draws, or moist, black earth fractured by the power of burgeoning daffodils. For Karen Sorenson it had to do with light. She marked the increase of daylight by the angle of the sun along the interstate as she drove back to Harney from Rapid City. In winter she knew she should be home before she needed headlights, before the reflectors along the shoulder began to snap at the edge of her vision. But a month ago she began to notice the sun lingering in her rearview mirror, and last week it was there full and red until she crossed the Cheyenne River.

Now it was there again as she began her descent into the Cheyenne River bottom, and she was reminded of a song she had liked years before. She watched the sun in the mirror. Cyrcle, she thought. The name of the group who sang the song was Cyrcle. *"I should have known you'd bid me farewell."* Karen did not sing the song. She recited the words and watched the sun as the car began to nose down into the deep, flat river bottom, where it was already dusk. By the time she was far enough down to see the cottonwoods along the interstate, the sun was gone, and she guessed at the time as she tried to remember the words to the song.

She had stayed too late in Rapid City. As the car reached the concrete bridge, Karen felt there was nothing between her and the water of the Cheyenne. The car rocketed out into space. Larry would be waiting for her; it was already after six o'clock. The tires hit the asphalt of the interstate and whined. Still another twenty miles, what was the use? Why had she come back at all? He was so preoccupied with his deals and angles, she wondered whether he would even miss her. The car began the climb out of the river bottom. *"You never cared for secrets I confide."* But he had missed Loni more than Karen imagined was possible, more than he would ever admit.

Karen looked in the rearview mirror for the sun as she came out onto the tableland to the east of the river. A sliver still hung in the corner. *"The morning sun was shining like a red rubber ball."* This was no morning sun; it was the evening sun, and it was staying up longer every day. Summer, Karen thought. And another summer after that, and again and again. The sun pulsed and was gone. It occurred to her that if she kept driving, the sun would be in her eyes in less than twelve hours. She would have to drive past Harney, she thought. A long way past Harney. Drive and drive. She could watch the sun rise in Iowa or Illinois.

FORTY-FOUR

Cleve Miller let Larry Sorenson into the Enchanted Forest through the side door. The Enchanted Forest was closed for the day. It was a good place to have a meeting, but the secrecy and the company made both men nervous.

Sorenson shook his head. "I'm getting nowhere with your neighbors," he said. "I thought this thing was going to be easy, but your Indian friends haven't been exactly cordial. The way that woman came into the bank, with Brady and that other guy, makes the Martinez place look more important."

Cleve held a finger up to stop Sorenson. "What other guy are you talking about?"

"I'm not sure, Cleve, he was an out-of-towner. Acted like an attorney." Cleve brought the finger back and laid it against the side of his mouth. He supported his chin with his thumb. The thought of an attorney bothered him. The fact that he was an outsider was frightening. "But it doesn't matter," Sorenson said. "We will get the woman's place. It's just a matter of when.

"Brady's loan is pretty well paid up." Sorenson was speaking to himself, but he was still watching Cleve, who sat with his hand under his chin. "It's best we work with the Indians first. What is it, Cleve?"

"I was just thinking about this other fellow."

"Stewart Bergman," Sorenson said.

Cleve's face slid down into his hand. The Jew, he thought, and he rubbed his eyes as if he were suddenly very tired. Now it made perfect sense. Now he could see why the woman was holding on, why Tuffy resisted Sorenson. The thought of bankruptcy came clear and cold to Cleve's mind. Did you declare bankruptcy at the courthouse? he wondered. Was there a way to keep it out of the newspaper?

Cleve did not speak. He watched Sorenson. If this deal fell apart, it would be Sorenson's fault. He was so naive. If they were beaten in this, it would be a victory of cunning intrigue over misplaced confidence and childish trust. Cleve made up his mind that instant that no matter what, he would not let that happen.

"Do you know him?" Sorenson asked.

Fool, Cleve thought. "Of course, I know him," Cleve said. He stood up and moved toward the door.

"Cleve, wait," Sorenson said. He came after Cleve. "What is it, Cleve? Wait."

But Cleve did not stop until he was out in the parking lot. Sorenson was right behind him. "Are you all right?" Sorenson asked.

Cleve sat in the driver's seat of his car, the window rolled down. "Yeah, Larry. I'm all right. But I'm wondering about you."

Sorenson stood over him looking down with concern. "We need one more of those ranches," he said. "Are you sure you're all right?"

Cleve smiled an exhausted smile. "We're playing in the big leagues now. You can forget about Brady's place. It belongs to the descendants of Cain."

Sorenson leaned toward Cleve. His hands were on the car door, and now he tried to laugh. "Come on, Cleve, it's not like that."

"Larry, you should read the Bible. The Lord says it plain in John eight forty-four. You've been a pawn for these people for so long that you can't recognize them when they come to your office." Cleve started his car. "I'm not going to let you blow this, Larry. I'm not going to just stand by."

"If you mean the Martinez place," Sorenson said, "I think it's a lost cause."

"I hope not, Larry." Cleve smiled up at Sorenson as if he felt sorry for him. "But we can't be fooled." He patted Sorenson's hand. "We have to stick together."

The car pulled out of the parking lot and passed briefly under a yellow streetlight. Sorenson stood looking after it, thinking that something made the night seem dreamy. The air was silent, peaceful. But the light in the street was a strange color. It had made the white car look odd.

▲

FORTY-FIVE

On the way back from Rapid City, Tuffy stopped at the Dust Buster. By the time he returned to his house, it was dark, and he tried not to look at anything except what was right in front of him. Clyde was meowing to get inside. There was something more than just hunger in the meow, so Tuffy opened the kitchen door slowly. Clyde remained in a crouch, his eyes very dark and his ears pointed forward for maximum effectiveness. When the door was open enough, he slipped in without a sound. Tuffy was drunk. Just like a fucking *ninja,* he thought, and peeked in after the cat.

The pack rat sat on the edge of the sink, hunched up like a squirrel eating a walnut. He was, in fact, eating what was left of a slice of bread. Tuffy cursed himself for leaving the .45 in the bedroom; it would have been an easy shot. But the way it was, with the rat between him and the hallway, the only chance was for Clyde to catch him when he jumped off the counter. But Clyde hadn't shown much stomach for tackling this rat, and seeing the size of it, silhouetted in the moonlight from the window, Tuffy could see why.

Clyde was somewhere in the darkened kitchen, and Tuffy couldn't stand at the door forever. He had taken only two cans of beer with him from the Dust Buster, and they were gone. There were more in the refrigerator, and if he was going to get one, he'd have to frighten the rat off the sink. He took a broom from the porch, just in case the rat came his way, and stepped into the kitchen.

273

The rat didn't leap madly to the floor. He eased down on all fours and watched Tuffy reach for the light switch. But before Tuffy could turn on the light, there was a violent movement, faster than the eye could follow, and the kitchen exploded into a cacophony of growls and high-pitched squeals. Clyde had leapt and snagged the rat from its perch on the sink. They tumbled to the floor as the light came on and rolled in a ball of yellow and brown fur. Tuffy stood above them with the broom at the ready, but there was no way to hit the rat without hitting Clyde.

"Get him, boy!"

They held each other with bared teeth, and Clyde tried to rake the rat's belly with his back claws. But the rat was powerful and fought back with squeals and lightning-fast bites to Clyde's face and neck. Finally the rat twisted away and escaped under the sink. Tuffy had time for one swing of the broom, but Clyde pursued closely as far as the cupboard. He put his face to the hole under the sink and let out a low yowl that rose in pitch, then trailed off to a growl.

"Good boy!" Tuffy said. He was drunk but could feel the rush of adrenaline as strongly as if he had been in the fight himself. "Damn." He knelt down and stroked Clyde's back. The cat was tense and felt wild. "Good boy." Tuffy took Clyde up in his arms and continued to stroke him. "He's gone. You can't get him. Settle down." More stroking and the cat began to purr. "That a boy."

Tuffy opened the refrigerator with his foot and took a six-pack from the first shelf. "Let's go outside and cool off," he said. Now the owl didn't frighten him. It had delivered its message and would not be back. Tuffy had done all he could anyway, and it was very important to him, just then, to be outside.

Clyde lay in his arms until Tuffy sat down on the back steps and then, as if he thought this affection had gone far enough, jumped down and walked toward the barn with his tail in the air. He moved halfway to the Harley-Davidson parked at the end of the walk and sat down to bathe himself. Tuffy popped the top on a can of beer. As was usually the case, it was a clear night. The moon was only about half full, but it lit the Harley and the area between the house and shed like a silvery black and white photo. This, Tuffy thought, was the best part of his life. He drank the first beer without a breath and opened another. He looked at the motorcycle and sipped the second beer.

It was a beautiful bike: wide, old handlebars, chrome pipes and heads, black leather saddlebags. If you didn't count the ranch or Bozo, it was about the nicest thing Tuffy had ever owned. It was a classic, an ageless machine. He tried to think how long he had owned the cycle, and suddenly the years all blended together. Tuffy couldn't even remember what year it was now. He knew the month was April because the moon was in the northeast and the air was chilly and clean, but he had no idea what year it was. The moonlight shone off the chrome and leather of the Harley and made it feel like 1979. Yes, he decided, 1979. Loni would start her last year of college in the fall. But he hadn't seen her since Christmas, when she passed in her Camaro full of college kids home on vacation. He hadn't talked to her for a year, just that long, wide-eyed stare as the Camaro accelerated past Thompson's Café, where Tuffy was leaning against a parking meter. Not a word in over a year, and now a telephone call. She'll be back in Harney for a week. That was all she could stand. But when her visit was over, she wanted to go away with you. You! Yes, you. Tuffy Martinez. Of course, you.

His mother was dead; his father was still alive but fading. It was hard for Tuffy to tell the old man, tottering around the ranch, keeping everything in perfect order, still speaking half-English half-Lakota, that he was going to the big motorcycle rally in Sturgis for five days. The old man shook his gray braids and told Tuffy for the ten thousandth time that this place was all that was important, that it was all Tuffy would ever have. But thinking back, Tuffy knew his father had been wrong. Once long ago he had had Loni Sorenson, if only for five days.

Tuffy emptied the second beer, and he could almost see her there on the back of the Harley. Everything about Loni was long and smooth. Everything was clean and light. She clung to him as they streaked down the interstate highway toward the Black Hills. Her blond hair flew, and her cheek and breasts pressed against his back as the sacred hills rose up ahead of them. Tuffy had been lean and hard then. He was not a drunk. It was the pinnacle of his life.

At every junction more motorcycles joined them, mostly Harleys, but Japanese and German bikes, too. Retired couples from the coasts on monster Electro Glides. Doctors from Atlanta on Gold Wings. A kid from Ohio on a Yamaha. And the loners and gangs from everywhere dressed in leathers with bandannas wrapped around their heads. Their colors flew, and with them came a half-breed Indian cowboy with a woman who made them all stop and stare.

But back then, Tuffy thought, it wasn't exactly a mismatch. His arms were heavy and hard as any of the thirty thousand bikers at Sturgis that year. His hair was black and long, his bare chest broad and strong. Though they had seldom touched before, Loni never let go of his arm as they walked the crowded strip of the tiny town on the northern edge of the Black Hills. She bought leather and chains and high-heeled boots with her father's money and wore halter tops that showed the curve of her breasts and the upturn of her nipples. They set up their tent in the trees at the west end of town, and after that first long, hot day, after they had waited a half hour in line for a two-dollar shower, she took him back to the tent and made love to him.

Tuffy opened another beer and took a swig. He thought about how sweet it was, how surprised he had been. Until then he had suspected that she saw him only as a way to spend five wild days away from her father. He thought that she might simply be using him. He found out later that he was being used, but that there was nothing simple about it. They rode the Harley up into the hills every day, walked the strip in the evening, and made love every night. On the last afternoon, a Saturday—Tuffy remembered it as if it were last week—the skies opened up, and the rain came in sheets. But later the rain tapered off to a gentle patter on the canvas tent, and the moon glowed behind the clouds, like tonight, in the northeast. They lay naked with the tent flap open, watching the rain and the halos around the lights in the town. She held his hand so tight that it ached, but he didn't care.

"You'll never see me again," she said. And Tuffy did not take his eyes off the lights in the rain. What she said was not a surprise. "I'll be going back to college as soon as we get back. My parents think I'm already there." Tuffy nodded; he knew that. She had left her Camaro in a huge parking lot in Rapid City where it could remain anonymous. "They won't see me again either. Something good is going to happen to me, and then I'm getting away from here forever."

"It's not such a bad place," Tuffy said. He had wanted to say more. He had wanted to say how truly beautiful it was, but she already knew what he was thinking.

"It's not the place," she said and turned his face to hers. She kissed him very gently. "And it's really not the men who live here." She looked back to the sky, and they both watched a living cloud pass between them and the moon. "It's what you men do to it." She squeezed the hand even tighter. "You play too rough," she said.

Then she pushed Tuffy's shoulder up so they were face-to-face and kissed him firmly. When she pushed again, he rolled onto his back, and she slid on top of him, squirming like an animal to bite his ear and neck. He could still remember her above him with the moon reflecting from her body and her blond hair falling down over her breasts. When he took her hair in his dark hands, it looked almost white. And when she gazed down on him with the moon in her eyes, it was with a look that he had never seen before, a look he knew he would never see again.

That was the way he remembered her now, and it took his breath away still. Tuffy finished his beer and opened the last one in the six-pack. He drank greedily and looked to the Harley-Davidson at the end of the walk. He was very drunk now and for a moment thought that it was Loni sitting on the seat. But it was Clyde. He was only a dark silhouette, and it was impossible to tell that he was really yellow.

Tuffy's head spun as he stood up. "Come on, Clyde, let's go to bed." The cat looked back but didn't move. "Come on."

Tuffy thought of throwing the beer can at the cat. But it was half-full, and Tuffy wanted to take it to bed with him, too. He picked up an empty and lobbed it over the bike. "Come on."

Clyde meowed sharply and jumped down. Amazingly, he trotted up the walk and through the door that Tuffy held open. Tuffy nodded. "That a boy," he said. "Damned right. Good boy." He felt a sadness coming on. It dulled his senses even more. Had he been more alert he might have taken one last look at the moon, might have seen summer's first bat twist past the pale oval in its frenzy for insects. He might have heard the nighthawk's foghorn voice or the car on the bench road, popping gravel under its tires as it moved steadily as time itself.

▲

FORTY-SIX

Idolatry, according to Paul, is the inordinate desire for the possessions of another. This desire is the nature of the mongrel races. Cleve Miller had learned this from his studies of the *Protocols of the Elders of Zion.* He had read the same thing in the hard-to-find writings of Henry Ford, but he had never before felt those writings to be alive and vital to his existence.

All the things he had read over the years—the pamphlets, the books, the Bible—combined with what he had experienced years before, and the constant nagging of his present financial situation created a physical pressure in his head. He had gone home from the Enchanted Forest with the intention of sleeping on it. There was a chance that it would all seem different in the light of a new day. But by the time he got to his driveway, he was not tired and did not even stop.

Sometimes driving quieted him. Perhaps the moon shining white on the gravel and the hum and vibration of the car would help. He drove past Ross Brady's place and already his mood mellowed. He passed John Kiser's and thought of the old man tended there by the girl. It felt best to let the Ford cruise slowly over the gravel. It followed the curves in the road as if it were alive.

As he passed Tuffy's driveway, Cleve thought of gold, wondered what it would look like if he could see it lying in the ground as it was at that very moment. When he came to the reservation line, he pulled over and let the car make a slow turn in the road. It came cleanly around and began to creep back along the bench road.

The driving helped. Cleve was calmer now. He told himself it would work out. He would talk to Tuffy, make a deal for his ranch, and it would all come together unless Sorenson had already fouled it up. He should never have trusted Sorenson to deal with Indians. Sorenson didn't understand how they thought.

Tuffy's mailbox appeared in his headlights, and Cleve pulled the Ford over and parked near where the driveway joined the road. He turned off the lights and the engine, rolled the window down, and breathed in the cool air. But there was still a knot in his chest. Deep inside he was sure that Stewart Bergman had figured it all out and had already gotten to Tuffy. If so, he'd never listen to reason. The engine ticked away the cylinder heat, and Cleve thought that this must be what it was like to be a wild animal lying dumb in the night, waiting.

But Cleve Miller was not an animal. He was a man with consciousness and responsibility. Nights like this were useful only for their beauty. He had always thought they calmed him, but as the ticking died away and silence folded over him, he felt a different sort of tension swell inside him. It was as if an otherwise undetected breeze were moving the hair at the back of his neck.

▲
FORTY-SEVEN

It was a drunkard's dream of all the land, the buttes, rolling hills, grass, cattle, birds, and trees twisting in a whirlpool that sucked all of it downward. And in the middle, placid except for the long, blond hair swirling behind, was the face of Loni Sorenson. Tuffy was sweating; the sheets constricted his legs like giant snakes. He was terrified but still tried not to awake. He didn't want the image of Loni to leave him. But finally the twisting and the sound of the earth being sucked away became too much, and he opened his eyes.

He did not jump or call out. He opened his eyes only to see a ceiling that he knew too well. But at first it didn't seem familiar, and he lay frozen in his bed, waiting for the headache to come and the ceiling to tell him where he was. Finally the fear that pressed on his chest began to slip away. The headache didn't come. It was too soon. He realized that he had been in bed only a short time, that he was still drunk. He rolled on his side to reach for the beer can that might hold one more swallow, but his hand stopped dead in the stale air of his bedroom.

The blue glow from the electric space heater spilled out onto the floor in front of the dresser. Something cast a black shadow through the blueness, and Tuffy blinked his eyes to make them focus. It could have been a wad of clothing or a boot, but as Tuffy squinted into the darkness, the shape moved. It put a foot down, took two steps, then sat back up and looked directly at Tuffy. It was the same way the pack rat had looked at him from the sink, and Tuffy continued his reach, but past the beer can. Gently he took the .45 from the bed stand and moved it at the end of a straight arm so he could see fur over the iron sights.

The sound of the .45 in the bedroom was much louder than Tuffy expected, and the concussion jolted him upright in the bed. The blue floor in front of the space heater was a tangle of fur and blood. A demonic growl and hiss filled the room, and Tuffy tore the covers away to get to the light switch.

The blue glow disappeared as the overhead light came on, and the movement and sounds faded to a quiver and moan. Tuffy, naked except for his underwear, stepped forward with the .45 still in his hand. He held it out, the pistol already cocked and ready to explode again. But when Tuffy's eyes adjusted to the new light, the .45 came down and he eased the hammer to safe. On the floor in front of him, head blown partially away, was Clyde.

Tuffy stared down at him for a long time before he sat on the bed. His arms dangled between his legs, and the .45 slipped onto the floor. He wanted to cry, wanted to bellow out his hate and frustration to the walls of his dingy room. But he wasn't sure any of it mattered. And if it did, this was not the place to cry. He pulled on a pair of pants and a T-shirt. He found his boots in the kitchen and squeezed his feet into them without socks. He took the .45 and Clyde's body with him as he left the bedroom. He carried the .45 as far as the porch. Only when he saw his saddlebags hanging on a peg did he remember the pistol was in his hand; he slipped it into the saddlebags.

The moon had not moved far. It was above the shed now, heading for its exit on the western horizon. Tuffy held his head up and let the moon see that now there were tears on his cheeks. Clyde lay in his arms bathed in the moonlight. It was cool but Tuffy still felt flushed. He walked down the driveway, past the Harley to the shed, where he found a shovel. He dug a shallow hole near the gas pump, laid Clyde in it, covered the body, and held his hands firmly on the freshly turned earth. Then he returned to the Harley.

For the first time that Tuffy could remember, it started on the first kick. The air was dead calm, and the hollow, slow popping of the two cylinders seemed to linger in the air, waiting for the next pop to send the first on its way. It took only a touch of the throttle to change the popping to a cracking sound. Tuffy tried it several times before he let it idle again and shifted into first.

The cool night air barely penetrated the numbness of Tuffy's skin. But there was nothing else to do. The Harley's headlight beamed ahead, the motorcycle crawled up the driveway, and Tuffy wondered what he would do. He did not see the car parked near his mailbox until after he had turned onto the bench road. Then the headlights came on behind him, and an engine roared. The sound and lights frightened him; he had shifted into third and accelerated before he had time to look over his shoulder.

Cleve had not been thinking of anything when the single headlight came up the driveway. Nothing had come into his mind until Tuffy pulled onto the road ahead of him. Cleve switched on the headlights and saw Tuffy jerk around. His face was startled in the light. It was the fear in Tuffy's face that made Cleve come to life. He started the car as a reaction to what he saw in Tuffy's face. The motorcycle and Indian looked helpless in the headlights, and when Tuffy accelerated, Cleve did, too.

The lights were too bright. Looking over his shoulder, Tuffy could not see beyond them. He gathered speed as he took the gradual turn where the road crossed the beginning of Cherry Creek. The gravel felt mushy under Tuffy's rear tire, and even if he had wanted to turn into Elizabeth's driveway, it would have been impossible. The road was straight there, and Tuffy opened up the throttle. The Harley fishtailed, and for an instant Tuffy thought he might lose control. But he came out of it and roared forward. The Ford could not accelerate like the Harley, but it pulled up easily at the slightest curve in the road.

Tuffy had to take the curves carefully, and when he did, the bright headlights seemed hot on the back of his head. He put his right foot out to help keep the bike upright, and the gravel flew. He could hear it hitting the front of the car, and he accelerated the instant it was safe. Not knowing who was back there in the darkness terrified him, and he twisted the accelerator all the way. A crazy thought came to him: if he could make it to Ross's house, he would be safe. It made no real sense, but there was comfort in the idea, and Tuffy began to believe it could work.

Then it was as if things slowed down. He knew he was rocketing down the road, but the fear diminished. It was as if someone else were steering the motorcycle and Tuffy were watching from above. He felt the wind in his face and the pressure at his wrist from holding the throttle open, but he wasn't really on the motorcycle. There was the sense that he would get away. But watching from above, he knew the Harley was going way too fast when he hit the loose gravel just past the missile silo. He saw the front wheel dig in and twist, then felt the weight from behind begin to swing around, and finally heard the rear wheel begin spraying gravel toward the ditch. For an instant he thought it would straighten out. But the headlights were on him again, and he saw his shadow cast on the Millers' sign. He was still going fifty miles per hour, and when he turned the handlebars, the wheel over-corrected, the rear wheel snapped back, and everything came off the ground.

He flew through the air with the sound of the Harley roaring and crumpling below him. For a while he was in the cone of light from the car, but then he was in the dark, and it didn't seem so bad. He floated, disoriented and oddly peaceful, until he hit one of the solid posts that held the sign, and everything went red.

He gasped for air and coughed the taste of blood. The world was pain and pressure. Finally the lungs filled with air again, and the panic subsided. One leg would move, then his lips and his eyes. He could feel the eyes blinking and knew that what could have been a woman's soft hair in his face was grass. Buffalo grass, he thought; gentle, tender buffalo grass. He could smell the spring shoots against his cheek. Then there was the swish of grass against pants' legs and boots, the white spot of a flashlight against his face.

The light moved up and down his body, evaluating the injuries. Now he could see it was Cleve, and a giddy joy came over him. He tried to talk, but the sounds would not form words. He moved his lips and felt the light on his face again. His eyes blinked, and he moved enough to look at Cleve. But the light was too bright to allow him to see, and when it flipped off, the night was dark enough to bring the panic back. His eyes continued to blink, but the flashlight beam was gone. He heard the swish of grass against boots again, And then the sound of the car's engine. At the road Tuffy saw the red taillights of the Ford. They hung on his horizon like radio towers in the distance. Then they began to move, slowly, accompanied by the sound of tires against gravel. The lights turned into the Millers' driveway and became smaller and smaller until the night went completely black.

▲

PART SIX

▲

FORTY-EIGHT

It was a damned poor time to kill yourself, Pete Rienrick thought. Getting drunk and driving a motorcycle off the road at sixty miles an hour was a goddamned stupid thing to do. Pete bumped through Red Willow Creek on the iron seat of Cleve Miller's backhoe. Cleve sat on the fender beside him holding a beer in his hand. It was the third beer he'd drunk since he picked Pete up at Elizabeth's mailbox. That was the first beer Pete had seen Cleve drink in years. He hoped Cleve wouldn't get drunk. It was getting dark, and this was a job they needed to get done.

On the other side of the creek, where they started up toward the burying hill, there was a washout, and they had to double back for a few hundred feet to get across it. That put them just fifty yards behind Tuffy's house. It looked different from that angle. Pete could see that the white paint was holding up better on that side. No sun, he thought. He was looking at the house from directly across Red Willow Creek, and there were a few cottonwoods and some ash trees growing on the slope. They served as a windbreak and shade for the house. Tuffy's house looked strange from that angle, and Pete tried to remember whether he had ever seen it from there before. He'd been on the place lots of times, lots of times when Tuffy was just a kid and his parents were still alive. But he couldn't remember ever seeing the house from that side.

Cleve had jumped down to open a gate and was talking about something as he pushed on the gatepost. But Pete's attention was fixed on the house. Cleve crawled back up on the fender and peeled the top off a new beer from the six-pack between his feet. Tuffy's killing himself had Cleve stirred up, Pete thought. He popped the clutch, and the backhoe bucked through the gate and started up to the burying hill. They took it easy, but still the rear bucket bounced heavy and hard as they crossed the roughest part of the pasture. The light was dull because the sun was behind a cloud bank that hung in the west. They should have started the job a couple hours earlier.

Pete had heard about the fence they had put up around old man Martinez and his wife. It didn't look bad, though Pete had liked it better the way it was before; just a couple head-stones on a hill. He understood, of course. Cattle had rubbed the stones over several times. He imagined that Tuffy had hated resetting them. Maybe he had worried that there would be no one to set his stone back upright. The fence made sense, made it more like a proper bone yard. Cleve got off to take a fence panel down. He took his beer with him, and Pete backed the machine up to the fence.

The burying was the next day, and the sun was already getting low. If they didn't get the hole dug, if the backhoe broke down, and it might, they'd have a mess on their hands. "Tough to bury someone without a hole," Pete said out loud.

"What?" Cleve yelled over the backhoe's engine.

"Nothing," Pete yelled back. He imagined people following a long, black hearse out from town, gathering around the wrought-iron fence, and all of them peering over to find there was no hole. He imagined himself and Cleve, both in greasy coveralls, lying under the backhoe, working on the transfer case, while all the people stood dressed in their Sunday best with their heads bowed to the cold north wind and the coffin just dumped out on the ground because the hearse had another burying to get to.

"Hey," Cleve said, "hand me a pair of pliers out of that toolbox. I can't get the goddamned pin out."

Pete dug into the toolbox. "And hand me a beer," Cleve said. "Take one yourself." Pete handed the pliers to Cleve. He took two beers from the paper bag beside the toolbox.

"Let's get this over with," Cleve said.

He went back to work on the fence, and when Pete looked around, John Kiser was sitting on the fender. "Should have started this job earlier," John said.

"Yeah, I know it, but there's a lot to do this time of year: feed cattle, fix fence, get ready to brand the calves, haying equipment to get ready. You checked out. No more work for you. Easy to say a man should have done this, should have done that, should have gotten started sooner. You're right; going to take hours. Tuffy would have wanted this hole at least six feet."

"You bet your ass and all its fixtures." Pete spun to his left. Tuffy sat on the other fender.

"Swell," Pete said. "Meeting of the Retired Cowboys Club."

"Who the hell you talking to? Back that son of a bitch up." Cleve had swung one of the fence panels away and stood waving Pete through. "Watch out you don't run over Mrs. Martinez."

Pete backed into the graveyard and jockeyed a couple times to get lined up right. The sun was nearing the horizon, casting a yellow light under the clouds. It gave the short spring grass an illusion of height. "Beats being buried alongside a bunch of strangers," Tuffy said.

"Leave me alone. I'm trying to dig you a hole." Pete lowered the hydraulic feet, and the rear tires came off the ground. Cleve was standing in front of the backhoe, drinking his beer and motioning toward the space alongside Mrs. Martinez.

"Dig her right in here," Cleve said.

"No shit," Pete mumbled as he situated himself in front of the controls.

"A man falls in love with a country," Tuffy said. "Dying is kind of like a divorce."

John laughed. "It's the land that does the choosing. And there's no such thing as divorce. Separation maybe, but never divorce."

"Leave me alone," Pete said.

"Relax," Tuffy said. "Just take a look out there. Ain't it about the best view you ever saw?"

Pete had to look. The yellow light spread under the clouds and lit the Badland buttes to the east. They were purple. Far in the distance Pete could see someone's cattle. They were black whiteface, and there was a calf alongside each one.

"What the fuck are you looking at?" Cleve yelled.

"Just lookin'. Is there a goddamned law against it?" Pete dropped the front bucket hard, and the machine became stable. He touched one of the boom levers, and the heavy iron hoe clanked out over the area Cleve had indicated. It had been a long time since Pete had run a backhoe, and by rights Cleve should have done it. But Cleve was half-drunk, and even with his bad arm Pete had always been good at running dirt-moving machines. He played with the controls a little to get the feel back. The hoe moved back and forth in jerks. When he felt comfortable, he leaned over and set the throttle for more RPMs. "Not too fast," Tuffy said. He was sitting on one rear tire, and John was on the other. "I want this hole straight and deep."

"This is going to be a hole, not a fucking piano," Pete said. "I ain't retired. I got more work to do than I can get done."

"Take it easy," John said. "Don't let life pass you by." John and Tuffy laughed.

"Sure, you guys can say that. You got nothing to do but torment people. I got a ranch to run. Me and Elizabeth. The kid's gone, you know. Who the hell's going to brand them calves? Think me and Elizabeth can rope, brand, vaccinate, castrate, and hold them down all at once? We're going to need some help."

"Maybe I'll help," John said. "I'd like roping a few calves."

"What are you waiting for?" Cleve had crawled up onto the backhoe and stood behind Pete. His eyes were wild. Tuffy and John were gone. "It's getting dark," Cleve said.

"Right," Pete said. "Happens every shittin' day about this time." He forced one of the levers forward, and the heavy hoe, with its broken, case-hardened teeth, began to bash a hole through the tough prairie sod and into the warm earth below.

▲

FORTY-NINE

They were not able to find Kyle. He had ridden in Billings the week before, but no one knew which way he and Delbert went from there. He'd been in the money at Billings and could be a long way from the Badlands of South Dakota. He probably couldn't have made it back in time for the funeral anyway.

Tracy, Louis, and the kids got to Elizabeth's about noon. The funeral was at two o'clock, and they were all dressed up. The baby was crying and needed changing when Tracy brought her in. The boys had obviously been told not to ruin their good clothes and sat quietly on the living-room couch. Louis searched the cupboard for a bottle of whiskey.

After the baby was changed, Tracy went with Elizabeth into her bedroom. "It really is a shame," she said as Elizabeth pulled on a dress and braided her hair.

"He was a good friend," Elizabeth said.

"Yeah. Of course, we all knew he'd end up doing something like this." Elizabeth didn't speak. She was tying yellow ribbons in her braids. "You can't carry on like that and not expect it to catch up with you."

"Well," Elizabeth said, "he's dead now. There's no sense making it worse than it is."

"I feel bad. Yesterday was terrible for me. I spent all day thinking back on all those times in school."

"Tuffy wouldn't want to ruin your day." Elizabeth didn't want to talk about this with Tracy and was thankful when she heard a pickup in the driveway. She finished with the last bow, brushed on a tiny bit of makeup, and looked at herself in the mirror. She could see Tracy watching her from behind. "That's Ross," Elizabeth said as she turned toward the bedroom door. "I'm going to ride with him." She walked past Tracy, who followed closely.

"I thought we'd go over together. Like a family," Tracy said. Elizabeth stopped just outside the front door. The boys had already run out and were climbing in the pickup with Ross and Stewart.

"I told the boys to ride with Ross," Louis said as he moved past Elizabeth. Ross was watching her from the pickup. "Pete's going to stay with John. You come on and ride with us." Elizabeth smiled weakly at Ross and he smiled back. "We can use the help with the baby."

There were eight or ten vehicles at Tuffy's place, and most of them still had people sitting in them. Ross recognized the Millers' pickup and a couple from the reservation. Ruth Albertson sat in her old Buick. Ross had never seen it anywhere but parked behind the Dust Buster. A small group of Indians stood around a dented Ford Fairlane. An uncle from Oglala had seen to the arrangements. He was a very old man and stood in the center of the group around the Fairlane. Ross recognized Santee among the men.

They had been parked only a few minutes when the hearse rolled to a stop in the center of the cars. Tuffy's uncle walked stiffly to the driver's side and talked briefly to the driver. Then the old man returned to the Fairlane and got in on the passenger's side. One of the other men drove, and they led the hearse out into the pasture.

The whole procession wound its way through the bottom of Red Willow Creek and up the other side. One of the cars spun on the new grass, and the passengers got out and rode the rest of the way in the back of one of the pickups. The vehicles parked at the bottom of the hill, and the people followed the pallbearers up on foot. Twice someone stepped in to help the pallbearers as they struggled under the load. Finally they made it to the top and laid the casket beside the grave.

Cleve Miller crawled onto the seat of the backhoe, which was pulled back away from the graves but ready to fill the hole. He looked exhausted. He hadn't shaved, and his eyes were set deep and ringed with dark skin. The rest of the mourners stood outside the fence. Elizabeth was closest to the fence and watched the medicine man approach the casket. He spoke in Lakota and began by asking the winds to come and help them pray. Elizabeth felt Ross move up beside her as the medicine man said Mother Earth was taking Tuffy back. That made Elizabeth feel better. She glanced at Ross and caught him watching her.

When the medicine man finished, the pallbearers placed the casket on four ropes stretched across the grave and lowered Tuffy into the earth. The people began to move, some going to the grave to toss in a handful of dirt but most simply wandering down the hill to their vehicles. Ross and Elizabeth walked together. "How you doing?" Ross asked.

"OK. How about you?"

"OK."

Louis, Tracy, and the kids waited for them. Stewart leaned against the pickup. "You leave for Denver tomorrow," Elizabeth said. Ross nodded. A tall, well-dressed Indian was approaching them. "Will you come to see me tonight?" she asked.

The Indian was very close, but Ross did not take his eyes off Elizabeth. He nodded again. "Yes," he said. The tall Indian was right beside them.

"Excuse me," he said. "Are you Ross Brady?"

"Yes."

"If you have a moment, I'd like to speak with you." The

Indian stretched out his hand. "I'm a cousin of Tuffy's. Phil Bordeaux."

They walked away from the rest, toward Bordeaux's car, which was parked off by itself. "Guess you were a pretty good friend of Tuffy's," Bordeaux said.

"Yeah, we were good friends. We spent a lot of time together the last few years."

"He knew he was going to die, Mr. Brady." They had reached Bordeaux's car. "He thought a lot of you. From what he told me, he thought more of you than about anyone on earth."

Ross didn't know what Bordeaux was getting at. He watched him lean into his car and take a document from a briefcase. "He had me make up a will. The Catholic church lost this time. He left the whole place to you."

Ross did not look at the document that Bordeaux pushed his way. He looked at Bordeaux. "What do you mean?"

"It's here in this copy. I've got the original at my office. He gave the ranch to you. He didn't tell me exactly why."

Ross took the copy but didn't look at it. Bordeaux had moved around and was getting into his car. Most of the other vehicles had already left, and Bordeaux started his engine, took the brake off, and put the transmission in drive. "There will be some details," he said. "But no real hurry. My office is in the Rapid City phone book."

Ross watched him drive after the other cars. Still without looking, he folded the document and slid it into his coat pocket. He could hear that Cleve had started the backhoe. When he turned, only his pickup was left. Stewart leaned against it, and Tracy and Louis's boys sat in the cab. Behind the pickup at the top of the hill the backhoe's iron arm pushed dirt into Tuffy's grave.

When they got to the house, the people from the reservation were setting up tables to feed anyone who was hungry. The old uncle and a couple of helpers were bringing Tuffy's possessions from the house and sheds for the traditional give-away. Ross, Elizabeth, and Stewart stood together in the short line for soup and homemade bread. The rest of the people talked and joked in hushed tones. The uncle circulated, giving pots and pans to old women and boots and clothes to the men. Ross had just finished his soup and was ready to leave when the old man came to him with Tuffy's saddlebags. He said nothing. He only held the saddlebags out to Ross.

"Take them," Elizabeth said softly.

The old man nodded and said, "Thank you." Then he was off to pass out the tools from Tuffy's shop.

The saddlebags seemed heavy to Ross, and when he looked, he saw the .45 was inside. He closed the flap quickly, but not before Elizabeth had seen the pistol. She watched his expression, and when she saw his jaw muscles tighten, she moved close enough to touch his arm without anyone seeing.

▲
FIFTY

When they got home, Ross asked Stewart to come with him to Denver, but Stewart wanted to stay and take care of the cattle. "Pete Rienrick said he'd do the chores," Ross said. "You don't have to stay."

"I want to."

"Linda thinks you're coming with me."

"Eight hours is too long a drive for me. When I leave here, I'm flying."

They were just finishing up the chores, throwing hay to the only heifer left to calve. It was a warm April evening with only enough clouds in the west to make the sunset interesting. To the east the moon was rising brightly. "If I went to Denver with you, I'd have to go back to LA from there. I'm not quite ready."

"Haven't had enough of summer camp yet?"

"If you had to go back to LA and spend two months going around to all your old customers convincing them that the system and company you sold them last year is not as good as the new system and company that you're working for, summer camp would sound good to you, too."

Ross pitched a forkful of hay to the heifer. "Maybe," he said. "But the Caribbean sounds more like camp to me."

"Club Med? Jesus."

"Well, OK. If you want to watch things, that's great, but I'll be leaving in the morning. Be gone three days. If you change your mind, we can always call Pete."

They walked to the house, and Stewart started to cook while Ross took a shower. When Ross reappeared, he had changed his clothes and combed his hair back. Stewart was just bringing the macaroni and cheese to the table. He caught the scent of Ross's aftershave. "You must be heading for town," he said.

"I thought I'd go over to Elizabeth's and see how she's doing." Stewart nodded his head but said nothing. He put the macaroni on the table and went for dishes and silverware while Ross pulled on his boots.

"Now, where are you guys going to be in Denver?" Stewart asked.

"The Brown Palace," Ross said. "The rest of the dancers are staying somewhere else, but Linda thought the Brown Palace would be nice."

"Very nice. Classy. Big time in the big city."

"Country mouse comes to town."

"Country mouse. Right, Ross. I can't say this in LA. It might be taken wrong. But you can go both ways. You know that."

"Let's hope so. If I use the wrong fork, your sister will send me home."

"I don't think so." Stewart shook his head. "Hey, what's the deal? You don't like my cooking?" He pointed to Ross's plate.

"No, it's great. Really. It's the kind of meal I like." He picked up his fork. "Only one fork. No chance to screw up."

But Ross still had not finished his macaroni by the time Stewart went to watch the news. It was Ross's turn to clean up, and he cleared the dishes as soon as Stewart was gone. It was just the two plates and silverware. He washed them quickly and put them in the rack to dry. The television crackled in the other room, and Ross considered asking Stewart whether he wanted to come along to Elizabeth's. But when he poked his head into the living room, it was only to tell Stewart he was leaving.

The night had stayed warm, and the moon was huge. Ross drove slowly with the window down. When he had returned home from the funeral, he hung the saddlebags in the tack room and read through the copy of Tuffy's will. It was very simple: there was a preface in legal jargon and then a statement giving the ranch to Ross. It was only a page and a half long, but its meaning was clear. Ross now had two ranches, and he was not sure he wanted even one. Tuffy's, at least, had no big loan against it. Maybe the two of them together would be worth enough to give him a good start someplace else.

There was an extra truck parked in front of Elizabeth's house. It cast a long shadow from the moonlight, and Ross did not recognize it at first. But when he got closer, he saw that it was Tracy and Louis's. Ross felt a surge of disappointment. He glanced at his watch. It was almost eight o'clock. They should have been on their way home by now. He stopped his pickup beside Louis's and sat looking at the house. He saw the two boys run past a window, and then a light spilled out into the yard from the side door. The light disappeared, but Ross could make out Elizabeth coming toward him. She moved quickly and carried something in her arms. When she was closer, he could see that she held a star quilt.

Then she was beside the pickup. The moon colored her face a rich brown; her braids were tied with the red ribbons she had chosen for Ross's visit. She and Ross looked at each other through Ross's window for several seconds before Ross moved. He stepped out and shut the door quickly to extinguish the pickup's overhead light. They stood in the dark for another moment. When Ross leaned to kiss her, Elizabeth met him tentatively, but a tiny sigh escaped into the night.

They held each other until a dizziness forced them to open their eyes. "Come on," Elizabeth said. "I know a place."

She took his hand and led him away from the buildings toward the cottonwoods of Cherry Creek. The giant trees loomed above them, silvered by the moonlight, and they moved beneath them like shadows. They veered to their left, through the smaller ash trees and into the bottom of Cherry Creek. The moon's reflection shattered into a thousand pieces of gold as they crossed the shallow water. They stopped on the opposite bank to watch the water flatten and the pale disk reappear, shimmering, as if they had never disturbed it.

Ross lifted the top wire of the fence to the bull pasture and pushed the middle wire down with his boot to let Elizabeth slip through. She held the star quilt tightly, as if it were a baby, and they moved toward the large, flat rock that stood brilliantly white at the center of the pasture. They laughed quietly as they climbed, but once Elizabeth spread the quilt over the soft, thick buffalo grass that grew in the hidden pocket of earth on top of the rock, they sat silently and let the night come in close against them.

There was no wind. Badger's Ridge stretched across the northern horizon, but the moon had taken away their ability to judge distance, and the ridge seemed miles off. There were stars, and a satellite moved at the edge of the horizon. When Elizabeth turned to Ross, she found him staring at her. He took her face in his hands and kissed her gently. She returned his kiss and they pressed together. Then Elizabeth relaxed and let Ross lower her until she felt the star quilt against her back. He kissed her neck and shoulders, then pulled back far enough to see her eyes. There was no fear, just deep, dark Lakota eyes reflecting the moon and moist, full lips, parted in an expression of wonder.

They watched each other as Ross unbuttoned her blouse and his own shirt. When he fumbled with the bra snap, Elizabeth sat up and unfastened it herself. Seeing her smooth, brown skin and dark nipples made Ross quiver. Elizabeth sat unashamed with her hands folded in her lap and her eyes still wide. Her black braids fell across her breasts, and she reached out to Ross, pulled him in, and held him there like a child.

He awoke once during the night, when the moon was straight above them, and found her awake. She stroked his hair. "Sleep," she said. "Sleep." And something in the way she said it gave him no choice. He tightened his grip on her, snuggled deeper into the star quilt, and savored the cool prairie air that dried the moisture from his skin.

Then it was dawn, and they could hear the sound of meadowlarks in the grass and robins in the draw. They were wrapped in the quilt, and there was just enough light to see that the colors around them were deep greens and blues. It was cool, and Ross could feel Elizabeth move against him for warmth. He moved, too, and pressed her closer still, along the length of his body. He watched the light growing in the east, and just as the sun pulsed for the first time above the distant buttes, he felt Elizabeth's tears on his chest.

He raised her chin and saw that she was smiling. But still he shook his head. "No," he said and kissed at the tears.

She laughed. "It's not that I'm sad," she said. "It's just that it's a big day for me. A day every little girl thinks about." Ross rolled up on one elbow and questioned her with a look. "It was lovely," Elizabeth said. She turned away shyly for the first time in days. "It's really my first time."

"Come on," Ross said and gave her shoulder a gentle shove. But she didn't look up at him. "Come on."

This time when he turned her face, her chin quivered. She sunk her face into his chest and sobbed. Ross was surprised, but he wrapped his arms around her, and they began to rock.

"You're the first to love me," she whispered. "The time before was more like hate." She shivered as she remembered it and bit her lip to keep the memory inside. But when Ross stroked her hair, it erupted from deep in her chest. Ross was the person who should know. He was someone to depend on. "He was so drunk he's never even remembered. I was just a girl, and he pushed me down in the straw of my parents' barn."

"Kyle's father?"

Elizabeth's cheek was still against Ross's chest. He rocked her, wanting her to know it was all right to talk. She nodded. "Yes. No one knows, but it was Louis. Before they were married. He'd come looking for Tracy and found me collecting eggs in the barn."

Ross continued to hold her. "And you've never told anyone?"

"Only you. It would only hurt people."

Ross pulled the quilt up over her shoulder and kissed her forehead. "Thank you," he said.

He looked out over the prairie. The sun shone on the underside of the low, flat clouds and turned them orange and red. "Look at the sun," Ross said. She looked out from between the quilt and Ross's chest. She kept her eyes on the sun but turned her face enough to kiss Ross's collarbone.

"And there," she said, raising slightly and pointing. "Badger."

They looked at Badger's Ridge and saw the husky black and gray animal standing on his hind legs, watching them seriously. The ridge was much closer than it had seemed in the moonlight, and they could see the dark hair above his eyes and the shiny black of his nose. He seemed to squint in their direction. Then, satisfied with what he saw, he lowered himself to all fours and hustled off to the other side of the ridge.

▲

FIFTY-ONE

Since Larry Sorenson found out about Tuffy Martinez's death, he had been busy. His greatest fear was that the ranch would go into some protracted probate and force them simply to forget about it. He did not want to have to deal with Ross Brady, but after a few phone calls, he realized that Tuffy's place now belonged to Ross. He now owned half the bench. It was time to bring him in on the deal. Sorenson had tried to explain that to Cleve on the phone but had not been able to get him to understand. Cleve acted strangely, distant and untypically cynical. But it was not until Cleve came into Sorenson's office that Sorenson realized something was wrong with him.

Cleve's eyes seemed more deeply set in his skull. His big back was hunched, turning him inward and making him look as if he were in pain. He wore a sports jacket that Sorenson had never seen before. It was buttoned in the front and fit him poorly. When Sorenson told him that he thought Ross Brady should be approached, Cleve spoke flatly. "He's already on the other side," he said. "To salvage anything we have to move on the girl."

"He might come around," Sorenson said. Cleve shook his head, but Sorenson went on. "You're right, of course," he said. "We were much better off before that accident."

Cleve glared at him, and Sorenson looked at the sunken eyes. "Are you all right?"

"I'm fine, Larry. I know exactly what I'm about. I'm going

to see that this deal goes through, and that makes me fine. How about you? Are you all right?"

Sorenson nodded. "Yes, I'm all right."

"Then you better get moving on that Indian girl." Cleve was standing now and turned to look out the window.

He was out of line, pushing like that, and Sorenson was annoyed. "We will do everything we can," he said.

Cleve turned from the window and looked down at Sorenson sitting at his desk. He seemed to have calmed himself; his face looked nearly normal. "I sure agree with you, Larry. We have to do everything we can." He unbuttoned his coat and revealed the handle of a pistol tucked into an ancient shoulder holster. "Everything."

The sight of the pistol startled Sorenson, and he slid back in his chair. He sat at arm's length from his desk and stared at Cleve. He stammered and finally spoke. "Have you lost your mind, Cleve? That's not necessary."

The ill-fitting coat was rebuttoned. Cleve looked only a little tired and spoke in his usual, even tone. "In a situation like this," he said, "it's hard to tell what is necessary." He sat down calmly across from Sorenson. "Now let's get some papers drawn up on the Kiser place. It's time we finished this thing."

▲
FIFTY-TWO

The area along a stream where trees grow is called riparian habitat. Most people don't think much about riparian habitat, but in the grasslands it is the foundation for all life. Think of the ribbons of trees and brush that branch out as you move up a water shed as arteries connected directly to the heart of the land. Riparian areas are the home of deer, grouse, a hundred kinds of songbirds, coyotes, badgers, and almost everything else. They hide in the draws, have their young there, feed there, and find shelter there from winter storms. Without the draws and river courses nothing could live on the prairie. Everything ends up in the draws: the wildlife, the humans, even gold washes into and collects in the draws.

Ross Brady knew all of that, and it came instantly to mind when Larry Sorenson told him who was interested in the ranches along the bench. He had received a call from Sorenson just as he was leaving for Denver. The banker made it sound important, so he drove through Harney instead of going south to Milo. Sorenson already knew that Tuffy had left his ranch to Ross. It only took a moment for Ross to figure out that this was why Sorenson was being so nice.

"I think we could offer you a fair price for both places. Of course, this is confidential. We wouldn't want everyone in the country to find out yet." Sorenson raised an eyebrow and smiled at Ross as if they were old friends.

"You think there really is gold out there?"

"There is reason to suspect there is. It would certainly be a boon to the area if there was."

"And how would they get it out?"

Sorenson shrugged. "I really don't know. Bulldozers, I suppose."

"For jewelry." Ross spoke more to himself than to Sorenson.

"Excuse me?"

"Never mind."

"Yes," Sorenson tapped a finger on his desk. "It would be a nifty way for you to take care of your debt to this bank," he said. "There is a tremendous opportunity here, and we're going to be moving on it very soon."

Ross stood up. "I can see the opportunity," he said. "But right now I'm on my way to Denver."

"Denver?" Sorenson said. "How nice. And when will you be back?"

"A few days."

"That will be fine. There should be some further development by then." He thrust out his hand. "Give it some serious thought."

Ross took the hand, but as soon as he turned away, he did his best not to think about what Sorenson had said. What he said was important; but Ross could think about only so many important things at a time.

It's nearly four hundred miles from the Badlands of South Dakota to Denver. The drive takes over seven hours, and most of that time is spent on two-lane highways winding down through Nebraska and Wyoming. It's a long, lonely drive. Sometimes an hour will pass without seeing another car. But Denver is still the closest real city to the small ranches along the bench.

The people of the Badlands watch Denver television stations; they root for the Broncos and the Nuggets. Without meaning to, they keep up on the mayoral races and the debate over a city convention center. They know that Colfax Avenue is where the hookers and drug dealers hang out. They know that the Capitol Hill area harbors a rapist and that the Museum of Natural History has a good collection of Egyptian artifacts in the basement. Not everyone from the Badlands is interested in Egypt, but most of them have a secret wish just to take off some winter and go snowmobiling or try out snow skiing in the Rockies above Denver. Some picture themselves in chic, colorful ski clothes, but they never talk about it because it's silly. But almost all of them talk about going to see the stock show. They see the winners of the cattle and horse judgings on the evening news and shake their heads. Next year, they say.

But very few ever go to Denver. It's too far, too expensive, and too different. The city of Denver—any city, really—frightens them. But they see it on television. They see "Dynasty" and advertisements for pizza places that bring the pizza right to your door. If they don't get it there on time, you get the pizza free. No one believes that; they figure there must be a catch. After a while Denver becomes unreal. It becomes like any other television show.

But Ross Brady always knew that Denver was real. He had gone to Denver several times a year since he started living on the bench. Linda and he would weekend there doing things that they couldn't do in Harney: a football game if they could get tickets, the symphony once, movies, a Pakistani restaurant on Euclid Avenue. Driving down through the corner of Nebraska, Ross remembered every trip they made. He remembered where they stayed, what they did, where they ate. As he drove, Ross found himself longing for this time with Linda. He needed it very much. He avoided thoughts of Sorenson but could not hold off the thoughts of the night before with Elizabeth. He wondered what was happening to him.

He passed through Torrington, Wyoming, and the feel and warmth of Elizabeth's skin was there, close against him, but he could see only the image of Linda's coy smile.

None of it would leave him, and as he passed through Hawk Springs, on the way to Cheyenne, he remembered how Elizabeth had carried the folded quilt as they walked back to the house in the first light of day. She had held his arm as they walked to his pickup. When they saw that Tracy and Louis were already up and waiting for her on the porch, she had whispered, "Boy, oh boy, I'm in trouble now." But when he looked at her face, her lips were contorted, trying to hold back a smile, and her eyes sparkled. She left him at the pickup, but not before she kissed him quickly on the cheek. Tracy and Louis stared as she walked toward them. But Elizabeth didn't stop. She walked past them, smiling all the way.

By then he had begun to worry about what he would say to Stewart. But he need not have worried. When he got home, Stewart had already started the chores and acted as if he didn't even know that Ross had not come home the night before. As they fed the cattle, they talked only about what Stewart should do while Ross was gone. Stewart had seemed anxious for Ross to leave, and by nine thirty Stewart had the place to himself.

Ross's mind had begun to race as soon as he pointed the pickup southwest, and in twenty minutes he was in the driving daze that lasted until the traffic doubled on Interstate 25 just north of Denver. At Fort Collins he had to start paying attention. The highway widened to eight lanes, and the city began to appear in clusters of buildings at the interchanges. The Rocky Mountains towered to the west, and the brown haze that hung over Denver rose up ahead. The highway took a slight turn at Thornton, and when it straightened out again, the skyline of Denver suddenly appeared. Somehow Ross had lost more than seven hours. He rubbed his face, then put both hands on the wheel. The traffic doubled again before he reached the city limits.

▲
FIFTY-THREE

Stewart was taking a short break after feeding the only heifer left to calve when Elizabeth pulled up in front of the house. The coffee was nearly finished perking, and from the kitchen window Stewart thought Elizabeth looked as if she could use a cup. She was moving from her pickup to the house and seemed a little lost.

Stewart stepped from the doorway. "You missed him," he called out, "but there's coffee on."

Elizabeth looked a little embarrassed, then smiled. "Coffee sounds good."

"Have yourself a sit down," Stewart said as he pulled a chair from the table. "How about breakfast?" he asked. "You had breakfast? I'll cook."

"It's closer to lunchtime."

"We'll have brunch." He pointed at her and closed one eye. "You look like an eggs Benedict and mimosa girl."

Elizabeth frowned. "Speak English."

"Scrambled eggs and bacon?"

"That's more like it. Sure."

Stewart went to work frying bacon and cracking eggs. He had mastered the cast-iron skillets that hung above the stove and had made a note to try to buy some for his own kitchen. The bacon sizzled, and Stewart and Elizabeth talked about little things.

Then Elizabeth said that her sister was mad at her. "She

said she wasn't going to the Yuwipi with me tomorrow. She thinks that hurts my feelings."

"The what?" Stewart was mixing eggs with milk and Worcestershire sauce.

"Yuwipi. It's at my mother's house. You should come with me."

"What is it?"

"A kind of religious ceremony. There will be food and a get-together. You might like it."

"Sounds nice," Stewart said. He poured some of the grease off, emptied the eggs into the skillet beside the bacon, and began buttering toast.

"You should come. You couldn't go to the ceremony itself, but you could meet my mother and aunts."

"Why couldn't I go to the ceremony?"

"You're *wasicu.*" Elizabeth laughed. "You have to prepare for a Yuwipi."

"Oh, this is a serious religion. I know about that."

"Pretty serious," Elizabeth said as Stewart stirred the skillet a couple times, then scraped the eggs onto the plates. He put the plates on the table along with the coffeepot. The plates were heaped high with eggs, a half dozen pieces of bacon, and four slices of toast. Elizabeth looked at the plate in amazement. "Do I look like a truck driver?"

"You have to eat," Stewart said. "We've got cattle to feed, fence to fix, horses to ride." He took a big mouthful of scrambled eggs, chewed for a moment, and swallowed. "When is this weepy deal?"

"U-weep-e. Tomorrow. I'll be leaving about two in the afternoon. You can have everything done by then."

Stewart chewed and thought. "I'll give you a call. Depends on how things go today. I'm going to check the cattle." He smiled. "All by myself. From horseback."

"Whoa," Elizabeth said and rolled her eyes. "Watch out for the wolves and Indians."

"No problem. They don't call me the Redondo Kid for nothing."

"Right."

"Why'd your sister get mad?"

Elizabeth told him about her fight with Tracy. Stewart watched her as she talked. He expected her to be upset. But she laughed. "I just told them to pack their kids up and clear out. It's the first time I can remember Tracy without anything to say."

Stewart was a little lighthearted. "I've got a sister," he said. "My policy is to never do anything to make her mad."

They looked at each other over forks full of scrambled eggs. Elizabeth put her fork down and looked away. "Do you think your sister would be mad if she knew you'd cooked breakfast for me?" she asked.

Stewart reached across the table and touched her arm. "Hey," he said. "It's not my business." He squeezed the arm. "I guess I can make breakfast for a friend if I want." She looked up. "Now eat," he said. "We got broncs to bust, cows to rope, dogies to move along."

▲
FIFTY-FOUR

Stewart hauled the saddle he'd been using from the tack room about one thirty. He'd meant to ride out among the cattle long before then, but he'd talked with Elizabeth until almost one o'clock. He carefully tipped the saddle up so it balanced near the hitching rail with only the front fenders and horn touching the ground. It was exactly the way Ross had taught him to handle it. He laid the saddle pads over the rail and took the bridle with him to catch his horse. He had always ridden Lady when Ross and he checked the cattle. Ross had ridden Bozo, and Stewart had been impressed with the way they seemed to do everything effortlessly. But he had always gotten along well with Lady. She was easygoing, and though not as powerful, responsive, or willing as Bozo, she was much more of a horse than he was a rider. Ross said that Lady took care of her riders, and that had been very attractive to Stewart. He felt safe on Lady, liked her, and thought she liked him. So he surprised himself, when the two horses came up to him, by slipping the bridle over Bozo's soft brown nose.

Bozo was larger than Lady, so he had to adjust the bridle to fit. Both horses stood close to him with their heads down, swatting the few flies that only a day before had begun to appear. Lady's eyes were partially closed, and she rubbed the side of her face absently against Stewart's back as he lengthened the ear loop and pushed Bozo's ear through. It was nice, Stewart thought, standing there in the corral with the horses so close and friendly.

As he led Bozo from the corral, Stewart wondered whether he should be doing this. Ross had not told him he couldn't ride Bozo, and he'd known that Stewart was fascinated with the horse. Ross probably wouldn't mind, but maybe Bozo was too much horse. But that was the attraction. Bozo was a little like the Jaguar that was parked in Linda's garage, and Stewart could understand someone wanting to take it for a spin.

He tied Bozo to the hitching rail and brushed out some mud that had dried on his back and legs. He talked while he worked. "Now I'm just a novice," he said. "I want you to take it easy and give me a good ride."

Bozo stood hipshot with his head down and his eyes half-closed. He seemed to be enjoying the brushing and the conversation. He didn't move when Stewart put the saddle pads on his back. Even the heavy saddle didn't concern him. It occurred to Stewart that he might be trying to lull him into a sense of false security or conserving his energy for some rotten deed he was planning in that thick equine head. Stewart had heard stories of horse tricks. Ross had talked of being scraped off on trees and fence posts, of horses that bucked or ran away when you least expected it, and of horses that shied at rocks or stumps they had seen hundreds of times before. Stewart had never heard anyone accuse Bozo of any of these things, but he had a reputation for quickness and a thing they called cow sense. Ross had once said that you had to pay attention when you rode a horse like Bozo, because he could turn out from under you in an instant. Stewart tried to imagine what having a horse turn out from under you would look like. All that came to mind was a picture of a surprised cowboy suspended high above a rocky pasture with his horse conspicuously absent.

By the time Stewart had finished cinching the saddle down he had managed to frighten himself and was reluctant to put a foot in the stirrup. Bozo still stood with his head down, slowly chewing at his bit. Stewart remembered the rodeo and Kyle's ride on Psycho. He pushed that image out of his mind and replaced it with one of Ross and Bozo bringing a cow and her calf back to the barn. That was the image he wanted; smoothness, easy motion. He held the reins and the saddle horn with his left hand, stretched his left leg up into the stirrup. "OK," he said, "let's light this rocket," and he swung his right leg over and into the other stirrup.

He gathered the reins and the saddle horn quickly in both hands and forced himself tight into the saddle. Nothing happened. Bozo stood as before, head down, making a faint sucking sound like a sleeping baby. Stewart lifted the reins tentatively with his right hand but kept his left on the horn. Bozo's head came up, but he still felt relaxed. Stewart moved the reins to the left and touched the horse's right side with his bootheel. Bozo spun ninety degrees and started trotting before Stewart could get both hands back on the horn.

They were through the first gate, past the haystacks, and halfway to the feeding grounds by the time Stewart realized Bozo was simply going out to check the cattle the way he had so many times that spring. Stewart was concentrating on putting more weight on his legs when Bozo stopped, throwing Stewart forward, almost into painful contact with the horn. Bozo put his head down again and seemed to go to sleep. They were at the pasture gate, and Bozo was waiting for Stewart to get off and open it.

After Stewart had shut the gate behind them, he remounted and touched Bozo's ribs gently with both heels. When he broke into a trot, Stewart touched him again and felt the slow lope that he'd heard Ross and Tuffy talking about. It was as they said: smooth as a porch swing. Stewart took his free hand off the saddle horn and pulled his hat down so the wind wouldn't take it. He reined Bozo to the left, to the right. The horse never broke out of the slow lope. They loped down a gradual hill, and Stewart felt Bozo's power as they started up the other side. He leaned forward and tried to help.

They turned west at the top of the hill, and Stewart eased the reins back only an inch before Bozo was trotting along a ridge with a hundred miles of rolling prairie below. The sky was the clear blue Stewart had become used to. Far to the west there were four small white clouds. The wind was fresh in their faces. There were a few stark buttes in the distance, and Ross's cattle grazed in the foreground. It was a long way from the offices where Stewart sold long-distance telephone systems. From the ridge above the Cheyenne River, Stewart saw no telephone wires, no microwave towers, nothing man-made except the faint, distant line of fence that separated Ross's land from Cleve Miller's. Stewart looked at the fence, then at the ridge they were following. A little farther up the ridge widened, and Stewart could see that if they stuck to the right side, the fence would be out of sight.

He moved the reins and his heels at the same time, and Bozo sped up. When Stewart reached the right side, he stopped Bozo and turned to face the landscape. Now it was perfect, he thought: white-faced cows with calves at their sides under a sky that cut the world in half. And wind. It touched his face and felt almost alive as it moved the hair that was not tucked under his hat.

▲
FIFTY-FIVE

The Brown Palace Hotel is a triangular building in downtown Denver. It was built in 1892 with money from the rich ore mines of Colorado. It is made of Colorado red granite and Arizona sandstone, and in 1892 it was the largest building in Denver. It is nine stories high and occupies the entire triangular block formed by Tremont Place, Broadway, and Seventeenth Street. The Brown Palace is still the only building on that triangle, but now many larger, steel-and-glass buildings tower above it.

Rush hour was just beginning when Ross exited Interstate 25 and made his way downtown. He was not familiar enough with Denver to find the hotel on the first try. He knew approximately where he was going. Linda and he had walked past the Brown Palace several times and had always meant to go inside for a drink. But it is an expensive hotel, and there had never been money to spend on that kind of lodging. They had stayed at a Super 8 in Arvada. He knew that Linda's choice of hotels said a lot about the importance she attached to this rendezvous. The dance performance was not until the next evening. As Ross drove the maze of streets trying to find the hotel, Linda was at rehearsal. She would be back at the Brown Palace around six o'clock, and they had agreed to meet then. She had the evening off.

Ross crossed Seventeenth Street and saw the Brown Palace to the right. But Seventeenth was one-way going the wrong way. He drove down another block and doubled back.

Finally he saw a parking garage that was close, pulled in, took his bag from the rear of the pickup, and walked the rest of the way. The doorman watched him come down the sidewalk, but not until Ross turned to enter the hotel did he step up and reach for his bag. His name tag read Felix, and Ross let him take the bag. But immediately he wished he hadn't. The bag was not heavy. The front desk was not far.

Felix was very friendly. He chatted busily as he held the doors and directed Ross into an enormous lobby, open to the very top of the building, where a huge stained-glass roof let in daylight, which filtered down past six tiers of iron balconies. Behind the iron panels Ross could see the woodwork of the room doors, six floors of them. He stood among the giant potted plants of the lobby and looked up. "It's really something, isn't it?" Felix said. He had placed Ross's bag on a dolly and stood near the check-in desk.

"Nice," Ross said. "I like the little iron balconies."

"There's over seven hundred panels," Felix said. He raised an eyebrow. "Two of them were installed upside down."

"Which two?"

"I don't know. I've never really looked for them. It's just one of the interesting little facts about the hotel."

Ross nodded and looked at the closest panels. There was something like a face at the top of each one. All the panels in view were installed right side up. Felix was still standing beside the desk, and Ross realized he was waiting for a tip. He dug a dollar from his pocket. "Thanks."

"Have a nice stay," Felix said. "And let me know if you find those two panels."

The woman at the desk was expecting him. "Mr. Brady. Here is your key. Your wife has already checked in and left this message." The woman smiled warmly as she slid the envelope across the marble countertop. She tapped a bell, and a young black man stepped up to take Ross's bag.

This time Ross took the bag. "It's OK," he said.

The room was on the fifth floor, and as he walked from the elevator, Ross watched the iron panels. They reminded him of the fence Tuffy had erected around his family graveyard. It occurred to him that the graveyard now belonged to him. He didn't want it. He didn't even want to think about it and instead inspected the panels of the balcony. None was upside down. He probably passed twenty between the elevator and his room. Before he opened the door, he looked over the balcony. The panels were above and below and across from him. He could see only a few well enough to know whether they were installed properly.

The room was large with a king-sized bed and French-styled desk and dresser. The bathroom was rich, old white tile from floor to ceiling, and the bathtub was wide and deep and stood on lion's feet clutching spheres that could have been tiny globes. There was a familiar smell in the room, and it took only a moment for Ross to place it. It was Linda's smell. Her bags were open, and her clothes hung neatly in the closet. He put his bag down beside hers and sat on the bed to read the note she had left at the desk. "Welcome to Denver," it said, "I'm so anxious to see you." She thought the rehearsal would be over by six thirty. She had dinner reservations for eight. It was signed "with all my love."

Ross lay back on the bed. It had already been turned down for the night. The sheets felt like satin, and there was a mint on each pillow. It was a firm mattress that felt as if only the top couple inches were padded. Yet Ross seemed to sink into it. He stared at the ceiling for a moment, fatigued from the drive. He should get up. It wouldn't do to have Linda find him asleep. With effort he pulled himself to a sitting position and came face-to-face with his image in the mirror. He looked out of place in the room. Maybe he should take a shower and change into something other than blue jeans and boots. No. There would be enough time spent in a coat and tie. He stood up and tucked in his shirt. He needed to kill some time. Maybe he'd go look for those two upside-down iron panels.

▲

FIFTY-SIX

It was late afternoon, but Pete and Elizabeth were still cleaning out the shed where the heifers had calved. They were forking the manure into the manure spreader because the shed was too low to get into with the loader tractor. They had been at it for two hours and were on the last load when they heard a car drive past on its way to the house.

She leaned her manure fork against the shed wall on her way to the door. Pete continued to fork the manure into the spreader as if he had not heard the car. At first she did not recognize the big shiny Ford or the man in the sports coat, but the other man was Larry Sorenson. They were already halfway to the house, and Elizabeth thought she might be able to duck back into the shed. But Cleve Miller saw her standing at the shed door and tapped Sorenson on the shoulder.

It was too late to get away. They turned and came toward where she stood framed and frozen in the doorway. There was a time in her life when she would have run anyway, a time when she would have done anything to get away and not have to listen to what they had to say. But now she reached out calmly and touched the weathered wood of the door frame. She felt the grain of the wood with the very tips of her fingers, then stepped out to meet the men.

They tipped their hats and smiled, but the smiles were false. There was a piece of paper in Sorenson's hand. She knew there would be, and when he held it out to her, she took it. "I hate to be the one to have to do this," Sorenson said, "but this is a less painful way." He nodded to the paper in Elizabeth's hand.

"What is it?" she asked.

"It's a proposal to solve your financial problem," Sorenson said. Elizabeth nodded but did not take her eyes off him. "It's a good way. It's not like a bankruptcy. There's no stigma attached." Still she watched him. "It's a proposal to accept a quit claim deed in lieu of payment of the outstanding debt."

"You're taking the place?"

"This will save a lot of time and embarrassment. We would forgive the deficit in return for not having to go through the courts." Sorenson tried to match her stare but could not. Standing next to him, Cleve Miller smiled, but his eyes were not friendly.

Then the eyes shifted to something behind her, and Elizabeth knew that Pete had come to the shed door. She did not turn, but by watching the two men, she knew what they were seeing. Pete was standing behind her, two buttons missing from his sweat-soaked flannel shirt, a manure fork in his hand. He had not shaved for several days, and his hair was wild. Cleve and Sorenson had already taken a step backward when she heard Pete's voice. It came from somewhere far away, guttural and savage. "Go on," he said. "Fuck off. Leave her be."

▲
FIFTY-SEVEN

The restaurant in the Brown Palace was called the Palace Arms. It was decorated with late-eighteenth- and early-nineteenth-century flags. There were French hunting prints on the walls and an array of Napoleonic memorabilia. There were dueling pistols, armor, and horse tack. The maître d' was Iranian, but his name was Luki, after his Italian grandfather. He said one set of pistols had belonged to Napoleon himself. Another pair had belonged to Napoleon's wife, Louisa.

Luki seated Ross and Linda at a corner table. He flirted with Linda, commenting on her earrings and the color of her dress, and Linda smiled and thanked him with just enough delight to make him know his flirting had been appreciated. The candles made her eyes sparkle, and her skin looked as smooth as Ross knew it was. She thrived in this setting and read the wine list aloud to Ross as if each entry were rare and wonderful. When she came to the 1980 Santenary Burgundy, she reached across and grabbed the sleeve of Ross's sport coat and shook it with excitement. "Look." She pointed to the page but Ross was watching her.

"Perfect," he said. She looked up and saw that he was paying no attention to the wine list. She kissed him quickly, just as the waiter stepped up to the table.

They ordered the Santenary, then, for appetizers, the salmon mousse in a cracker cup and chilled grape soup. A small, very serious dark man named Mario made the Caesar salad. Ross ordered the rack of lamb and Linda, the chef's special roast duck. For dessert they shared a chocolate truffle and a slice of strawberry cheesecake.

The coffee was rich and nutty. They leaned toward each other as they talked. Ross was not to worry; Linda's father was picking up the check for their weekend. He wanted them to have a good time.

"What you mean is he wants us to get things straightened out," Ross said.

Linda nodded. "I'm sure that was what he had in mind."

They sat quietly sipping their coffee until Ross felt he had to speak. "I don't know much more than I did when you left," he said.

Linda looked at her coffee. "You make it sound like I deserted you."

"No. I understand why you left. You had to." Ross tapped the side of his coffee cup nervously.

"We have to talk this out," Linda said, "but not now. It's our first night together in a long time." She didn't know how to tell Ross that she'd left not only for the dancing and the city. It would be difficult to say that she'd left for his good. As long as she was there, he had no need to face up to the fact that he was really hiding. She had felt since before she left that she was making things harder for him, that he'd never take an honest look at his life as long as she supported him in it.

They walked arm in arm to the elevator and kissed as they rushed upward. On the way to the room Ross again watched for the panels that had been installed upside down. He'd nearly given up when they came to their room and he looked directly across the lobby and up one floor. There it was, an upside-down panel. Once he saw it, it seemed obvious. He hesitated but said nothing to Linda. She walked past him on her way to the room. His eyes were on the distant panel, but he could smell her perfume and hear the fabric of her dress as she moved.

▲
FIFTY-EIGHT

Stewart and Elizabeth left the bench after they finished their chores. They traveled south across the northern part of the Pine Ridge Reservation. Elizabeth named the buttes. "Snake Butte," she said. "Eagle Nest Butte."

"Are there eagles up there?"

Elizabeth laughed. "There are eagles everywhere."

"No," Stewart said. "They're endangered or extinct or something."

"No," Elizabeth said. "You watch. We'll see at least one today. I've never been to a Yuwipi where an eagle did not come."

"Right."

They descended the bluff into Bear in the Lodge Creek. The cottonwoods were fully leafed out; the chokecherry and buffalo-berry bushes were in bloom. White and yellow flowers streaked the moist draws that meandered up from the creek bottom, and Stewart and Elizabeth rolled the windows down to let the pickup cab fill with the sweet smell. They raced on through the shabby reservation communities of Wanblee and Longvalley toward the small house of the Bad Wound girls.

Elizabeth had been wondering how Stewart would react to the inhabited parts of the reservations: the unpaved streets, trashy yards, and neglected homes. She watched from the corner of her eye as they passed through Norris. Stewart did not speak. He watched the tattered homes and deserted automobiles. Just as they came onto the Rosebud Reservation, before

327

they started down into the Little White River breaks, there was a tiny log house set not far off the road. A young girl, perhaps three years old, stood in the last mud puddle left from the snow melt, a stick in her hand. One of many reservation dogs they saw that day stood beside the puddle and wagged its tail furiously. But the little girl paid no attention. Her eyes were fixed on the pickup as it sped past. Stewart swiveled in his seat and watched her until the pickup topped a rise and she dipped out of sight.

Before they saw the house, they saw the cars and pickups. At first Stewart thought it was some sort of wrecking yard. He had seen hundreds of old cars already that day, some jacked up with the wheels missing, some completely stripped, and some that looked like swamp creatures, partly submerged in head-light-high grass. When they were closer, Stewart could see that at least some of these cars were not junkers. A few, in fact, were fairly new. Then Stewart realized that these were the vehicles of the people here for the Yuwipi.

Children began to come around the house and stand shyly in groups of two and three. When Stewart stepped out of the pickup, two small boys took one look and disappeared around the front of another pickup. He heard one say that word again, *wasicu.* But then someone recognized Elizabeth, and the children drifted her way. They did not rush up but moved slowly with their eyes intent on the ground. Elizabeth spoke to them in Lakota and English. A few smiled, and when they were close enough, she hefted a little girl up onto her hip.

It was Beverly, and she bit her own finger to hide a smile but would not look at her aunt. "This is Stewart," Elizabeth said. The little girl smiled more broadly but still would not look up. More people came to the front of the house: two teenage girls, an old man, a heavyset, pockmarked young man in a black cowboy hat. They all greeted Elizabeth.

Then Agnes and Sarah were there. "Come along," Agnes said. "The men are going into the sweat. Rachel is preparing the room. The meal is cooking."

"Mother, this is Stewart. He is a relative of a good friend."

The two old women looked Stewart over from head to toe, then nodded. "Come along. Come along."

Behind the house two canvas tarps were stretched over wooden frames and set up near a pit where a fire blazed. Two young men with their shirts off tended the fire. Other men were stripping down to shorts and crawling under one of the canvas domes. Some of the younger women entered the other dome. Sarah watched the women going into the sweat lodge and waved her hands at the whole thing. "It's bad medicine," she said.

Elizabeth teased her. "You have to stay up with the times."

Sarah shook her head. "Nonsense," she said.

As they started toward the house, the two young men began pulling rocks from the fire with pitchforks and moving them into the canvas domes.

The main room was being transformed. Two men with staple guns tacked blankets over the windows. The furniture was being hauled outside, and a young woman scattered small, leafy limbs on the floor. The room smelled of something Stewart recognized. He picked up one of the small branches and smelled it. "Sage," Elizabeth said, "to purify."

Three men sat in the corner on pillows and tapped on a small drum. They tested their voices and joked. In the center of the room a girl, Rachel, and two young men were very busy with what looked like coffee cans filled with dirt, small colored flags, and long strings of tiny cloth bundles. Elizabeth and her mother looked at each other and nodded. "We should leave," Agnes said.

"This is where the Yuwipi will be," Elizabeth said. "Aunt Rachel is preparing the camp circle." Stewart nodded and tried not to look confused.

Already men and women were emerging from the sweat lodges and drying with towels as they laughed at things others said in mumbled tones. They walked toward a very old man sitting on a folding chair under the fresh pine boughs of the shade house. Elizabeth and Agnes shook his hand and talked to him in Lakota. His face was wrinkled and his voice weak. He was very frail. The skin on the backs of his thin hands was nearly transparent. "That's Ernest Yellow Robe," Elizabeth said as they walked away. "He is very sick. The Yuwipi is mostly for him."

"His boy Bobby is on the hill," Agnes said.

"He's been on a high place for two days now," Elizabeth said, "waiting for a vision, trying to help his father."

Stewart nodded again and looked back at the old man. He sat all alone on his folding chair. He was wrapped in a star quilt. "The Yuwipi is to make him well?"

"Him mostly," Elizabeth said softly as if she did not want her mother to hear.

"The Yuwipi is for everyone," Agnes said. Then to Elizabeth, "Did you talk to your Aunt Rachel?"

"No."

"Well, I did," the old woman said and nodded her head as if it were final. But then she winked and patted her daughter's cheek. She winked again at Stewart. "Sarah is going to sit with you during the Yuwipi," she said. Then to Elizabeth, "Says she's on her moon." Agnes laughed. Elizabeth smiled but looked embarrassed. Stewart nodded.

An hour later the area around the Bad Wound girls' house was deserted. It was late afternoon, and the cooking fires were beginning to give off a glow. Smoke trailed up from the dying fire, where the stones for the sweat lodge had been heated. Stewart and Sarah sat under the pine boughs of the shade house. Stewart was seated in the same chair Ernest Yellow Robe had used earlier. The house was dark and silent.

"They have the light on," Sarah said, "but the room is completely sealed. When they turn the light out, it will be dark as the inside of a black cat. It's so the spirits will come and not be seen."

"Why aren't you in with the rest?" Stewart asked.

"It's my moon, my period."

Stewart was immediately uncomfortable. But Sarah seemed so relaxed that he had to find out. "How old are you?"

"I'll be sixty-nine in August. I been having periods for a very long time. Once a month," she said, "just like paying the rent." Stewart rubbed his forehead. He wanted to say something but he didn't know what. "Women in my condition are not allowed at a Yuwipi."

Stewart exhaled. "We have something like that, too. Is it considered unclean?"

Sarah laughed heartily. "Hah," she said and punched Stewart's arm. "You're a joker. I'm too powerful at this time. The spirits can't handle it."

Then a drumbeat began to sound from the house, and a high voice joined in, changing pitch after a half dozen beats. The singer sang in Lakota, and it was impossible for Stewart to know whether it was a man or a woman. "The Filling the Pipe Song," Sarah said. "Rachel has explained her power. They will bundle her up now and turn off the light."

"Bundle her up?"

"In a blanket. You know, tied with rawhide and sage." Another song began and Sarah closed her eyes and smiled. "This is my favorite." She kept her eyes closed and sang along in English: "Friend, I send my voice, so hear me. In the west

331

I call a black stone friend. In the north I call a red stone friend. In the east I call a yellow stone friend. In the south I call a white stone friend. On Earth I call a spider friend. Above I call a spotted eagle friend."

She opened her eyes and smiled at Stewart. "You're a nice boy," she said. But then she jumped up and pulled his arm. "Come along. We have to keep the food hot. Everyone has a job." She squeezed his arm to size his biceps as they moved toward the fires. "You're a man," she said. "You split wood."

Stewart hustled along toward the woodpile. The evening was coming and the sunset had begun, but above them there was still a wide section of blue. In the blue a large, dark bird circled on an unseen updraft. Stewart pointed. "What is it?"

Sarah stopped beside him and sighted along his arm. "An eagle," she said. "It's a spotted eagle."

They ate until no one could hold any more. There was way too much food, and as people began to get ready to go home, Tupperware, plastic bags, and mason jars appeared to consume the leftovers. Sleeping children wrapped in star quilts were carried to old cars and pickup trucks. People hugged and joked. A line of vehicles began to wind its way over the rutted driveway and out to the gravel road.

The moon was only half but still bright and hung above the road ahead as Stewart and Elizabeth made their way back across the reservation to the bench. On the dash Elizabeth had placed a string of the small cloth bundles and several sprigs of sage. In the moonlight the cloth was red, and the sage was silver. "What is it?" Stewart asked.

"Tobacco bundles and sage from the Yuwipi."

"And what's it for?"

Elizabeth didn't answer for several seconds. "Aunt Rachel

gave it to me during the Yuwipi. It's medicine. I have to take it to a special place."

"Are you sick?"

"No, not like Ernest Yellow Robe. Just problems."

"You mean the bank?"

"They came to the house yesterday. They brought a paper."

"What kind of paper?"

"I don't know. It says if I give them the place, they won't take me to court."

"Shit. They can't do that." Stewart waved his hand as if to dismiss the idea. But Elizabeth's face told him that she believed they could. "They can't do that," Stewart said again.

A sad smile came to Elizabeth's lips. "They've done it thousands of times before."

"Well, you can't let them. You have to fight." But Elizabeth said nothing. They were at the Milo junction. A few cars were parked outside the Dust Buster. They turned and started down the bench road.

"Is this what you're going to fight with?" Stewart touched the tobacco bundles and sage.

"No," Elizabeth said. "That's for another problem."

Stewart said nothing more until Elizabeth pulled to a stop in front of Ross's house. Even then Stewart made no move to get out. He sat thinking. He rubbed his face, then looked out into the moonlit yard. Beneath the cottonwoods there were shadows of a hundred different depths. Where there were no trees, the land was as silver as the sage on the dashboard. Finally Stewart pulled the door handle, and the door popped open. But he didn't let it open enough to turn on the overhead light.

"It really is beautiful." He said it more to himself than to Elizabeth. Then, "I'm driving Miller's old flatbed pickup. I'll come over and get you tomorrow evening," he said. "I'll have a surprise for you. I'll cook dinner."

The overhead light came on then for an instant before Elizabeth turned the pickup around between the house and barn. She moved steadily away, but in the rearview mirror she could see that Stewart was not walking toward the house. He was standing in the driveway with his hat in one hand, looking up at the moon.

She drove back up the bench road and turned in at her place but did not drive all the way to the house. She stopped near the shed and got out holding the string of tobacco bundles and the sprigs of sage. She moved to the back of the shed and through the fence, then went the same way she had gone a thousand times: down through the ash and cottonwood trees to the water of Cherry Creek, up the other side through the fragrance of blooming chokecherry and out into the bull pasture.

The bulls were waiting for her and rose to their feet one by one as she passed. She climbed the rock to her favorite place and sat for a moment watching the bulls settle back to the ground below her. Then she laid the string of tobacco bundles out in a circle with the sage in the center, just the way her Aunt Rachel had instructed her to do it. She made sure it was perfect, then sat down. She watched Badger's Ridge. She could not stay long. There were a million things to do the next day, and she needed her rest. But there was a little time. She would watch for a while. The old man might get word that she was there and waddle out to say hello.

▲

FIFTY-NINE

When Ross and Linda returned to the Brown Palace after the performance and reception, there was a message for Linda to call Stewart. It was not late. They had broken away from the party because this would be their last night together. Ross was driving back in the morning.

He had forgotten what it was like to watch Linda dance. He felt a tremendous sense of pride, which was tempered by a hint of resentment that several hundred other people were watching her, too. Ross had not missed what one woman at the reception had called "the special dynamic" between Linda and Jonathan. They had stolen the show, but since the previous night he did not feel insecure in their relationship. He did not know exactly what he felt about the relationship or the future, but he was sure that they still loved each other. He felt awkward at the reception, as if his clothes did not fit. He did not like the people, and it was only a short time before he found himself longing to leave. Even when they got to their room, he was not sure whether he had wanted to leave to get away from the people or so they could be alone.

He watched Linda sit on the bed, cross her legs under a gown more beautiful than the one she had worn the night before, toss her head, and remove one of the long, dangling earrings so she could more easily talk on the telephone. She laughed at something Stewart said when he answered, and for an instant it seemed to Ross that this beautiful woman was a stranger.

He had had that sensation before. Many times during the rough times in their past he awoke to watch her sleeping and thought that she was too good, too understanding, to be with him. But here he was, looking on as she laughed and moved to her briefcase on the desk, the phone tucked easily at her shoulder. She took out a notebook and read a couple names and telephone numbers to her brother. She laughed again. "Yes," she said, "a wonderful time."

Then she handed the phone to Ross. "Everything is going well, but he's got a question for you."

"What's a *wasicu?*" Stewart said.

Ross laughed. "Who's been calling you that? It's kind of derogatory. It means "white man" but comes from when the French first came up the Missouri River and brought bacon into the country for the first time. Literally it means "the man who brings the fat; the pork eater.""

"You're kidding!"

"Fact."

Ross hung up with a smile on his face. But when he looked at Linda, he forgot about Stewart. She sat on the bed and watched him with a fondness Ross had nearly forgotten. Ross's smile faded as he looked back at her. Her head was tilted now as she unfastened her other earring. But her eyes were on him. "Penny for your thoughts," she said. But he didn't know what to say. He could only purse his lips and shake his head.

"Then let me tell you mine," Linda said. She laid the earrings on the stand beside the bed and held out her hands to him. He let her guide him onto the bed beside her. "I thought you'd follow me to California," she said. "I hoped you'd decide to come without my asking, thought you'd miss me and just show up one day."

"I can't just leave the ranch."

"In a way I'm part of that ranch, too. I say just put it up

for sale, and take whatever you can get. Don't you see it's no good for us, that you're using it as a place to hide?"

Ross looked away. "I'm not sure."

"Look at it honestly. It's not really your country. You don't belong there. You've made no commitment there." She reached up with her right hand and turned his face back toward her. "Your commitment is with me."

▲
SIXTY

Stewart was up early. He fed the cattle, cleaned out the flatbed pickup, and was in Harney by eight thirty. He ate biscuits and gravy at the Badlands Café, then sat by the front window drinking coffee until a Federal Express truck pulled up outside. The driver was in a hurry and jumped from the truck carrying only one small envelope and a clipboard.

Stewart stood up slowly and dug in his pocket for change to leave as a tip. By the time he got to the front door of the First Bank of Harney, the Federal Express driver was hurrying out. Stewart had to step out of his way. Before he went inside, he looked up at the time-and-temperature sign. It was one minute after nine, and the temperature was fifty-two degrees.

There were already two old men in line at the tellers' windows, but there was a young woman sitting at a desk who was not busy. "I believe you have an envelope for me," Stewart said. "Bergman."

The woman looked up in surprise. "I was wondering," she said. "I couldn't for the life of me . . ." She pulled the envelope from the top drawer of her desk. Stewart already had identification out to show her. He opened the envelope as he walked to Sorenson's office. He didn't bother to knock.

Sorenson stood up as Stewart came in. He started to say something but Stewart held up his hand. "I'm here to pay off Elizabeth Janis's loan. I know the principle. Go figure the interest up to today."

Sorenson stood but was not able to speak for a moment.

338

"That debt," he finally said, "is in excess of forty thousand dollars."

Stewart shrugged and pulled a cashier's check from the Federal Express envelope. "I sold a car," he said. "This money's burning a hole in my pocket."

"Your car?"

Stewart smiled. "It was a pretty nice car, but just a car."

Sorenson was dazed as he walked to the desk of the same woman who had helped Stewart moments earlier. He explained that they needed a current balance on the Janis loan and stood staring at Stewart. Stewart tapped the cashier's check against the desktop to a jazz beat in his head and smiled at Sorenson.

"Forty-one thousand six hundred and twenty-six dollars," the woman announced.

Stewart picked up a pen from her desk, did a quick calculation on a piece of scrap paper, and signed the check. He handed it to Sorenson. "I'll want a copy of the loan marked paid," he said. "And by my figures you owe me eleven hundred and twenty-four dollars. Large bills will be fine."

Sorenson took the check but had trouble taking his eyes off Stewart. He looked at the check for only a moment. Suddenly it was as if he had to get away from Stewart. He handed the check to the woman. "Take care of this," he said. "Give him what he wants."

He spun away from the desk and did not look back. He walked directly into his office and shut the door. Then he went to the window and put his hands on the sill. Everything seemed out of control. Nothing in this deal had worked as he had planned. Sorenson stood at his window and watched a pickup truck pulling a horse trailer move past on the street outside. He had to think.

He would have to call Cleve and let him know what had happened. But the whole thing had gone far enough. He was afraid of what Cleve might do and knew it was time to put a stop to all of it. He would call Higgins, too, get a meeting with him for that afternoon. They would just have to come out with it, get a commitment from Brome Mining Company to buy the ranches. Get them to pay a good price for them. Lay it all on the table. He rubbed his hands and watched a few more cars pass on the street. Nothing had gone right for a long time, and he couldn't figure out why.

It was time to set things right. He had thought the same thing as he ate his breakfast that morning and watched Karen getting ready to go to Rapid City. She never even told him she was going anymore. It was as if it weren't worth the bother. He had felt like saying something to her. He had wanted to just stop the foolishness, make a fresh start. And now he felt the same way about this whole mining deal. He pushed away from the window and picked up the telephone.

▲
SIXTY-ONE

Ross put Linda on the dance-company bus in Denver at ten o'clock in the morning. Their next performance was in Santa Fe. Now she was traveling south on Interstate 25; he was traveling north. He stopped for gas in Cheyenne and turned onto Highway 85 a few miles farther north.

They had talked late into the night. It began with remembering the first years in Vancouver, the university, the small apartment, and the crazy friends. Linda talked about people they had known and wondered what happened to them. But remembering those times always brought back to Ross the memory of sleepless nights, the vague panic, and the dull ache in his chest that Linda had done so much to ease. He didn't bring those things up, but as Linda talked, he remembered that when sleep did come, it often came with dreams of the prairie he had driven through on the trip from Fort Sill, Oklahoma, to Fort Lewis, Washington.

The last thing they talked about was the future. She wanted him to leave the ranch. She said it frightened her and she was probably right. Maybe Sorenson's offer was serious. But Ross didn't tell her about any of that. "You don't have to hide out there anymore. I've talked with Dad. There are lots of things you can do."

He nodded when she said that, but the nod was no more intended for her than the nodding he did in the pickup, all alone, moving seventy-five miles per hour between Lingle and Lusk, Wyoming. Again he recalled that long trip toward Fort

Lewis, Washington. The country he passed through now was different, but there was something very similar about the hollow feeling in his abdomen. As he drove through the center of Washington those many years ago, he had felt numb. Like today he was driving too fast. But it didn't matter. He was a soldier that day, basic and advanced infantry training behind him, Fort Lewis ahead, and a field full of C-130 cargo airplanes loading troops and equipment for Vietnam.

He could see the sacred Black Hills from just north of Lusk. He would turn before he got to them. That day in Washington he had driven through the coastal range, the Wenatchee and Snoqualmie national forests. He remembered that their dark, damp trees frightened him and that fear weighed him down and compounded on the downhill run into Seattle. Fort Lewis was near Tacoma, only forty miles south. He began seeing signs long before he got to Seattle and planned to turn. But as he got closer, the word *Tacoma* began to look odd to him. It became foreign and dangerous. When the sign for Vancouver appeared, he had already decided he would not go to Tacoma. Canada, it said. Vancouver, Canada. And he guided the car off the ramp with an ease that exhilarated him. Two hours later a Canadian border guard waved him through and winked. It would be years before he would cross that line again, but during all that time he thought about the land he had driven through in the center of the nation, the rolling grass, and the remoteness of the Badlands.

Now he turned off Highway 85 and drove toward those same Badlands. It was afternoon, and the sun was behind him, projecting the shadow of his own pickup far ahead on the highway. The Black Hills were to his left, and he drove through a small town before coming to the Cheyenne River. He would cross it twice more before he was home. He felt as if he were running for home. Crossing the Cheyenne that last time would be like slamming the door behind him. That made him remember what Linda had said. She said he could stop hiding. He had never thought of it that way, and it bothered him to know she saw it like that. He had known at the time he should have said something, tried to explain what she didn't understand. But he hadn't, and that was all right because they had agreed to talk again when Linda's tour was over.

She had told him to think about what she said on his way back to the ranch. She had taken his face in her hands and said not to think about it just then, to enjoy the time they had left together. And he had done as she asked, lying soft in her arms until she fell asleep. But he could not sleep, and very late, long after the hotel was quiet, he had moved out of her arms and slipped into his pants and shirt.

He thought he needed fresh air and that he would walk along the streets of Denver. But once out of the room, the wrought-iron balcony panels caught his eye. He still had not found the second improperly installed panel, and so instead of going outside, he walked all the balconies again, but still found only one upside-down panel. It was so easy to see once you knew where to look, but somehow he had missed its mate. He walked the floors again. Still nothing.

He walked past each room in the hotel two more times. He stopped thinking and simply looked at the panels. But he didn't find the one he was looking for, and finally he was tired. He made his way back to their room, and as he slipped the key into the lock, he looked over his shoulder at the panel directly in front. There it was, only ten feet away, the panel closest to where he would sleep.

▲
SIXTY-TWO

Sorenson was at the Hilton at a quarter after four. His meeting with Higgins was at four thirty. He sat at the end of the bar sipping coffee and thinking about how he would approach this deal if he had it to do over. Brady hadn't said it, but the idea of digging up the creeks had upset him. Brady had failed to see the importance, had his priorities mixed up. Ideas like that were one thing Sorenson would address if he had it to do over. They should have laid it out economically and openly, let the people in on the profits from the start. When Higgins showed up, he intended to begin the process, to get a commitment from Higgins simply to buy the four ranches on the bench at a good price.

The bartender asked whether Sorenson would like a drink. "Sun's below the yardarm," he said and looked out the window. Sorenson shook his head but followed the bartender's nod. The front window of the lounge was large, and the sun was easy to see just over the tall elm trees of a residential section of town. There were a few clouds that looked as if they might contain some rain. The light filtered through the clouds and made the new leaves of the elms look pale green. Sorenson knew the ranchers in his part of the world would be needing rain soon. He also knew that it was impossible to brand calves when they were wet, and so they would want the rain to hold off for a couple weeks. He found himself hoping that the rain would do just that. Still, the clouds were fascinating.

He was watching the clouds when Higgins's assistant tapped him on the shoulder. Sorenson turned with a start to find the rigid, white face of a young man who seemed very out of place. Higgins stood at the door as if he did not want to be seen in a bar. "We have a meeting room reserved," the young man said. "Just a small one."

Sorenson nodded. "A small room should be fine," he said.

Higgins took his hand as they stepped into the hall outside the lounge. "Nice to see you," Higgins said in his Australian accent. "You sounded upset on the telephone, Larry."

Sorenson couldn't remember Higgins calling him Larry before. He wasn't sure how he felt about it. He should have returned that small intimacy, but just then he couldn't remember Higgins's first name. "Yes," he finally said. "We need to talk."

The assistant led the way down the wide hall that opened into the spacious hotel lobby. Sorenson and Higgins walked side by side. They were nearly to the elevators that led upstairs to the guest rooms when a well-dressed older man and a woman started down the hallway from the lobby. They laughed as they came toward Sorenson and Higgins. They seemed very happy, and something in the scene attracted Sorenson's attention.

At first he thought it was the carefree way they moved or the obvious joy they found in each other's company. They were only ten feet away, the older man pressing the elevator button with good-natured impatience, when Sorenson realized what had attracted him. The woman smiled at the man, then looked up as Sorenson, Higgins, and the assistant approached. The elevator bell sounded just as Karen Sorenson recognized her husband. But she hesitated only for a moment before she took the man's arm and stepped into the elevator. They turned and faced Sorenson as the doors closed, and he was left standing in the hallway, Higgins and the assistant a few steps ahead and looking back at him as he stared at the closed doors.

He was not surprised to find his wife with another man. All the signs had been there. What amazed him was the man's age. He was at least as old as Sorenson, but younger around the eyes, energetic, with more life left inside. The lights above the doors lit in sequence as the elevator rose, but Sorenson did not take his eyes off the doors. He felt Higgins and the assistant watching him and knew he had to move on.

Higgins came back toward him and asked whether he was all right. Sorenson nodded; he had to talk to Higgins. This meeting was very important. It was a chance to set things straight. Sorenson reached out with his left hand and touched the elevator doors. What he needed, he thought, more than anything, was a chance to set things straight.

▲
SIXTY-THREE

Stewart picked up Elizabeth just after five o'clock. She was sitting at the kitchen table making a list of all the things they would need to brand the calves: numbered ear tags, disinfectant for the castrating, vaccine for red nose and blackleg, plenty of syringes, something for grubs and lice, a full bottle of propane to run the branding stove, and dehorning paste. There was more but she couldn't think just then. One missing ingredient was enough help to get all the jobs done. It was bad enough that Tuffy was gone, but Elizabeth hadn't heard from Kyle in weeks. She could count him out. She also had a nagging feeling that Ross would not be there that year either. When she thought about the branding, the biggest job of the year, she was nearly relieved when her thoughts eventually got around to the possibility that she would not even be on the ranch the next week, that it would be someone else's headache.

She had worried herself into desperation by the time Stewart knocked on the front door. She almost didn't get up. There was only one man's knock that would make her jump to her feet, and he was in Denver with his wife. The thought of that made her shudder, and rather than dwell on it, she let Stewart into her house.

"You ready for the dinner of your life?"

"I don't know, Stewart. I should make something for Pete and John."

"Leave some sandwich makings. Pete's a big boy; he can handle things."

"Big, but he gets younger every day."

"Look, I already shopped. My version of chicken Parmesan, a bottle of wine. Harney's got a hell of a selection, by the way." He rolled his eyes. "We have something to celebrate. If you were a different kind of girl, I'd have gotten cream cheese and bagels for breakfast."

"Bagels?"

"OK, cream cheese and English muffins. Come on, we'll have a big time."

"I don't know."

"We really do have something to celebrate. Come on, you're coming over to our place." Stewart took her hand and pulled.

"Is Ross coming home?"

Stewart looked down and shook his head but didn't let go of the hand. "As a matter of fact, he might make it back tonight. But that's not what we have to celebrate." He shrugged. "Come on, give me a break. Hell, give yourself a break."

On the way to Ross's place Elizabeth commented on how clean the flatbed was. Stewart explained that he had been to town on business. He raised his eyebrows to let her know that the business had to do with the celebration, but he didn't say any more until he was twisting the lid off the bottle of wine.

"Finest wine in town," he said as he poured the Chablis into coffee cups. "But then Ross's crystal leaves something to be desired, too." He was acting very gallant, and Elizabeth was forced to laugh. The chicken breasts were broiling, and the Parmesan cheese was beginning to melt.

"Here's what I did," Stewart said after they had toasted and sipped from the wine. He handed Elizabeth the paid note on her ranch and took another sip of wine.

"What is it?" Elizabeth asked after seeing it was an official paper.

"It amounts to the title of your ranch. You own it. You can

do anything you want with it now. You don't have to listen to anyone. You don't even have to let them on the place."

Elizabeth looked at the paper, then back at Stewart. "But how?"

"Look. I paid it off. It's a much bigger deal to you than it is to me. I was glad to do it."

"You can't."

"I did. Don't say another word."

The chicken Parmesan sizzled loudly, and Stewart turned to tend it. "It won't be long," he said. "I have to get the asparagus going."

Elizabeth was still a little dumfounded. "Can I help?"

"No, this is my baby. But I'll tell you what. There's one heifer left in the barn to calve. Ross said to check it every six hours, and it's already been seven. Would you mind?"

It had begun to cool off for the night, and so before Elizabeth left the house, she took Ross's old canvas coat from a peg and slipped it on. It was too big but it felt good. It smelled like Ross and horses and cows. When she stepped into the barn, the heifer bawled a greeting. She was not ready to have her calf, but Elizabeth could see by her bag that it would come soon. She would tell Stewart to keep a close eye on her.

There was a pile of hay near the pen, and Elizabeth forked some to the heifer. The barn door at the other end was open, and the late-afternoon light shone in at a flat angle. Elizabeth could see the new leaves of the trees and shrubs of Sweet Grass Creek. She stood looking past the heifer toward the creek for several minutes. Then there was the sound of a vehicle on the driveway, and she spun toward the door to see whether it was Ross.

She had taken three or four steps from the barn by the time she realized that it was not Ross. It was the long Ford

Crown Victoria, and it pulled up near the house. Elizabeth ducked through the closest door and found herself in the tack room, surrounded by halters, saddles, ropes, and bridles and watching Cleve Miller through a crack in the door. She stood petrified in the gloom of the tack room as Cleve stepped from the car. The interior of the tack room was so still she could hear herself breathe.

Stewart had come from the house and stood on the porch smiling and wiping his hands on a dish towel. He nodded to Cleve as the taller man stepped onto the porch. Elizabeth stood still in the gloom of the tack room and watched Cleve shake his head sadly and move close to Stewart.

It was too far for Elizabeth to make out what Cleve was saying, but he moved his hands as if he were earnestly trying to convince Stewart of something. He continued to shake his head. Then, suddenly, there was a rush of violence on the porch and Cleve drove his fist hard into Stewart's stomach.

Even from the tack room Elizabeth heard the air go out of Stewart as he crashed backward through the screen door. Cleve followed him in and Elizabeth could hear furniture breaking. She was too scared to move but tried to think. She looked desperately around the tack room for a weapon, but by the time her eyes found Tuffy's saddlebags, Cleve had pulled Stewart from the house and was dragging him toward the car.

Elizabeth rushed to the saddlebags and found the .45 where Ross had left it. The Ford was pulling away before she realized that she did not know how the military weapon worked. Through the crack in the door, she watched the car disappear down the driveway.

When it was gone, she ran for the house. The pocket of Ross's coat was big enough for the .45, and she tucked it away just as she came into the wreckage of the living room. The couch was tipped over, the television smashed. There was a dark stain on the rug, and when she touched it, she knew it was blood. She ran for the telephone though she had no idea whom she would call. It was dead, the cord pulled from the wall.

The sun was nearly down when she came back into the yard. She checked the pickup, but there were no keys. Nervously she spun in the driveway, then started out toward the road. She ran as far as the mailbox, but there was no traffic on the bench road, no reason to expect anyone would come along soon. The car tracks turned to the north, toward town, but Elizabeth wandered southward, along the bench road, toward her own house. She was exhausted by the time she came to the place Tuffy had died. Her boots hurt her feet, and her fear had turned to despair. The missile silo was only a little way off the road, and she wandered as far as the locked chain link gate. Helplessly, she hung her fingers through the wire. The gate was tall and strong, and she shook it weakly. Finally she pressed her face against the wire and let her eyes go closed.

▲
SIXTY-FOUR

Ross had been driving for over seven hours when he came to Milo. His mind had raced all day, and now, with less than a half hour more to drive, he tried to come to some conclusions. But as soon as he turned onto the bench road, his thoughts for the future jumbled with memories, and conclusions became impossible. He passed Tuffy's old place and thought about him buried now, on the small hill between his parents. Red Willow Creek fell away from the road, and Ross imagined what it would be like after the miners were finished. Without the creeks there would be nothing. But what was there now?

When he came to Elizabeth's place he turned in without thinking. He was halfway to the house before he started wondering what he would say. But Elizabeth was gone. Pete came to the door chewing on a sandwich. John Kiser sat motionless behind him, a napkin tucked into his shirt below his chin. When Pete saw Ross, he stopped chewing and stared with one eye squinted. "It's Ross," Ross said.

"Ross."

"Yeah, is Elizabeth here?"

"No. She left with that young fellow a couple hours ago. I had to fix the supper." Ross backed away. Pete went on talking, but not to Ross. "Something ain't right," he said. "Just ain't right." He moved back into the house. "Something ain't right," he said.

Ross was nearly to the missile silo when he saw someone

duck off the road ahead and vanish into a draw that led down toward Old Woman Creek. A person on foot was strange enough on the bench road, but the last rays of pink sunlight made the escaping figure eerie. Ross stopped where the person had left the road. He peered down the draw, then stepped out of the pickup. When he came to the edge of the road, he heard the brush breaking below him and saw Elizabeth flush from her hiding place and head for the next clump of brush. He called her name, but she didn't stop. Then he was running after her, the brush slapping his face and the roots trying to trip him. But suddenly there was no brush; there were no roots. He ran faster than he had ever run in his life. And he caught her and took her down just as she started into the next draw.

They rolled, and she beat at him until she heard him calling her name. By then they were very close, and she turned his face up to hers. When she recognized him, she pulled him to her and they held each other tightly, but only for an instant. "I thought you were him," Elizabeth said.

"Who?"

"He took Stewart. Beat him up." Now she was on her feet. "Come on."

She explained what happened on the way back to the pickup. "The tracks turned north out of the driveway," she said. "He must have taken him to town."

▲
SIXTY-FIVE

Cleve Miller sat in the dark. They would be coming soon, and he would turn on the light so they would know he was there. But for now he wanted it dark, wanted a chance to gather his strength, wanted to be alone with God.

He had always felt that if the time came to defend what was good, he would rise to the task. It never occurred to him that he would have doubts, that he might be afraid, that he might question what must be done. Even now he was sure the sick feeling in his stomach would pass. This time of waiting was a sort of test that he was determined to pass. He would finally be able to do what was required.

Thinking back over the events of the last weeks, he was proud. It had been a simple land deal. But the Zionists who controlled things couldn't see someone like him make a profit. It was this Stewart Bergman and his kind's greed that turned it into something much bigger. He felt some guilt for breaking the law, but there were higher laws than those of the governments of men, and those were the laws he had followed when he kidnapped Bergman and beat him with his fists. And those higher laws proved themselves to be the true laws because he found that Bergman did not have superhuman strength. Bergman had whimpered and cried for help, and this had given Cleve heart.

Yes. He would be able to do what was required. He would be the tool that drove Satan's people from this good land. He would drive them all out, and if they didn't go, he would kill them. There was no real choice. But it would not be easy. No one would understand. They would say he was insane. They would prosecute him for what he had to do and send him to jail. But he would not be the first, or the last, to be sacrificed in this battle.

He should be happy to be chosen for this, and in a way he was. But still there was a sadness. Why had he alone been given such clear insight? It was a heavy burden, but a burden he would shoulder.

When he thought of Edith he had to cover his face with his hands. He hoped she would understand. He was doing it for her. He was doing it for everyone, for everything clean and decent. And they would turn on him, call him crazy, and he would never be able to get them to understand. But he couldn't think about that. What mattered was his resolve. He would sit in the dark awhile longer.

SIXTY-SIX

The road flattened out across the grasslands and headed straight north. It was nearly dark. There should be something to say, Ross thought, but neither he nor Elizabeth could think of anything. Twenty minutes later the lights of the town appeared, but still there was nothing to say. They crossed over the interstate highway and entered Harney where Murray's gas-station sign jetted up to lure tourists into town.

"We should call the sheriff," Ross said. He looked at Elizabeth as he said it, hopeful that she would think it was a good idea. The lights from the town flicked over her face as they moved down Main Street. She looked back at him with an expression that told him what he already knew: the sheriff probably would not listen to anything they said. They would be wasting time. They drove down Main Street pretending to look for Cleve's car, but somehow they knew where they would find it.

The Ford was parked at the extreme end of town, squarely in front of the Enchanted Forest. When they pulled up beside it, Ross was sweating, and he could feel a tremor at the back of his throat. For a moment they sat and waited, Ross looking straight ahead and Elizabeth watching him from the side. Then she reached out and touched his shoulder. When he looked, she reached into the pocket of the coat and brought out Tuffy's .45. Ross shook his head and wiped the sweat from his face. "No," he said. Then, with great effort, he pushed his door open. "Let's get in there."

356

The door to the Enchanted Forest opened easily, and Ross and Elizabeth entered between the gift shop and the snack bar. The empty hallway seemed wider than it ever had before, the wooden floor hollow and hard. The Taiwanese souvenirs in the gift shop window were illuminated by a dim light spilling into the hallway from the snack bar. There was also a faint metallic tapping. They moved to the door, and just before they stepped from the shadows and into the light they looked at each other. Elizabeth's eyes were wide, and for the first time Ross saw that they could have been Asian. She could have been a woman from anywhere, but she was Elizabeth, a woman from the grasslands, and all Ross wanted to do was look at her. Again she touched his shoulder, but this time she nodded as if she knew what was going through his mind. He found himself nodding back, and then he stepped from the shadows and into the light.

Cleve sat at a table with a cup of coffee in front of him and his hands spread on the table. Very near the coffee cup was a .38 revolver. The tapping continued, and now they could see it was the ring on Cleve's left hand hitting the table as his finger moved with a distracting lack of rhythm. The light came from a small lamp on the table. It was built like a tiny covered wagon. The bulb was inside the wagon, and the canvas glowed with a gray light. Cleve smiled and his teeth were dark. "Ross," he said. "I was hoping you'd show up." He nodded to Elizabeth. "Brought your little squaw with you, too. That's good." Cleve spoke softly, with a note of regret.

Ross leaned forward. "What the hell are you doing, Cleve? Have you gone crazy?"

Cleve smiled and shook his head. "No," he said. "Just the opposite."

"Where's Stewart?"

"He's here," Cleve said. "We'll get to that in a minute. First I want to talk about you." For the first time he looked directly at Ross. The face was old and tired. "You know, when you first moved in here we all wondered what your game was. Nobody liked it much when you bought the old Swenson place, brought that fancy wife of yours around." Cleve sipped his coffee and waited a moment before going on. "There were all kinds of rumors: you were a Russian spy keeping an eye on the missile silos; she was a California hippie. Course that was all bullshit. Turned out you were a goddamned deserter, and she was a Jew." Cleve stared at Ross and his temples pulsed.

"What have you done with Stewart?"

"He's OK," Cleve said. "A little sore is about all." He took the revolver from the table and let it dangle loose from his right hand. The tired smile was back on his face. "We're not stupid out here. We know about Jews and the plans they have to steal all the land from us Christians. And we're not cowards either." Cleve's shoulders slumped with exhaustion. "Would you like to see Stewart? Would you like to take him home? I hope so, because that's what I want. I want you to take him and his dirty money back to California, or Israel, or wherever the hell he came from." Cleve had moved closer. He was big and haggard and spoke so softly that he could barely be heard. But Ross could smell his sour breath. "And I want your chickenshit ass to go right along with him."

"Just take us to Stewart," Ross said.

Cleve shrugged, then motioned with the pistol for them to lead the way.

They walked out into the Enchanted Forest. The pillars of petrified stone were otherworldly. They cast irregular shadows across the path and made the crushed-rock walkway appear liquid. They walked past the Pirates' Hideaway and around the Oasis, where cactus grew in grotesque tangles. A single flower was open to the moon, but its color was only gray.

Cleve switched on the lights of the tower and motioned for them to step through the ornamental iron door. There were a few benches and chairs scattered around the stone floor, and at first neither Ross nor Elizabeth saw Stewart. It was not until Cleve pushed over one of the chairs that they saw him. He cowered in the corner but looked up when the chair crashed down beside him. His shirt was soaked with blood, and one eye was battered and bruised shut. His lips were split, but when he realized who it was, he managed to speak. "Ross," he said.

▲
SIXTY-SEVEN

Larry Sorenson's drive back to Harney seemed to take forever. Fatigue had settled in his bones. He knew that Karen would not be at home when he got there and wondered whether she would ever come back. It would be a terrible thing, he thought, if he never got to talk to her again. He was sure he had something to say, but as he turned onto Main Street, he could not imagine what it could be.

The street was nearly deserted, and as he drove past Thompson's Café, he noticed no one was at the counter. He passed Ottmyer's clothing store and the Blue Note Lounge. The sign on the bank said seven thirty. It was fifty-nine degrees; the sign said sixty-one. He saw Cleve Miller's car a full block before he came to the Enchanted Forest, recognized the pickup parked beside it, but did not want to admit it belonged to Ross Brady.

He stopped beside the two vehicles and knew there was something very wrong going on inside. He exhaled and rubbed his face. He needed to fix things. Now was a good time to begin.

"Say hi to your brother-in-law," Cleve said, prodding Stewart with the toe of his boot. "He's come to take you back to California. And I hope you'll decide to stay there." He nudged Stewart harder.

"That's enough," Ross said and started forward.

"Hold on, Ross," Cleve said and raised the pistol. "You will be taking him home, won't you?"

Ross stopped, paralyzed by the pistol. "You're crazy, Cleve," he said.

Cleve nudged Stewart harder with his boot just as Sorenson stepped through the door. "What's going on here?" Sorenson's face was pinched, revolted by what he saw. He moved to the center of the room and looked at everyone to demand an explanation. No one spoke, and finally he went to Stewart. He looked at Cleve in disbelief. "What have you done to this man?"

Cleve smiled. "I'm protecting what's ours, Larry."

Sorenson was standing now. "This has gone far enough. I talked with Higgins today. He's going to buy these people's ranches for what they are worth."

"It's gone beyond that, Larry. We've been controlled long enough," Cleve said. "We've got to make a stand. Show them we can't be pushed around."

Sorenson shook his head and looked sadly at Cleve. "You'll make out," Sorenson said quietly.

"That's not the point anymore."

Sorenson ignored Cleve and faced Ross. "It will be top dollar. You'll see. You can get out of here with money in your pocket." Everyone was looking at Ross, but Sorenson turned back to Cleve. "It's over, Cleve."

"It is not over," Cleve said. "There's principle here. These people are trying to steal what's ours. It's us against them, and you're falling right in with them." He stopped for an instant. Then, "The Lord gives his people strength, and, Larry, you've gone weak." He turned with purpose and kicked Stewart hard. Sorenson moved between them, and Elizabeth's hand tightened on Ross's. He did not understand her touch until she guided his hand into the coat pocket.

"Stop!" Sorenson said. "Stop!" He grabbed Cleve by the arms and tried to push him back. But Cleve fought. The two men clung to each other, pushing back and forth as the others looked on. They were two older men, friends for thirty years, and the sound of their exertion was pitiful in the hollow stone room. No one realized the danger until Cleve's .38 exploded in Sorenson's stomach.

Sorenson hunched and clung to Cleve. His eyes were wide open, and his mouth gasped for air. He began to slide toward the floor. "Jesus," he said to Cleve. The lips worked to form more words, but all he could say was "Jesus Christ."

Cleve let him slump to the floor. His head was bowed, and the .38 was still in his hand. The others watched and could see his breathing deepen. His jaw muscles pulsed, and when he looked up, his eyes glittered with wildness. He pulled back the hammer of the .38 as he raised the muzzle and turned to face them.

But the revolver never came all the way up. With an easy, practiced motion, Ross armed the .45, squared his stance, and quickly fired three slugs into Cleve's heart. The sound was deafening, but Cleve did not go down. He looked at his chest, where blood was beginning already to soak through his shirt, and a noise came from deep in his throat. He may have been trying to raise the .38 again, but no one would ever know. Ross's next shot took him at the base of the neck and sent him backward into the corner of the room, where he stood for only a second before sliding to the floor.

And then there was complete silence, and Elizabeth and Stewart looked at Ross. He did not take his eyes off the body in the corner. But when he was sure Cleve was dead, he lowered the .45, slid it to safe, and placed it gently on the floor at his feet.

▲

PART SEVEN

▲
SIXTY-EIGHT

Elizabeth has been up since four thirty this morning. It is the day of the branding. She has not seen Ross since the night Sorenson and Cleve were killed. He has been at a Rapid City hospital with Stewart. The nurse on the ward told Elizabeth that Stewart was improving, that he would be flying back to California soon. Elizabeth would like to see him before he leaves, but Linda is there, too. She and Ross have been together for three days.

They learned that the mining company wanted to dig out the trees along the creeks and take away the gold. Brome wasted no time in offering Elizabeth a good price for the ranch. She told them no but remembers what Sorenson said to Ross before he was killed, about getting top dollar for his land, and now she can't help thinking that Ross will not be coming back. It is probably better that way, she thinks as she stands at the top of the large, white rock in the bull pasture in the predawn. She tells herself that she is all right alone.

Maybe she has everything she needs. But still it is difficult. She dreads the days to come. It is really only she and Pete to do all the work, and she isn't sure they can manage. Pete was worse than usual when she saw him a half hour earlier. He'd been talking about the people who were coming to help. She tried to explain that there was no one else, but he didn't seem to understand. It was true that Kyle had finally called from Bismark, North Dakota, and said he would try to make it. But she and Pete will be riding out to gather the cattle in an hour, and still there is no Kyle.

There isn't much time, so Elizabeth kneels down at the edge of the ring of tobacco bundles she laid there several days before and reaches in to take up a sprig of sage. She rubs her hands with the sage and spreads the clean fragrance through her hair. She remains kneeling, with her head bowed, as long as she thinks she can. But there is a day filled with very hard work ahead. She stands and looks around before she starts back. There is a faint hope that she will see the badger before she goes back to help Pete get the horses ready, but it is still too dark. The moon is only a sliver.

▲
SIXTY-NINE

Ross and Linda sat up with Stewart during the tough time. He had suffered a concussion, and for two days the doctors were not sure just what damage had occurred. But by the third night he was better. He could recognize people and spoke a few words. But he was exhausted and slept most of the time. When the doctors said it looked as if he would make a full recovery, fatigue overtook Linda, and she left Ross sitting at the bedside while she went back to the motel and slept for a few hours.

She awakes just after dark, showers, dresses, and has just started across the street to a restaurant when a man steps out of a car and calls her name. He is a pleasant-looking, well-dressed older man with an accent she will learn later is Australian. "Mrs. Brady?" he asks. Linda nods. "My name is John Higgins. I have something I'd like very much to talk to you about."

"I was just on my way to get something to eat."

Higgins smiles. "Wonderful," he says. "Let me buy."

Two hours later Linda appears at the door of Stewart's room. She stands there for a minute and looks at her brother and husband. They both sleep like babies, and for an instant she thinks of them as exactly that and feels something like a need to protect them. What is going through their heads? she wonders. What do men dream of?

She moves to Ross's side and looks down at him, her husband, and wants to lean over, kiss him lightly, and let him sleep. But she cannot. She sits in the chair beside him and puts her hand on his shoulder.

When she shakes him awake, his eyes open but give little sign of recognition. They stare at each other for a moment before Linda exhales. "We can get away from here," she whispers. "I talked to Higgins and it would be easy."

Ross shakes his head. "Not easy," he says. "Not now."

Linda says no more. She looks at her husband and notices that the eyes have changed. They are harder; the skin of his face is cut with wrinkles she never noticed before, and she knows the land has somehow finally seeped inside of him. A sense of loss comes over her, and she thinks for an instant she might cry. But there is no real reason. She continues to look into the eyes and knows that Ross will be all right, that now he might be better than ever.

▲
SEVENTY

Watch old Pete Rienrick lead Barney and Jake from the corral beside the tack room. It is still dark, and Elizabeth hears him swear as he wraps the lead ropes around the hitching rail. He acts as if he doesn't recognize Elizabeth until she is very close. His eyes roll in his head, and she notices that his shirt is buttoned all wrong. She fights back a tiredness that threatens to engulf her.

"What's that?" Pete asks, his eyes wild in the gray light.

"What, Pete?"

"That pickup. You hear it. Sounds like John's coming home from town. Son of a bitch always did get drunk the night before branding. Better have coffee for him, or he won't be worth a damn."

Elizabeth stands square in front of Pete. The morning light is crawling into the yard, and when she looks, she can see John Kiser sitting at the kitchen window where she left him. She takes Pete's shoulders tight in her hands. "Pete, now listen to me. John can't ride. He's been sick for a long time." Pete looks at her seriously, then squints one eye and cocks his head to listen.

Now Elizabeth hears it, too. Hear it? A pickup with a sticky valve lifter. When Elizabeth turns, she sees Tuffy's pickup coming down the driveway. Kyle is driving and blows the horn when he sees them. Delbert Benson sits in the passenger seat, and the trailer with Delbert's horse bounces along behind.

369

Just as you would do, she runs to squeeze her son. "Is there a branding here today?" Kyle says with a laugh. "There must be. Aunt Tracy and Uncle Louis are right behind us. Come on, Mom." Elizabeth has not let him go.

"We don't work without coffee," Delbert says.

"We left Bismark at midnight last night," Kyle says. Elizabeth holds him out at arm's length. He seems bigger and stronger than he did only a few weeks before. "Coffee, Mom. You got to give me coffee before I climb on a horse."

"Either that or up the prize money," Delbert says.

"I'll give you coffee," Elizabeth says.

While she is making a second pot of coffee, Tracy and Louis arrive. Louis goes to help Pete, and Tracy comes into the house. She is dressed in her work clothes and carrying a casserole dish. "Brought some lunch," she says.

The sisters look at each other until smiles come to their faces. "Thank you," Elizabeth says.

Elizabeth is busy loading the branding stove, so she doesn't notice that Edith Miller has stepped up behind her. When she turns, Edith is there, tears in her eyes and very close. "I'm ashamed," she says, and her voice threatens to crack. "But I want to help. I want to help you with the branding. Help with the food." The women gaze at each other. See how they look deep inside?

Elizabeth begins to nod before the words come. "Sure," she says. "Of course."

Now we have action. Horses are being unloaded, strategies planned, jokes being played, tools and lunches being loaded into the back of pickup trucks. Elizabeth stands at the rear of her own pickup and goes over supplies for the hundredth time. Branding irons, syringes, vaccine, ear tags. They are nearly ready to go. But look at Kyle coming to his mother, shaking his head. "Mom," he says. "Pete's acting funny."

Elizabeth nods. "He's been getting worse, but he'll be all right."

"I don't know, Mom. I'm afraid he's going to get hurt. He's putting a saddle on Dancer."

This is too much. It is dangerous, so Elizabeth drops what she is doing and moves to the corral. She stands near the gate and watches the old man swing a saddle onto the elegant black horse who is tied to the fence. He strokes the horse's neck and talks to him as if he were an old friend. The rest of the men stand behind Elizabeth. They are not sure what to do. They are not sure what Pete has in mind.

When the old man unties the reins from the corral rail and leads the horse outside, Elizabeth moves to meet him. "Pete? What are you doing?"

"Saddlin' Dancer; what's it look like?"

"We won't need him, Pete. There are plenty of other horses." Elizabeth stays in front of him and reaches out for the reins. Pete's eyes roll again and he jerks away in confusion. Elizabeth feels a sickness in her stomach. People are milling behind her, and she hears a pickup door slam. Look there. Look who's coming.

"Bullshit," Pete says. He is struggling now to understand what is going on. "I counted. Everyone's got a horse but John." He gives his head a quick nod. "John needs a horse."

Elizabeth bites her lip, then speaks softly. "John is staying in the house. We won't need Dancer." She nods toward the house, and some of the people glance with her to the old man at the window, who stares back without so much as a blink.

Pete's eyes shift nervously, then stick on something behind Elizabeth. He does not look back to Elizabeth but speaks with certainty. "'Bout time you showed up," he says. "Hell, we're ready to go." He holds Dancer's reins out in front of him and steps past Elizabeth. "Get your butt up in that saddle. Let's go round up those cattle."

Now Elizabeth turns and sees Ross take the reins from Pete. But Ross is looking at her. Pete walks on past and unties Barney from the fence. The other men go to their horses, and the area becomes alive again. But watch the two in the center. Ross and Elizabeth stand looking at each other. It is not until everyone is mounted that Ross looks at Dancer. The horse chews at his bit and stamps a front foot. But see how he quiets when Ross rubs his forehead? Ross touches him gently on the shoulder, then down the front left foreleg. Finally he loops the reins over Dancer's head.

No one moves as he swings into the saddle. He finds the stirrup on the other side and settles in to see what the horse will do. The others form a circle around Ross and Dancer. The horse prances to one side and tosses his head. Ross moves easily with him and in a moment reaches out and strokes his neck. Then he looks up. But his eyes focus over the heads of the people and lock for an instant on the old mattered eyes of John Kiser. See how these men gaze at each other, then look on past? They see the same thing you may see now: the horizon, the buttes just going purple in the morning light, and the green ribbons of trees winding down toward the unseen river beyond.

Now you can start your car.

Leave these people as they are, preparing to ride out and gather their cattle. But save the scene. Pack it up tight for the kids, and take it on out the driveway and up the bench road. Travel with it away from the Badlands and over the interstate highways. Take it home with you to Newark and Santa Barbara. Keep it as a reminder of all that's off the beaten track, all that is under the surface of this country of ours.

When you get home, remember the early-morning sun,

the way it stretches the shadows and spreads golden light on the land. Remember that gold as you put on your jewelry and think about chokecherry draws and purple buttes and weather. Think about the beauty and the evil, and know that all of it is a legacy, a living part of every one of us. Think of the grasslands of North America, the way the wind pushes the grass in waves, waves of grass, one after the other forever. The wind is the breath of Mother Earth. Let it move through your mind and keep you calm.

AVON BOOKS

___ **The Brave Cowboy** by Edward Abbey	$10.00 US/$12.00 Can	71459-0
___ **Fire on the Mountain** by Edward Abbey	$10.00 US/$12.00 Can	71460-4
___ **The Fool's Progress:** **An Honest Novel** by Edward Abbey	$11.00 US/$13.00 Can	70856-6
___ **The Monkey Wrench Gang** by Edward Abbey	$12.50 US/$15.00 Can	71339-X
___ **Bones of the Moon** by Jonathan Carroll	$7.95 US/$9.95 Can	70688-1
___ **An American Romance** by John Casey	$9.95 US/$11.95 Can	71240-7
___ **Spartina** by John Casey	$8.95 US/$10.95 Can	71104-4
___ **Testimony and Demeanor** by John Casey	$8.95 US/$10.95 Can	71239-3
___ **A Model World and Other** **Stories** by Michael Chabon	$10.00 US/$12.00 Can	71099-4
___ **The Last to Go** by Rand Richards Cooper	$7.95 US/$9.95 Can	70862-0
___ **Rumor Has It** by Charles Dickinson	$9.00 US/$11.00 Can	71346-2
___ **The Widows' Adventures** by Charles Dickinson	$8.95 US/$10.95 Can	70847-7
___ **Tours of the Black Clock** by Steve Erickson	$8.95 US/$10.95 Can	70944-9
___ **Winterchill** by Ernest J. Finney	$8.95 US/$10.95 Can	71101-X
___ **The Twenty-Seventh City** by Jonathan Franzen	$8.95 US/$10.95 Can	70840-X
___ **The New Twilight Zone** edited by Martin H. Greenberg	$10.00 US/$12.00 Can	75926-8
___ **The Eye of the Heart** edited by Barbara Howes	$10.95 US/$12.95 Can	70942-2
___ **Migrant Souls** by Arturo Islas	$8.95 US/$10.95 Can	71440-X
___ **The Rain God** by Arturo Islas	$8.95 US/$10.95 Can	76393-1
___ **Me and Brenda** by Philip Israel	$9.00 US/$11.00 Can	71537-6
___ **Foreign Affairs** by Alison Lurie	$7.95 US/$9.95 Can	70990-2
___ **Imaginary Friends** by Alison Lurie	$8.95 US/$10.95 Can	71136-2

TRADE PAPERBACKS

___	Only Children by Alison Lurie	$7.95 US/$9.95 Can	70875-2
___	The Truth About Lorin Jones by Alison Lurie	$9.00 US	70807-8
___	The War Between the Tates by Alison Lurie	$8.95 US/$10.95 Can	71135-4
___	The Music Room by Dennis McFarland	$8.95 US/$10.95 Can	71456-6
___	Afterlife by Paul Monette	$10.00 US/$12.00 Can	71197-4
___	Lies of Silence by Brian Moore	$9.00 US	71547-3
___	The Expendables by Antonya Nelson	$8.00 US/$10.00 Can	71452-3
___	A Trail of Heart's Blood Wherever We Go by Robert Olmstead	$11.00 US/$13.00 Can	71548-1
___	Call and Response by T.R. Pearson	$10.95 US/$12.95 Can	71163-X
___	Gospel Hour by T.R. Pearson	$11.00 US/$13.00 Can	71036-6
___	Lights Out in the Reptile House by Jim Shepard	$10.00 US/$12.00 Can	71413-2
___	The Ballad of Peckham Rye by Muriel Spark	$7.95 US	70936-8
___	A Far Cry From Kensington by Muriel Spark	$7.95 US	70786-1
___	The Girls of Slender Means by Muriel Spark	$7.95 US	70937-6
___	Loitering With Intent by Muriel Spark	$7.95 US	70935-X
___	Memento Mori by Muriel Spark	$7.95 US	70938-4
___	The Lady at Liberty by Hudson Talbott	$9.95 US/$11.95 Can	76427-X
___	The Fugitive by Pramoedya Ananta Toer	$8.95 US/$10.95 Can	71496-5
___	Failure to Zigzag by Jane Vandenburgh	$8.95 US/$10.95 Can	71019-6
___	Girl With Curious Hair by David Wallace	$9.95 US/$11.95 Can	71230-X
___	Calm at Sunset, Calm at Dawn by Paul Watkins	$8.95 US/$10.95 Can	71222-9
___	Night Over Day Over Night by Paul Watkins	$7.95 US/$9.95 Can	70737-3
___	Winning the City by Theodore Weesner	$9.00 US/$11.00 Can	71554-6